PETER BENCHLEY

COLLECTION

Reader's Digest
CONDENSED
BOOKS

PETER BENCHLEY

COLLECTION

The Reader's Digest Association, Inc.
New York, NY / Montreal

We are committed to both the quality of our products and the service we provide to our customers. We value your comments, so please feel free to contact us.

The Reader's Digest Association, Inc.
Select Editions
44 South Broadway
White Plains, NY 10601

Reader's Digest Select Editions, also known as Condensed Books, is an ongoing series published every two to three months. The typical volume contains four outstanding books by different authors in condensed form. Anyone may receive this service by writing The Reader's Digest Association, Inc., 44 South Broadway, White Plains, NY 10601, visiting the web at www.rd.com/freebook, or calling our toll-free number: 800-463-8820.

For more Reader's Digest products and information, visit our website:
www.rd.com (in the United States)
www.readersdigest.ca (in Canada)

ISBN 978-1-62145-054-2 (hardcover)
ISBN 978-1-60652-550-0 (paperback)

Printed in the United States of America

CONTENTS

JAWS

Part One

1

THE great fish moved silently through the night water, propelled by short sweeps of its crescent tail, the mouth open just enough to permit a rush of water over the gills. There was little other motion: an occasional correction of the apparently aimless course by the slight raising or lowering of a pectoral fin—as a bird changes direction by dipping one wing and lifting the other.

The senses transmitted nothing extraordinary to the small, primitive brain. The fish might have been asleep, save for the movement dictated by millions of years of instinctive continuity: lacking the flotation bladder common to other fish and the fluttering flaps to push oxygen-bearing water through its gills, it survived only by moving. Once stopped, it would sink to the bottom and die of anoxia.

The land along the south shore of Long Island seemed almost as dark as the water, for there was no moon. All that separated sea from shore was a long, straight stretch of beach—so white that it shone. From a house behind the grass-splotched dunes, lights cast yellow glimmers on the sand.

The front door to the house opened, and a man and a woman stepped out onto the wooden porch. They stood for a moment staring at the sea, embraced quickly, then ran together to the beach.

"First a swim," said the woman, "to clear your head."

"Forget my head," said the man. Giggling, he fell backward onto the sand, pulling the woman down with him. Urgently they fumbled with each other's clothing.

Afterward the man lay back and closed his eyes. The woman looked at him and smiled. "Now, how about that swim?" she said.

"You go ahead. I'll wait for you here."

The woman rose and walked naked to where the gentle surf washed over her ankles. The water was colder than the night air, for it was only mid-June. She called back, "Sure you don't want to come in?" But there was no answer from the man, who had fallen asleep.

She backed up a few steps and ran at the water. At first her strides were long and graceful, but then a small wave crashed into her knees. She faltered, regained her footing and walked until the water covered her shoulders. Then she began to swim—with the jerky, head-above-water stroke of the untutored.

A hundred yards offshore the fish sensed a change in the sea's rhythm. It did not see the woman, nor yet did it smell her. Running within the length of its body were thin canals filled with mucus and dotted with nerve endings, and these nerves detected vibrations and signaled the brain. The fish turned toward shore.

The woman continued to swim away from the beach, stopping now and again to check her position by the lights shining from the house. The tide was slack, so she had not drifted. But she was tiring, so she rested for a moment, treading water, and then started for shore.

The vibrations were stronger now, and the fish recognized prey. The sweeps of its tail quickened, thrusting the giant body forward with a speed that agitated the tiny phosphorescent animals in the water and cast a mantle of sparks over the fish.

The fish closed on the woman and hurtled past, a dozen feet to the side and six feet below the surface. She felt only a wave of pressure that seemed to lift her up and ease her down again.

The fish smelled her now, and began to circle close to the surface. Its dorsal fin broke water, and its tail, thrashing back and forth, cut the glassy surface with a hiss.

For the first time the woman felt fear, though she did not know why. Adrenaline shot through her body, urging her to swim faster. She was about fifty yards from shore. She could see the lights in the house, and for a comforting moment she thought she saw some-one pass by one of the windows.

The fish was about forty feet from the woman, off to the side, when it turned suddenly to the left, dropped entirely below the sur-face and, with two quick thrusts of its tail, was upon her.

There was no initial pain, only one violent tug on the woman's right leg. At first she thought she had snagged it on a rock. She reached down to touch her foot. She could not find it. She reached higher, and then she was overcome by a rush of nausea and diz-ziness. Her groping fingers had found a nub of bone and tattered flesh. She knew that the warm, pulsing flow over her fingers in the chill water was her own blood.

Pain and panic struck together. The woman threw her head back and screamed a guttural cry of terror.

Now the fish turned again, homing on the stream of blood from the woman's femoral artery. This time it attacked from below. The great conical head struck the woman like a locomotive, knocking her out of the water, and the gaping jaws snapped shut around her torso. The fish, with the woman's body in its mouth, smashed down on the water, spewing foam and blood and phosphorescence in a gaudy shower.

THE man awoke, shivering in the early morning cold. The sun had not yet risen, but a line of pink on the eastern horizon told him that daybreak was near. He stood and began to dress. He was annoyed that the woman had not wakened him when she went back to the house, and he found it curious that she had left her clothes on the beach. He picked them up and walked to the house.

He tiptoed across the porch and opened the screen door. The deserted living room was littered with glasses, ashtrays and dirty plates. He walked across it and turned right, down a hall, past two closed doors. The door to the room he shared with the woman was open, and a bedside light was on. Both beds were made. He tossed the woman's clothes on one of them.

There were two more bedrooms in the house. The owners slept in one. Two other houseguests occupied the other. As quietly as possible the man opened the door to the first bedroom. There were two beds, each containing only one person. He closed the door and moved to the next room. The host and hostess were asleep on either side of a king-size bed. The man closed the door and went to check the bathroom. It was unoccupied. Then he went back to his room to find his watch. It was nearly five o'clock.

He sat on one bed and stared at the bundle of clothes on the other. He was certain the woman wasn't in the house. He began to consider the possibility of an accident.

Very quickly the possibility became a certainty. He returned to the hosts' bedroom, hesitated for a moment beside the bed, and then placed his hand on a shoulder. "Jack," he said. "Hey, Jack."

The man sighed and opened his eyes. "What?"

"It's me. Tom. I hate like hell to wake you up, but have you seen Chrissie?"

"What do you mean? Isn't she with you?"

"No. And I can't find her."

Jack sat up and turned on a light. His wife stirred and covered her head with a sheet.

"I'm sorry," Tom said. "Do you remember when you saw her last?"

"Sure I remember. She said you were going for a swim, and you both went out on the porch. When did *you* see her last?"

"On the beach. Then I fell asleep. Didn't she come back?"

"Not before we went to bed, and that was around one."

"I found her clothes on the beach."

"You looked in the living room?"

Tom nodded. "And in the Henkels' room. I checked the whole house."

"So what do you think?"

"What I'm beginning to think," said Tom, "is that maybe she had an accident. Maybe she drowned."

Jack looked at him for a moment, then glanced at his watch. "I don't know what time the police in this town go to work," he said, "but I guess this is as good a time as any to find out."

WHEN the phone rang Patrolman Leonard Hendricks was at his desk in the Amity police station reading a detective novel called *Deadly, I'm Yours*.

He picked up the phone. "Amity Police, Patrolman Hendricks," he said. "Can I help you?"

"This is Jack Foote, over on Old Mill Road. I want to report a missing person. Or at least I think she's missing."

"Say again, sir?" Hendricks had served in Vietnam as a radioman, and he was fond of military terminology.

"One of my houseguests went for a swim at about one this morning," said Foote. "She hasn't come back yet. Her date found her clothes on the beach."

Hendricks scribbled on a pad. "What is her name?"

"Christine Watkins."

"Age?"

"I don't know. Say around twenty-five."

"Height and weight?"

"Wait a minute." There was a pause. "We think about five feet seven, between one twenty and one thirty pounds."

"Color of hair and eyes?"

"Listen, Officer, why do you need all this? If the woman's drowned, she's probably the only one tonight. Right?"

"Who said she drowned, Mr. Foote? Maybe she went for a walk."

"Stark-naked at one in the morning? Have you had any reports about a woman walking around naked?"

Hendricks relished the chance to be insufferably cool. "Not yet. But once the summer season starts you never know what to expect. Color of hair and eyes?"

"Her hair is . . . oh, dirty blond, I guess. I don't know what color her eyes are. Let's say hazel."

"Okay, Mr. Foote. As soon as we find out anything we'll contact you."

Hendricks hung up and looked at his watch. It was 5:10, and he wasn't anxious to wake the chief for something as vague as a missing-person report. But if she was washed up somewhere, Chief Brody would want the whole thing taken care of before the body was found by some nanny with a couple of young kids.

Judgment, that was what the chief kept telling him he needed; that was what made a good cop. The cerebral challenge of police work had played a part in Hendricks's decision to join the Amity force after he returned from Vietnam. He was convinced that as soon as he could get sprung from this midnight-to-eight shift, he would start to enjoy his work. But Chief Brody liked to break in his young men slowly—at a time of day when they wouldn't be overtaxed.

Eight a.m. to four p.m. was the business shift, and it called for experience and diplomacy. Six men worked that shift. One handled the traffic intersection at Main and Water streets. Two patrolled in squad cars. One manned the phones at the station house. One handled the clerical work. And the chief handled the public: ladies who complained that they hadn't been able to sleep because of the din coming from the Randy Bear or Saxon's, the town's two gin mills; homeowners who complained that bums were disturbing the peace; and the vacationing bankers or lawyers who stopped in to discuss their various plans for keeping Amity a pristine and exclusive summer colony.

Four to midnight was the trouble shift, when young studs from the nearby Hamptons would flock to the Randy Bear and get involved in a fight, or speed drunkenly along the Montauk Highway; when, very rarely, a couple of predators from Queens would lurk in the dark side streets and mug passersby; and when, about twice a month in the summer, the police would feel obliged to stage a pot bust at one of the huge waterfront homes. The six largest men on the force worked four to midnight.

Midnight to eight was usually quiet. Normally, during the summer, it was manned by three officers. One, however, young Dick Angelo, was taking his two weeks' leave before the season began to swing. The third was a thirty-year veteran named Henry Kimble, who held a daytime job as a bartender at Saxon's.

Hendricks tried to raise Kimble on the radio, but he knew the attempt was hopeless. As usual, Kimble would be asleep in a squad car parked behind the Amity Pharmacy. Hendricks picked up the phone and dialed Chief Brody's home number.

Martin Brody was in that fitful state of semiconsciousness before waking. On the second ring of the phone he rolled over and picked up the receiver. "Yeah?"

"Chief, this is Hendricks. I hate to bother you this early, but I think we've got a floater on our hands."

"A floater? What the hell is a floater?"

Hendricks had picked up the word from his night reading. "A drowning," he said, embarrassed. He told Brody about the call from Foote. "I didn't know if you'd want to check it out before people start swimming. It looks like it's going to be a nice day."

Brody heaved an exaggerated sigh. "Where's Kimble?" he said. "Oh, never mind. It was a stupid question. One of these days I'm going to fix that radio of his so he can't turn it off."

Hendricks said, "Like I said, Chief, I hate to bother—"

"Yeah, I know, Leonard. You were right to call. I'll take a look along the beach in front of Old Mill and Scotch, then I'll go out and talk to Foote and the girl's date. I'll see you later."

Brody hung up the phone and stretched. He looked at his wife, lying next to him in the double bed. She had stirred when the phone rang, but soon lapsed back into sleep.

Ellen Brody was thirty-six, five years younger than her husband. The fact that she looked barely thirty, though a source of pride to Brody, was also one of annoyance. She had been able, despite the strains of bearing three children, to keep her good looks, whereas Brody—though hardly fat at six feet one and two hundred pounds—was beginning to be concerned about his blood pressure and his thickening middle. Sometimes he would catch himself gazing with idle lust at the young, long-legged girls who pranced around town during the summer. But he never enjoyed the sensation, for it made him wonder if Ellen felt the same stirring when she looked at the tanned, slim young men.

Summers were bad times for Ellen Brody, for in summer she was tortured by thoughts of chances she had missed. She saw boarding-school classmates, now married to successful husbands, summering in Amity and wintering in New York, graceful women who stroked tennis balls and enlivened conversations with equal ease, women who (Ellen was convinced) joked among themselves about Ellen Shepherd marrying that policeman.

Ellen had been twenty-one when she met Brody. She had just finished her junior year at Wellesley and was spending the summer in Amity with her parents—as she had done for the previous eleven summers. Though she'd enjoyed the modest wealth her father had earned, she had not been eager to live a life like her parents'. The petty social problems had bored her.

Her first contact with Brody was professional. Late one night she was being driven home very fast by an extremely drunk young man. The car was stopped by a policeman who impressed Ellen with his youth, his looks and his civility. After issuing a summons he confiscated the car keys and drove Ellen and her date to their respective homes. The next morning Ellen wrote Brody a thank-you note, and also a note to the chief of police commending young Martin Brody. Brody telephoned to thank her.

When he asked her out to dinner and the movies on his night off, she accepted out of curiosity. She had scarcely ever talked to a policeman, let alone gone out with one. Brody was nervous, but Ellen seemed so interested in him and his work that he eventually calmed down enough to have a good time. Ellen found him delightful: strong, simple, kind—sincere. He had been a policeman for six years. He said his ambition was to be chief of the Amity force, to have sons to take duck shooting in the fall and enough money for a vacation every second or third year.

They were married that November.

There were some awkward moments during the first years. Ellen's friends would ask them to dinner, and Brody would feel ill at ease and patronized. When they got together with Brody's friends, Ellen's past seemed to stifle fun. Gradually, as new acquaintance-ships developed, the awkwardness disappeared. But they never saw Ellen's old friends anymore.

Until about four years ago she had been too busy and too happy to let the estrangement bother her. But when her last child started school she found herself adrift, and she began to dwell on memo-ries of how her mother had lived: shopping excursions (fun because there was money to spend), lunches with friends, tennis games, cocktail parties, weekend trips. What had once seemed shallow and tedious now loomed in memory like paradise.

At first she tried to reestablish bonds with friends she hadn't seen in ten years, but all common interests had long since van-ished. Ellen talked gaily about local politics, about her job as a vol-unteer at the Southampton Hospital. Her old friends talked about New York politics, about art galleries, painters and writers they knew. Most conversations ended with feeble pledges about getting together again.

Once in a while she would try to make friends among the sum-mer people she hadn't known, but the associations were forced and brief. Ellen was self-conscious about her house and about her hus-band's job. She made sure that everyone she met knew she had started her Amity life on an entirely different plane. She was aware of what she was doing and hated herself for it, because in fact she loved her husband deeply, adored her children and—most of the year—was quite content with her lot. But somehow the resentments and the longings lingered.

Brody rolled over toward Ellen, raising himself on one elbow and resting his head on his hand. With his other hand he flicked away a strand of hair that was tickling her nose and making it twitch. He debated rousing her, but he knew her early morning moods were more cantankerous than romantic. Still, it would be fun. There had not been much sex in the Brody household recently. There seldom was when Ellen was in her summer moods.

Just then Ellen's mouth fell open and she began to snore. Brody got up and walked into the bathroom.

IT WAS nearly 6:30 and the sun was well up when he turned onto Old Mill Road. From the road there was no view of the beach. All Brody could see were the tops of the dunes. So every hundred yards or so he had to stop the squad car and walk up a driveway to a point from which he could survey the shore.

There was no sign of a body. All he saw on the broad white expanse were pieces of driftwood, a can or two and a yard-wide belt of seaweed pushed ashore by the southerly breeze. There was practically no surf, so if a body had been floating on the surface it would have been visible.

By seven o'clock Brody had covered the whole beach along Old Mill and Scotch roads. He turned north toward town on Bayberry Lane and arrived at the station house at 7:10.

"No luck, Chief?" Hendricks said.

"That depends on what you mean by luck, Leonard. If you mean did I find a body, the answer is no."

Brody poured himself a cup of coffee, walked into his office and began to flip through the morning papers—the early edition of the New York *Daily News* and the Amity *Leader*.

Kimble arrived a little before eight o'clock, looking, aptly enough, as if he had been sleeping in his uniform, and had a cup of coffee with Hendricks while they waited for the day shift to appear. Hendricks' replacement came in at eight sharp, and Hendricks was about to leave when Brody came out of his office.

"I'm going out to see Foote, Leonard," Brody said. "You want to come along? I thought you might want to follow up on your . . . floater." He smiled.

"Sure, I guess so," said Hendricks. "I got nothing else going today, so I can sleep all afternoon."

At the Footes' house the door opened almost before Brody

finished knocking. "I'm Tom Cassidy," said a young man. "Did you find her?"

"I'm Chief Brody. This is Officer Hendricks. No, Mr. Cassidy, we didn't find her. Can we come in?"

"Sure. Go on in the living room. I'll get the Footes."

Within five minutes Brody had learned everything he needed to know. Then, to be thorough, he looked through the missing woman's clothes. "She didn't have a bathing suit with her?"

"No," said Cassidy. "It's in the top drawer over there."

"I see," said Brody. "We'd better go down to the beach. You don't have to come. Hendricks and I can handle it."

"I'd like to come, if you don't mind."

On the beach Cassidy showed the policemen where he had fallen asleep—and where he had found Christine Watkins's clothes.

Brody looked up and down the mile-long stretch. For as far as he could see, clumps of seaweed were the only dark spots on the white sand. "Let's take a walk," he said. "Leonard, you go east as far as the point. Mr. Cassidy, let's you and I go west. You got your whistle, Leonard? Just in case."

"I've got it," said Hendricks. "You care if I take my shoes off? It's easier walking on the sand."

"I don't care," said Brody. "You can take your pants off if you want. Of course then I'll arrest you for indecent exposure."

Hendricks started eastward, the wet sand cool on his feet. He walked with his head down, looking at the tiny shells and tangles of seaweed. A few little black beetles skittered out of his path, and when the wave wash receded he saw minute bubbles pop above the holes made by sandworms. He enjoyed the walk. It was a funny thing, he thought, that when you lived in a place you almost never did the things that tourists did—like walk on the beach or go swimming in the ocean.

Once Hendricks turned around to see if Brody and Cassidy had found anything. He guessed that they were nearly half a mile away. As he started walking again, he saw ahead of him an unusually large clump of kelp. When he reached it he bent down to pull some of the weed away. Suddenly he stopped, frozen rigid. He fumbled in his pants pocket for his whistle, blew it weakly, then staggered back and fell to his knees, vomiting.

Snarled within the weed was a woman's head, still attached to her shoulders, part of an arm and about a third of her trunk.

HENDRICKS was still on his knees when Brody and Cassidy got to him. Brody was several steps ahead of Cassidy, and he said, "Mr. Cassidy, stay back there a second, will you?" He pulled apart some of the weeds, and when he saw what was inside he felt bile rise in his throat. He swallowed and closed his eyes. After a moment he said, "You might as well look now, Mr. Cassidy, and tell me if it's her or not."

Cassidy shuffled forward reluctantly. Brody held back a piece of weed, to give him a clear look at the gray and gaping face. "Oh, my God!" said Cassidy, and he put a hand to his mouth.

"Is it her?"

Cassidy nodded. "What happened to her?"

"Offhand, I'd say she was attacked by a shark," said Brody.

Cassidy's knees buckled, and as he sank to the sand he said, "I think I'm going to be sick."

Brody knew instantly that he had lost his struggle for control. "Join the crowd," he said, and he vomited, too.

2

SEVERAL minutes passed before Brody felt well enough to stand, walk back to his car and call for an ambulance from the Southampton Hospital. By eleven o'clock he was back in his office, filling out forms about the accident. He had completed everything but cause of death when the phone rang.

"Carl Santos, Martin," said the voice of the coroner.

"Yeah, Carl. What have you got for me?"

"Unless you have any reason to suspect a murder, I'd have to say shark."

"I don't think it's a murder, Carl. I've got no motive, no murder weapons and—unless I want to go off into left field—no suspect."

"Then it's a shark. A big one. Even the screw on an ocean liner wouldn't have done this. It might have cut her in two, but—"

"Okay, Carl," said Brody. "Spare me the gore."

"Sorry, Martin. Anyway, I'd say shark attack makes the most sense to put down, unless there are . . . other considerations."

"No. Not this time, Carl. Thanks for calling." He hung up, typed "shark attack" on the forms, and leaned back in his chair.

The possibility of other considerations hadn't occurred to Brody. Those considerations were the touchiest part of his job, forcing him constantly to assess the best means of protecting the commonweal without compromising either himself or the law.

It was the beginning of the summer season, and Brody knew that on the success or failure of those twelve brief weeks rested the fortunes of Amity for a whole year. The winter population of Amity was about a thousand; in a good summer the population jumped to nearly ten thousand. And those nine thousand summer visitors kept the thousand permanent residents alive for the rest of the year.

Local merchants—from the owners of the hardware store and the sporting-goods store and the two gas stations to the local pharmacist—needed a boom summer to support them through the lean winter. Charter fishermen needed every break they could get: good weather, good fishing and, above all, crowds.

Even after the best of summers Amity winters were rough. Three of every ten families went on relief. Dozens of men were forced to move for the winter to the north shore of Long Island, where they shucked scallops for a few dollars a day.

Brody knew that one bad summer would nearly double the relief rolls. And two or three bad summers in a row—a circumstance that fortunately hadn't occurred in more than two decades—could wreck the town. If people didn't have enough money to pay for clothes or food or repairs, then business firms would have to close down. The town would lose tax revenue, municipal services would deteriorate and people would begin to move away. So everyone was expected to do his bit to make sure that Amity remained a desirable summer community.

Generally, Brody's contribution—in addition to maintaining the rule of law—consisted of suppressing rumors and, in consultation with Harry Meadows, the editor of the Amity *Leader*, keeping a certain perspective on the rare unfortunate occurrences that qualified as news.

If one of the wealthier summer residents was arrested for drunken driving, Brody was willing to book him for driving without a license, and that charge would be duly reported in the *Leader*. But Brody made sure to warn the driver that the second time he would be booked and prosecuted for drunk driving.

When youngsters from the Hamptons caused trouble, Harry Meadows was handed every fact—names, ages and charges lodged. When Amity's own youth made too much noise at a party, the *Leader* usually ran a one-paragraph story without names.

But Brody wanted full disclosure of the shark incident. He intended to close the beaches for a couple of days, to give the shark time to travel far from the Amity shoreline.

He knew there would be a strong argument against publicizing the attack. So far Amity's summer was shaping up as a mediocre one. Rentals were up from last year, but they were not "good" rentals. Many were "groupers," bands of ten or fifteen young people who came from the city and split the rent on a big house. At least a dozen of the expensive shorefront properties had not yet been rented. Sensational reports of a shark attack might turn the season into a disaster.

Still, Brody thought, one death would certainly have less effect than three or four. The fish might have disappeared already, but Brody wasn't willing to gamble lives on the possibility. He dialed Meadows' number. "Free for lunch, Harry?" he said.

"Sure," said Meadows. "My place or yours?"

"Yours," he said. "Why don't we order out from Cy's?"

"Fine with me," said Meadows. "Cy's Thursday special okay?"

Suddenly Brody wished he hadn't called at mealtime. The thought of food nauseated him. "No, just egg salad, I guess, and a glass of milk. I'll be right there."

HARRY Meadows was an immense man; the mere act of drawing breath caused perspiration to dot his forehead. He was in his late forties, ate too much, chain-smoked cheap cigars, drank bonded bourbon and was, in the words of his doctor, the Western world's leading candidate for a huge coronary infarction.

When Brody arrived Meadows was standing beside his desk, waving a towel at the open window. "In deference to what your lunch order tells me is a tender stomach," he said, "I am trying to clear the air of essence of White Owl."

"I appreciate that," said Brody. He glanced around the small, cluttered room and found a chair. He pulled it over to Meadows's desk and sat down.

Meadows rooted around in a large brown paper bag, pulled out a paper cup and a plastic-wrapped sandwich, and slid them across the desk to Brody. Then he began to unwrap his own lunch: a large meatball sandwich, a carton of fried potatoes and a quarter of a lemon meringue pie. He reached behind his chair and from a small refrigerator took a can of beer.

"Amazing," said Brody. "I must have had about a thousand meals with you, Harry, but I still can't get used to it."

"Everyone has his little quirks, my friend," Meadows said as he lifted his sandwich. "Some men chase other people's wives. Some lose themselves in whiskey. I find my solace in nature's own nourishment."

They ate in silence for a few moments. Brody finished his sandwich and lit a cigarette. Meadows was still eating, but Brody knew his appetite wouldn't be diminished by a discussion of Christine Watkins's death.

"About the Watkins thing," he said. "I have a couple of thoughts, if you want to hear them." Meadows nodded. "First, it seems to me that the cause of death is cut-and-dried. Santos thinks it was a shark attack, and if you'd seen the body, you'd agree."

"I did see it."

"So you agree?"

"Yes. I agree that's what killed her. But there are a few things I'm not so sure of."

"Like what?"

"Like why she was swimming at that time of night. Do you know what the temperature was around midnight? Sixty. And the water was about fifty. You'd have to be out of your mind to go swimming under those conditions."

"Or drunk," said Brody, "which she probably was."

"You're probably right. There's one other thing that bothered me, though. It seemed damn funny that we'd get a shark around here when the water's still this cold."

"Maybe there are sharks who like cold water. Who knows about sharks?"

"I know a lot more about them than I did this morning. After I saw what was left of Miss Watkins, I called a young guy I know up at the Woods Hole Oceanographic Institution. I described the body to him, and he said it's likely that only one kind of shark would do a job like that."

"What kind?"

"A great white. Others attack people, like tigers and hammerheads and maybe makos and blues, but this fellow, Matt Hooper, told me that to cut a woman in half you'd have to have a fish with a mouth like this"—he spread his hands about three feet apart—"and the only shark that grows that big *and* attacks people is the great white. There's another name for them—man-eaters."

"What did he say about the cold water?"

"That it's quite common for a great white to come into water this cold. Some years ago a boy was killed by one near San Francisco. The water temperature was fifty-seven."

Brody said, "You've really been checking into this, Harry."

"It seemed to me a matter of public interest to determine exactly what happened and the chances of it happening again."

"And did you determine those chances?"

"I did. They're almost nonexistent. From what I can gather, this was a real freak accident. According to Hooper, there's every reason to believe that the shark is long gone. There are no reefs around here. No fish-processing plant or slaughterhouse that dumps blood or guts into the water. So there's nothing at all to keep the shark interested." Meadows looked at Brody. "So it seems to me, Martin, there's no reason to get the public all upset over something that's almost sure not to happen again."

"That's one way to look at it, Harry. Another is that since it's not likely to happen again, there's no harm in telling people that it did happen this once."

Meadows sighed. "Journalistically, you may be right. But I don't think it would be in the public interest to spread this around. I'm not thinking about the townspeople; they'll know about it soon enough, the ones that don't know already. But what about the people who read the *Leader* in New York or Philadelphia or Cleveland? A lot of the summer people subscribe year-round. And you know what the real estate situation is like this season. If I run a story saying that a young woman was bitten in two by a monster shark off Amity, there won't be another house rented in this town. Sharks are like axe murderers, Martin. People react to them with their guts."

Brody nodded. "I can't argue with that, and I don't want to tell the people that there *is* a killer shark around. You're probably right. That shark has probably gone a hundred miles away and won't ever show up again. But suppose—just suppose—we don't say a word, and somebody else gets hit by that fish. What then? I want you to run the story, Harry. I want to close the beaches for a couple of days, just for insurance. If we tell people what happened and why we're doing it, I think we'll be way ahead."

Meadows sat back in his chair. "There won't be any story about the attack in the *Leader,* Martin."

"Just like that."

"Well, not exactly. I'm the editor of this paper and I own a piece of it, but not a big enough piece to buck certain pressures."

"Such as?"

"I've already gotten six phone calls. Five were from advertisers—a restaurant, a hotel, two real estate firms and an ice-cream shop. They were most anxious that we let the whole thing fade quietly away. The sixth call was from Mr. Coleman in New York, who owns fifty-five percent of the *Leader.* It seems Mr. Coleman had received a few phone calls himself. He told me there would be no story in the *Leader.*"

"Well, Harry, where does that leave us? You're not going to run a story, so as far as the good readers of the *Leader* are concerned, nothing ever happened. I'm going to close the beaches and put up a few signs saying why."

TEN minutes after Brody returned to his office a voice on the intercom announced, "The mayor's here to see you, Chief."

Brody smiled. The mayor. Not Lawrence Vaughan of Vaughan & Penrose Real Estate; not Larry Vaughan, just calling to check in. But Mayor Lawrence P. Vaughan, the people's choice. "Send His Honor in," Brody said.

Larry Vaughan was a handsome man in his early fifties, with a full head of salt-and-pepper hair and a body kept trim by exercise. A native of Amity, he had made a great deal of money in real estate speculation, and he was the senior partner (some thought the *only* partner) in the most successful agency in town. He dressed with elegant simplicity, in timeless British jackets, button-down shirts and Gucci loafers. Unlike Ellen Brody, who had descended from summer folk to winter folk, Vaughan had ascended smoothly from winter folk to summer folk. As a local merchant he was not one of them, so he was never asked to visit them in New York or Palm Beach. But in Amity he moved freely among all but the most aloof members of the summer community, which, of course, was very good for business.

Brody liked Vaughan. He didn't see much of him during the summer, but after Labor Day, Vaughan and his wife, Eleanor, would occasionally ask Brody and Ellen out to dinner at one of the better restaurants in the Hamptons. The evenings were special treats for Ellen, and that in itself was enough to make Brody happy. Vaughan seemed to understand Ellen. He always treated her as a club mate and comrade.

Vaughan walked into Brody's office and sat down. "I just talked to Harry Meadows," he said. "Where are you going to get the authority to close the beaches?"

Vaughan was obviously upset, which surprised Brody. "Officially, I'm not sure I have it," Brody said. "The code says I can take whatever actions I deem necessary in the event of an emergency, but I think the selectmen have to declare an emergency. I don't imagine you want to go through all that rigmarole."

"Not a chance. But I don't want you to close the beaches. The Fourth of July isn't far off, and that's the make-or-break weekend. We'd be cutting our own throats."

"I know the argument, and I'm sure you know my reasons. It's not as if I have anything to gain by closing the beaches."

"No. I'd say quite the opposite is true. Look, Martin, this town doesn't need that kind of publicity."

"It doesn't need any more people killed, either."

"Nobody else is going to get killed. All you'd be doing by closing the beaches is inviting a lot of reporters to come snooping around where they don't have any business."

"So? They'd come out here, and when they didn't find anything worth reporting, they'd go home again."

"Suppose they did find something. There'd be a big to-do that couldn't do anybody any good."

"Like what, Larry? What could they find out? I don't have anything to hide. Do you?"

"No, of course not. Look, if you won't listen to reason, will you listen to me as a friend? I'm under a lot of pressure from my partners. Something like this could be very bad for us."

Brody laughed. "That's the first time I've heard you admit you *had* partners, Larry. I thought you ran that shop like an emperor."

Vaughan was embarrassed, as if he felt he had said too much. "My business is complicated," he said. "There are times I'm not sure *I* understand what's going on. Do me a favor. This once."

Brody looked at Vaughan, trying to fathom his motives. "I'm sorry, Larry, I have to do my job."

"If you don't listen to me," said Vaughan, "you may not have your job much longer."

"You haven't got any control over me. You can't fire any cop in this town."

"Not off the force, no. But believe it or not, I do have discretion over the job of chief of police." From his jacket pocket he took a copy of Amity's corporate charter. He found the page he sought and handed the pamphlet to Brody. "What it says, in effect, is that even though you were elected by the people, the selectmen have the power to remove you."

Brody read the paragraph Vaughan had indicated. "You're right," he said. "But I'd love to see what you put down for 'good and sufficient cause.' "

"I dearly hope it doesn't come to that, Martin. I had hoped you'd go along, once you knew how I and the selectmen felt."

"All the selectmen?"

"A majority."

"Like who?"

"I'm not going to sit here and name names for you. All you have to know is that I have the board behind me, and if you won't do what's right, we'll put someone in your job who will."

Brody had never seen Vaughan in a mood so aggressively ugly. He was fascinated, but he was also slightly shaken. "You really want this, don't you, Larry?"

"I do." Sensing victory, Vaughan said evenly, "Trust me, Martin. You won't be sorry."

Brody sighed. "I don't like it," he said. "It doesn't smell good. But okay, if it's that important."

"It's that important." Vaughan smiled. "Thanks, Martin."

BRODY ARRIVED HOME A LITTLE before five o'clock. His stomach had settled down enough to permit him a beer or two before dinner. Ellen was in the kitchen, still dressed in the uniform of a hospital volunteer. Her hands were busy, making a meat loaf.

"Hello," she said, turning her head so Brody could plant a kiss on her cheek. "What was the crisis?"

"You were at the hospital. You didn't hear?"

"No. I was stuck in the Ferguson wing."

"A girl got killed off Old Mill. By a shark." He reached into the refrigerator for a beer.

Ellen stopped kneading meat and looked at him. "A shark! I've never heard of that around here. You see one once in a while, but they never do anything."

"Yeah, I know. It's a first for me, too."

"So what are you going to do?"

"Nothing."

"Really? Is that sensible? Isn't there anything you can do?"

"Sure, there are some things I could do. Technically. But the powers that be are worried that it won't look nice if we get all excited just because one stranger got killed by a fish. They're willing to take the chance that it won't happen again."

"What do you mean, the powers that be?"

"Larry Vaughan, for one. He said he'd have my job if I closed the beaches."

"I can't believe that, Martin. Larry isn't like that."

"I didn't think so, either. Hey, what do you know about his partners?"

"In the business? I didn't think there were any. I thought he owned the whole thing."

"Apparently not."

"Well, it makes me feel better to know you talked to Larry. He tends to take a wider, more overall view of things than most people. He probably does know what's best."

Brody felt the blood rise in his neck. He tore the metal tab off his beer can, flipped it into the garbage, and walked into the living room to turn on the evening news.

3

FOR the next few days the weather remained clear. A gentle breeze rippled the surface of the sea but made no whitecaps. Only at night was there a crispness to the air, and after days of constant sun the earth and sand had warmed.

Sunday was the twentieth of June. About noon, on the beach in front of Scotch and Old Mill roads, a boy of six was skimming flat stones into the water. He stopped, walked up to where his mother lay dozing, and flopped down next to her. "Hey, Mom," he said. "I don't have anything to do."

"Why don't you go throw a ball?"

"With who? There's nobody here. Can I go swimming?"

"No. It's too cold. Besides, you know you can't go alone."

"Will you come with me?"

"Alex, Mom is pooped, absolutely exhausted. Can't you find anything else to do?"

"Can I go out on my raft? I won't go swimming. I'll just lie on my raft."

His mother sat up and looked along the beach. A few dozen yards away a man stood in waist-deep water with a child on his shoulders. She looked in the other direction. Except for a few couples in the distance, the beach was empty. "Oh, all right," she said. "But don't go too far out." To show she was serious she lowered her sunglasses so the boy could see her eyes.

"Okay," he said. He grabbed his rubber raft and dragged it down to the water. When the water reached his waist, he held the raft in front of him and leaned forward. A swell lifted it, with the boy aboard. He paddled smoothly, with both arms, his feet hanging over the rear of the raft. He moved out a few yards, then began to paddle up and down, parallel to the beach. Though he didn't notice it, a gentle current carried him slowly offshore.

Fifty yards farther out, the ocean floor sloped precipitously. The depth of the water increased from fifteen feet to twenty-five, then forty, then fifty, leveling off at about a hundred feet until the true ocean depths began.

IN THIRTY-FIVE feet of water the great fish swam slowly, its tail waving just enough to maintain motion. It saw nothing, for the water was murky with motes of vegetation. The fish had been moving parallel to the shoreline, too. Now it turned and followed the bottom upward.

The boy was resting, his arms dangling down, his feet and ankles dipping in and out of the water with each small swell. His head was turned toward shore, and he noticed that he had been carried out beyond what his mother would consider safe. He could see her lying on her towel, and the man and child playing in the wave wash. He began to kick and paddle toward shore. His arms displaced water almost silently, but his kicking feet made erratic splashes and left swirls of bubbles in his wake.

The fish did not hear the sound but rather registered the sharp and jerky impulses emitted by the kicks. It rose, slowly at first, then gaining speed as the signals grew stronger.

The boy stopped for a moment to rest, and the signals ceased. The fish slowed, turning its head from side to side, trying to recover them. The boy lay perfectly still, and the fish passed beneath him, skimming the sandy bottom. Again it turned.

The boy resumed paddling. He kicked only every third or fourth stroke, but the occasional kicks sent new signals to the fish. This time it needed to lock on them only an instant, for it was almost directly below the boy.

The fish rose. Nearly vertical, it now saw the commotion on the surface. There was no conviction that what thrashed above was food, but the fish was impelled to attack. If what it swallowed was not digestible, it would be regurgitated. The mouth opened, and with a final sweep of the sickle tail the fish struck.

The boy had no time to cry out. The fish's head drove the raft out of the water. The jaws smashed together, engulfing head, arms, shoulders, trunk, pelvis and most of the raft.

On the beach the man with the child shouted, "Hey!" He was not sure what he had seen. He had been looking toward the sea, then started to turn his head when an uproar caught his eye. He jerked his head back seaward again, but by then there was nothing to see but the waves made by the splash. "Did you see that?" he cried. "Did you see that?"

"What, Daddy, what?" His child stared up at him, excited.

"Out there! A shark or a whale or something! Something huge!"

He ran toward the boy's mother, who was half asleep on her towel. She opened her eyes and squinted at the man. She didn't understand what he was saying, but he was pointing at the water, so she sat up and looked out to sea. At first the fact that she saw nothing didn't strike her as odd. Then she said, "Alex."

BRODY was having lunch at home when the phone rang.

"Bixby, Chief," said the voice from the station house. "I think you'd better come down here. I've got this hysterical woman on my hands."

"What's she hysterical about?"

"Her kid. Out by the beach."

A twinge of unease shot through Brody's stomach. "What happened?"

"It's . . ." Bixby faltered, then said quickly, "Thursday."

Brody understood. "I'll be right there." He hung up the phone. Fear and guilt and fury blended in a thrust of gut-wrenching pain. He felt at once betrayed and betrayer, a criminal forced into a crime. He had wanted to do the right thing; Larry Vaughan had forced him not to. But if he couldn't stand up to Vaughan, what kind of cop was he? He should have closed the beaches.

"What is it?" asked Ellen.

"A kid just got killed."

"How?"

"By a goddam shark."

"Oh, no! If you had closed the beaches—"

"Yeah, I know."

Harry Meadows was waiting for Brody in the parking lot behind the station house. "So much for the odds," he said.

"Yeah. Who's in there, Harry?"

"A man from the *Times*, two from *Newsday*. And the woman. And the man who says he saw it happen."

"How did the *Times* get hold of it?"

"Bad luck. He was on the beach. So was one of the *Newsday* guys. They're both staying with people for the weekend. They were on to it within two minutes."

"Do they know about the Watkins thing?"

"I doubt it. They haven't had any digging time."

"They'll get on to it, sooner or later."

"I know," said Meadows. "It puts me in a difficult position."

"*You!* Don't make me laugh."

"Seriously, Martin. If the *Times* prints that Watkins story in tomorrow's paper, along with today's attack, the *Leader* will look like hell. I'm going to have to use it, to cover myself, even if the others don't."

"Who are you going to say ordered it hushed up? Vaughan?"

"I'm not going to say anybody ordered it hushed up. There was no conspiracy. I'm going to talk to Carl Santos. If I can put the right words in his mouth, we may all be spared a lot of grief."

"What about telling the truth? Say that I wanted to close the beaches and warn people, but the selectmen disagreed. And say that because I was too much of a chicken to fight and put my job on the line, I went along with them."

"Come on, Martin, it wasn't your fault. It wasn't anybody's. We took a gamble and lost. That's all there is to it."

"Terrific. Now I'll just go tell the kid's mother that we're terribly sorry we had to use her son for chips."

Brody entered his office through a side door. The boy's mother was sitting in front of the desk, clutching a handkerchief. She was wearing a short robe over her bathing suit. Her feet were bare. Brody looked at her nervously, once again feeling the rush of guilt. He couldn't tell if she was crying, for her eyes were masked by large, round sunglasses.

A man was standing by the back wall. Brody assumed he was the one who claimed to have witnessed the accident.

Brody had never been adept at consoling people, so he simply introduced himself and started asking questions. The woman said she had seen nothing: one moment the boy was there, the next he was gone, "and all I saw were pieces of his raft." Her voice was weak but steady. The man described what he thought he had seen.

"So no one actually saw this shark," Brody said, courting a faint hope in the back of his mind.

"No," said the man. "But what else could it have been?"

"Any number of things." Brody was lying to himself as well as to them, testing to see if he could believe his own lies. "The raft could have gone flat and the boy could have drowned."

"Alex is a good swimmer," the woman protested. "Or . . . was."

"And what about the splash?" said the man.

Brody realized that the exercise was futile. "Okay," he said. "We'll probably know soon enough, anyway."

"What do you mean?" said the man.

"One way or another, people who die in the water usually wash up somewhere. If it was a shark, there'll be no mistaking it." The woman's shoulders hunched forward, and Brody cursed himself for being a clumsy fool. "I'm sorry," he said. The woman shook her head and wept.

Telling them both to wait in his office, Brody walked out into the front of the station house. Meadows was by the outer door, leaning against the wall. A young man in swim trunks and a short-sleeved shirt was gesturing at Meadows and seemed to be asking questions. Two men were sitting on a bench. One wore swim trunks, the other a blazer and slacks.

"What can I do for you?" Brody said.

The young man next to Meadows stepped forward and said, "I'm Bill Whitman, from the *New York Times*. I was on the beach."

"What did you see?"

One of the others—obviously from *Newsday*—answered. "Nothing. I was there, too. Nobody saw anything. Except maybe the guy in your office."

The *Times* man said, "Are you prepared to list this as a shark attack?"

"I'm not prepared to list this as anything, and I'd suggest you don't either, until you know a lot more about it."

The *Times* man smiled. "Come on, Chief, what do you want us to do? Call it a mysterious disappearance? Boy lost at sea?"

Brody said, "Listen, Mr. Whitman. We have no witnesses who saw anything but a splash. The man inside thinks he saw a big silver-colored thing that may have been a shark, but he says he has never previously seen a live shark, so that's not what you'd call expert testimony. We have no body, no real evidence that anything violent happened to the boy—"

Brody stopped at the sound of tires grinding on gravel. A car door slammed, and Hendricks charged into the station house, wearing swim trunks. "Chief, there's been another attack!" he said.

The *Times* man quickly asked, "When was the first one?"

Before Hendricks could answer, Brody said, "We were just discussing it, Leonard. I don't want you or anyone else jumping to conclusions. After all, the boy could have drowned."

"Boy?" said Hendricks. "What boy? This was a man, an old man. Five minutes ago. He was just beyond the surf, and suddenly he screamed bloody murder and his head went underwater and it came up again and he screamed something else and then he went down again. There was all this splashing around, and the fish kept coming back and hitting him again and again. That's the biggest fish I ever saw, big as a station wagon. I went in and tried to get to the guy, but the fish kept hitting him."

Hendricks paused, staring at the floor. His breath squeezed out of his chest in short bursts. "Then the fish quit," he said. "Maybe it went away, I don't know. I waded out to where the guy was floating. His face was in the water. I took hold of one of his arms and pulled. . . . It came off in my hand." Hendricks looked up, his eyes red and filling with tears of exhaustion and fright.

"Did you call the ambulance?"

Hendricks shook his head.

Brody said, "Bixby, call the hospital. Leonard, are you up to doing some work?" Hendricks nodded. "Then go put on some clothes and find some notices that close the beaches."

WHEN Brody arrived at his office in the station house on Monday morning the *New York Times* lay in the center of his desk. About three-quarters of the way down the right-hand side of page one he saw the headline and began to read:

SHARK KILLS TWO ON LONG ISLAND
BY WILLIAM F. WHITMAN
Special to the New York Times

AMITY, L.I., June 20—A 6-year-old boy and a 65-year-old man were killed today in separate shark attacks that occurred within an hour of each other near the beaches of this resort community on the south shore of Long Island.

Though the body of the boy, Alexander Kintner, was not found, officials said there was no question that he was killed by a shark. A witness, Thomas Daguerre, of New York, said he saw a large silver-colored object rise out of the water and seize the boy and his rubber raft and disappear into the water with a splash.

Amity coroner Carl Santos reported that traces of blood found on shreds of rubber recovered later left no doubt that the boy had died a violent death.

At least 15 persons witnessed the attack on Morris Cater, 65, which took place at approximately 2 p.m. a quarter of a mile down the beach from where young Kintner was attacked. Mr. Cater called out for help, but all attempts to rescue him were in vain.

These incidents are the first documented cases of shark attacks on bathers on the Eastern Seaboard in more than two decades.

According to Dr. David Dieter, an ichthyologist at the New York Aquarium at Coney Island, it is logical to assume—but by no means a certainty—that both attacks were the work of one shark.

Dr. Dieter said the shark was probably a "great white" (*Carcharodon carcharias*), a species known throughout the world for its voraciousness and aggressiveness.

In 1916, he said, a great white killed four bathers in New Jersey on one day—the only other recorded instance of multiple shark-attack fatalities in the United States in this century.

Brody finished reading the article and put down the paper. There were three people dead now, and two of them could still be alive, if only Brody had . . .

Meadows was standing in the doorway. "You've seen the *Times*," he said.

"Yeah, I've seen it. They didn't pick up the Watkins thing."

"I know. Kind of curious, especially after Leonard's little slip of the tongue."

"But you did use it."

"I had to. Here." Meadows handed Brody a copy of the Amity *Leader*.

The banner headline ran across all six columns of page one: TWO KILLED BY MONSTER SHARK OFF AMITY BEACH. Below that, in smaller type, a subhead: NUMBER OF VICTIMS OF KILLER FISH RISES TO THREE.

The victims were Alexander Kintner, age 6, who lived with his mother in the Goose Neck Lane house owned by Mr. and Mrs. Richard Packer, and Morris Cater, 65, who was spending the weekend at the Abelard Arms Inn. Patrolman Leonard Hendricks, who by sheer coincidence was taking his first swim in five years, made a valiant attempt to rescue the struggling Mr. Cater, but the fish gave no quarter. Mr. Cater was dead by the time he was pulled clear of the water.

The *Leader*'s account of the killings continued:

Last Wednesday night, Miss Christine Watkins, a guest of Mr. and Mrs. John Foote of Old Mill Road, went for a swim and vanished.

Thursday morning, Police Chief Martin Brody and Officer Hendricks recovered her body. According to coroner Carl Santos, the cause of death was "definitely and incontrovertibly shark attack." Asked why the cause of death was not made public, Mr. Santos declined to comment.

Brody looked up from the paper and said, "What about the beaches not being closed? Did you go into that?"

"*You* did. Read on."

Asked why he had not ordered the beaches closed until the marauding shark was apprehended, Chief Brody said, "The Atlantic Ocean is huge. Fish don't always stay in one area, especially an area like this where there is no food source. What were we going to do? Close our beaches, and people would just drive up to East Hampton and go swimming there. And there's just as good a chance that they'd get killed in East Hampton as in Amity."

After yesterday's attacks, however, Chief Brody did order the beaches closed until further notice.

"My God, Harry," said Brody. "You really put it to me. You've got me arguing a case I don't believe, then being proved wrong and *forced* to do what I wanted to do all along. That's a pretty dirty trick."

"It wasn't a trick. I had to have someone give the official line. I tried to get hold of Larry Vaughan, but he was away for the week-end. So you were the logical one. You admit you agreed to go along with the decision, so—reluctantly or not—you supported it."

"I suppose. Anyway, it's done. Is there anything else I should read in this?"

"No. I just quote Matt Hooper, that fellow from Woods Hole. He says it would be remarkable if we ever have another attack. But he's a little less sure than he was the last time."

"Does he think one fish is doing all this?"

"He doesn't know, of course, but offhand, yes. He thinks it's a big white."

"I do, too. I mean, I think it's one shark."

"Why?"

"I'm not sure, exactly. Yesterday afternoon I called the Coast Guard out at Montauk. I asked them if they'd noticed a lot of sharks around here recently, and they said they hadn't seen a one so far this spring. They said they'd send a boat down this way later on and give me a call if they saw anything. I finally called them back. They said they had cruised up and down this area for two hours and hadn't seen a thing. So there sure aren't many sharks around."

"Hooper said there was one thing we could do," Meadows said. "We could chum. You know, spread fish guts and goodies like that around in the water. If there's a shark around, he said, that will bring him running."

"Oh, great. And what if he shows up? What do we do then?"

"Harpoon him."

"Harry, I don't even have a police boat, let alone a boat with harpoons on it."

"There are fishermen around. It seems to me—" A commotion out in the hall stopped Meadows in midsentence.

They heard Bixby say, "I told you, ma'am, he's in conference."

Then a woman's voice said, "I don't care! I'm going in there."

The door to Brody's office flew open, and standing there clutch-ing a newspaper, tears streaming down her face, was Alexander Kintner's mother.

Meadows offered her a chair, but she ignored him and walked up to Brody.

"What can I do—"

The woman slapped the newspaper across his face. It made a sharp report that rang deep into his left ear. "What about this?" Mrs. Kintner screamed. "What about it?"

"What about what?" said Brody.

"What they say here. That you knew it was dangerous to swim. That somebody had already been killed by that shark. That you kept it a secret."

Brody couldn't deny it. "Sort of," he said. "I mean yes, it's true, but it's . . . Look, Mrs. Kintner—"

"You killed Alex!" She shrieked the words, and Brody was sure they were heard all over Amity. He was sure his wife heard them, and his children.

He thought, Stop her before she says anything else. But all he could say was, "Sssshhh!"

"You did! You killed him!" Her fists were clenched at her sides, and her head snapped forward as she screamed, "You won't get away with it!"

"Please, Mrs. Kintner," said Brody. "Calm down. Let me explain." He reached to touch her shoulder and help her to a chair, but she jerked away.

"Keep your hands off me!" she cried. "You knew! You knew all along, but you wouldn't say. And now a six-year-old boy, a beautiful six-year-old boy, my boy . . ." Tears seemed to pulse from her eyes. "You knew! Why didn't you tell? Why?"

"Because we didn't think it could happen again." Brody was surprised by his brevity. That was it, really, wasn't it?

The woman was silent for a moment, letting the words register in her muddled mind. She said, "Oh," then slumped into the chair next to Meadows and began to weep in gasping, choking sobs.

Meadows tried to calm her, but she didn't hear him. She didn't hear Brody tell Bixby to call a doctor. And she saw, heard and felt nothing when the doctor came into the office, gave her a sedative, led her to his car and drove her to the hospital.

When she had left, Brody said, "I could use a drink."

"I have some bourbon in my office," said Meadows.

Brody smiled. "No. If this was any indication of how the day's going to go, I better not louse up my head."

The phone rang. It was answered in the other room, and a voice on the intercom said, "It's Mr. Vaughan."

Brody pushed the lighted button, picked up the receiver and said, "Hi, Larry. Did you have a nice weekend?"

"Until about eleven o'clock last night," said Vaughan, "when I turned on my car radio driving home. I was tempted to call you, but I figured you had had a rough enough day without being bothered at that hour."

"That's one decision I agree with."

"Don't rub it in, Martin. I feel bad enough."

Brody wanted to scrape the wound raw, to unload some of the anguish onto someone else, but he knew it was impossible, so all he said was, "Sure."

"I had two cancellations already this morning. Big leases. Good people. I'm scared to answer the phone. I still have twenty houses that aren't rented for August."

"I wish I could tell you different, Larry, but it's going to get worse with the beaches closed."

"You know that next weekend is the Fourth of July. It's already too late to hope for a good summer, but we may be able to salvage something—if the Fourth is good."

Brody couldn't read the tone in Vaughan's voice. "Are you arguing with me, Larry?"

"No. I guess I was thinking out loud. Anyway, you plan to keep the beaches closed until when? Indefinitely?"

"I haven't had time to think that far ahead. Let me ask you something, Larry. Just out of curiosity."

"What?"

"Who are your partners?"

It was a long moment before Vaughan said, "Why do you want to know? What does that have to do with anything?"

"Like I said, just curiosity."

"You keep your curiosity for your job, Martin. Let me worry about my business."

"Sure, Larry. No offense."

"So what are you going to do? We can't just sit around and hope the thing will go away."

"I know. A fish expert, friend of Harry's, says we could try to catch the fish. How about getting up a couple of hundred dollars to charter Ben Gardner's boat for a day or two? I don't know that he's ever caught any sharks, but it might be worth a try."

"Anything's worth a try, just so we get rid of that thing and go back to making a living. Go ahead. Tell him I'll get the money from somewhere."

Brody hung up the phone and said to Meadows, "I'd give a lot to know more about Mr. Vaughan's business affairs."

"Why?"

"He's a very rich man. No matter how long this shark thing goes on, he won't be badly hurt. But he's taking all this as if it was life and death—and I don't mean just the town's. His."

4

Thursday afternoon Brody sat on the beach, his elbows resting on his knees to steady the binoculars in his hands. When he lowered the glasses he could barely see the boat—a white speck that disappeared and reappeared in the ocean swells.

"Hey, Chief," Hendricks said, walking up to Brody. "I was just passing by and I saw your car. What are you doing?"

"Trying to figure out what the hell Ben Gardner's doing."

"Fishing, don't you think?"

"That's what he's being paid to do, but I've been here an hour, and I haven't seen anything move on that boat."

"Can I take a look?" Brody handed him the glasses. Hendricks raised them and looked out to sea. "Nope, you're right. How long has he been out there?"

"All day, I think. He said he'd be taking off at six this morning."

"You want to go see? We've got at least two more hours of daylight. I'll borrow Chickering's boat."

Brody felt a shimmy of fear skitter up his back. He was a very poor swimmer, and the prospect of being on top of—let alone in— water above his head gave him what his mother used to call the whim-whams: sweaty palms, a persistent need to swallow and an ache in his stomach—essentially the sensation some people feel about flying. "Okay," he said. "I guess we should. Maybe by the time we get to the dock he'll already have started in. You go get the boat ready. I'll telephone his wife to see if he's called in on the radio."

Hendricks was standing in Chickering's Aquasport, the engine running, when Brody came along the town dock and climbed down into the boat.

"What did she say?" asked Hendricks.

"She hasn't heard a word. She's been trying to raise him for half an hour, but she figures he must have turned off the radio."

"Is he alone?"

"As far as she knows. His mate had an impacted wisdom tooth that had to be taken out today."

Hendricks cast off the hawser at the bow, walked to the stern, uncleated the stern line and tossed it onto the deck. He moved to the control console and pushed a knobbed handle forward. The boat lurched ahead, chugging.

Brody grabbed a steel handle on the side of the console. "Are there any life jackets?" he asked.

"Just the cushions," said Hendricks. "They'd hold you up all right, if you were an eight-year-old boy."

"Thanks."

The breeze had died, but there were small swells, and the boat took them roughly, smacking its prow into each one, recovering with a shudder that unnerved Brody. "This thing's gonna break apart if you don't slow down," he said.

Hendricks smiled. "No worry, Chief. If I slow down, it'll take us a week to get out there."

Gardner's boat was anchored about three-quarters of a mile from shore, its stern toward them. As they drew nearer, Brody could make out the black letters on the flat wooden transom: *FLICKA*.

Fifty yards from the *Flicka*, Hendricks throttled down, and the boat settled into a slow roll. They saw no signs of life. There were no rods in the rod holders. "Hey, Ben!" Brody called. There was no reply.

"Maybe he's below," said Hendricks.

When the bow of the Aquasport was only a few feet from the *Flicka*'s port quarter, Hendricks pushed the handle into neutral, then gave it a quick burst of reverse. The Aquasport stopped and, on the next swell, Brody grabbed the gunwale.

Hendricks made a line fast to the other boat, then both men climbed into the *Flicka*'s cockpit. Brody poked his head through the forward hatch. "You in there, Ben?" He looked around, withdrew his head and said to Hendricks, "He's not on board. No two ways about it."

"What's that stuff?" said Hendricks, pointing to a bucket in one corner of the stern.

Brody walked to the bucket and bent down. A stench of fish and oil filled his nose. "Must be chum—fish guts," he said. "You spread it around in the water and it's supposed to attract sharks. He didn't use much of it. The bucket's almost full."

Suddenly a voice crackled over the radio. "This is the *Pretty Belle*. You there, Jake?"

"He never turned off his radio," said Brody.

"I don't get it, Chief. He didn't carry a dinghy, so he couldn't have rowed away. He swam like a fish, so if he fell overboard he would've just climbed back on."

Brody was standing at the starboard gunwale when the boat moved slightly, and he steadied himself with his right hand. He felt something strange and looked down. There were four ragged screw holes where a cleat had been. The wood around the holes was torn. "Look at this, Leonard."

Hendricks ran his hand over the holes. He looked to the port side, where a ten-inch steel cleat still sat securely on the wood. "What would it take to pull a thing as big as that out?" he said.

"Look here, Leonard." There was an eight-inch scar on the gunwale. "It looks like someone took a file to this wood."

Brody walked to the stern and leaned on his elbows on the gunwale. As he gazed down at the transom a pattern began to take shape, a pattern of holes, deep gouges in the wood, forming a rough semicircle more than three feet across. Next to it was another, similar pattern. And at the bottom of the transom, just at the waterline, were three short smears of blood. Please, God, thought Brody, not another one. "Come here, Leonard," he said.

Hendricks walked to the stern and looked over. "What?"

"If I hold your legs, you think you can lean over and take a look at those holes and try to figure out what made them?"

"I guess so." Hendricks lay on the top of the transom. Brody took one of his legs under each arm and lifted.

"Okay?" said Brody.

"A little more. Not too much! You just dipped my head in the water."

"Sorry. How's that?" Brody said.

"Okay, that's it." Hendricks began to examine the holes. "If some shark came along he could grab me right out of your hands."

"Don't think about it. Just look."

In a moment Hendricks said, "Hey, pull me up. I need my pocketknife."

"What is it?" Brody asked when Hendricks was back aboard.

"There's a white chip or something stuck into one of the holes," Hendricks replied. Knife in hand, he allowed himself to be lowered over the rail again. He worked briefly, his body twisting from the effort. Then he called, "Okay. I've got it. Pull."

Brody hoisted Hendricks over the transom. "Let's see," he said, and Hendricks dropped a triangle of glistening white denticle into his hand. It was nearly two inches long. The sides were tiny saws. Brody scraped the tooth against the gunwale, and it cut the wood.

"It's a tooth, isn't it?" said Hendricks. "My God! You think the shark got Ben?"

"I don't know what else to think," said Brody. He dropped the tooth into his pocket. "We might as well go. There's nothing we can do here."

"What do you want to do with Ben's boat?"

"It's getting dark. We'll leave it here. No one's going to need this boat before tomorrow, especially not Ben Gardner."

THEY arrived at the dock in late twilight. Harry Meadows and another man, unknown to Brody, were waiting for them. As Brody climbed the ladder onto the dock Meadows gestured toward the man beside him. "This is Matt Hooper. Matt Hooper, Chief Brody."

The two men shook hands. "You're the fellow from Woods Hole," Brody said, trying to get a look at him in the fading light. He was young—mid-twenties, Brody thought—and handsome: tanned, hair bleached by the sun. He was about as tall as Brody, an inch over six feet, but leaner.

"That's right," said Hooper.

Meadows said, "I called him. I thought he might be able to figure out what's going on."

Brody sensed resentment in himself at the intrusion, the complication that Hooper's expertise was bound to add, the implicit division of authority that Hooper's arrival had created. And he recognized the resentment as stupid. "Sure, Harry," he said.

"What did you find out there?" Meadows asked.

Brody started to reach in his pocket for the tooth, but he stopped. "I'm not sure," he said. "Come on back to the station house and I'll fill you in."

"Is Ben going to stay out there all night?"

"It looks that way, Harry." Brody turned to Hendricks, who had finished tying up the boat. "You going home, Leonard?"

"Yeah. I want to clean up before I go to work."

Brody arrived at police headquarters before Meadows and Hooper. It was almost eight o'clock. He had two phone calls to make—to Ellen, to see if there were any dinner leftovers, and, the call he dreaded, to Sally Gardner. He called Ellen first; the pot roast could be reheated. It might taste like a sneaker, but it would be warm. He hung up, checked the phone book for the Gardner number and dialed it.

"Sally? This is Martin Brody." Suddenly he regretted having called without thinking about what he should tell her.

"Where's Ben, Martin?" The voice was calm, but pitched slightly higher than normal.

"I don't know, Sally. He wasn't on the boat."

"You went on board? You looked all over it? Even below?"

"Yes." Then a tiny hope. "Ben didn't carry a dinghy, did he?"

"No. How could he not be there?" The voice was shriller now.

Brody wished he had gone to the house in person. "Are you alone, Sally?"

"No. The kids are here."

Brody dug at his memory for the ages of the Gardner children. Twelve, maybe; then nine, then about six. Who was the nearest neighbor? The Finleys. "Just a second, Sally." He called to the officer at the front desk. "Clements, call Grace Finley and tell her to get over to Sally Gardner's house. Tell her I'll explain later." As he turned back to the phone Meadows and Hooper walked into the office. He motioned them to chairs.

"But where could he be?" said Sally Gardner. "You don't just get off a boat in the middle of the ocean."

"No."

"Maybe someone came and took him off in another boat. Maybe the engine wouldn't start. Did you check the engine?"

"No," Brody said, embarrassed.

"That's probably it, then." The voice was subtly lighter, almost girlish, coated with a veneer of hope that, when it broke, would shatter like iced crystal. "And if the battery was dead, that would explain why he couldn't call on the radio."

"The radio was working, Sally."

"Wait a minute. . . . Who's there? Oh, it's you." Brody heard Sally talking to Grace Finley. Then Sally came back on the line. "Grace says you told her to come over here. Why?"

"I thought—"

"You think he's dead, don't you?" She began to sob.

"I'm afraid so, Sally. That's all we can think at the moment. Let me talk to Grace, will you please?"

A couple of seconds later Grace's voice said, "Yes, Martin?"

"Can you stay with her for a while?"

"Yes. All night."

"That might be a good idea."

"Is it that . . . *thing* again?"

"Maybe. That's what we're trying to figure out. But do me a favor, Grace. Don't say anything about a shark to Sally. It's bad enough as it is." He replaced the phone and looked at Meadows. "You heard."

"I gather that Ben Gardner has become victim number four."

Brody nodded. "I think so." He told Meadows and Hooper about his trip with Hendricks. Once or twice Meadows interrupted with a question. Hooper listened, his angular face placid and his eyes— a light, powder blue—fixed on Brody. At the end of his tale Brody reached into his pants pocket. "We found this," he said. "Leonard dug it out of the wood." He flipped the tooth to Hooper, who turned it over in his hand.

"What do you think, Matt?" said Meadows.

"It's a great white."

"How big?"

"Fifteen, twenty feet. That's some fantastic fish." He looked at Meadows. "Thanks for calling me. I could spend a whole lifetime around sharks and never see a fish like that."

Brody asked, "How much would a fish like that weigh?"

"Five or six thousand pounds."

Brody whistled. "Three tons."

"Do you have any thoughts about what happened?" Meadows asked Hooper.

"From what the chief says, it sounds like the fish killed Mr. Gardner."

"How?" said Brody.

"Any number of ways. Gardner might have fallen overboard. More likely, he was pulled over. His leg may have gotten tangled in a harpoon line. He could even have been taken while he was leaning over the stern."

"How do you account for the teeth in the stern?"

"The fish attacked the boat."

"What the hell for?"

"Sharks aren't very bright, Chief. They exist on instinct and impulse. The impulse to feed is powerful."

"But a thirty-foot boat—"

"To him it wasn't a boat. It was just something large."

"And inedible."

"Not till he'd tried it. You have to understand. There's nothing in the sea this fish would fear. Other fish run from bigger things. That's their instinct. But this fish doesn't run from anything."

"Do you have any idea why he's hung around so long?" said Brody. "I don't know how much you know about the water here, but—"

"I grew up here."

"You did? In Amity?"

"No, Southampton. I spent all my summers there."

"*Summers.* So you didn't really grow up there." Brody was groping for something with which to reestablish his parity with, if not superiority to, the younger man, and what he settled for was reverse snobbism, a defensive attitude not uncommon to year-round residents of resort communities. It was an attitude that, in general, Brody found both repugnant and silly. But he felt somehow threatened by the younger man.

"Okay," Hooper said testily, "so I wasn't born here. But I've spent a lot of time in these waters, and I wrote a paper on this coastline. Anyway, you're right. This isn't an environment that would normally support a long stay by a shark. On the other hand, anyone who'd risk money—not to mention his life—on a prediction about what a shark will do is a fool. There are things that could cause him to stay here—natural factors, caprices."

"Like what?"

"Changes in water temperature or current flow or feeding patterns. As food supplies move, so do the predators. Last summer, for example, off Connecticut and Rhode Island, the coastline was suddenly inundated with menhaden—fishermen call them bunker. They coated the water like an oil slick. Bluefish and bass feed on menhaden, so all of a sudden there were masses of bluefish right off the beaches. Then the big predators came—tuna, four, five, six hundred pounds. Deep-sea fishing boats were catching bluefin tuna within a hundred yards of the shore. Then suddenly it stopped. The menhaden went away, and so did the other fish. I spent three weeks up there trying to figure out what was going on. I still don't know."

"But this is even weirder," said Brody. "This fish has stayed in one chunk of water only a mile or two square for over a week. He hasn't touched anybody in East Hampton or Southampton. What is it about Amity?"

"I don't know. I doubt that anyone could give you an answer."

Meadows said, "Minnie Eldridge has the answer."

"Who's Minnie Eldridge?" asked Hooper.

"The postmistress," said Brody. "She says it's God's will, or something like that. We're being punished for our sins."

Hooper smiled. "Right now, anyway, that's as good an answer as I've got."

"That's encouraging," said Brody. "Is there anything you plan to do to *get* an answer?"

"There are a few things. I'll take water samples here and in East Hampton. I'll find out how other fish are behaving—and I'll try to find that shark. Which reminds me, is there a boat available?"

"Yes, I'm sorry to say," said Brody. "Ben Gardner's. Do you

really think you can catch that fish, after what happened to him?"

"I don't think I'd want to try to catch it. Not alone, anyway."

Brody looked into Hooper's eyes and said, "I want that fish killed. If you can't do it, we'll find someone who can."

Hooper laughed. "You sound like a mobster. 'I want that fish killed.' So go get a contract out on him. Who are you going to get to do the job?"

"I don't know. What about it, Harry? You're supposed to know everything that goes on around here. Isn't there any fisherman on this whole damn island equipped to catch big sharks?"

Meadows thought for a moment before he spoke. "There may be one. I don't know much about him, but I think his name is Quint, and I think he operates out of a private pier somewhere around Promised Land. I can find out a little more about him if you like."

"Why not?" said Brody. "He sounds like a possible."

Hooper said, "Look, Chief, that shark isn't evil. It's not a murderer. It's just obeying its instincts. Trying to get retribution against a fish is crazy."

"Listen, you . . ." Brody was growing angry—an anger born of frustration and humiliation. He knew Hooper was right, but he felt that right and wrong were irrelevant to the situation. The fish was an enemy. It had come upon the community and killed two men, a woman and a child. The people of Amity would demand the death of the fish. They would need to see it dead before they could feel secure enough to resume their normal lives. Most of all, Brody needed it dead, for the death of the fish would be a catharsis for him. But he swallowed his rage and said, "Forget it."

The phone rang. "Mr. Vaughan, Chief," Clements called.

"Oh, swell. That's just what I need." Brody picked up the receiver. "Yeah, Larry."

"Hello, Martin. How are you?" Vaughan was friendly, almost effusive. Brody thought, He's probably had a couple of belts.

"As well as can be expected, Larry."

"I heard about Ben Gardner. Are you sure it was the shark?"

"Yeah, I guess so. Nothing else seems to make any sense."

"Martin, what are we going to *do?* I'm getting cancellations every day. I haven't had a new customer in here since Sunday."

"So what do you want *me* to do?"

"Well, I thought . . . I mean, what I'm wondering is, maybe we're overreacting to this whole thing."

"You're kidding. Tell me you're kidding."

There was a moment of silence, and then Vaughan said, "What would you say to opening the beaches, just for the Fourth of July weekend?"

"Not a chance."

"Now listen—"

"No, you listen, Larry. The last time I listened to you we had two people killed. If we catch that fish, if we kill him, then we'll open the beaches. Until then, forget it."

"What about patrols? We could hire people to patrol up and down the beaches in boats."

"That's not good enough, Larry. What is it with you, anyway? Are your partners on you again?"

"That's none of your business, Martin. For God's sake, man, this town is dying!"

"I know it, Larry," Brody said softly. "And as far as I know, there's not a damn thing we can do about it. Good night." He hung up the phone.

Meadows and Hooper rose to leave. Brody walked them to the front door of the station house. As they started out Brody said to Meadows, "Hey, Harry, you left your lighter inside. Come on back and I'll give it to you." He waved to Hooper. "See you."

When they were back in Brody's office Meadows took his lighter from his pocket and said, "I trust you had something to say."

Brody shut the door. "You think you can find out something about Larry's partners?"

"I guess so. Why?"

"Ever since this thing began Larry has been after me to keep the beaches open. And now, after all that's just happened, he says he wants them open for the Fourth. The other day he said he was under heavy pressure from his partners. I told you about it."

"And?"

"I think we should know who it is who has enough clout to drive Larry crazy. He's the mayor of this town, and if there are people telling him what to do, I think I ought to know who they are."

Meadows sighed. "Okay, Martin. I'll do what I can. But digging around in Larry Vaughan's affairs isn't my idea of fun."

Brody walked Meadows to the door, then went back to his desk and sat down. Vaughan had been right about one thing, he thought: Amity was showing all the signs of imminent death. And it wasn't just the real estate market.

Two new boutiques that had been scheduled to open the next day had had to put off their debuts until July third. The sporting-goods store had advertised a clearance sale—a sale that normally took place over the Labor Day weekend. The only good thing about the Amity economy, as far as Brody was concerned, was that Saxon's was doing so badly that it had laid off Henry Kimble. Now that he didn't have his bartending job, he could occasionally get through a shift of police work without a nap.

Beginning on Monday morning—the first day the beaches had been closed—Brody had posted men on them. Since then there had been four reports of shark sightings by members of the public. One had turned out to be a floating log. Two, according to fishermen, were schools of jumping baitfish. And one, as far as anyone could tell, was a flat nothing.

On Tuesday evening at dusk Brody had received an anonymous phone call telling him that a man was dumping shark bait into the water off the beach. It turned out to be not a man, but a woman in a man's raincoat—Jessie Parker, one of the clerks at Walden's Stationery Store. She admitted she had tossed a paper bag into the surf. It contained three empty vermouth bottles.

"Why didn't you throw them in the garbage?" Brody had asked.

"I didn't want the garbageman to think I'm a heavy drinker."

"Then why didn't you throw them in someone else's garbage?"

"That wouldn't be nice," she had said. "Garbage is . . . sort of private, don't you think?"

Brody had told her that from now on she should take her empty bottles, put them in a plastic bag, put that bag in a brown paper bag, then smash the bottles with a hammer until they were ground up. Nobody would ever know they had been bottles.

Brody looked at his watch. It was after nine o'clock. Before he left the office he called the Coast Guard station at Montauk and told the duty officer about Ben Gardner. The officer said he would dispatch a patrol boat at first light to search for the body.

"Thanks," said Brody. "I hope you find it before it washes up." He was suddenly appalled at himself. "It" was Ben Gardner, a friend.

"We'll try," said the officer. "Boy, I feel for you guys. You're having some summer."

"I only hope it isn't our last," said Brody. He hung up, turned out the light in his office and walked out to his car.

As HE turned into his driveway Brody saw the familiar blue-gray light of television shining from the windows. He walked through the front door and poked his head into the living room. His oldest boy, Billy, fourteen, lay on the couch. Martin, age twelve, lounged in an easy chair. Eight-year-old Sean sat on the floor, his back against the couch. "How goes it?" said Brody.

"Good, Dad," said Bill, without shifting his gaze from the tube.

"Where's your mom?"

"Upstairs. She said to tell you your dinner's in the kitchen."

"Okay. Not too late, Sean, huh? It's almost nine thirty."

Brody went into the kitchen and got a beer from the refrigerator. The remains of the pot roast sat on the counter in a roasting pan. He sliced a thick slab of meat and made a sandwich. He put it on a plate, picked up his beer and climbed the stairs to his bedroom.

Ellen was sitting up in bed, reading a magazine. "Hello," she said. "A tough day? You didn't say anything on the phone."

"You heard about Ben Gardner? I wasn't positive when I talked to you." He put the plate and the beer on the dresser and sat down to remove his shoes.

"Yes. I got a call from Grace Finley asking if I knew where Dr. Craig was. She wanted to give Sally a sedative."

"Did you find him?"

"No. But I had one of the boys take some Seconal over to her."

"I didn't know you were taking sleeping pills."

"I don't often. Just every now and then. I got them from Dr. Craig, when I went to him last time about my nerves. I told you."

"Oh." Brody began to eat his sandwich.

Ellen said, "It's so horrible about Ben. What will Sally do?"

"I don't know," said Brody. "Have you ever talked money with her?"

"There can't be much. She's always saying she'd give anything to be able to afford meat more than once a week, instead of having to eat the fish Ben catches. Will she get Social Security?"

"I'd think so, but it won't amount to much. There may be something the town can do. I'll talk to Vaughan about it."

"Have you made any progress?"

"You mean about catching that damn thing? No. Meadows called that friend of his down from Woods Hole, so he's here."

"What's he like?"

"He's all right, I guess. A bit of a know-it-all, but he seems to know the area. As a kid he spent his summers in Southampton."

"Working?"

"I don't know, living with the parents probably." He finished his sandwich in silence as Ellen aimlessly turned the pages of her magazine.

"You know," she said, "we should give the boys tennis lessons."

"What for? Have they said they want to play tennis?" Brody rose, undressed, and went to find his pajamas in the closet.

"No. Not in so many words. But it's a good sport for them to know. It will help them when they're grown-up."

"Where are they going to get lessons?"

"I was thinking of the Field Club. I think we could get in. I still know a few members."

"Forget it. We can't afford it. I bet it costs a thousand bucks to join, and then it's at least a few hundred a year."

"We have savings."

"Not for tennis lessons! Come on, let's drop it." He walked to the dresser to turn out the light.

"It would be good for the boys."

Brody let his hand fall to the top of the dresser. "Look, we're not tennis people. We wouldn't feel right there. *I* wouldn't feel right there." He switched off the light, walked over to the bed and slid in next to Ellen. "Besides," he said, nuzzling her neck, "there's another sport I'm better at."

Ellen yawned. "I'm so sleepy," she said. "I took a pill before you came home."

"What for?" Brody asked.

"I didn't sleep well last night, and I didn't want to wake up if you came home late."

"I'm going to throw those pills away." He kissed her cheek, then tried to kiss her mouth.

"I'm sorry," she said. "I'm afraid it won't work."

Brody turned onto his back and lay staring at the ceiling.

In a moment Ellen said, "What's Harry's friend's name?"

"Hooper."

"Not David Hooper."

"No. I think his name is Matt."

"Oh. I went out with a David Hooper a long, long time ago. I remember . . ." Before she could finish the sentence her eyes shut, and soon she slipped into the deep breathing of sleep.

Part Two

5

ON HER way home Friday noon, after a morning of volunteer work at the Southampton Hospital, Ellen stopped at the post office to buy a roll of stamps and get the mail. There was no home delivery in Amity.

The post office, just off Main Street, had 500 mailboxes, 340 of which were rented to permanent residents. The other 160 were allotted to summer people according to the whims of the postmistress, Minnie Eldridge. Those she liked were permitted to rent boxes for the summer. Those she didn't like had to wait in line at the counter.

It was generally assumed that Minnie Eldridge was in her early seventies and that she had somehow convinced the authorities in Washington that she was well under compulsory retirement age. She was small and frail-looking, but able to hustle packages and cartons nearly as quickly as the two young men who worked with her. She never spoke about her past. The only common knowledge about her was that she had been born on Nantucket Island. But she had been in Amity for as long as anyone could remember.

Ellen sensed that Minnie didn't like her, and she was right. Minnie felt uneasy with Ellen because she was neither summer folk nor winter folk. She hadn't earned her year-round mailbox, she had married it.

Minnie was sorting mail when Ellen arrived.

"Morning, Minnie," Ellen said.

Minnie looked up at the clock and said, "Afternoon."

"Could I have a roll of eights, please?" Ellen put a five-dollar bill and three ones on the counter.

Minnie gave Ellen a roll of stamps and dropped the bills into a drawer. "What's Martin going to do about that shark?" she said.

"I don't know. I guess they'll try to catch it."

"Canst thou draw out leviathan with an hook?"

"I beg your pardon?"

"Book of Job," said Minnie. "No mortal man's going to catch that fish."

"Why do you say that?"

"We're not meant to catch it, that's why."

"I see." Ellen put the stamps in her purse. "Well, maybe you're right. Thanks, Minnie."

Ellen walked to Main Street and stopped at Amity Hardware. There was no immediate response to the tinkle of the bell as she opened the door.

She walked to the back of the store, to an open door that led to the basement. She heard two men talking below.

"I'll be right up," called the voice of Albert Morris. "Here's a whole box of them," Morris said to the other man. "Look through and see if you find what you want."

"Cleats," Morris said as he climbed to the top of the stairs.

"What?" said Ellen.

"Cleats. Fella wants cleats for a boat. Size he's looking for, he must be captain of a battleship. What can I do for you?"

"I want a rubber nozzle for my kitchen sink."

"Up this way." Morris led Ellen to a cabinet in the middle of the store. "This what you had in mind?" He held up a rubber nozzle.

"Perfect."

As he rang up the sale Morris said, "Lots of people upset about this shark thing. Maybe this fish expert can help us out."

"Oh, yes. I heard he was in town."

"He's down cellar. He's the one wants the cleats."

Just then Ellen heard footsteps on the stairs. She saw Hooper coming through the door and felt a surge of girlish nervousness, as if she were seeing a beau she hadn't seen in years.

"I found them," said Hooper, holding up two large stainless-steel cleats. He smiled politely at Ellen, and said to Morris, "These'll do fine." He handed Morris a twenty-dollar bill.

Ellen hoped Albert Morris would introduce them, but he seemed to have no intention of doing so. "Excuse me," she said to Hooper, "but I have to ask you something."

Hooper looked at her and smiled again—a pleasant, friendly smile. "Sure," he said. "Ask away."

"You aren't by any chance related to David Hooper, are you?"

"He's my older brother. Do you know David?"

"Yes," said Ellen. "Or rather, I used to. I went out with him a long time ago. I'm Ellen Brody. I used to be Ellen Shepherd."

"Oh, sure. I remember you."

"You don't."

"I do. No kidding. Let me see. . . . You wore your hair shorter then, sort of a pageboy. You always wore a charm bracelet. It had a big charm that looked like the Eiffel Tower. And you always used to sing that song—what was it called?—'Sh-boom,' right?"

Ellen laughed. "My heavens, you have quite a memory."

"It's screwy the things that impress kids. You went out with David for what—two years?"

"Two summers," Ellen said. "They were fun."

"Do you remember me?"

"Vaguely. You must have been about nine or ten then."

"About that; David's ten years older than I am. Another thing I remember: everybody called me Matt, but you called me Matthew. You said it sounded more dignified. I was probably in love with you."

"Oh?" Ellen reddened, and Albert Morris laughed.

Morris handed Hooper his change, and Hooper said to Ellen, "I'm going down to the dock. Can I drop you anywhere?"

"Thank you. I have a car. So now you're a scientist," she said as they walked out together.

"Kind of by accident. I started out as an English major. But then I took a course in marine biology to satisfy my science requirement, and—bingo!—I was hooked."

"On what? The ocean?"

"Yes and no. I was always crazy about the ocean. But what I got hooked on was fish, or, to be really specific, sharks."

Ellen laughed. "It's like having a passion for rats."

"That's what most people think," said Hooper. "But they're wrong. Sharks are beautiful. They're like an impossibly perfect piece of machinery. They're as graceful as any bird. They're as mysterious as any animal on earth. No one knows for sure how long they live or what impulses—except for hunger—they respond to. There are more than two hundred and fifty species of shark, and every one is different from every other." He stopped, looked at Ellen and smiled. "I'm sorry. I don't mean to lecture."

"You must be the world's greatest living shark expert."

"Hardly," Hooper said with a laugh. "But after graduate school I spent a couple of years chasing sharks around the world. I tagged them in the Red Sea and dove with them off Australia."

"You dove with them?"

Hooper nodded. "In a cage mostly, but sometimes not. I know what you must think. A lot of people think I've got a death wish, but if you know what you're doing, you can reduce the danger to almost nil."

"Tell me about David," Ellen said. "How is he?"

"He's okay. He's a broker in San Francisco. He's been married twice. His first wife was—maybe you know this—Patty Fremont."

"Sure. I used to play tennis with her."

"That lasted three years, until she latched on to someone else. So David found himself a girl whose father owns most of an oil company. She's nice, but she's got the IQ of an artichoke. If David had had any sense he would have held on to you."

Ellen blushed and said softly, "You're nice to say it."

"I'm serious. That's what I'd have done."

"What did you do? What lucky girl finally got you?"

"None, so far. I guess there are girls around who just don't know how lucky they could be." Hooper laughed. "Tell me about yourself. No, don't. Let me guess. Three children. Right?"

"Right. I didn't realize it showed that much."

"No, no. I don't mean that. It doesn't show at all. Not at all. Your husband is—let's see—a lawyer. You have an apartment in town and a house on the beach in Amity."

Ellen shook her head, smiling. "Not quite. My husband is the police chief in Amity."

Hooper let his surprise show for only an instant. Then he said, "Of course—Brody. I never made the connection. Your husband seems like quite a guy."

Ellen thought she detected a flicker of irony in Hooper's voice, but then she told herself, Don't be stupid. You're making things up. "Do you live in Woods Hole?" she said.

"No. In Hyannis Port. In a little house on the water. I have a thing about being near the water. Say, do you still dance?"

"Dance?"

"Yeah. David used to say you were the best dancer he ever went out with. You won a contest, didn't you?"

The past was suddenly swirling around in her head, showering her with longing. "A samba contest," she said. "At the Beach Club. I'd forgotten. No, I don't dance anymore. Martin doesn't dance, and even if he did, nobody plays that kind of music anymore."

"That's too bad. Well, I should get down to the dock. You're sure I can't drop you anywhere?"

"Positive, thank you. My car's just across the street."

"Okay." Hooper held out his hand. "I don't suppose I could get you out on a tennis court late some afternoon."

Ellen laughed. "Oh, my. I haven't held a tennis racquet in my hand since I can't remember when. But thanks for asking."

"Okay. Well, see you." Hooper hurried off to his car. As he pulled out into the street and drove past her she raised her hand and waved, tentatively, shyly. Hooper waved back. Then he turned the corner and was gone.

A terrible sadness clutched at Ellen. More than ever before she felt that her life—the best part of it, at least—was behind her. Recognizing the sensation made her feel guilty, for she read it as proof that she was an unsatisfactory mother, an unsatisfied wife. She thought of a line from a song Billy played on the stereo. *I'd trade all my tomorrows for a single yesterday.* Would she make a deal like that? She wondered.

A vision of Hooper's smiling face flashed across her mind. Forget it, she told herself.

WITH the beaches closed, Amity was practically deserted on the weekend. Hooper cruised up and down offshore in Ben Gardner's boat, but the only signs of life he saw in the water were a few schools of baitfish and one small school of bluefish. By Sunday night he told Brody he was ready to conclude that the shark had gone back to the deep.

"What makes you think so?" Brody had asked.

"There's not a sign of him," said Hooper. "And there are other fish. If there was a big white in the neighborhood, everything else would vanish. That's one thing divers say about whites. When they're around there's an awful stillness in the water."

"I'm not convinced," said Brody. "At least not enough to open the beaches. Not yet." He almost wished Hooper had seen the fish. This was nothing but negative evidence, and to his policeman's mind that was not enough.

On Monday afternoon Brody was sitting in his office when Ellen phoned. "I'm sorry to bother you," she said. "But what would you think about giving a dinner party? I can't even remember when our last one was."

"Neither can I," said Brody. But it was a lie. He remembered their last dinner party all too well. Three years ago, when Ellen was in the midst of a crusade to reestablish her ties with the summer community, she had asked three summer couples. They were nice enough people, Brody recalled, but the conversations had been stiff and uncomfortable. Brody and the guests had few common interests, and after a while the guests had fallen back on talking among themselves. When they had left, and after Ellen had done the dishes, she said twice to Brody, *"Wasn't* that a nice evening!" Then she shut herself in the bathroom and wept.

"Well, what do you think?" said Ellen.

"I guess it's all right. Who are you going to invite?"

"First of all, I think we should have Matt Hooper."

"What for? He eats over at the Abelard, doesn't he? It's all included in the price of the room."

"That's not the point. He's alone in town, and he's very nice."

"I didn't think you knew him."

"I ran into him in Morris's on Friday. I'm *sure* I mentioned it to you, because it turns out he's the brother of the Hooper I used to know."

"Uh-huh. When are you planning this shindig for?"

"I was thinking about tomorrow night. And it's not going to be a shindig. I simply thought we could have a nice, small party with a few couples. What about the Baxters? Would they be fun?"

"I don't think I know them."

"Yes, you do. Clem and Cici Baxter. She was Cici Davenport. They live out on Scotch. He's taking some vacation now."

"Okay. Try them if you want. How about the Meadowses?"

"But Matt Hooper already knows Harry."

"He doesn't know Dorothy."

"All right," said Ellen. "I guess a little local color won't hurt."

"I wasn't thinking about local color," Brody said sharply. "They're our friends."

"I know. I didn't mean anything."

"If you want local color, all you have to do is look on the other side of your bed."

"I *know.* I said I was sorry."

"What about a girl?" said Brody. "I think you should try to find some nice young thing for Hooper."

There was a pause before Ellen said, "All right. I'll see if I can think of somebody who'd be fun for him."

WHEN BRODY ARRIVED HOME THE next evening Ellen was setting the dinner table. He kissed her and said, "It's been a long time since I've seen that silver." It was Ellen's wedding silver, a gift from her parents.

"I know. It took me hours to polish it."

"And will you look at this?" Brody picked up a tulip wineglass. "Where did you get these?"

"I bought them at the Lure."

"How much?" Brody set the glass down on the table.

"Twenty dollars. But that was for a whole dozen."

"You don't kid around when you throw a party."

"We didn't have any decent wineglasses," she said defensively.

Brody counted the places set. "Only six?" he said.

"The Baxters couldn't make it. Clem had to go into town on business, and Cici thought she'd go with him. They're spending the night." There was a fragile lilt to her voice, a false insouciance.

"Oh," said Brody. "Too bad." He dared not show that he was pleased. "Who'd you get for Hooper, some nice young chick?"

"Daisy Wicker. She works at the Bibelot. She's a nice girl."

"What time are people coming?"

"The Meadowses and Daisy at seven thirty. I asked Matthew for seven. I wanted him to come early so the kids could get to know him. I think they'll be fascinated."

Brody looked at his watch. "If people aren't coming till seven thirty, we won't be eating till eight thirty or nine. I think I'll grab a sandwich." He started for the kitchen.

"Don't stuff yourself," said Ellen. "I've got a delicious dinner coming."

Brody sniffed the kitchen aromas, eyed the clutter of pots and packages and said, "What are you cooking?"

"It's called butterfly lamb. I hope I don't botch it."

"Smells good," said Brody. "What's this stuff in the pot by the sink? Should I throw it out?"

Ellen hurried into the kitchen. "Don't you dare—" She saw the smile on Brody's face. "Oh, you rat." She slapped him on the rear. "That's gazpacho. Soup."

Brody shook his head. "Old Hooper's going to wish he ate at the Abelard," he said.

"You're a beast," she said. "Wait till you taste it. You'll change your tune."

At 7:05 the doorbell rang, and Brody answered it. He was wearing a blue madras shirt, blue uniform slacks and black cordovans. He felt crisp and clean. But when he opened the door for Hooper, he felt outclassed. Hooper wore bell-bottom blue jeans and Weejun loafers with no socks. It was the uniform of the young and rich in Amity.

"Hi," said Brody. "Come in."

"Hi," said Hooper. He extended his hand, and Brody shook it.

Ellen came from the kitchen in a long batik skirt and a silk blouse. She wore the cultured pearls Brody had given her as a wedding present. "Matthew," she said. "I'm glad you could come."

"I'm glad you asked me," Hooper said, shaking Ellen's hand. He turned and said to Brody, "Do you mind if I give Ellen something?"

"What do you mean?" Brody said. He thought, Give her what? A kiss? A box of chocolates? A punch in the nose?

"A present. Nothing, really. Just something I picked up."

"No, I don't mind," said Brody.

Hooper dug into the pocket of his jeans and handed Ellen a small package wrapped in tissue. "For the hostess," he said.

Ellen tittered and carefully unwrapped the paper. Inside was what seemed to be a pendant, an inch or so across.

"It's a tiger-shark tooth," said Hooper. "The casing's silver."

"Where did you get it?"

"In Macao. I passed through there a couple of years ago on a project. There's a superstition that if you keep it with you, you'll be safe from shark bite. Under the present circumstances, I thought it would be appropriate."

"Completely," said Ellen. "Do you have one?"

"I have one," said Hooper, "but I don't know how to carry it. I don't like to wear things around my neck, and if you carry a shark tooth in your pants pocket, you end up with a gash in your pants."

Ellen laughed and said to Brody, "Martin, could I ask a huge favor? Would you run upstairs and get that silver chain out of my jewelry box? I'll put Matthew's shark tooth on right now."

Brody started up the stairs, and Ellen said, "Oh, and Martin, tell the boys to come down."

As he rounded the corner at the top of the stairs Brody heard Ellen say, "It *is* such fun to see you again."

Brody walked into the bedroom and sat down on the edge of the bed, clenching and unclenching his right fist. He felt as if an intruder had come into his home, possessing subtle weapons he could not cope with: looks and youth and sophistication and, above all, a communion with Ellen born in a time which, Brody knew, Ellen wished had never ended. He felt that Ellen was trying to impress Hooper. He didn't know why. It demeaned her, Brody thought; and it demeaned Brody that she should try, by posturing, to deny her life with him.

"To hell with it," he said aloud. He stood up, opened Ellen's jewelry box and took out the silver chain. Before going downstairs he poked his head into the boys' rooms and said, "Let's go, troops."

Ellen and Hooper were sitting on the couch, and as Brody walked into the room he heard Ellen say, "Would you rather that I not call you Matthew?"

Hooper laughed. "I don't mind. It sort of brings back memories."

"Here," Brody said to Ellen, handing her the chain.

"Thank you." She unclasped the pearls and tossed them onto the coffee table. "Now, Matthew, show me how this should go."

Brody went into the kitchen to make drinks. Ellen had asked for vermouth on the rocks, Hooper for a gin and tonic. He poured the vermouth and mixed Hooper's drink, then started to make a rye and ginger for himself. By habit he began to measure the rye with a shot glass, but then he changed his mind and poured until the glass was a third full. He topped it off with ginger ale, dropped in a few ice cubes and reached for the two other glasses. The only convenient way to carry them in one hand seemed to involve sticking his index finger down inside one glass.

The boys, neatly dressed in sport shirts and slacks, had joined Ellen and Hooper in the living room. Billy and Martin were crowded onto the couch with them and Sean was sitting on the floor. Brody heard Hooper say something about a pig, and Martin said, "Wow!"

"Here," said Brody, handing Ellen the glass with his finger in it.

"No tip for you, my man," she said. "It's a good thing you decided against a career as a waiter."

Brody looked at her, considered a rude remark and settled for, "Forgive me, Duchess." He handed the other glass to Hooper.

"Matt was just telling us about a shark he caught," said Ellen. "It had almost a whole pig in it."

"No kidding," said Brody. He took a long swallow of his drink.

"And that's not all, Dad," said Martin. "There was a roll of tar paper, too."

"And a human bone," said Sean.

"I said it looked like a human bone," said Hooper. "There was no way to be sure at the time. It might have been a beef rib."

"Hey, Dad," said Billy. "You know how a porpoise kills a shark?"

"With a gun?"

"No, man. It butts him to death. That's what Mr. Hooper says."

"Terrific," said Brody, and he drained his glass. "I'm going to have another drink. Anybody else ready?"

"On a weeknight?" said Ellen. "My!"

"Why not? It's not every night we throw a no-kidding, go-to-hell dinner party." Brody started for the kitchen but was stopped by the doorbell. He opened the door and saw Dorothy Meadows, wearing a dark blue dress and a single strand of pearls. Behind her was a girl Brody assumed was Daisy Wicker—a tall, slim girl with long, straight hair. She wore slacks and sandals and no makeup. Behind her was the unmistakable bulk of Harry Meadows.

"Hello, there," said Brody. "Come on in."

"Good evening, Martin," said Dorothy Meadows. "We met Miss Wicker as we came into the driveway."

"I walked," said Daisy Wicker. "It was nice."

"Good, good. Come on in." Brody led them into the living room and turned them over to Ellen for introduction to Hooper. He took drink orders, but before fixing them he made a fresh one for himself and sipped it while preparing the others. By the time they were ready he had finished half his drink, so he poured in a generous splash of rye and a dash more ginger ale.

Brody took Dorothy's and Daisy's drinks first, and returned to the kitchen for Meadows's and his own. He was taking one last swallow before rejoining the company when Ellen came in.

"Don't you think you better slow down?" she said.

"I'm fine," he said. "Don't worry about me." As he spoke he realized she was right: he had better slow down. He walked into the living room.

The children had gone upstairs. Dorothy Meadows was chatting with Hooper about his work, while Harry listened. Daisy Wicker was standing alone, on the other side of the room, gazing about with a subdued smile on her face. Brody strolled over to her.

"You're smiling," he said.

"Am I? I guess I was just interested. I've never been in a policeman's house before."

"And what have you decided? It looks just like a normal person's house, doesn't it?"

"I guess so." She took a sip of her drink and said, "Do you like being a policeman?"

Brody couldn't tell whether or not there was hostility in the question. "Yes. It's a good job, and it has a purpose to it."

"What's the purpose?"

"What do you think?" he said, slightly irritated. "To uphold the law."

"Don't you feel alienated?"

"Why the hell should I feel alienated? Alienated from what?"

"From the people. I mean, the only thing that justifies your existence is telling people what not to do. Doesn't that make you feel freaky?"

For a moment Brody thought he was being put on, but the girl never smiled or shifted her eyes from his. "No, I don't feel freaky," he said. "I don't see why I should feel any more freaky than you do, working at the whatchamacallit."

"The Bibelot."

"Yeah. What do you sell there, anyway?"

"We sell people their past. It gives them comfort."

"What do you mean, their past?"

"Antiques. They're bought by people who hate their present and need the security of their past. If not theirs, someone else's. I bet that's important to you, too."

"What, the past?"

"No, security. Isn't that supposed to be one of the heavy things about being a cop?"

Brody glanced across the room and noticed that Harry Meadows's glass was empty. "Excuse me," he said. "I have to tend to the other guests."

Brody took Meadows's glass and his own into the kitchen. Ellen was checking the meat in the broiler.

"Where the hell did you find that girl?" he said. "She's a spook. She's just like some of the kids we bust who start smart-mouthing us in the station." He made a drink for Meadows, then poured another for himself. He looked up and saw Ellen staring at him.

"What's the matter with you?" she said.

"I guess I don't like people coming into my house and insulting me." He picked up the two drinks and started for the door.

Ellen said, "Martin . . ." and he stopped. "For my sake . . . please."

"Calm *down*," he said. "Everything'll be fine."

He refilled Hooper's glass and Daisy Wicker's. Then he sat down and nursed his drink through a long story Meadows was telling

Daisy. Brody felt all right—pretty good, in fact—and he knew that if he didn't have anything more to drink before dinner, he'd be fine.

At 8:30 Ellen brought the soup plates out from the kitchen and set them around the table. "Martin," she said, "would you open the wine for me while I get everyone seated? There's a bottle of white in the refrigerator and there are two reds on the counter. You may as well open them all. The red will need time to breathe."

"Of course it will," Brody said as he stood up. "Who doesn't?"

In the kitchen he found the corkscrew and went to work on the two bottles of red wine. He pulled one cork cleanly, but the other crumbled, and pieces slipped into the bottle. He took the bottle of white out of the refrigerator, uncorked it and took it into the dining room.

Ellen was seated at the end of the table nearest the kitchen. Hooper was at her left, Meadows at her right. Next to Meadows, Daisy Wicker, then an empty space for Brody at the far end of the table, and, opposite Daisy, Dorothy Meadows.

When he had poured the wine Brody sat down and took a spoonful of the soup in front of him. It was cold, and it didn't taste anything like soup, but it wasn't bad.

"I love gazpacho," said Daisy, "but it's such a pain to make that I don't have it very often."

"Mmmm," said Brody, spooning another mouthful.

"Have you ever tried a G and G?"

"Can't say as I have."

"You ought to try one. Of course, you might not enjoy it since it's breaking the law."

"What is it?"

"Grass and gazpacho. Instead of herbs, you sprinkle a little marijuana over the top. It's really wild."

Brody didn't answer right away. He scooped out the last little bit of his soup, drained his wineglass in one draft and looked at Daisy, who was smiling sweetly at him. "You know," he said, "I don't find—"

"I bet Matt's tried one." Daisy raised her voice and said, "Matt, excuse me." The conversation at the other end of the table stopped. "I was just curious. Have you ever tried a G and G? By the way, Mrs. Brody, this is terrific gazpacho."

"Thank you," said Ellen. "But what's a G and G?"

"I tried one once," said Hooper. "But I was never really into that."

"Matt'll tell you," said Daisy to Ellen, and she turned to talk to Meadows.

Brody cleared away the soup bowls and Ellen followed him into the kitchen. "I'll need some help carving," she said.

"Okeydoke," said Brody, and Ellen hefted the lamb onto the carving board.

"Slices about three-quarters of an inch thick, the way you'd slice a steak," she said.

Brody searched through a drawer for a carving knife and fork. That Wicker dame was right about one thing, he thought as he slashed the meat: I sure feel alienated right now. A slab of meat fell away, and he said, "Hey, I thought you told me this was lamb."

"It is."

"It isn't even done. Look at that." He held up a piece he had sliced. It was pink and, toward the middle, almost red.

"That's the way it's supposed to be."

"Not if it's lamb, it isn't. Lamb's supposed to be well-done."

"Martin, believe me. It's all right to cook butterfly lamb sort of medium. I promise you."

Brody raised his voice. "I'm not gonna eat raw lamb!"

"Ssshhh!" said Ellen. "It's done! If you don't want to eat it, don't eat it, but that's the way I'm going to serve it."

"Then cut it yourself." He dropped the knife and fork on the board, picked up the two bottles of red wine and left the kitchen.

"There'll be a short delay," he said as he approached the table, "while the cook kills our dinner. She tried to serve it as it was, but it bit her on the leg."

Brody filled the wineglasses and sat down. He took a sip of his wine, said, "Good," then took another.

Ellen came in with the lamb. She returned to the kitchen, and came back carrying two vegetable dishes. "I hope it's good," she said. "I haven't tried it before."

"What is it?" asked Dorothy Meadows. "It smells delicious."

"Butterfly lamb. Marinated."

"Really? What's in the marinade?"

"Ginger, soy sauce, a whole bunch of things." She put a slice of lamb, some asparagus and some summer squash on each plate.

When everyone had been served and Ellen had sat down, Hooper raised his glass and said, "A toast to the chef."

The others lifted their glasses, and Brody said, "Good luck."

Meadows took a bite of meat and said, "Fantastic. It's like a very tender sirloin, only better. What a flavor!"

"From you, Harry," said Ellen, "that's a special compliment."

"It's delicious," said Dorothy. "Will you promise to give me the recipe? Harry will never forgive me if I don't give this to him at least once a week."

"He better rob a bank," said Brody.

"But it is delicious, Martin, don't you think?"

Brody didn't answer. He had started to chew a piece of meat when a wave of nausea hit him. He felt detached, as if his body were controlled by someone else. His fork felt heavy, and for a moment he feared it might slip from his fingers. It was the wine. It had to be. With exaggerated precision he reached forward to push his wineglass away from him. He sat back and took a deep breath. His vision blurred. He tried to focus his eyes on a painting above Ellen's head, but he was distracted by the image of Ellen talking to Hooper. Every time she spoke she touched Hooper's arm—lightly, but, Brody thought, intimately, as if they were sharing secrets. He didn't hear what anyone was saying. The last thing he remembered hearing was, "Don't you think?" Who had said it? He looked at Meadows, who was talking to Daisy. Then he looked at Dorothy and said thickly, "Yes."

She looked up at him. "What did you say, Martin?"

He couldn't speak. He wanted to stand and walk out to the kitchen, but he didn't trust his legs. Just sit still, he told himself. It'll pass.

And it did. His head began to clear, and by the time dessert was served he was feeling well. He had two helpings of the coffee ice cream in a pool of crème de cacao and chatted amiably with Dorothy.

They had coffee in the living room, and Brody offered drinks, but only Meadows accepted. "A tiny brandy, if you have it," he said.

Brody poured Meadows's drink and thought briefly of having one, too. But he resisted, telling himself, Don't press your luck.

At a little after ten o'clock Meadows yawned and said, "Dorothy, I think we had best take our leave."

"I should go, too," said Daisy. "I have to be at work at eight. Not that we're selling very much these days."

Meadows stood up. "Well, let's hope the worst is over," he said. "From what I gather from our expert here, there's a good chance the leviathan has left."

"A chance," said Hooper. "I hope so." He rose. "I should be on my way, too."

"Oh, don't go!" Ellen said. The words came out much stronger than she intended, and she added quickly, "I mean, it's only ten."

"I know," said Hooper. "But if the weather's good, I want to get out on the water early. I can drop Daisy off on my way home."

Daisy said, "That would be fun."

"The Meadowses can drop her," Ellen said.

"True," said Hooper, "but I really should go so I can get up early. But thanks for the thought."

They said their good-byes at the front door. Hooper and Daisy were the last to leave, and when he extended his hand to Ellen she took it in both of hers and said, "Thank you *so* much for my shark tooth."

"You're welcome. I'm glad you like it."

"We'll see you again before you go?"

"Count on it."

"Wonderful." She released his hand. He said a quick good-night to Brody and walked to his car.

Ellen waited at the door until both cars had pulled out of the driveway, then she turned off the outside light. Without a word she began to pick up the glasses, cups and ashtrays.

Brody carried a stack of dessert dishes into the kitchen, set them on the sink and said, "Well, that was all right."

"No thanks to you," said Ellen. "You were awful."

He was surprised at the ferocity of her attack. "What are you talking about?"

"I don't want to talk about it."

"Just like that. You don't want to talk about it. Look . . . okay, I was wrong about the damn meat. I'm sorry. Now—"

"I said I don't want to talk about it!"

Brody was ready for a fight, but he said only, "Well, I'm sorry about that." He walked out of the kitchen and climbed the stairs.

As he was undressing, the thought occurred to him that the cause of all the unpleasantness was a fish: a mindless beast that he had never seen. The ludicrousness of it made him smile.

He crawled into bed and fell into a dreamless sleep.

6

Brody awoke with a start, jolted by a signal that told him something was wrong. He threw his arm across the bed to touch Ellen. She wasn't there. He sat up and saw her sitting in a chair by the window. Rain splashed against the panes, and he heard the wind whipping through the trees.

"Lousy day, huh?" he said. She didn't answer, continuing to

stare fixedly at the drops sliding down the glass. "How come you're up so early?"

"I couldn't sleep." She seemed subdued, sad.

"What's the matter?"

"Nothing."

"Whatever you say." Brody got out of bed.

When he had shaved and dressed he went down to the kitchen. The boys were finishing breakfast, and Ellen was frying his egg. "What are you guys gonna do on this crummy day?" he said.

"Clean lawnmowers," said Billy, who worked during the summer for a local gardener. "Boy, do I hate rainy days."

"And what about you two?" Brody said to Martin and Sean.

"Martin's going to the Boys Club," said Ellen, "and Sean's spending the day at the Santoses'."

"And you?"

"I've got a full day at the hospital. Which reminds me: I won't be home for lunch. Can you get something downtown?"

"Sure. I didn't know you worked a full day Wednesdays."

"I don't, usually. But one of the girls is sick, and I said I'd fill in. Could you drop Sean and Martin off on your way to work? I want to do a little shopping on my way to the hospital."

"No problem."

After they had left, Ellen looked at the kitchen clock. It was a few minutes to eight. Too early? Maybe. But better to catch him now, before he went off somewhere. She held out her right hand and tried to steady the fingers, but they quivered uncontrollably. She went upstairs to the bedroom and picked up the green phone book. She found the number for the Abelard Arms Inn, hesitated for a moment, then dialed.

"Abelard Arms."

"Mr. Hooper's room, please."

Ellen heard the phone ring once, then again. She could hear her heart beating, and she saw the pulse throb in her right wrist. Hang up, she told herself. Hang up. There's time.

"Hello?" said Hooper's voice.

Ellen swallowed and said, "Hi. It's me . . . I mean it's Ellen."

"Oh, hi."

"I hope I didn't wake you."

"No. I was just going for breakfast."

"Good. It's not a very nice day. Will you be able to work?"

"I don't know. I was trying to figure that out."

"Oh." She paused, fighting the dizziness that was creeping up on her. Do it, she said to herself. The words spilled from her mouth. "I was wondering, if you can't work today . . . if there was any chance you'd like to . . . if you're free for lunch."

"Lunch?"

"Yes. You know, if you have nothing else to do."

"You mean you and the chief and I?"

"No, just you and I. Martin usually has lunch at his desk. I don't want to interfere with your plans or anything. . . ."

"No, no. That's okay. What did you have in mind?"

"There's a wonderful place up in Sag Harbor. Banner's. Do you know it?" She hoped he didn't. She didn't know it, but she had heard that it was good and quiet and dark.

"Sag Harbor," said Hooper. "That's quite a hike for lunch."

"It's only about fifteen or twenty minutes. I could meet you there whenever you like."

"Anytime's all right with me."

"Around twelve thirty, then?"

"Twelve thirty it is. See you then."

Ellen hung up the phone. Her hands were still shaking, but she felt elated, excited. Her senses seemed alive and incredibly keen. She felt more intensely feminine than she had in years.

She took a shower. Then she stood before the full-length mirror examining herself. Would the offering be accepted? She had worked to keep in shape, to preserve the smoothness and sinuousness of youth. She could not bear the thought of rejection.

She dressed in her hospital clothes. From the back of her closet she took a plastic shopping bag, into which she put fresh underthings, a lavender summer dress and a pair of low-heeled pumps.

She carried the bag to the garage, tossed it into her Volkswagen and drove to the Southampton Hospital.

She didn't know exactly when she had decided on this rash, dangerous plan. She had been thinking about it—and trying not to think about it—since the day she first met Hooper. She had weighed the risks and somehow calculated that they were worth taking. She wanted to be reassured that she was desirable—not just to her husband, but to the people she saw as her real peers, the people among whom she still numbered herself. The thought of love never entered her mind. Nor did she want a relationship either profound or enduring. She sought only to be restored.

Ellen was grateful that her work at the hospital demanded concentration and conversation, for it prevented her from thinking. At 11:45 she told the supervisor of volunteers that she didn't feel well. Her thyroid was acting up again, she said, and she thought she'd probably go home and lie down.

SHE drove most of the way to Sag Harbor, then stopped at a gas station. When the tank was full and the gas paid for, she used the ladies' room to change her clothes.

It was 12:20 when she arrived at Banner's, a small steak-and-seafood restaurant on the water. The parking lot was concealed from the street, for which she was grateful; someone she knew might drive by, and she didn't want her car in plain view.

The restaurant was dark, with a bar on the right as she walked in. The bartender, a young man with a Vandyke beard and a button-down shirt, sat by the cash register, reading the New York *Daily News,* and a waitress stood at the bar, folding napkins. Apart from one couple at a table, they were the only people in the room. Ellen looked at her watch. Almost 12:30.

The waitress saw Ellen and said, "Hello. May I help you?"

"Yes. I'd like a table for two, please. That corner booth, if you don't mind."

"Sure," said the waitress. "Anywhere you like." She led Ellen to the booth, and Ellen slipped in with her back to the door. Hooper would be able to find her. "Can I get you a drink?"

"Yes. A gin and tonic, please."

The waitress brought the drink, and Ellen drank half of it immediately, eager to feel the relaxing warmth of alcohol. It was the first time since her wedding that Ellen had had a drink during the day. Every few seconds she checked the door and looked at her watch. It was almost 12:45. He's not going to come, she thought. What will I do if he doesn't come?

"Hello." Hooper slid into the seat opposite her and said, "I'm sorry I'm late. I had to stop for gas, and the station was jammed." He looked into her eyes and smiled.

Ellen looked down at her glass. "You don't have to apologize. I was late myself."

The waitress came over, and Hooper, noticing Ellen's glass, ordered a gin and tonic.

"I'll have another," said Ellen. "This one's almost finished."

The waitress left, and Hooper said, "I don't normally drink at lunch."

"Neither do I."

"After about three drinks I say stupid things. I never did hold my liquor very well."

Ellen nodded. "I know the feeling. I tend to get sort of . . ."

"Impetuous? So do I."

"Really? I thought scientists weren't ever impetuous."

Hooper smiled. "Beneath our icy exteriors," he said, "we are some of the raunchiest people in the world."

They chatted about old times, about people they had known, about Hooper's ambitions in ichthyology. They never mentioned the shark or Brody or Ellen's children. It was an easy, rambling conversation, which suited Ellen. Her second drink loosened her up, and she felt happy and in command of herself.

She wanted Hooper to have another drink, and she knew he was not likely to take the initiative and order one. She picked up a menu and said, "Let me see. What looks good?"

Hooper picked up the other menu, and after a minute the

waitress strolled over to the table. "Are you ready to order?"

"Not quite yet," said Ellen. "Why don't we have one more drink while we're looking?"

Hooper pondered for a moment. Then he nodded his head and said, "Sure. A special occasion."

The waitress brought their drinks and said, "Ready?"

"Yes," said Ellen. "I'll have the shrimp cocktail and the chicken."

Hooper said, "Are these really bay scallops?"

"I guess so," said the waitress. "If that's what it says."

"All right. I'll have the scallops."

"Anything to start?"

"No," said Hooper, raising his glass. "This'll be fine."

In a few minutes the waitress brought Ellen's shrimp. When she had left, Ellen said, "Do you know what I'd love? Some wine."

"That's a very good idea," Hooper said, looking at her. "But remember what I said about impetuousness. I may become irresponsible."

"I'm not worried." Ellen felt a blush crawl up her cheeks.

"Okay," Hooper said, "but first I'd better check the treasury." He reached in his back pocket for his wallet.

"Oh, no. This is my treat."

"Don't be silly."

"No, really. I asked you to lunch." She began to panic. She didn't want to annoy him by sticking him with a big bill.

"I know," he said. "But I'd like to take *you* to lunch."

She toyed with the one shrimp left on her plate. "Well . . ."

"I know you're only being thoughtful," Hooper said, "but don't be. Didn't David ever tell you about our grandfather?"

"Not that I remember. What about him?"

"Old Matt was known—and not very affectionately—as the Bandit. If he were alive today, I'd probably be at the head of the pack calling for his scalp. But he isn't, so all I've had to worry about was whether to keep the bundle of money he left me or give it away."

"What did your grandfather do?"

"Railroads and mining. Technically, that is. Basically he was a robber baron. At one point he owned most of Denver. He was the landlord of the red-light district." Hooper laughed. "And from what I hear, he liked to collect his rent in trade."

"That's supposed to be every schoolgirl's fantasy," Ellen ventured playfully.

"What is?"

"To be a . . . you know . . . to sleep with a whole lot of different men."

"Was it yours?"

Ellen laughed to cover her blush. "I don't remember if it was exactly that," she said. "But I guess we all have fantasies of one kind or another."

Hooper smiled and called the waitress. "Bring us a bottle of cold Chablis, would you, please?"

Something's happened, Ellen thought. She wondered if he could sense the invitation she had extended. Anyhow, he had taken the offensive. All she had to do was avoid discouraging him.

Their entrées came, followed a moment later by the wine. Hooper's scallops were the size of marshmallows. "Flounder," he said after the waitress had left.

"How can you tell?" Ellen asked.

"They're too big, for one thing. And the edges are too perfect. They were obviously cut."

"I suppose you could send them back." She hoped he wouldn't; a quarrel with the waitress could spoil their mood.

"I might," said Hooper, and he grinned at Ellen. "Under different circumstances." He poured her a glass of wine, then filled his own and raised it. "To fantasies," he said. He leaned forward until his face was only a foot from hers. His eyes were a bright, liquid blue and his lips were parted in a half smile.

Impulsively, Ellen said, "Let's make our own fantasy."

"Okay. How do you want to start?"

"What would we do if we were going to . . . you know."

"That's a very interesting question," he said with mock gravity. "Before considering the what, however, we'd have to consider the where. I suppose there's always my room."

"Too dangerous. Everybody knows me at the Abelard. Anywhere in Amity would be too dangerous."

"There must be motels between here and Montauk."

"All right. That's settled."

ELLEN arrived home a little before 4:30. She went upstairs, into the bathroom, and turned on the water in the tub. After her bath she put on a nightgown and climbed into bed. She closed her eyes and gave in to her fatigue.

Almost instantly, it seemed, she was awakened by Brody saying, "Hey, there, are you okay?"

She yawned. "What time is it?"

"Almost six."

"Oh-oh. I've got to pick up Sean. Phyllis Santos must be having a fit."

"I got him," said Brody. "I figured I'd better, once I couldn't reach you."

"You tried to reach me?"

"A couple of times. I tried you at the hospital at around two. They thought you'd come home. Then I tried to reach you here."

"My, it must have been important."

"No. If you must know, I was calling to apologize for whatever I did that got you upset last night."

A twinge of shame struck Ellen, and she said, "You're sweet, but don't worry. I'd already forgotten about it."

"Oh," said Brody. "So where were you?"

"I came home and went to bed. My thyroid pills aren't doing what they should."

"And you didn't hear the phone? It's right there." Brody pointed to the table near the other side of the bed.

"No, I . . . I took a sleeping pill. The moaning of the damned won't wake me after I've taken one of them."

Brody shook his head. "I really am going to throw those things down the john. You're turning into a junkie." He went into the bathroom. "Have you heard from Hooper?" he called to her.

Ellen thought for a moment about her response, then said, "He called this morning to say thank you. Why?"

"I tried to get hold of him today. The hotel said they didn't know where he was. What time did he call here?"

"Just after you left for work."

"Did he say what he was going to be doing?"

"He said . . . he said he might try to work on the boat, I think. I really don't remember."

"Oh? That's funny."

"What is?"

"I stopped by the dock on my way home. The harbor master said he hadn't seen Hooper all day."

On Thursday morning Brody got a call summoning him to Vaughan's office for a noon meeting of the board of selectmen. He knew what the subject of the meeting was: opening the beaches for the weekend—the Fourth of July weekend. Brody was convinced that opening the beaches would be a gamble. They would never know for certain that the shark had gone away.

The town hall was an imposing, pseudo-Georgian affair—red brick with white trim and two white columns framing the entrance. The rooms inside were as preposterously grandiose as the exterior: huge and high-ceilinged, each with its own elaborate chandelier. Mayor Vaughan's office was on the southeast corner of the second floor, overlooking most of the town.

Vaughan's secretary, a wholesome, pretty woman named Janet Sumner, sat at a desk outside his office. Brody was paternally fond of Janet, and he was idly mystified that—at age twenty-six—she was still unmarried. He usually made a point of inquiring about her love life, but today he said simply, "Are they all inside?"

"All that's coming." Brody started into the office, and Janet said, "Don't you want to know who I'm going out with?"

He stopped, smiled and said, "Who is it?"

"Nobody. I'm in temporary retirement. But I'll tell you one

thing." She lowered her voice and leaned forward. "I wouldn't mind playing footsie with that Mr. Hooper."

"Is he in there?"

Janet nodded.

"I wonder when he was elected selectman."

"I don't know," she said. "But he sure is cute."

As soon as he was inside the office Brody knew he would be fighting alone. The only selectmen present were longtime allies of Vaughan's: Tony Catsoulis, a contractor who was built like a fire hydrant; Ned Thatcher, a frail old man whose family owned the Abelard Arms Inn; Paul Conover, owner of Amity Liquors; and Rafe Lopez (pronounced Loaps), a dark-skinned Portuguese elected to the board by the town's black community.

The selectmen sat around a coffee table at one end of the room. Hooper stood at a southerly window, staring out at the sea.

"Where's Albert Morris?" Brody said to Vaughan after greeting the others.

"He couldn't make it," said Vaughan. "I don't think he felt well."

"And Fred Potter?"

"Same thing. There must be a bug going around." Vaughan stood up. "Well, I guess we're all here. Grab a chair and pull it over by the coffee table."

He looks awful, Brody thought. Vaughan's eyes were sunken and dark. His skin looked like mayonnaise.

When everyone was seated Vaughan said, "You all know why we're here. And I guess it's safe to say that there's only one of us that needs convincing about what we should do."

"You mean me," said Brody.

Vaughan nodded. "Look at it from our point of view, Martin. The town is dying. People are out of work. Stores that were going to open aren't. People aren't renting houses, let alone buying them. And every day we keep the beaches closed, we drive another nail into our own coffin."

"Suppose you do open the beaches for the Fourth, Larry," said Brody. "And suppose someone gets killed."

"It's a calculated risk, but I think—we think—it's worth taking."

"Why?"

Vaughan said, "Mr. Hooper?"

"Several reasons," said Hooper. "First of all, nobody's seen the fish in a week."

"Nobody's been in the water, either."

"That's true. But I've been on the boat looking for him every day—every day but one."

"I meant to ask you about that. Where were you yesterday?"

"It rained," said Hooper. "Remember?"

"So what did you do?"

"I just . . ." He paused, then said, "I studied some water samples. And read."

"Where? In your hotel room?"

"Part of the time, yeah. What are you driving at?"

"I called your hotel. They said you were out all afternoon."

"So I was out!" Hooper said angrily. "I don't have to report in every five minutes, do I? You're not even paying me!"

Vaughan broke in. "Come on. This isn't getting us anywhere."

"Anyway," said Hooper, "I haven't seen a trace of that fish. Not a sign. And the water's getting warmer every day. It's almost seventy now. As a rule great whites prefer cooler water."

"So you think he's gone farther north?"

"Or out deeper, into colder water. He could even have gone south. You can't predict what these things are going to do."

"That's my point," said Brody. "All you're doing is guessing."

Vaughan said, "You can't ask for a guarantee, Martin."

"Tell that to Christine Watkins. Or the Kintner boy's mother."

"I know, I know," Vaughan said. "But we have to do something. God isn't going to scribble across the sky, 'The shark is gone.' We have to weigh the evidence and make a decision."

"The decision's already been made," said Brody.

"You could say that, yes."

"And when someone else gets killed? Who's taking the blame?

Who's going to talk to the husband or the mother or the wife and tell them, 'We were just playing the odds, and we lost'?"

"Wait a minute, Martin."

"If you want the authority for opening the beaches, then you take the responsibility, too."

"What are you saying?"

"I'm saying that as long as I'm chief of police in this town those beaches will not be open."

"I'll tell you this, Martin," said Vaughan. "If those beaches stay closed over Fourth of July weekend, you won't have your job very long. Twenty minutes after they hear you won't open the beaches the people of this town will impeach you, or find a rail and run you out on it. Do you agree, gentlemen?"

"I'll give 'em the rail myself," said Catsoulis.

"My people got no work," said Lopez. "You don't let them work, you're not gonna work."

Brody said flatly, "You can have my job anytime you want it."

A buzzer sounded on Vaughan's desk. He stood up angrily and picked up the phone. There was a moment's silence, then he said to Brody, "There's a call for you. Janet says it's urgent. You can take it here or outside."

"I'll take it outside," Brody said, wondering what could be urgent enough to call him out of a meeting with the selectmen. Another attack? He left the room and closed the door behind him. Janet handed him the phone on her desk, but before she could release the "hold" button Brody said, "Tell me, did Larry call Albert Morris and Fred Potter this morning?"

Janet looked away from him. "I was told not to say anything."

"Tell me, Janet. I need to know."

"The only ones I called were the four in there."

"Press the button." Janet did, and Brody said, "Brody."

Inside his office Vaughan saw the light stop flashing and he gently eased his finger off the circuit button and placed his hand over the mouthpiece. He looked around the room, searching each face for a challenge. No one returned his gaze.

"It's Harry, Martin," said Meadows. "I know you're in a meeting so I'll be brief. Larry Vaughan is up to his tail in hock."

"I don't believe it."

"A long time ago, maybe twenty-five years, before Larry had any money, his wife got sick. It was serious. And expensive. My memory's a little hazy on this, but I remember him saying afterward that he had been helped out by a friend, gotten a loan to pull him through. It must have been for several thousand dollars. Larry told me the man's name. It was Tino Russo."

"Get to the point, Harry."

"I am. Now jump to the present. A couple of months ago, before this shark thing ever began, a company was formed called Caskata Estates. It's a holding company. The first thing it bought was a big potato field just north of Scotch Road. When the summer didn't shape up well, Caskata began to buy a few more properties at low prices. It was all perfectly legitimate. But then—as soon as the first newspaper reports about the shark thing came out—Caskata really started buying. The lower the real estate prices fell, the more they bought—with very little money down. All short-term promissory notes. Signed by Larry Vaughan, who is listed as the president of Caskata. The executive vice-president is Tino Russo, whom the *Times* has been naming for years as a second-echelon crumb in one of the five Mafia families in New York."

Brody whistled through his teeth. "And Vaughan has been moaning about how nobody's been buying anything from him. I still don't understand why he's being pressured to open the beaches."

"I'm not sure. He may be arguing out of personal desperation. I imagine he's way overextended. The only way he can get out without being ruined is if the market turns around and the prices go up. Then he can sell what he's bought and get the profit. Or Russo can get the profit, however the deal's worked out. If prices keep going down—in other words, if the beaches are still officially unsafe—he can't possibly meet his notes when they come due. He'll lose his cash, and the properties will either revert to the original owners or else get picked up by Russo if he can raise the cash. My guess is that Russo still has hopes of big profits, but the only way he has a chance of getting them is if Vaughan forces the beaches open. As far as I can tell, Russo doesn't have a nickel in cash in this outfit. It's all—"

"You're a damned liar, Meadows!" Vaughan's voice shrieked into the phone. "You print one word of that and I'll sue you to death!" There was a click as he slammed down the phone.

"So much for the integrity of our elected officials," said Meadows.

"What do you think I ought to do, Harry? I offered them my job before I came out to talk to you."

"Don't quit, Martin. We need you. If you quit, Russo will get together with Vaughan and handpick your successor. If I were you, I'd open the beaches. You're going to have to open them sometime. You might as well do it now."

"And let the mob take their money and run."

"What else *can* you do? You keep them closed, and Vaughan'll get rid of you and open them himself. Then you'll be no use to anybody. This way, if you open the beaches and nothing happens, the town might have a chance. Then, maybe later, we can find a way to pin something on Vaughan."

"All right, Harry, I'll think about it," said Brody. "But if I open them, I'm gonna do it my way."

When Brody went back into Vaughan's office Vaughan said, "The meeting's over."

"What do you mean, over?" said Catsoulis. "We ain't decided anything."

Vaughan said, "Don't give me any trouble, Tony! It'll work out all right. Just let me have a private chat with the chief. Okay?"

Hooper and the four selectmen left the office. Vaughan shut the door, walked over to the couch and sat down heavily. He rested his elbows on his knees and rubbed his temples with his fingertips. He said, "I swear to you, Martin, if I had any idea how far this would go, I'd never have gotten into it."

"How much are you into him for?"

"The original amount was ten thousand. I've tried to pay it back, but I could never get them to cash my checks. When they came to me a couple of months ago, I offered them a hundred thousand dollars—cash. They said it wasn't enough. They didn't want the money. They wanted me to make a few investments. Everybody'd be a winner, they said."

"And how much are you out now?"

"Every cent I had. More than every cent. Close to a million." Vaughan took a deep breath. "Can you help me, Martin?"

"The only thing I can do for you is put you in touch with the DA. If you'd testify, you might be able to slap a loan-sharking rap on these guys."

"I'd be dead before I got home from the DA's office, and Eleanor would be left without anything. That's not the kind of help I meant."

Brody looked down at Vaughan, a huddled, wounded animal, and felt compassion. He began to doubt his own opposition to opening the beaches. How much was self-protection, and how much was concern for the town? "I'll tell you what, Larry. I'll open the beaches. Not to help you, because I'm sure if I didn't open them you'd find a way to get rid of me and open them yourself. I'll do it because I'm not sure I'm right anymore."

"Thanks, Martin. I appreciate that."

"I'm not finished. Like I said, I'll open them. But I'm going to post men on the beaches. And I'm going to have Hooper patrol in the boat. And I'm going to make sure every person who comes down there knows the danger."

"You can't do that!" Vaughan said. "You might as well leave the damn things closed. Nobody's going to the beach if it's crawling with cops."

"I can do it, Larry, and I will. I'm not going to make believe nothing ever happened."

"All right, Martin." Vaughan rose. "You don't leave me much choice. If I got rid of you, you'd probably go down to the beach as a private citizen and run up and down yelling '*Shark!*' So all right. But be subtle—if not for my sake, for the town's."

BRODY ARRIVED HOME THAT afternoon at 5:10. As he pulled into the driveway the back door to the house opened and Ellen ran toward him. She had been crying, and she was still visibly upset.

"Thank God you're home!" she said. "Come here. Quick!" She led him to the shed where they kept the garbage cans. "In there." She pointed to a can. "Look."

Lying in a twisted heap atop a bag of garbage was Sean's cat—a big, husky tom named Frisky. The cat's head had been twisted completely around, and the yellow eyes overlooked its back.

"How the hell did that happen?" said Brody. "A car?"

"No, a man." Ellen's breath came in sobs. "Sean was right there when it happened. A man got out of a car over by the curb. He picked up the cat and broke its neck. Then he dropped it on the lawn, got back in his car and drove away."

"Did he say anything?"

"I don't know. Sean's inside. He's hysterical, and I don't blame him. Martin, what's *happening*?"

Brody slammed the top back on the can. "Son of a *bitch!*" he said. He clenched his teeth. "Let's go inside."

Five minutes later Brody marched out the back door. He tore the lid off the garbage can and pulled out the cat's corpse. He took it to his car, pitched it through the open window and climbed in. He backed out of the driveway and screeched away.

It took him only a couple of minutes to reach Vaughan's Tudor-style mansion just off Scotch Road. He got out of the car, dragging the dead cat by one of its hind legs, mounted the front steps and rang the bell.

The door opened, and Vaughan said, "Hello, Martin. I—"

Brody raised the cat and pushed it toward Vaughan's face. "What about this, you bastard? One of your friends did this. Right in front of my kid. They murdered my cat! Did you tell them to do that?"

"Don't be crazy, Martin." Vaughan seemed genuinely shocked. "I'd never do anything like that. Never."

Brody lowered the cat and said, "Did you call your friends after I left?"

"Well . . . yes. But just to say that the beaches would be open tomorrow."

"That's all you said?"

"Yes. Why?"

"You damned liar!" Brody hit Vaughan in the chest with the cat and let it fall to the floor. "You know what the guy said after he strangled my cat? You know what he told my eight-year-old boy?"

"No, of course I don't know. How would I know?"

"He said the same thing you did. He said, 'Tell your old man this—be subtle.' "

Brody turned and walked down the steps, leaving Vaughan standing over the gnarled bundle of fur.

7

FRIDAY was cloudy, with scattered light showers, and the only people who swam were a young couple who took a quick dip early in the morning just as Brody's man arrived at the beach. Hooper patrolled for six hours and saw nothing. On Friday night Brody called the Coast Guard for a weather report. He wasn't sure what he hoped to hear. He knew he should wish for beautiful weather for the holiday weekend, but privately he would have welcomed a three-day blow that would keep the beaches empty. The report was for clear and sunny skies, with light southwest winds. Well, Brody thought, maybe that's for the best. If we have a good weekend and nobody gets hurt, maybe I can believe the shark is gone. And Hooper's sure to leave.

He wanted Hooper to go back to Woods Hole. It was not just that Hooper was always there, the expert voice to contradict his caution. Brody sensed that somehow Hooper had come into his home.

He knew Ellen had talked to Hooper since the party: young Martin had mentioned the possibility of Hooper taking them on a beach picnic to look for shells. Then there was that business on Wednesday. Ellen had said she was sick, and she certainly had looked worn-out when he came home. But where had Hooper been that day? Why had he been so evasive when Brody had asked him about it? For the first time in his married life Brody was wondering.

He went to the kitchen phone to call Hooper at the Abelard Arms. Ellen was washing the supper dishes. Brody saw the phone book buried beneath a pile of bills and comic books on the counter. He started to reach for it, then stopped. "I have to call Hooper," he said. "You know where the phone book is?"

"The number is six five four three," said Ellen.

"How do you know?"

"I have a memory for phone numbers. You know that."

He did know it, and he cursed himself for playing stupid tricks. He dialed the number and asked for Hooper's room.

"This is Brody," he said when Hooper answered.

"Yeah. Hi."

"I guess we're on for tomorrow," Brody said. "The weather report is good."

"Yeah, I know."

"Then I'll see you down at the dock at nine thirty. Nobody's going swimming before then."

"Okay. Nine thirty."

"By the way," Brody said, "did things work out with Daisy Wicker?"

"What?"

Brody wished he hadn't asked the question. "I was just curious. You know, about whether you two hit it off."

"Well . . . yeah, now that you mention it. Is that part of your job, to check up on people's sex life?"

"Forget it. Forget I ever mentioned it." He hung up the phone and turned to Ellen. "I meant to ask you. Martin said something about a beach picnic. When's that?"

"No special time," she said. "It was just a thought."

"Oh." He looked at her, but she didn't return the glance. "I think it's time you got some sleep."

"Why do you say that?"

"You haven't been feeling well. And that's the second time you've washed that glass."

SATURDAY noon, Brody stood on a dune overlooking the Scotch Road beach, feeling half secret agent, half fool. He was wearing a polo shirt and swim trunks. In a beach bag by his side were binoculars, a walkie-talkie, two beers and a sandwich. Offshore the *Flicka* moved slowly eastward. Brody watched the boat and said to himself, At least I know where *he* is today.

The Coast Guard had been right: the day was cloudless and warm, with a light onshore breeze. The section of beach below him was not crowded. A few couples lay dozing, and a dozen or so teenagers were scattered about in their ritual rows. A family was gathered around a charcoal fire, and the scent of grilling hamburger drifted to Brody's nose.

Brody reached into the beach bag and took out the walkie-talkie. He pressed a button and said, "You there, Leonard?"

In a moment the reply came rasping through the speaker. "I read you, Chief. Over." Hendricks had volunteered to spend the weekend on the beach, as the third point in the triangle of watch.

"Anything happening on your part of the beach?" said Brody.

"Nothing we can't handle, but there are some TV guys here interviewing people. Over."

"How long have they been there?"

"Most of the morning. I don't know how long they'll hang around, especially since no one's going in the water. Over."

"As long as they're not causing any trouble."

"Nope. Over."

"Okay. Hey, Leonard, you don't have to say over all the time. I can tell when you're finished speaking."

"Just procedure, Chief. Keeps things clear. Over and out."

Brody waited a moment, then pressed the button again and said, "Hooper, this is Brody. Anything out there?" There was no answer. "This is Brody calling Hooper. Can you hear me?" He was about to call a third time when Hooper answered.

"Sorry. I was out on the stern. I thought I saw something."

"What did you think you saw?"

"I can't really describe it. A shadow, maybe. Nothing more."

"You haven't seen anything else?"

"Not a thing. All morning."

"Let's keep it that way. I'll check with you later."

"Fine. I'll be near the beach in a minute or two."

Brody put the walkie-talkie back in the bag, sat down and unwrapped his sandwich.

By 2:30 Brody's section of the beach was almost empty. People had gone to play tennis, to sail, to have their hair done. The only ones left were half a dozen teenagers.

Brody's legs had begun to sunburn, so he covered them with his towel. He took the walkie-talkie out of the beach bag and called Hendricks. "Anything happening, Leonard?"

"Not a thing, Chief. Over."

"Anybody go swimming?"

"Nope. Wading, but that's about it. Over."

"Same here. What about the TV people?"

"They're gone. They left a few minutes ago. They wanted to know where you were. Over."

"Did you tell them?"

"Sure. I didn't see why not. Over."

"Okay. I'll talk to you later." Brody stood up, wrapped his towel around his waist to keep the sun from his legs and, carrying the walkie-talkie, strolled toward the water.

Hearing a car engine, he turned and walked to the top of the dune. A white panel truck was parked on Scotch Road. The lettering on its side said WNBC-TV News. The driver's door opened, and a man got out and trudged through the sand toward Brody. He was young, with long hair and a handlebar mustache.

"Chief Brody?" he said when he was a few steps away.

"That's right."

"Bob Middleton, Channel Four News. I'd like to interview you."

"About what?"

"The whole shark business. How you decided to open the beaches."

Brody thought, What the hell; a little publicity can't hurt the town, now that the chances of anything happening—today, at least—are pretty slim. "All right," he said. "Where?"

"Down on the beach. It'll take a few minutes to set up, so I'll give a yell when we're ready." He went back to the truck.

Brody walked down toward the water. As he passed the group of teenagers he heard a boy say, "What about it? Anybody got the guts? Ten bucks is ten bucks."

A girl said, "Come on, Limbo, lay off."

Brody stopped, feigning interest in something offshore.

Another boy said, "If you're such hot stuff, why don't *you* go?"

"I'm the one making the offer," said the first boy. "Nobody's gonna pay *me* to go in the water. Well, what do you say?"

There was a moment's silence, and then the other boy said, "How far out do I have to go?"

"Let's see. A hundred yards. Okay?"

"You've got a deal." The boy stood up.

The girl said, "You're crazy, Jimmy. Why do you want to go in the water? You don't need ten dollars."

"You think I'm scared?"

The boy turned and began to jog toward the water. Brody said, "Hey!" and he stopped.

Brody walked over to the boy. "What are you doing?"

"Going swimming."

Brody showed the boy his badge. "Do you want to go swimming?" he said.

"Sure. Why not? It's legal, isn't it?"

Brody nodded. Then he lowered his voice and said, "Do you want me to order you not to?"

The boy looked past him at his friends. He hesitated, then shook his head. "No, man. I can use the ten bucks."

"Don't stay in too long," said Brody.

"I won't." He scampered into the water and began to swim.

Brody heard running footsteps behind him. Bob Middleton dashed past him and called out to the boy, "Hey! Come back!"

The boy stopped swimming and stood up. "What's the matter?"

"I want some shots of you going into the water. Okay?"

"Sure, I guess so," said the boy. He started back toward shore.

Two men came up beside Brody. One was carrying a camera and a tripod. The other carried a rectangular box covered with dials and knobs. Around his neck was a pair of earphones.

"Right there's okay, Walter," said Middleton. He took a notebook from his pocket and began to ask the boy some questions.

The sound man handed a microphone to Middleton, who looked into the camera and said, "We have been here on the Amity beach since early morning, and no one has yet ventured into the water, although there has been no sign of the shark. I'm standing here with Jim Prescott, a young man who has just decided to take a swim. Tell me, Jim, do you have any worries about what might be swimming out there with you?"

"No," said the boy. "I don't think there's anything out there."

"So you're not scared."

"No."

Middleton held out his hand. "Well, good luck, Jim. Thanks for talking to us."

The boy ran into the water and began swimming.

"How much do you want of this?" said the cameraman, tracking the boy as he swam.

"A hundred feet or so," said Middleton. "But let's stay here till he comes out. Be ready, just in case."

Brody had become so accustomed to the far-off, barely audible hum of the *Flicka*'s engine that his mind no longer registered it as a sound. But suddenly the engine's pitch changed from a low murmur to an urgent growl. Brody looked beyond the swimming boy and saw the boat in a tight, fast turn, nothing like the slow, ambling sweeps it had been making. He put the walkie-talkie to his mouth, pressed the button and said, "You see something, Hooper?" The boat slowed, then stopped.

"Yes," said Hooper's voice. "It was that shadow again. But I can't see it now. Maybe my eyes are getting tired."

Middleton called to the cameraman, "Get this, Walter." He walked to Brody and said, "Something going on, Chief?"

"I don't know," said Brody. "I'm trying to find out." He said into the walkie-talkie, "There's a kid swimming out there."

"Where?" said Hooper.

Middleton shoved the microphone at Brody, sliding it between his mouth and the walkie-talkie. Brody brushed it aside, but Middleton quickly jammed it back.

"Thirty, maybe forty yards out. I better tell him to come in." Brody tucked the walkie-talkie into the towel at his waist, cupped his hands around his mouth and called, "Hey, come on in!"

The boy did not hear the call. He was swimming straight away from the beach.

Brody grabbed the walkie-talkie and called Hooper. "He doesn't hear me. You want to toot in here and tell him to come ashore?"

"Sure," said Hooper. "I'll be there in a minute."

THE fish had sounded now, and was meandering a few feet above the sandy bottom, eighty feet below the *Flicka*. For hours its sensory system had been tracking the strange noise above. It had not felt compelled either to attack the "creature" passing overhead or to move away.

Brody saw the boat, which had been heading west, swing toward shore and kick up a shower of spray from the bow.

"Get the boat, Walter," Middleton said to the cameraman.

Below, the fish sensed a change in the noise, which grew louder, then faded as the boat moved away. The fish turned, banking smoothly, and followed the sound toward the beach.

The boy stopped swimming and looked toward shore, treading water. Brody waved his arms and yelled, "Come in!" The boy waved back and started swimming. He swam well, rolling his head to catch a breath, kicking in rhythm with his arm strokes. Brody guessed he was sixty yards away and that it would take him another minute to reach shore.

It took Hooper only thirty seconds to cover the couple of hundred yards and draw near the boy. He stopped just beyond the surf line, letting the engine idle. He didn't dare go closer for fear of being caught in the waves.

The boy heard the engine and raised his head. "What's the matter?" he called to Hooper.

"Nothing," Hooper answered. "Keep swimming."

The boy lowered his head and swam. A swell moved him faster, and with two or three more strokes he was able to stand.

"Come on!" said Brody.

Middleton spoke into the microphone. "Something is going on, ladies and gentlemen, but we don't know exactly what. All we know for sure is that Jim Prescott went swimming, and then suddenly a man on a boat out there saw something. Now Police Chief Brody is trying to get Jim to come ashore. It could be the shark; we just don't know."

Hooper put the boat in reverse, to back away from the surf. As he looked off the stern he saw a silver streak moving in the gray-blue water. For a second Hooper did not realize what he was seeing. When the realization struck he cried, "Look out!"

"What is it?" yelled Brody.

"The fish! Get the kid out! Quick!"

The boy heard Hooper, and he tried to run. But in the chest-deep water his movements were slow and labored.

Brody ran into the water and reached out. A wave hit him in the knees and pushed him back.

Middleton said into the microphone, "The man on the boat just said something about a fish. I don't know if he means a shark."

The boy was pushing through the water faster now. He did not see the fin rise behind him, a sharp blade of brownish gray.

"There it is, Walter!" said Middleton. "See it?"

"I'm zooming," said the cameraman. "Yeah, I've got it."

"Hurry!" said Brody. He reached for the boy. The boy's eyes were wide and panicked. Brody's hand touched the boy's, and he pulled. He grabbed the boy around the chest, and together they staggered out of the water.

The fin dropped beneath the surface, and, following the slope of the ocean floor, the fish moved into the deep.

Brody stood with his arm around the boy. "Are you okay?"

"I want to go home." The boy shivered.

"I bet you do," Brody said.

Middleton came up. "Can you repeat that for me?"

"Repeat what?"

"Whatever you said to the boy. Can we do that again?"

"Get out of my way!" Brody snapped. He took the boy to his friends, and said to the one who had offered the money, "Take him home. And give him his ten dollars." The other boy nodded, pale and scared.

Brody saw his walkie-talkie in the wave wash and retrieved it. He pressed the "talk" button. "Leonard, can you hear me?"

"I read you, Chief. Over."

"The fish has been here. If anybody's in the water down there, get them out. Right away. The beach is officially closed."

As Brody went to pick up his beach bag Middleton called to him, "Hey, Chief, can we do that interview now?"

Brody sighed and returned to where Middleton stood with his camera crew. "All right," he said. "Go ahead."

"Well, Chief Brody," said Middleton, "that was a lucky break, wouldn't you say?"

"It was very lucky. The boy might have died."

"So where do you go from here?"

"The beaches are closed. For the time being that's all I can do."

"I guess it isn't yet safe to swim here in Amity."

"I'd have to say that, yes."

"What does that mean for Amity?"

"Trouble, Mr. Middleton. We are in big trouble."

"Chief, how do you feel about having opened the beaches?"

"How do I *feel?* What kind of question is that? Angry, annoyed, confused. Thankful that nobody got hurt. Is that enough?"

"That's just fine, Chief," Middleton said with a smile. "Thank you, Chief Brody." He paused, then said, "Okay, Walter, that'll wrap it. Let's get home and start editing this mess."

AT SIX o'clock Brody sat in his office with Hooper and Meadows. He had already talked to Larry Vaughan, who had called—drunk and in tears—and muttered about the ruination of his life. Brody's buzzer sounded, and he picked up the phone.

"Fellow named Bill Whitman to see you, Chief," said Bixby. "Says he's from the *New York Times*."

"Oh, for . . . Okay. Send him in."

The door opened, and Whitman stood there. He said, "Am I interrupting something?"

"Nothing much," said Brody. "What can we do for you?"

"I was wondering," said Whitman, "if you're sure this is the same fish that killed the others."

Brody gestured toward Hooper, who said, "I can't be positive. But in all probability it's the same fish. It's too far-fetched—for me, anyway—to believe that there are two big man-eating sharks off the south shore of Long Island at the same time."

Whitman said to Brody, "What are you going to do, Chief? I mean, beyond closing the beaches."

"I'd be happy to hear any suggestions. Personally, I think we're going to be lucky if there's a town left after this summer."

"Isn't that a bit of an exaggeration?"

"I don't think so. Do you, Harry?"

"Not really," said Meadows. "At the least—the very least—next winter is going to be the worst in our history, we're going to have so many people on the dole."

"I still don't see why the shark can't be caught," said Whitman.

"Maybe it can be," said Hooper. "But I don't think by us. At least not with the equipment we have here."

"Do you know anything about some fellow named Quint?" said Whitman.

"I've heard the name," Brody said. "Did you ever look into the guy, Harry?"

"I read what little there was. As far as I know, he's never done anything illegal."

"Well," said Brody, "maybe it's worth a call."

"You're joking," said Hooper. "You'd do business with him?"

"You got any better ideas?" Brody took a phone book from his desk and opened it to the Q's. He ran his finger down the page. "Here it is. Quint. That's all it says. No first name. But it's the only one on the page. Must be him." He dialed the number.

"Quint," said a voice.

"Mr. Quint, this is Martin Brody. I'm the chief of police in Amity. We have a problem."

"I've heard. I thought you might call."

"Can you help us?"

"That depends."

"On what?"

"On how much you're willing to spend, for one thing."

"We'll pay whatever you charge by the day."

"I don't think so," said Quint. "I think this is a premium job."

"What does that mean?"

"My usual rate's two hundred. But I think you'll pay double."

"Not a chance."

"Good-bye."

"Wait a minute! Come on. Why are you holding me up?"

"You got no place else to go."

"There are other fishermen."

Brody heard Quint laugh—a short, derisive bark. "Sure there are," said Quint. "You already sent one. Send another one. Send half a dozen more. Then when you come back to me again, maybe you'll even pay triple. I got nothing to lose by waiting."

"I'm not asking for any favors," Brody said. "But can't you at least treat me the way you treat regular clients?"

"You're breaking my heart," said Quint. "You got a fish needs killing, I'll try to kill it for you. No guarantees, but I'll do my best. And my best is worth four hundred dollars a day."

Brody sighed. "I don't know that the selectmen will give me the money."

"You'll find it somewhere."

Brody paused. "Okay," he said. "Can you start tomorrow?"

"Nope. Monday's the earliest. I got a charter party tomorrow."

"Can't you cancel them?" Brody asked.

"Nope. They're regular customers. You're just a one-shot deal. And there's one more thing," said Quint. "I'm gonna need a man with me. My mate's quitting, and I wouldn't feel comfortable taking on that big a fish without an extra pair of hands."

"Why is your mate quitting?"

"Nerves. Happens to most people after a while in this work."

"But it doesn't happen to you."

"No. I know I'm smarter'n the fish."

"And that's enough, just being smarter?"

"Has been so far. I'm still alive. What about it? You got a man for me?"

"Who are you going to use tomorrow?"

"Some kid. But I won't take him out after a big white."

Brody said casually, "I'll be there." He was shocked by the words as soon as he said them.

"You? Ha!"

Brody smarted. "I can handle myself," he said.

"Maybe. But I still need a man who knows something about fishing. Or at least about boats."

Brody looked across his desk at Hooper. The last thing he wanted was to spend days on a boat with Hooper, especially in a situation in which Hooper would outrank him in knowledge, if not authority. He could send Hooper alone and stay ashore himself. But that, he felt, would be admitting his inability to conquer the strange enemy that was waging war on his town.

Besides, maybe—over the course of a long day on a boat— Hooper might make a slip that would reveal what he had been do- ing last Wednesday. Brody was becoming obsessed with finding out where Hooper was that day it rained. He wanted to *know* that Hooper had not been with Ellen.

He cupped his hand over the mouthpiece and said to Hooper, "Do you want to come along? He needs a mate."

"Yes," said Hooper. "I'll probably live to regret it, but I want to see that fish, and I guess this is my only chance."

Brody said to Quint, "Okay, I've got your man."

"Does he know boats?"

"He knows boats."

"Monday morning, six o'clock. You know how to get here?"

"Route Twenty-seven to Cranberry Hole Road, right?"

"Yeah. About a hundred yards past the last houses take a left on a dirt road. Leads right to my dock. Mine's the only boat there. It's called the *Orca*."

"All right. See you Monday."

"One more thing," said Quint. "Cash. Every day. In advance."

"All right," said Brody. "You'll have it." He hung up and said to Hooper, "Monday, six a.m., okay?"

"Okay. What's the name of his boat?"

"I think he said *Orca*," said Brody. "I don't know what it means."

"It doesn't *mean* anything. It *is* something. It's a killer whale."

Meadows, Hooper and Whitman rose to go. At the door Hooper turned and said, "Thinking of orca reminds me of something. You know what Australians call great white sharks?"

"No," said Brody, not really interested. "What?"

"White death."

"You had to tell me, didn't you?" Brody said as he closed the door behind them.

Part Three

8

THE sea was as flat as gelatin. There was no whisper of wind to ripple the surface. The boat sat still in the water, drifting imperceptibly in the tide. Two fishing rods, in rod holders at the stern, trailed wire lines baited with squid into the oily slick that spread westward behind the boat. Hooper sat at the stern, a twenty-gallon garbage pail at his side. Every few seconds he dipped a ladle into the pail and spilled chum overboard into the slick.

Forward, in two rows that peaked at the bow, lay ten red wooden barrels the size of quarter kegs. Around each was wrapped several thicknesses of three-quarter-inch hemp, which continued in a hundred-foot coil beside the barrel. Tied to the end of each rope was the dart-shaped steel head of a harpoon.

Brody sat in the swivel fighting chair bolted to the deck, trying to stay awake. He was hot and sticky. They had been sitting for six hours, and the back of his neck was badly sunburned.

Brody looked up at the figure on the flying bridge: Quint. He wore a white T-shirt, faded blue-jean trousers, white socks and a pair of graying Top-Sider sneakers. Brody guessed Quint was about fifty. He was six feet four and very lean—perhaps a hundred and eighty or a hundred and ninety pounds. When, as now, the sun was high and hot, he wore a Marine Corps fatigue cap. His face, like the rest of him, was hard and sharp. It was ruled by a long, straight nose. When he looked down from the flying bridge, he seemed to aim his eyes—the darkest eyes Brody had ever seen— along the nose as if it were a rifle barrel. His skin was permanently browned and creased by wind and salt and sun. He gazed off the stern, rarely blinking, his eyes fixed on the slick.

Brody tried to stare at the slick, but the reflection of the sun on the water hurt his eyes, and he turned away. "I don't see how you do it, Quint," he said. "Don't you ever wear sunglasses?"

"Never." Quint's tone did not invite conversation.

Brody looked at his watch. It was a little after two o'clock; three or four more hours before they would give up for the day and go home. "Do you have a lot of days like this, when you just sit and nothing happens?"

"Some."

"And people pay you even though they never get a bite?"

Quint nodded. "That doesn't happen too often. There's generally something that'll take a bait." He stopped. "Something's taking one of them now."

Brody and Hooper watched as the wire on the starboard fishing rod began to feed overboard with a soft metallic hiss.

"Take the rod," Quint said to Brody. "And when I tell you, throw the brake and hit him."

"Is it the shark?" said Brody. The possibility that at last he was going to confront the beast, the monster, the nightmare, made his heart pound. He wiped his hands on his trousers, took the rod out of the holder and stuck it in the swivel between his legs.

Quint laughed—a short, sour yip. "That thing? No. That's just a little fella. Give you some practice for when your fish finds us." He watched the line for a few seconds, then said, "Hit it!"

Brody pushed the small lever on the reel forward, then pulled back on the rod. It bent into an arc. Brody began to turn the crank to reel in the fish, but the line kept speeding out.

"Don't waste your energy," said Quint.

Brody held on to the rod with both hands. The fish had gone

deep and was moving slowly from side to side, but it was no longer taking line. Brody cranked quickly as he picked up slack, then hauled backward. "What the hell have I got here?" he said.

"A blue," said Quint.

"He must weigh half a ton."

Quint laughed. "Maybe a hundred 'n' fifty pounds."

Brody hauled, until finally Quint said, "You're getting there. Hold it." Brody stopped reeling.

With a smooth, unhurried motion Quint swung down the ladder from the flying bridge. He had a rifle in his hand, an old army M1. He stood at the gunwale and looked down. "You want to see the fish?" he said. "Come look."

In the dark water the shark was indigo blue. It was about eight feet long, slender, with long pectoral fins. It swam slowly from side to side, no longer struggling.

"He's beautiful, isn't he?" said Hooper.

Quint flicked the rifle's safety to "off" and when the shark came within a few inches of the surface he squeezed off three quick shots. The bullets made clean round holes in the shark's head, drawing no blood. The shark shuddered and stopped moving.

"He's dead," said Brody.

"He's stunned, maybe, but that's all," said Quint. He took a glove from one of his hip pockets, slipped his hand into it, and grabbed the wire line. From a sheath at his belt he took a knife. He hoisted most of the shark out of the water, and with a single, swift motion slit its belly. Then he cut the leader with a pair of wire cutters, and the fish slid overboard.

"Now watch," said Quint. "If we're lucky, in a minute other blues'll come around, and there'll be a real feeding frenzy. That's quite a show. The folks like that."

Brody saw a flash of blue rise from below. A small shark—no more than four feet long—snapped at the body of the disemboweled fish. Its jaws closed on a bit of flesh, and its head shook violently from side to side. Soon another shark appeared, and another, and the water began to roil. Fins crisscrossed on the surface, tails whipped the water. Amid the sounds of splashes came an occasional grunt as fish slammed into fish.

The frenzy continued for several minutes, until only three large sharks remained, cruising back and forth beneath the surface.

"My God!" said Hooper.

"You don't approve," said Quint.

"I don't like to see things die for people's amusement. Do you?"

"It ain't a question of liking it or not," said Quint. "It's what feeds me." He reached into an ice chest and took out a baited hook and another leader. Using pliers, he attached the leader to the end of the wire line, then dropped the bait overboard.

Hooper resumed his routine of ladling the chum into the water. Brody said, "Anybody want a beer?" Both Quint and Hooper nodded, so he went below and got three cans from a cooler. As he left the cabin Brody noticed two old, cracked and curling photographs thumbtacked to the bulkhead. One showed Quint standing hip-deep in a pile of big, strange-looking fish. The other was a picture of a dead shark lying on a beach. There was nothing else in the photograph to compare the shark to, so Brody couldn't determine its size.

Brody left the cabin, gave the others their beers and sat down in the fighting chair. "I saw your pictures down there," he said to Quint. "What are all those fish you're standing in?"

"Tarpon," said Quint. "That was a while back, in Florida. I never seen anything like it. We must have got thirty, forty big tarpon in four nights' fishing."

"And you kept them?" said Hooper. "You're supposed to throw them back."

"Customers wanted 'em. For pictures, I guess. Anyway, they don't make bad chum, chopped up."

"What you're saying is, they're more use dead than alive."

"Sure. Same with most fish. And a lot of animals, too. I never did try to eat a live steer." Quint laughed.

"What's the other picture?" said Brody. "Just a shark?"

"Well, not *just* a shark. It was a big white—about fourteen, fifteen feet. Weighed over three thousand pounds."

"How did you catch it?"

"Ironed it. But I tell you"—Quint chuckled—"for a while there it was a question of who was gonna catch who."

"What do you mean?"

"Damn thing attacked the boat. No provocation, no nothing. My mate and a customer and I were sitting out here minding our own business, when whammo! It felt like we was hit by a freight train. Knocked my mate right on his ass, and the customer started screaming bloody murder that we were sinking. Then the bastard hit us again. I put an iron in him and we chased him—we must have chased him halfway across the Atlantic."

"Why didn't he go deep?" asked Brody.

"Couldn't. Not with that barrel following him. They float. He dragged it down for a while, but before too long the strain got to him, and he came to the surface. So we just kept following the barrel. After a couple of hours we got another two irons in him, and he finally came up, real quiet, and we threwed a rope around his tail and towed him to shore."

"You wouldn't try to catch the fish we're after on a hook and line, would you?" asked Brody.

"Hell, no. From what I hear, the fish that's been bothering you makes the one we got look like a pup."

"Then how come the lines are out?"

"Two reasons. First, a big white might just take a little squid bait like that. It'd cut the line pretty quick, but at least we'd know he was around. The other reason is, we might run into something else that'll take the bait. If you're paying four hundred bucks, you might as well have some fun for your money."

"Suppose the big white did come around," said Brody. "What would be the first thing you'd do?"

"Try to keep him interested enough so he'd stick around till we could start pumping irons into him. And that's where we'll have a little trouble. The squid isn't enough to keep him interested. Fish that size'll suck a squid right down and not even know he's et it. So we'll have to give him something special that he can't turn down, something with a big ol' hook in it that'll hold him at least until we can stick him once or twice."

From the stern, Hooper said, "What's something special, Quint?"

Quint pointed to a green plastic garbage can nestled in a corner amidships. "Take a look for yourself. It's in that can."

Hooper walked over to the can, flipped the metal clasps and lifted the top. He gasped at what he saw. Floating in the can full of water was a tiny bottle-nosed dolphin, no more than two feet long. Sticking out from a puncture on the underside of the jaw was the eye of a huge shark hook, and from a hole in the belly the barbed hook itself curled forward. Hooper clutched the sides of the can and said, "A baby."

"Even better," Quint said with a grin. "Unborn. I got it from the mother."

Hooper gazed into the can again, then slammed the top back on and said, "Where did you get the mother?"

"Oh, I guess about six miles from here, due east. Why?"

"You killed her."

"No." Quint laughed. "She jumped into the boat and swallowed a bunch of sleeping pills." He paused, waiting for a laugh, and when none came he said, "Sure I killed her. You can't rightly buy them, you know."

Hooper stared at Quint. He was furious, outraged. "You know they're protected by law."

"What's your line of work, Hooper?"

"I'm an ichthyologist. I study fish. That's why I'm here."

"Okay, you study fish for a living. If you had to work for a living—I mean the kind of work where the amount of money you make depends on the amount of sweat you put in—you'd know more about what laws really mean. That law wasn't put in to stop Quint from taking one or two porpoise for bait. It was meant to stop big-time fishing for them, to stop nuts from shooting them for sport. So you can moan all you want, Hooper, but don't tell Quint he can't catch a few fish to help him make a living."

"I get your message," said Hooper. "Take it while you can, and if after a while there's nothing left, why, we'll just start taking something else. It's so stupid!"

"Don't overstep, son," said Quint. His voice was flat, toneless, and he stared into Hooper's eyes. "Don't go calling me stupid."

"I didn't mean that, for God's sake. I just meant—"

On his perch midway between the two men Brody decided it was time to stop the argument. "Let's drop it, Hooper, okay?" he said. "We're not out here to have a debate on ecology."

"What do you know about ecology, Brody?" said Hooper. "I bet all it means to you is someone telling you you can't burn leaves in your backyard."

"Listen, damn you! We're out here to stop a fish from killing people, and if using one porpoise will help us save God knows how many lives, that seems to me a pretty good bargain."

Hooper smirked and said to Brody, "So now you're an expert on saving lives, are you? Let's see. How many could have been saved if you'd closed the beaches after the—"

Brody was on his feet moving at Hooper before he consciously knew he had left his chair. "You shut your mouth!" he said. Then he stopped short.

A quick, sharp laugh from Quint broke the tension. "I seen that coming since you came aboard this morning," he said.

THE second day of the hunt was as still as the first. The boat lay motionless on the glassy sea, like a paper cup in a puddle.

Brody had brought a book along to pass the time, a sex mystery borrowed from Hendricks. He did not want to have to fill time with conversation, which might lead to a repeat of yesterday's scene with Hooper. It had embarrassed him—Hooper, too, he thought. Today they seldom spoke to one another, directing most of their comments at Quint.

By noon the lines had been in the chum slick for over four hours. The men ate lunch—sandwiches and beer—and when they were finished Quint loaded his M1. For the next hour they sat in silence—Brody dozing in the fighting chair, a hat protecting his face; Hooper at the stern, ladling chum and occasionally shaking his head to keep awake, and Quint on the flying bridge, watching the slick, his Marine Corps cap tilted back on his head.

Suddenly Quint said, his voice soft, "We've got a visitor."

Brody snapped awake. Hooper stood up. The starboard line was running out, smoothly and very fast.

"Take the rod," Quint said. He removed his cap and dropped it onto the bench.

Brody took the rod, fitted it into the swivel and held on.

"When I tell you," said Quint, "you throw that brake and hit him." The line stopped running. "Wait. He's turning. He'll start again." But the line lay dead in the water, limp and unmoving. After several moments Quint said, "Reel it in."

The line came clear of the water and hung at the tip of the rod. There was no hook, no bait, no leader. The wire had been neatly severed. Quint hopped down from the bridge and looked at it. "I think we've just met your friend," he said. "This wire's been bit clean through. The fish probably didn't even know he had it in his mouth. He just sucked the bait in and closed his mouth."

"So what do we do now?" said Brody.

"We wait and see if he takes the other one, or if he surfaces."

"What about using the porpoise?"

"When I know it's him," said Quint, "then I'll give him the porpoise. I don't want to waste a prize bait on some little runt."

They waited. The only sound was the liquid plop of the chum Hooper ladled overboard. Then the port line began to run.

Brody was both excited and afraid, awed by the thought of a creature swimming below them whose power he could not imagine. Hooper stood at the gunwale, transfixed by the running line.

The line stopped and went limp.

"He done it again," said Quint. He took the rod out of the holder and began to reel. The severed line came aboard exactly as the other one had. "We'll give him one more chance," said Quint, "and I'll put on a tougher leader. Not that that'll stop him, if it's the fish I think it is." From a drawer in the cockpit he took a four-foot length of three-eighth-inch chain.

"That looks like a dog's leash," said Brody.

"Used to be," said Quint.

"What's next if this doesn't work?"

"Don't know yet. I could take a four-inch shark hook and a length of chain and drop it overboard with a bunch of bait on it. But if he took it, I wouldn't know what to do with him. He'd tear out any cleat I've got on board." Quint flipped the baited hook overboard and fed out a few yards of line. "Come on, you bastard," he said. "Let's have a look at you."

The three men watched the port line. Hooper bent down, filled his ladle with chum and tossed it into the slick. Something caught his eye and made him turn to the left. What he saw sucked from him a throaty grunt that made the others turn to look.

"My God!" said Brody.

No more than ten feet off the stern, slightly to starboard, was the conical snout of the fish. It stuck out of the water perhaps two feet. The top of the head was sooty gray, pocked with two black eyes. The mouth was open not quite halfway, a dim cavern guarded by huge, triangular teeth.

Fish and men confronted each other for perhaps ten seconds. Then Quint yelled, "Get an iron!" and, obeying himself, he dashed forward for a harpoon. Just then the fish slid quietly backward into the water. The long, scythed tail flicked once, and the fish disappeared.

"He's gone," said Brody.

"Fantastic!" said Hooper. "That fish is everything I thought. And more. He's fantastic! That head must have been four feet across."

"Could be," said Quint, walking aft to deposit in the stern two harpoon heads and two barrels with their coils of rope.

"Have you ever seen a fish like that, Quint?" Hooper asked.

"Not quite," said Quint.

"How long was he, would you say?"

"Twenty feet. Maybe more. With them things, it don't make much difference. Once they get to six feet, they're trouble."

"I hope he comes back," said Hooper.

Brody felt a chill. "He looked like he was grinning," he said.

"Don't make him out to be more than he is," said Quint. "He's just a dumb garbage bucket."

"How can you say that?" said Hooper. "That fish is a beauty. It's the kind of thing that makes you believe in a god."

A noise behind Hooper made him turn. Knifing the water thirty feet away was a triangular dorsal fin over a foot high, followed by a towering tail that swatted left and right in cadence.

"It's attacking the boat!" cried Brody. Involuntarily he backed into the seat of the fighting chair.

"Hand me that iron," said Quint.

The fish was almost at the boat. It raised its head, gazed vacantly at Hooper with one of its black eyes, and passed under the boat. Quint raised the harpoon and turned back to the port side. The throwing pole struck the fighting chair, and the dart dislodged and fell to the deck.

"Damn!" shouted Quint. "Is he still there?" He reached down, grabbed the dart and stuck it back on the end of the pole.

"Your side!" yelled Hooper. "He's passed this side already."

Quint turned as the gray-brown shape of the fish pulled away and began to dive. He dropped the harpoon, snatched up the rifle and emptied the clip into the water behind the fish. "Bastard!" he said. "Give me some warning next time." Then he put the rifle down and laughed. "At least he didn't attack the boat," he said. He looked at Brody. "Gave you a bit of a start."

"More'n a bit," said Brody. He shook his head, as if to reassemble his thoughts. "I'm still not sure I believe it." His mind was full of images of a torpedo shape streaking upward in the blackness and tearing Christine Watkins to pieces; of the boy on the raft, unknowing, unsuspecting, until suddenly seized by a nightmare creature. "You think he'll come back?"

"I don't know," said Quint. "You never know what they're going to do." From a pocket he took a note pad and a pencil. He
extended his left arm and pointed it toward shore. He closed his
right eye and sighted down the index finger of his left hand, then
scribbled on the pad. He moved his hand a couple of inches to the
left, sighted again and made another note. Anticipating a question
from Brody, Quint said, "Taking bearings so if he doesn't show up
for the rest of today, I'll know where to come tomorrow."

Brody looked toward shore. "What are you taking them on?"

"Lighthouse on the point and the water tower in town. They line
up different ways depending where you are."

Hooper smiled. "Do you really think he'll stay in one place?"

"He sure as hell stayed around Amity," said Brody.

"That's because he had food," said Hooper. There was no irony
in his voice, no taunt. But the remark was like a needle stabbing
into Brody's brain.

They waited, but the fish never returned. At a little after five
o'clock Quint said, "We might as well go in."

"You don't think we should spend the night, to keep the slick
going?" said Brody.

Quint thought for a moment. "Nope. First, the slick would be
big and confusing, and that would foul us up for the next day. Second, I like to get this boat in at night."

"I guess I can't blame you," said Brody. "Your wife must like it
better, too."

Quint said flatly, "Got no wife."

"Oh. I'm sorry."

"Don't be. I never saw the need for one." Quint turned and
climbed the ladder to the flying bridge.

ELLEN was fixing the children's supper when the doorbell rang.
She heard the screen door open, heard Billy's voice, and a moment
later saw Larry Vaughan standing at the kitchen door. It had been
less than two weeks since she had last seen him, yet the change in
his appearance was startling. As always he was dressed perfectly,

but he had lost weight, and the loss showed in his face. His skin looked gray, and appeared to droop at the cheekbones.

Embarrassed when she found herself staring, Ellen lowered her eyes and said, "Larry. Hello."

"Hello, Ellen. I stopped by to say farewell."

Ellen said, "You're going away? For how long?"

"Perhaps for good. There's nothing here for me anymore."

"What about your business?"

"That's gone. Or it soon will be. What few assets there are will belong to my . . . partners." He spat the word and then he said, "Has Martin told you about . . ."

"Yes." Ellen looked down at the chicken she was cooking.

"I imagine you don't think very highly of me anymore."

"It's not up to me to judge you, Larry. How much does Eleanor know?"

"Nothing, poor dear. I want to spare her, if I can. That's one reason I want to move away." Vaughan leaned against the sink. "You know something? Sometimes I've thought that you and I would have made a wonderful couple."

Ellen reddened. "What do you mean?"

"You're from a good family. You know all the people I had to fight to get to know. We would have fit in Amity. You're lovely and good and strong. You would have been a real asset to me. And I could have given you a life you would have loved."

Ellen smiled. "I'm not as strong as you think, Larry."

"Don't belittle yourself. I only hope Martin appreciates the treasure he has. Anyway, no point in dreaming." He walked across the kitchen and kissed the top of Ellen's head. "Good-bye, dear," he said. "Think of me once in a while."

Ellen looked at him. "I will." She kissed his cheek. "Where are you going?"

"I don't know. Vermont, maybe, or New Hampshire. I might sell land to the skiing crowd."

"Send us a card so we'll know where you are."

"I will. Good-bye." Vaughan left the room, and Ellen heard the screen door close behind him.

When she had served the children their supper Ellen went up-stairs and sat on her bed. "A life you would have loved," Vaughan had said. What would it have been like? There would have been money and acceptance. She would never have missed the life she led as a girl, for it would never have ended. There would have been no craving for renewal and self-confidence and confirmation of her femininity, no need for a fling with someone like Hooper. But it would have been a life without challenge, a life of cheap satisfactions.

As she pondered what Vaughan had said she began to recognize the richness of her relationship with Brody. It was more rewarding than any Larry Vaughan would ever experience, an amalgam of minor trials and tiny triumphs that added up to something akin to joy. And as her recognition grew so did a regret that it had taken her so long to see the waste of time and emotion in trying to cling to her past. Suddenly she felt fear—fear that she was growing up too late, that something might happen to Brody before she could savor her awareness. She looked at her watch: 6:20. He should have been home by now.

She heard the front door open. She ran down the stairs, wrapped her arms around Brody and kissed him hard on the mouth.

"My God!" he said when she let him go. "That's some welcome."

9

"YOU'RE not putting that thing on my boat," said Quint.

They stood on the dock in the brightening light. The sun had cleared the horizon, but it lay behind a low bank of clouds. The boat was ready to go. The engine chugged quietly, sputtering bubbles as tiny waves washed against the exhaust pipe.

Quint, with his back to the boat, faced Brody and Hooper, who stood on either side of an aluminum cage slightly over six feet tall, six feet wide and four feet deep. Inside it were a scuba tank, an airflow regulator, a face mask and a neoprene wet suit.

"What the hell is it, anyway?" said Quint.

"It's a shark cage," said Hooper. "Divers use them to protect themselves when they're swimming in the open ocean. I phoned last night and my friends brought it down from Woods Hole."

"And what do you plan to do with it?"

"When we find the fish I want to go down in the cage and take some pictures."

"Not a chance," said Quint. "A fish that big could eat that cage for breakfast."

"But *would* he? I think he might bump it, might even mouth it, but I don't think he'd seriously try to eat it."

"Well, forget it."

"Look, Quint, this is a chance of a lifetime. I never thought of doing it until I saw the fish yesterday. Even though people have filmed great whites before, no one's ever filmed a twenty-foot white swimming in the open ocean. Never."

"He said forget it," said Brody. "So forget it. We're out here to kill that fish, not make a home movie about it."

Hooper said to Quint, "I'll pay you."

Quint smiled. "Oh, yeah? How much?"

"A hundred dollars. Cash. In advance, the way you like it." He reached into his back pocket for his wallet.

"I said no!" said Brody.

"I don't know," said Quint. Then he said, "Hell, I don't guess it's my business to keep a man from killing himself if he wants to."

"You put that cage on the boat," Brody said to Quint, "and you don't get your four hundred." If Hooper wants to kill himself, Brody thought, let him do it on his own time.

"And if the cage doesn't go," said Hooper, "I don't go."

"We'll find another man," said Brody.

"Can't do it," said Quint. "Not on this short notice."

"Then the hell with it!" said Brody. "We'll go tomorrow. Hooper can go back to Woods Hole and play with his fish."

Hooper was angry—angrier, in fact, than he knew, for before he could stop himself, he had said, "That's not all I might . . . Oh, forget it."

A leaden silence fell over the three men. Brody stared at Hooper, unwilling to believe what he had heard. Then suddenly he was overcome by rage. He reached Hooper in two steps, grabbed both sides of his collar and rammed his fists alongside Hooper's neck. "What was that?" he said. "What did you say?"

Hooper clawed at Brody's fingers. "Nothing!" he said, choking.

"Where were you last Wednesday afternoon?"

"Nowhere!" Hooper's temples were throbbing. "Let me go!"

"Where were you?" Brody twisted his fists tighter.

"In a motel! Now let me go!"

Brody eased his grip. "With who?" he said.

"Daisy Wicker." Hooper knew it was a weak lie. Brody could check it out with no trouble. But it was all he could think of. He could stop on the way home and phone Daisy Wicker, beg her to corroborate his story.

"I'll check," said Brody. "You can count on it."

"Well, what do you say?" said Quint. "We going today or not? Either way, Brody, it'll cost you."

Brody was tempted to cancel the trip, to return to Amity and discover the truth. But he said to Quint, "We'll go."

"With the cage?"

"With the cage. If this ass wants to kill himself, let him."

"Okay by me," said Quint. "Let's get this circus on the road."

"I'll get in the boat," Hooper said hoarsely. "You two can lean the cage over toward me, then one of you come down and help me stow it."

Brody and Quint slid the cage across the wooden dock, and Brody was surprised at how light it was. Even with the diving gear inside, it couldn't have weighed more than two hundred pounds. They tipped it toward Hooper, who held it until Quint joined him in the cockpit. The two men loaded the cage on deck and secured it under the overhang of the flying bridge.

"Uncleat the stern line, will you?" Quint called to Brody. Then, as Brody jumped aboard, Quint pushed the throttle forward and headed the boat toward the open sea.

Gradually, as the *Orca* fell into the rhythm of the long ocean swells, Brody's fury dulled. Maybe Hooper was telling the truth. He was sure Ellen had never cheated on him before. But, he told himself, there's always a first time. And once again the thought made his throat tighten. He climbed up to the flying bridge and sat on the bench next to Quint.

Quint chuckled. "What is it, you think Hooper's been fooling around with your wife?"

"None of your damn business," Brody said.

"Whatever you say. But if you ask me, he ain't got it in him."

"Nobody asked you." Anxious to change the subject, Brody said, "Are we going back to the same place?"

"Same place. Won't be too long now."

"What are the chances the fish will still be there?"

"Who knows? But it's the only thing we can do."

"You said something the other day about being smarter than the fish. Is that all there is to it?"

"That's all there is. It's no trick. They're stupid as sin."

"But there are fish you can't catch, aren't there?"

"Oh, sure, but that only means they're not hungry, or they're too fast for you, or you're using the wrong bait."

Quint fell silent for a moment, then spoke again. "Once," he said, "a shark almost caught *me*. It was about twenty years ago, I gaffed a fair-sized blue, and he gave a big yank and hauled me overboard."

"What did you do?"

"I come up over that transom so fast I don't think my feet touched anything between water and deck."

Quint pulled back on the throttle, and the boat slowed. He took a piece of paper from his pocket, read the notes and, sighting along his outstretched arm, checked his bearings. "Okay, Hooper," he said. "Start chuckin' the stuff overboard."

Hooper mounted the transom and began to ladle the chum into the sea.

By ten o'clock a breeze had come up—not strong, but fresh enough to ripple the water and cool the men, who sat and watched and said nothing. Brody was again in the fighting chair, struggling to stay awake. He yawned, then he stood, stretched and went down the three steps into the cabin. "I'm going to have a beer," he called. "Anybody want one?"

"Sure," said Quint.

Brody took out two beers, and had started to climb the stairs when he heard Quint's flat, calm voice say, "There he is."

Hooper jumped off the transom. "Wow! He sure is!"

Brody stepped quickly onto the deck. It took his eyes a moment to adjust, but then, off the stern, he saw the fin—a brownish gray triangle that sliced through the water, followed by the tail sweeping left and right. The fish was at least thirty yards away, Brody guessed. Maybe forty.

Quint walked forward and fastened a harpoon head to the wooden shaft. He set a barrel on the transom to the left of Hooper's bucket and arranged the coiled rope beside it. Then he climbed up on the transom and stood, his right arm cocked, holding the harpoon. "Come on, fish," he said. "Come on in here."

The fish cruised slowly back and forth, but he would come no closer than fifty feet.

"I don't get it," said Quint. "He should come in and take a look at us. Brody, throw those squid bait overboard. And make a big splash. Let him know something's there."

Brody did as he was told. But still the fish stayed away.

Hooper said, "What about the porpoise?"

"Why, Mr. Hooper," said Quint. "I thought you didn't approve."

"Never mind that," Hooper said excitedly. "I want to see that fish!"

"We'll see," said Quint. "If I have to use it, I will."

They waited—Hooper ladling, Quint poised on the transom, Brody standing by one of the rods.

"Hell," said Quint. "I guess I got no choice." He set the harpoon down and jumped off the transom. He flipped the top off the garbage can next to Brody, and Brody saw the lifeless eyes of the tiny porpoise as it swayed in the briny water. The sight repelled him, and he turned away.

"Well, little fella," said Quint. "The time has come." He took out a dog-leash chain and snapped one end of it into the hook eye protruding from beneath the porpoise's jaw. To the other end of the chain he tied several yards of three-quarter-inch hemp. Then he made the rope fast to a cleat on the starboard gunwale.

"You said the shark could pull out a cleat," said Brody.

"It might just," said Quint. "But I'm betting I can get an iron in him and cut the rope before he pulls it taut enough to yank the cleat." Quint carried the porpoise over to the transom and cut a series of shallow slashes in its belly before tossing it into the water. He let out six feet of line, then put the rope under his foot on the transom.

"Why are you standing on the rope?" asked Brody.

"To keep the little fella where I can get a shot at the shark. But I don't want to cleat it down that close. If the shark took it and didn't have any running room, he could thrash around and beat us to pieces."

The shark was still cruising back and forth, but coming closer to the boat with every passage. Then it stopped, twenty or twenty-five feet away. The tail dropped beneath the surface; the dorsal fin slid backward and vanished; and the great head reared up, mouth open in a slack, savage grin, eyes black and abysmal. Brody stared in mute horror.

"Hey, fish!" Quint called. He stood on the transom, legs spread, his hand curled around the shaft of the harpoon that rested on his shoulder. "Come see what we've got for you!"

For another moment the fish hung in the water, watching. Then soundlessly the head slid down and disappeared.

"He'll be coming now," said Quint.

Suddenly the boat lurched violently to the side. Quint's legs skidded out from under him, and he fell backward on the transom. The harpoon dart separated from the shaft and clattered to the deck. Brody tumbled sideways, grabbed the back of the chair as it swiveled around. Hooper slammed into the port gunwale.

The rope attached to the porpoise tautened and shivered. Then it snapped backward and lay slack in the water.

"I'll be damned!" said Quint. "I never have seen a fish do that before. He either bit right through the chain, or else . . ." He walked over to the starboard gunwale and grabbed the chain. It was intact, but the hook it was attached to was nearly straight.

"He did that with his mouth?" said Brody.

"Bent it out nice as you please," said Quint. "Probably didn't slow him down for more than a second or two."

Brody felt light-headed. He sat down in the chair and drew several deep breaths, trying to stifle his mounting fear.

"Where do you suppose he's gone?" said Hooper.

"He's around here somewhere," said Quint. "That porpoise wasn't any more to him than an anchovy is to a bluefish. He'll be looking for more food." He reassembled the harpoon and re-coiled the rope. "I'll tie up some more squid and hang 'em overboard."

Brody watched Quint as he wrapped twine around each squid and dropped it overboard. When a dozen squid had been placed around the boat, Quint climbed to the flying bridge and sat down.

Brody looked at his watch: 11:05. At 11:30 he was startled by a sharp, resonant *snap*. Quint leaped down the ladder and across the deck, and picked up the harpoon. "He's back," he said. "He took one of the squid." A few inches of limp twine hung from a cleat amidships.

As Brody looked at the remnant he saw another piece of twine— a few feet farther up the gunwale—go limp. "He must be right underneath us," he said.

"Let's put the cage overboard," said Hooper.

"You're kidding," said Brody.

"No, I'm not. It might bring him out."

"With you in it?"

"Not at first. Let's see what he does. What do you say, Quint?"

"Might as well," said Quint. "Can't hurt just to put it in the water." He laid the harpoon down.

He and Hooper tipped the cage onto its side, and Hooper opened the top hatch and removed the scuba gear, face mask and wet suit. They stood the cage upright again, slid it across the deck and secured it with two lines to cleats on the starboard gunwale.

"Okay," said Hooper. "Let's put her over." They lifted the cage overboard, and it sank until the ropes stopped it, a few feet beneath the surface.

"What makes you think this'll bring him out?" said Brody.

"I think he'll come and have a look at it, to see whether he wants to eat it," said Hooper.

But the cage lay quietly in the water, unmolested.

"There goes another squid," said Quint. "He's there, all right."

Hooper said, "Oh, well," and went below. He reappeared moments later, carrying an underwater movie camera and a stick with a thong at one end.

"What are you doing?" Brody said.

"I'm going down there. Maybe that'll bring him out."

"You're out of your mind. What are you going to do if he does come out?"

"First, I'm going to take some pictures of him. Then I'm going to try to kill him."

"With what, may I ask?"

"This." Hooper held up the stick. "It's called a bang stick or a power head. Basically it's an underwater gun." He pulled both ends of the stick, and it came apart in two pieces. "In here," he said, pointing to a chamber, "you put a twelve-gauge shotgun shell." He took one from his pocket and pushed it into the chamber. "Then you jab it at the fish and the shell goes off. If you hit him right—the brain's the only sure place—you kill him."

"Even a fish that big?"

"I think so. If I hit him right."

"And if you don't? Suppose you miss by just a hair."

"What concerns me is that if I miss, I might drive him off," said Hooper. "He'd probably sound, and we'd never know if he died or not."

"Until he ate someone else," said Brody.

"That's right."

"You're plain crazy," said Quint.

"Am I, Quint? You're not having much success with this fish. I think he's more than you can handle."

"That right, boy? You think you can do better'n Quint? Fine and dandy. You're gonna get your chance."

Brody said, "Come on. We can't let him go in that thing."

"What are *you* bitchin' about?" said Quint. "From what I seen, you just as soon he went down there and never come up. At least that'd stop him from—"

"Shut your mouth!" Brody's emotions were jumbled. Could he really wish a man dead? No. Not yet.

"Go on," Quint said to Hooper. "Get in that thing."

"Right away." Hooper removed his shirt, sneakers and trousers and began to pull the neoprene suit over his legs. "When I'm inside the cage," he said, forcing his arms into the rubber sleeves of the jacket, "stand up here and keep an eye out. Maybe you can use the rifle if he gets close enough to the surface."

When he was dressed, Hooper fitted the airflow regulator onto the neck of the air tank and opened the valve. He sucked two breaths from the tank to make sure it was feeding air. "Help me put this on, will you?" he said to Brody.

Brody held the tank while Hooper slipped his arms through the straps and fastened a third strap around his middle. He put the face mask on his head. "I should have brought weights," he said.

Quint said, "You should have brought brains."

Hooper put his right wrist through the thong at the end of the power head, picked up the camera and walked to the gunwale. "If you'll each take a rope and pull the cage to the surface, I'll open the hatch and go in through the top."

Quint and Brody pulled on the ropes, and the cage rose in the water. When the hatch broke the surface Hooper said, "Okay, right there." He spat in the face mask, rubbed the saliva around on the glass and fitted the mask over his face. He reached for the regulator tube, put the mouthpiece in his mouth and took a breath. He unlatched the hatch and flipped it open, put a knee on the gunwale, then stopped and took the mouthpiece out of his mouth. "I forgot something." He walked across the deck and picked up his trousers. He rummaged through the pockets. Then he unzipped his wet-suit jacket.

"What's that?" said Brody.

Hooper held up a shark's tooth, a duplicate of the one he had given Ellen. He dropped it inside his wet suit. "Can't be too careful," he said, smiling. He replaced his mouthpiece, took a final breath and jumped overboard, passing through the open hatch as he hit the water.

Before his feet touched the bottom of the cage he curled around and pulled the hatch closed. Then he stood, looked up at Brody and put his thumb and index finger together in the okay sign.

Brody and Quint let the cage descend until the top was about four feet beneath the surface.

"Get the rifle," said Quint. He climbed onto the transom and lifted the harpoon to his shoulder.

Brody went below, found the rifle and hurried back on deck.

In the cage Hooper waited for the bubbly froth of his descent to dissipate, then checked his watch. He felt serene. He was alone in blue silence speckled with shafts of sunlight that danced through the water. He looked up at the gray hull of the boat. Even with the bright sunlight, the visibility in the murky water was poor— no more than forty feet. Hooper turned slowly around, trying to pierce the edge of gloom and grasp any sliver of color or movement. Nothing. He looked at his watch again, calculating that if he controlled his breathing, he could stay down for half an hour more.

Carried by the tide, one of the small white squid slipped between the bars and, tethered by twine, fluttered in Hooper's face.

He pushed it out of the cage. He glanced downward, started to look away, then snapped his eyes down again. Rising at him from the darkling blue—slowly, smoothly—was the shark.

Hooper stared, impelled to flee but unable to move. As the fish drew nearer he marveled at its colors: the top of the immense body was a hard ferrous gray, bluish where dappled with streaks of sun. Beneath the lateral line all was creamy white. Hooper wanted to raise his camera, but his arm would not obey.

The fish came closer, silent as a shadow, and Hooper drew back. The head was only a few feet from the cage when the fish turned and began to pass before Hooper's eyes, as if in proud display of its mass and power. The snout passed first, then the jaw, slack and smiling. And then the black, fathomless eye, seemingly riveted upon him. The gills rippled—bloodless wounds in the steely skin.

Tentatively, Hooper stuck a hand through the bars and touched the flank. It felt cold and hard. He let his fingertips caress the pectoral fins, the pelvic fin, the genital claspers—until finally they were slapped away by the sweeping tail.

Hooper heard faint popping noises, and he saw three straight spirals of angry bubbles speed from the surface, then slow and stop, well above the fish. Bullets. Not yet, he told himself. One more pass for pictures.

"What the hell is he doing down there?" said Brody. "Why didn't he jab him?"

Quint stood on the transom, harpoon clutched in his fist, peering into the water. "Come up, fish," he said. "Come to Quint."

The fish had circled off to the limit of Hooper's vision—a spectral blur. Hooper raised his camera and pressed the trigger. He wanted to catch the beast as it emerged from the darkness.

Through the viewfinder he saw the fish turn toward him. It moved fast, tail thrusting vigorously, mouth opening and closing. Hooper changed the focus. Remember to change it again, he told himself, when it turns.

But the fish did not turn. It struck the cage head-on, the snout ramming between two bars and spreading them. The snout hit

Hooper in the chest and knocked him backward. The camera flew from his hands, and the mouthpiece shot from his mouth. The fish turned on its side, and the pounding tail forced the great body farther into the cage. Hooper groped for his mouthpiece but couldn't find it. His chest was convulsed with the need for air.

"It's attacking!" screamed Brody. He grabbed one of the tether ropes and pulled, desperately trying to raise the cage.

"Damn your soul!" Quint shouted.

"Throw the iron!" Brody yelled. "Throw it!"

"I can't throw it! I gotta get him on the surface! Come up, you devil!"

The fish slid backward out of the cage and turned sharply to the right in a tight circle. Hooper reached behind his head and located the mouthpiece. He put it in his mouth and drew an agonized breath. It was then that he saw the wide gap in the bars, and saw the giant head lunging through it again. He raised his hands above his head, grasping at the escape hatch.

The fish rammed through the space between the bars, spreading them still farther. Hooper, flattened against the back of the cage, saw the mouth reaching, straining for him. He tried to lower his arm and grab the power head. The fish thrust again, and its jaws closed around his torso. Hooper felt a terrible pressure, as if his guts were being compacted. He jabbed his fist into the black eye. The fish bit down, and the last thing Hooper saw before he died was the eye gazing at him through a cloud of his own blood.

"He's got him!" cried Brody. "Do something!"

"The man is dead," Quint said.

"How do you know? We may be able to save him."

"He's dead."

Holding Hooper in its mouth, the fish backed out of the cage. Then, with a thrust of its tail, it drove itself upward.

"He's coming up!" said Brody.

"Grab the rifle!" Quint cocked his hand for the throw.

The fish broke water fifteen feet from the boat, surging upward in a shower of spray. Hooper's body hung from each side of the mouth. For a few seconds Brody thought he saw Hooper's glazed, dead eyes staring through his face mask.

Simultaneously, Brody reached for the rifle and Quint cast the harpoon. The target was huge, a field of white belly, and the distance was not too great for a successful throw above water. But as Quint threw, the fish slid downward and the iron went high.

Brody fired without aiming, and the bullets hit the water in front of the fish.

"Here, give me the damned thing!" Quint grabbed the rifle and in a single, quick motion raised it to his shoulder and squeezed off two shots. But the fish had already begun to slip beneath the surface. The bullets plopped harmlessly into the swirl.

The fish might never have been there. There was no noise save the whisper of a breeze. From the surface the cage seemed undamaged. The water was calm. The only difference was that Hooper was gone.

"What do we do now?" said Brody. "What in the name of God can we do now? There's nothing left. We might as well go back."

"We'll go back," said Quint. "For now."

"For now? What do you mean? There's nothing we can do. The fish is too much for us. It's not real, not natural."

"Are you beaten?"

"I'm beaten. All we can do is wait until God or nature or whatever the hell is doing this to us decides we've had enough. It's out of man's hands."

"Not mine," said Quint. "I am going to kill that thing."

"I'm not sure I can get any more money after what happened today."

"Keep your money. This is no longer a matter of money."

"What do you mean?"

Quint said, "I am going to kill that fish. Come if you want. Stay home if you want. But I am going to kill that fish." His eyes seemed as dark and bottomless as the eye of the fish.

"I'll come," said Brody. "I don't guess I have any choice."

"No," said Quint. "We got no choice."

When the boat was tied up, Brody walked toward his car. At the end of the dock there was a phone booth, and he stopped beside it, prompted by his earlier resolve to call Daisy Wicker. But what's the point? he thought. If there was anything, it's over now.

Still, as he drove toward Amity, Brody wondered what Ellen's reaction had been to the news of Hooper's death. Quint had radioed the Coast Guard before they started in, and Brody had asked the duty officer to phone Ellen.

BY THE time Brody arrived home Ellen had long since finished crying. She had wept angrily, grieving not so much for Hooper as in hopelessness and bitterness at yet another death. Hooper had been her lover in only the most shallow sense of the word. She had not *loved* him, she had used him.

She heard Brody's car pull into the driveway, and she opened the back door. Lord, he looks whipped, she thought. His eyes were red and sunken, and he seemed slightly hunched as he walked toward the house. At the door she kissed him and said, "You look like you could use a drink."

"That I could." He went into the living room and flopped into a chair.

"What would you like?"

"Anything. Just so long as it's strong."

She went into the kitchen, filled a glass with equal portions of vodka and orange juice, and brought it to him. She sat on the arm of his chair and said, "Well, it's over now, isn't it? There's nothing more you can do."

"We're going out tomorrow. Six o'clock."

"Why?" Ellen was stunned. "What do you think you can do?"

"Catch the fish. And kill it."

"Do you believe that?"

"I'm not sure. But Quint believes it. God, how he believes it."

"Then let him go. Let him get killed."

"I can't."

"Why not?"

Brody thought for a moment and said, "I don't think I can explain it. But giving up isn't an answer."

Tears spilled out of Ellen's eyes. "What about me and the children? Do you want to get killed?"

"No, God, no. It's just . . ."

"You think it's all your fault. You think you're responsible for that little boy and the old man. You think killing the shark will make everything all right again. You want revenge."

Brody sighed. "Maybe. I don't know. I feel . . . I believe the only way this town can be alive again is if we kill that thing."

"And you're willing to get killed trying to—"

"Don't be stupid! I'm not even willing—if that's the word you want to use—to go out in that goddamn boat. I'm so scared every minute I'm out there I want to puke."

"Then *why go?*" She was pleading with him, begging. "Can't you ever think of anybody but yourself?"

Brody was shocked at the suggestion of selfishness. "I love you," he said. "You know that . . . no matter what."

"Sure you do," she said bitterly. "Oh, sure you do."

AROUND midnight the wind began to blow hard from the northeast, whistling through the screens and soon bringing a driving rain. Brody got out of bed and shut the window. He tried to go back to sleep, but his mind refused to rest.

At five o'clock he got up and dressed quietly. Before he left the bedroom he looked at Ellen, who had a frown on her sleeping face. "I do love you, you know," he whispered, and he kissed her brow. He started down the stairs and then, impulsively, went and looked in the boys' bedrooms. They were all asleep.

10

WHEN he got to the dock Quint was waiting for him—a tall, impassive figure whose yellow oilskins shone under the dark sky.

"I almost called you," Brody said as he pulled on his slicker. "What does this weather mean?"

"Nothing," said Quint. "It'll let up after a while. Or even if it doesn't, he'll be there." He hopped aboard the boat.

"Is it just us? I thought you liked an extra pair of hands."

"You know this fish as well as any man, and more hands won't make no difference now. Besides, it's nobody else's business."

Brody undid the stern line, and was about to jump down to the deck when he noticed a canvas tarpaulin covering something in a corner. "What's that?" he said, pointing.

"Sheep." Quint turned the ignition key. The engine coughed once, caught, and began to chug evenly.

"What for?" Brody stepped down into the boat. "You going to sacrifice it?"

Quint barked a brief, grim laugh. "Might, at that," he said. "No, it's bait." He walked forward and cast off the bow line. Then he pushed the throttle forward, and the boat eased out of the slip.

The water off Montauk was rough, for the wind was at odds with the tide. The pounding bow cast a mantle of spray.

They had been around the point only fifteen minutes when Quint pulled back on the throttle and slowed the engine.

"We're not as far out as usual," Brody said. "We can't be more than a couple of miles offshore."

"Just about."

"So why are you stopping?"

Quint pointed to the left, to a cluster of lights farther down the shore. "That's Amity there. I think he'll be somewhere between here and Amity."

"Why?"

"I got a feeling. There's not always a why to these things."

"Two days in a row we found him farther out."

"Or he found us." Quint's tone was sly.

Brody bristled. "What kind of game are you playing?"

"No game. If I'm wrong, I'm wrong."

"And we try somewhere else tomorrow." Brody half hoped Quint would be wrong, that there would be a day's reprieve.

"Or later today. But I don't think we'll have to wait that long." Quint went to the stern and lifted a bucket of chum onto the transom. "Start chummin'," he said, handing Brody the ladle. He uncovered the sheep, tied a rope around its neck and laid it on the gunwale. He slashed its stomach and flung the animal overboard, letting it drift twenty feet from the boat before securing the rope to an after cleat. Then he went forward, unlashed two barrels and carried them and their coils of ropes and harpoon darts back to the stern. "Okay," he said. "Now let's see how long it takes."

The sky had lightened to full, gray daylight, and in ones and twos the lights on the shore flicked off. The stench of the mess Brody was ladling overboard made his stomach turn.

Suddenly he saw the monstrous head of the fish—not five feet away, so close he could have touched it with the ladle—black eyes staring at him, silver-gray snout pointing at him, gaping jaw grinning. "Quint!" Brody said. "There he is!"

Quint was at the stern in an instant. As he jumped onto the transom the fish's head slipped back into the water, and a second later it slammed into the transom. The jaws closed on the wood and the head shook violently from side to side. Brody grabbed a cleat and held on, unable to look away from the eyes. Quint fell to his knees. The fish let go and dropped beneath the surface, and the boat lay still again.

"He was waiting for us!" yelled Brody.

"I know," said Quint. "We've got him now."

"*We've* got *him?* Did you see what he did to the boat?"

"Give it a mighty good shake, didn't he?"

The rope holding the sheep tightened, shook, then went slack.

Quint stood and picked up the harpoon. "He's took the sheep. It'll be a minute before he comes back."

Brody saw fever in Quint's face—an anticipation that strummed the sinews in his neck and whitened his knuckles.

The boat shuddered again, and there was a dull, hollow thump.

"What's he doing?" said Brody.

"He's trying to chew a hole in the bottom of the boat, that's what! Look in the bilge." Quint raised high his harpoon. "Come out, you son of a bitch!"

Brody raised the hatch cover over the engine room and peered into the dark, oily hole. There was water in the bilges, but there always was, and he saw no new hole. "Looks okay to me," he said.

The dorsal fin and tail surfaced ten yards to the right of the stern and began to move again toward the boat. "There you come," said Quint, cooing. "There you come." He stood, right hand extended to the sky, grasping the harpoon. When the fish was a few feet from the boat, Quint cast his iron.

The harpoon struck the fish near the dorsal fin. Then the fish hit the boat, and Quint tumbled backward. His head struck the fighting chair, and a trickle of blood ran down his neck. He jumped up and cried, "I got you! I got you, you miserable bastard!"

The rope attached to the iron dart snaked overboard as the fish sounded. Then the barrel popped off the transom and vanished.

"He took it down with him!" said Brody.

"Not for long," said Quint. "He'll be back, and we'll throw another into him, and another, and another, until he quits." Quint pulled the twine attached to the wooden harpoon shaft and brought it back aboard. He fixed the shaft to a new dart.

His confidence was contagious, and Brody now felt ebullient, gleeful, relieved—free from the mist of death. Then he noticed the blood on Quint's neck, and he said, "Your head's bleeding."

"Get another barrel," said Quint, "and bring it back here."

Brody ran forward, unlashed a barrel, slipped the coiled rope over his arm and carried the gear to Quint.

"There he comes," said Quint, pointing to the left. The first barrel had come to the surface and bobbed in the water. Quint raised the harpoon above his head. "He's coming up!"

The fish broke water like a rocket lifting off. Snout, jaw and pectoral fins rose straight up, and Quint leaned into the throw. The second iron hit the fish in the belly, just as the great body began to fall. The belly smacked the water with a thunderous boom, and a blinding spray covered the boat.

The boat lurched once, and again, and there was the distant sound of crunching.

"Attack me, will you?" said Quint. He ran to push the throttle forward, and the boat moved away from the bobbing barrels.

"Has he done any damage?" said Brody.

"Some. We're riding a little heavy aft. He probably poked a hole in us. But we'll pump her out."

"That's it, then," Brody said happily.

"What's what?"

"The fish is as good as dead."

"Not quite. Look."

Following the boat, keeping pace, were the two red wooden barrels. They did not bob. Dragged by the great force of the fish, each cut through the water, pushing a wave before it.

"He's chasing us?" said Brody. "He can't still think we're food."

"No. He means to make a fight of it."

For the first time Brody saw a frown of disquiet on Quint's face. "Hell," Quint said, "if it's a fight he wants, it's a fight he'll get." He throttled down to idling speed, jumped to the deck and up onto the transom. He picked up another harpoon. Excitement had returned to his face. "Okay," he called. "Come and get it!"

The barrels kept coming—thirty yards away, twenty-five, twenty. Brody saw the flat plane of gray pass along the starboard side of the boat. "He's here!" he cried. "Heading forward."

Quint detached the harpoon dart from the shaft, snapped the twine that held the shaft to a cleat, hopped down from the transom and ran forward. When he reached the bow he bent down and tied the twine to a forward cleat, unlashed a barrel and slipped its dart onto the harpoon shaft. Then he stood, harpoon raised.

Thirty yards in front of the boat the fish turned. The head lifted out of the water, then dipped back in. The tail, standing like a sail, began to thrash back and forth. "Here he comes!" said Quint.

The fish hit the bow head-on with a noise like a muffled explosion. Quint cast his iron. It struck the fish atop the head, over the right eye, and it held fast. The rope fed slowly overboard as the fish backed off.

"Perfect!" said Quint. "Got him in the head that time."

There were three barrels in the water now, and they skated across the surface. Then they disappeared.

"*Damn!*" said Quint. "That's no normal fish that can sound with three irons in him and three barrels to hold him up."

The boat trembled, seeming to rise up, then dropped back. The barrels reappeared twenty yards from the boat.

"Go below," Quint told Brody, as he readied another harpoon. "See if he done us any dirt up forward."

Brody swung down into the cabin. He pulled back the threadbare carpet and opened a hatch. A stream of water was flowing aft. He went topside and said to Quint, "It doesn't look good. There's a lot of water under the cabin floor."

"I better go take a look. Here." Quint handed Brody the harpoon. "If he comes back, stick this in him for good measure."

Brody stood near the bow, holding the harpoon. The barrels twitched as the fish moved about below. How do you die? Brody said silently to the fish. He heard an electric motor start.

"No sweat," said Quint, walking forward. He took the harpoon from Brody. "The pumps should take care of it. When he dies we'll tow him in."

Brody dried his palms on the seat of his pants. "And until then?"

"We wait."

FOR THREE HOURS THEY WAITED. At first the barrels would disappear every ten or fifteen minutes, then their submergences grew rarer until, by eleven o'clock, they had not gone under for nearly an hour. By 11:30 the barrels were wallowing in the water.

"What do you think?" said Brody. "Is he dead?"

"I doubt it. But he may be close enough to it for us to throw a rope around his tail and drag him till he drowns."

Quint switched on the electric winch to make sure it was working, then turned it off again. He gunned the engine and moved the boat cautiously toward the barrels.

When he came alongside the barrels Quint reached overboard with a gaff, snagged a rope and pulled one of them aboard. He unsheathed his knife and cut the rope from the barrel. Then he stabbed the knife into the gunwale, freeing both hands to hold the rope and shove the barrel to the deck. He climbed onto the gunwale, ran the rope through a pulley and down to the winch. He took a few turns around the winch, then flipped the starter switch. As soon as the slack in the rope was taken up, the boat heeled hard to starboard, dragged down by the weight of the fish.

The winch turned slowly. The rope quivered under the strain, scattering drops of water on Quint's shirt.

Suddenly the rope started coming too fast. It fouled on the winch, coiling in snarls. The boat snapped upright.

"Rope break?" said Brody.

"Hell, no!" said Quint, and now Brody saw fear in his face. "The son of a bitch is coming up!"

The fish rose vertically beside the boat, with a great rushing *whoosh*, and Brody gasped at the size of the body. Towering overhead, it blocked out the light. The pectoral fins hovered like wings, stiff and straight, as the fish fell forward.

It landed on the stern with a shattering crash, driving the boat beneath the waves. Water poured in over the transom. In seconds Quint and Brody were standing in water up to their hips.

The fish's jaws were not three feet from Brody's chest. In the black eye, as big as a baseball, Brody thought he saw his own image.

"Damn your black soul!" screamed Quint. "You sunk my boat!" A barrel floated into the cockpit, the rope writhing like a worm. Quint grabbed the harpoon dart at the end of the rope and plunged it into the soft white belly of the fish. Blood poured from the wound and bathed Quint's hands. The boat was sinking. The stern was completely submerged, and the bow was rising. The fish rolled off the stern and slid beneath the waves. The rope, attached to the dart Quint had stuck into the fish, followed.

Suddenly Quint lost his footing and fell into the water. "The knife!" he cried. His left leg lifted above the surface, and Brody saw the rope coiled around Quint's foot.

Brody lunged for the knife stuck in the starboard gunwale, wrenched it free, and turned back, struggling to run in the deepening water. He could not move fast enough. He watched helplessly as Quint, arms reaching toward him, eyes wide and pleading, was pulled slowly down into the dark water.

For a moment there was silence, except for the sucking sound of the boat slipping gradually down. The water was up to Brody's shoulders when a seat cushion popped to the surface next to him. "They'd hold you up all right," Brody remembered Hendricks saying, "if you were an eight-year-old boy." But Brody grabbed the cushion.

He saw the shark's tail and dorsal fin break the surface twenty yards away. The tail waved once left, once right, and the dorsal fin moved closer. "Get away, damn you!" Brody yelled.

The fish kept coming, barely moving, closing in.

Brody tried to swim to the bow of the boat, which was almost vertical now. Before he could reach it, the bow slid beneath the surface. He clutched the cushion, and he found that by putting his forearms across it and kicking constantly he could stay afloat without exhausting himself.

The fish came closer. It was only a few feet away, and Brody screamed and closed his eyes, waiting for an agony he could not imagine.

Nothing happened. He opened his eyes. The fish was only a foot or two away, but it had stopped. And then, as Brody watched, the steel-gray body began to fall downward into the gloom.

Brody put his face into the water and opened his eyes. He saw the fish sink in a graceful spiral, trailing behind it the body of Quint—arms out, head thrown back, mouth open in mute protest.

The fish faded from view. But, kept from sinking farther by the bobbing barrels, it stopped somewhere beyond the reach of light, and Quint's body hung suspended, a shadow twirling slowly in the twilight.

Brody raised his head, cleared his eyes, and began to kick toward shore.

THE GIRL
OF THE SEA
OF CORTEZ

I

THE girl lay on the surface of the sea, looking into the water through a mask, and was afraid. She was surprised to feel fear—a true, deep fear that bordered on panic—for not in years had anything in the sea frightened her.

But then, never in her life had she been actively, aggressively menaced by an animal. Creatures had snapped at her, and some had circled her, hungry and curious, but always a show of strength and confidence had sent them on their way in search of more appropriate prey.

This animal, however, *did* look to her as if it wanted to hurt her. It had appeared with magical speed. One moment the girl was gazing into an empty blue haze; the next, she was staring at a sharp and pointed bill of bone that quivered three feet from her chest. The bill swooped back to a broadened base, and ended in two clam-size black eyes as cold as night.

This billfish had a dorsal sail covering most of its backbone, which could lie flat and be almost invisible, or stand in proud display. But when the fish was agitated, as now, the sail pulsed up and down, up and down, as the head of a serpent hypnotizes a rodent.

The girl did not know what to do, how to behave. Backing away was no answer. This was not territorial aggression, for this was not a territorial animal. It cruised the deep water of the open sea;

it knew no home. To move suddenly *at* it was no answer. The fish was supremely confident of its superiority over her—in speed and strength and agility—or it would not have approached her. She could not hope to shoo it away. And to stay where she was seemed to be no answer. Apparently she was somehow irritating the fish, for it shook its head, and its spear sliced the water and she felt its force against her chest. Its entire body was a cocked spring, ready at the release of an inner trigger to impale her on its bill.

Why?

It could not be malice; her father had taught her that malice did not exist in animals. Animals could be hungry, angry, frightened, hurt, sick, protective, or jealous—and in any of those states could become vicious or violent—but not malevolent.

What, then? What did it want?

Again the head shook and the spear slit the water.

She wondered if she could make it to her boat before the fish attacked. She fluttered her fingers and toes, hoping to propel herself backward, inch by inch, closer to her boat.

But how far away was the boat?

She turned her head, flicked her eyes over her shoulder, saw the boat, and turned immediately back to face the fish.

It was gone.

She had felt nothing, heard nothing, and now all she could see was the endless blue.

THERE was no electricity on Santa Maria Island, and kerosene lamps burned with a thick, greasy smoke that made some people sick, so the old man and the girl chose to sit in a room illuminated only by the light that leaked around the edges of the shaded windows. The old man kept the room dark because the slashing rays of the late afternoon sun pained his eyes and confused him. He had cataracts in both eyes, and sudden bursts of bright light felt like little explosions in his brain.

His name was Francisco, but everyone called him Viejo—Old

Man—even the children who might have called him Grandfather, because Viejo was an honor, a title as significant as Excellency or General. To attain old age was a true achievement.

The girl's name was Paloma—Dove—after the morning bird that cooed a prelude to the cock's crow. She was sixteen.

"I don't understand, Viejo," she said. "Nothing like that has ever happened to me before."

"You had never met a bad animal before. Now you have. It had to happen eventually."

"Forgive me, but . . ." She hesitated. "Papa always told me there was no such thing as a bad animal."

"Your father, Jobim, was a . . . a curious man." Viejo sought gentle words to describe his son-in-law, rather than those that came quickly to mind. "Of course there are bad animals, just as there are bad people. I am only grateful that the billfish you met today was not truly bad, or he would have run you through."

"I don't see why God would create a bad animal. It doesn't make sense."

"Who says you must understand everything?" Viejo said with a touch of pique. "For a human being to try to fathom all of God's works is a waste of time."

Paloma tried to retreat. "I didn't mean—"

"What is, is. And one of the things that is, is that there are good things and bad things." He paused. "They tell me you have been interfering with the fishermen again."

"No! I only—"

"They say you shout and make a fool of yourself."

"All I did was ask Jo and Indio and the others why they can't be more careful. They bring back fish they have no use for. They don't kill just for food. That I could understand. The way they fish, someday there will be nothing left."

"No. The sea is forever. And you must learn that man will hunt what he wishes, for whatever reason he wishes. His judgments are his own. For example, it has been judged that some animals are good, like the bonito and the tuna and the grouper. They feed other useful animals and they feed people. Some animals are bad, like the sea snake and the stonefish and the scorpion. All they do is cause pain and death. And then it has been judged that there are animals both good and bad, like barracuda—which one day feeds a man handsomely and the next day poisons him—and like sharks. Sharks bring us food and money, true, but now and again they kill people."

"What about an angelfish?" Paloma asked. "What could be good or bad about an angelfish? Or a puffer? Indio caught a puffer the other day, and you'd think he had caught a marlin. Why? We don't sell them. We don't eat them."

"The fishermen make their living from the sea," said Viejo, "and so they must become one with the sea and all its creatures. Sometimes, the only way to come to know a creature is to catch and kill it."

Because Paloma did not want to offend her grandfather, she did not argue further. So all she said was, "I hope nothing ever wants to get to know me that well."

Outside, Paloma looked to the western sky. The sun hovered over the horizon, as if about to be sucked beneath the shiny gray water.

She hurried to her rock, a narrow shelf of stone that jutted out over the western tip of the island. She came here at this time every day, and she loved both the place and the time of day, for this was where she felt at peace, close to nature, to life.

There were a few clouds overhead, and the setting sun painted them pink, but the horizon was cloudless, a blade beneath the red fireball that was slowly sliding downward. The bottom of the sun touched the horizon, and Paloma half expected to hear a hiss as the water quenched the fire. But smoothly and without a sound, it slipped faster and faster out of sight.

Paloma watched the sky for a moment more, enjoying the changes that happened with such speed only at the beginning and end of the day. The light was fading, following the sun to other parts of the world. Only the faintest splash of pink still touched the clouds.

She rose to her knees and was about to leave the rock when a flicker of movement made her look back at the water. What she saw made her stop and stare and catch her breath.

Rising clear of the water, twisting in a spasm of pure pleasure, was an enormous marlin. Its saber blade sliced through the air, its sickle tail arched upward, and in graceful slow motion the huge body slammed down upon the water.

It was a full second before Paloma heard the resonant boom, and by then all that remained as testimony to the acrobatics was a spreading ring of ripples on the sea.

Paloma felt suddenly calm and happy.

With a feeling of privilege, of being witness to nature reveling in itself, Paloma started for home. As she walked along the path, she looked down and saw her brother, Jo, and his friends, Indio and Manolo, approaching the dock in their skiff.

Paloma could see from the top of the hill that they had had a good day. The bow of their boat was heaped high with fish, a kaleidoscope of glistening colors in the fading light. And Paloma could see, even from where she stood, that they had taken fish indiscriminately. Whatever they could catch they had killed. There were angelfish and bonitos, puffers and stingrays, and even one of the rare and strange creatures called guitar sharks—harmless and, to fishermen, useless.

As Paloma watched, Jo shut off the outboard motor and guided the skiff toward the dock, while his mates culled the piles of dead fish, throwing overboard those that were not worth selling.

When Paloma had first seen them do this, she had erupted in fury, screaming at Jo, demanding to know why, if they intended to throw back the fish, they didn't do so as soon as they caught them, when the fish still had a chance to live.

Jo had been forthright in his response. "Early in the day, before we know the size of the catch, any fish is good. By the end of the day, if the catch has been rich, we can afford to keep only the best. So then we throw the others back."

Now she watched as Indio picked up a small fish and waved it at the other mate, Manolo. Though the twilight was deepening, she could tell them apart by the color of their hair. Indio always wore a hat out in the sun, so his hair had remained black. Manolo kept his head cool by pouring salt water on it, so his hair had been bleached to a light brown, just as Paloma's own auburn hair had been bleached nearly blond by salt and sun. Indio threw the fish at Manolo, who picked up another fish by its tail and whacked Indio on the head with it.

Yowling and cursing, the fishermen flung fish at one another. Most missed their targets and landed in the water, to float there belly up. To Paloma, striding down the hill, the fight was nauseating, the waste obscene. It offended her to see dead animals treated as if they had never been live beings.

She bent over and picked up a rock and called out, "Hey!" The three in the skiff looked up. "If you have to throw things at each other, throw these." She threw the rock as hard as she could, hoping it would strike the skiff and knock a hole in it. But the rock flew wide and plopped in the water, and Jo responded by laughing and ticking his thumbnail off his front teeth—the most insulting, contemptuous gesture he could make.

Paloma turned away.

Her father had explained the problem to her when she had first complained about the young men who fished without care. "This sea is too rich," he had said. "It has too much life. If fish were in short supply here, fishermen might fish with care, for fear of killing off their livelihood. But here nature seems to be showing off. People see no reason to be careful. One day they will, but by then it may be too late."

Paloma had loved the sea since the time of her earliest memories. Jobim, her father, had recognized the affinity between his firstborn child and the sea and had determined to nourish it. When she was a baby, he had bathed her in the sea and taught her to float, and then to swim, and to fear few living things but to respect them all.

And he had captivated her with his descriptions of the things that made their sea, the Sea of Cortez, unique.

The Sea of Cortez, he said, existed because of an ancient accident. Ages ago, the peninsula known as Baja California had been part of the Mexican mainland. Then, at some point in prehistory, the earth's surface had realigned itself and caused what must have been the most spectacular earthquake of all time.

"You know how you take an old ratty shirt and tear it up the back to make rags?" Jobim had said. "That's what happened to Mexico. It split along its main seam, the San Andreas Fault. And when the seam split, there was a big space and the Pacific Ocean rushed in, and a new sea was born."

The sea had had no name then. Jobim read to her from a book that said it was not until 1536 that the sea was named for the Spanish explorer Hernando Cortez, who discovered Lower California and the sea that separated it from the Mexican mainland.

"Nowadays," Jobim had said, "some people don't call it a sea anymore. They call it a gulf, the Gulf of California. But it doesn't need a name. It is the sea."

So to Paloma it was simply the sea—provider and friend. For it gave her most of what she loved in life. But it had also taken from her the one thing that she had cherished most in life.

Because of the peculiar combination of mountains and water, extreme dryness and extreme humidity, Pacific Ocean winds and high sierra winds, the Sea of Cortez was a breeding ground for sudden, violent low-pressure weather systems. With no warning at all, a fine day on the sea could turn mean. Over the horizon would race a black swirl of clouds. Beneath and before the clouds, the calm sea would begin to churn. A sound like a distant whisper would swell into a horrid wailing roar.

They were called chubascos, and unlike hurricanes and typhoons, they did not come from anywhere; they were created right there. Even if you had a radio, you could not hear a weather fore-cast about a chubasco approaching.

If you were on the water, you hoped to be able to notice the early signs—like a subtle shift in the wind or the sudden formation of a tower of black clouds—in time to run for a lee or, at least, to reach open water, where you could face the pounding waves with-out fear of being driven onto a rocky shore.

If you were so unlucky as to be underwater when the first signs formed, and did not see them until the storm was almost upon you, and were forced to scramble aboard your boat and start your motor—then all that was left to you was prayer.

Two summers before, after the terrible "chubasco of the full moon"—the moon was full and the tides were very high, which meant that the storm-driven water rose higher and did more dam-age—Jobim was found, drowned, washed up on the beach of a nearby island. He had surfaced from a dive, no doubt, to find his boat bucking and heaving in mountainous seas. He must have tried to board it and been knocked unconscious by the motor or the boat, for when he was found, there was a big blue dent in his forehead.

That was one reason Paloma tended to question the acceptance, by Viejo and others, that everything mysterious was somehow an integral part of God's master plan. She believed that Papa's death was an accident, a random blow, something that nothing had or-dained. She had conditioned her mind not to think beyond that, about what might lie behind randomness or luck.

AT SUPPER that evening Jo described for Paloma and their mother each of the triumphs of his day at sea. He boasted about how many fish they had caught, about how hard the grouper had fought, about how sharks had tried to steal his catch.

Paloma sat silently. Miranda, their mother, smiled and nodded and said, "That's nice."

With a glance at Paloma, Jo said, "I even threw my harpoon at a manta ray, a giant devilfish. I missed, but then—I swear—he turned and attacked the boat. It's a good thing I was quick, or I would've been rammed and sunk."

Paloma said quietly, "Manta rays don't attack boats."

"*This* one did. This was a real devilfish. I swear."

"Why do you want to harpoon a manta ray? They don't hurt anybody."

"So *you* say! The devilfish is evil! That's why he has horns."

Paloma said nothing, making an effort to look only at her bowl of fish soup. But she could not resist—it came almost as a reflex—shaking her head as Papa used to, in a way that manifested contempt.

Jo recognized the gesture and hated it. He started to shout. "You think you know so much. You don't know anything! The devilfish is evil. Everybody knows that. Everybody but you."

Miranda recognized the gesture, too, and could see in it Jobim and the conflict he had unknowingly built up between his children. Frightened, she said, "It is possible, Paloma."

Without looking up from her soup, Paloma said, "No, Mama."

"Don't listen to her," said Jo. "She doesn't know!" He spat toward the fireplace, the way the men of the island did to show that they had won an argument.

"You may think you know, Paloma," Miranda said, hoping to placate both her children. "There are times when I think I know something, when maybe I just—"

"Mama." Paloma wanted to stop Miranda. "Let's leave it."

The room was silent.

Paloma raised her eyes and looked into the taut, flushed face of her brother. His jaws twitched, and his arm—as big around as one of Paloma's thighs—trembled. She had wanted to avoid enraging Jo by arguing, and instead had enraged him by being silent—a silence that he interpreted as condescension.

Paloma tried to appear calm. She knew that if ever he was driven to act out his inner fury, he could take her apart as easily as he dismantled the engines he so loved to tinker with.

Jo was fifteen, seventeen months younger than Paloma, yet he had the physique of an adult. From hauling lines and nets since he was a young boy, he had developed massive shoulders and arms. From balancing in a tipping boat day after day, his calves and thighs were lined with sinews as tough as wire. He was short—five feet six—which suited working in boats, for a low center of gravity made quick movement easy.

Paloma was as lithe as Jo was compact. She was five feet eight inches tall, and weighed about one hundred and twenty pounds. While Jo looked very much of his people—dark of hair and skin and eyes—she did not. Everything about her was light, from her bones to her skin to her hair, for she was not so much of her people as of her father.

And there, she knew, lay the core of the problem between them. Jo felt that it should be he, not she, who was more like their father. After all, was he not a male? Was his name not made from Jobim's? And yet every day, what she said, what she did, her entire manner reminded him of how close Paloma had been to Papa and how far from him he himself had been.

Worst of all, they both knew that Jo had had a chance to be the one close to Papa. But it would have taken a superhuman boy to be the son Papa wanted, for, like all the boys on their island, he had a strange aversion to the water. And so Paloma, a girl and a kind of son by default, had been taught more patiently, forgiven more kindly, and praised more freely than Jo had been.

Once the core of enmity had been established between the brother and sister, almost every other aspect of their relationship seemed to provide new antagonism.

Without another word, Jo rose from the table and left the room. Miranda looked after him. When he had gone, she turned back and said, "Paloma—"

"I know, Mama. I know."

As USUAL, Paloma awakened just before daybreak, when the sun was sending its first gray messengers into the blackness of the eastern sky. She splashed water on her face and crept out of the house and trotted along a path to the cliffs that faced east.

Slowly the gray sky was suffused with orange, and then the first shimmering line of fire slipped over the lip of the world.

Paloma sat and watched the sea and tried to envision all the things that were happening below the flat, calm surface. She wished she could watch day break from underwater, for Jobim had told her that it was the time of most activity in the sea, of movement, change, and feeding.

This was true in all seas, he had said, but particularly in the Sea of Cortez. Here, deepwater fish fed in shallow water, animals that normally never saw light were swept up into bright sunlight, and the whole bustle of the sea was concentrated in a few areas. These areas were called seamounts.

Thousands—perhaps millions—of years after the earthquake that created the sea, other tremors occurred and caused volcanoes to heave up and erupt and, later, to collapse into the water. Some of them had melded back into the seabed, but others remained as seamounts—mountains that rose thousands of feet from the bottom to within fifty or sixty feet of the surface.

The seamounts were a major contributor to the abundance of life in the Sea of Cortez, for they created a kind of natural banquet that attracted animals of every species imaginable.

Deepwater currents that flowed along the bottom of the sea would strike a seamount and create an upwelling—the water would rush upward, carrying with it all the microscopic animals, the plankton, tiny shrimps, and thousands of other creatures on which larger animals feed. The larger animals would chase their food into shallower water, and they, in turn, would be pursued by the still larger animals that fed on them. Around a seamount, nature's whole food chain flourished.

Jobim had introduced Paloma to a seamount, one never visited by the fishermen because they didn't know it existed. There, only an hour's paddle in her pirogue from Santa Maria Island, she could spend her days watching and swimming and, in her fancies, imagining herself to be part of a rich undersea life.

Each morning after breakfast she walked down to the dock. She pretended to be there to run errands for the fishermen as they prepared for the day's journey; in fact, she was there to see them off, to make sure they left before she did, so there would be no chance they could follow her and discover her private place. In a single morning's fishing they could damage the delicate balance established by nature over countless years.

Jo and Indio and Manolo would never discover Paloma's seamount on their own, for, like almost all the islanders, they fished the shoals that had always been fished and seldom changed their locations by more than a few hundred yards. They had never had a need to move; the old grounds still yielded well. True, some species—especially the territorial ones, such as groupers—were growing scarce. But if you had a big enough boat, you could balance the marketability of your catch, making up in volume what you lost in quality.

A more compelling reason for staying on the familiar grounds was that Jo and the others had no way of finding new places. It would never occur to any of them to let themselves be towed behind a boat in the open sea, wearing a face mask so they could spot a seamount from the surface.

They spent their time *on* the sea, never under it; none of the island fishermen stuck his face underwater if he could avoid it. They claimed to know how to swim, but most disliked swimming and went into the water only by accident.

Jo had tried. But from the time when he was eighteen months old and Jobim had pitched him into the water off the dock and told him to swim, he had hated it. It was alien to him, and frightening. Jobim explained things to him, taught him, cajoled him, bellowed at him—hoping that through conditioning he could overcome this aversion to the sea. But finally Jobim had despaired of him and had turned to Paloma, who did not have to try. For swimming was as natural to her as breathing, and the more he taught her the more she begged to learn.

She did not understand how the others could live on the edge of an undiscovered world and have no curiosity about exploring it. Beneath their feet were wonders too exotic for them even to dream of. Secretly she was glad that they left it all to her.

This morning, Paloma tried to be more helpful than usual, to send Jo a message of truce. She did not enjoy hurting him. Besides, his foul humors made their mother tense, and when Miranda was tense, the whole house was, too.

But Jo wanted no part of a truce today. He rejected all Paloma's offers of help. When his gear and his mates were aboard, he started the motor and set out for the fishing grounds.

Jo and the others would start the day working with handlines. Periodically they would look through a glass-bottomed bucket to see if any big schools were in the neighborhood. If the school fish were there, they would set their net and wait and then gather it, spilling masses of fish into their boat.

If the big boat from La Paz was due that night or the next morning, the fish would be kept cool until they could be dumped into the boat's ice hold. If the boat was not due for a few days, the fish would have to be gutted and put on ice on the island, or they would spoil before the boat arrived.

Since Paloma was not a fisherman, she was not permitted to take up dock space for her little boat. She kept it beneath the dock, where it was out of the way.

When she judged that Jo's boat had traveled a safe distance, she reached beneath the dock and pulled out her pirogue. It was eight feet long and two feet wide and, basically, nothing more than a hollow log. It was Paloma's dearest possession.

Her father had made it for her thirteenth birthday. He had ordered the log from La Paz, for there were no trees on Santa Maria, and it had arrived on the boat that came to take away the fish. He had burned a cavity in the log, then attacked it with a chisel and a wooden mallet. Finally he had used coarse dried sharkskin to smooth the wood and erase the splinters.

She tossed a broad-brimmed hat into the pirogue; later, around midday, when the temperature was over one hundred degrees, to spend more than a few minutes on the water without a hat was to invite a pounding headache. She checked her mesh bag to make sure she had all her equipment: her face mask and flippers, a snorkel tube, her knife—a sharp, double-edged blade of stainless steel with a rubber hilt—and a mango for her lunch.

She did not carry the knife to defend herself—before yesterday's encounter with the testy billfish she had never felt menaced by anything under the water; if a shark was going to bite her, it would move so fast that a knife wouldn't do any good. The knife was more a tool than a weapon. Its primary use was to pry oysters free from the rocks on the seamount and to open them in her pirogue. Its less common but more important use was precautionary. Over the years fishermen had lost a lot of monofilament fishing line. Made of nylon, the line did not degrade in water; colorless, it was almost impossible to see underwater. Anchored to boulders, it was a trap; if her hand or foot became entangled, she could not hold her breath long enough to strip away every thread and wiggle free. She would have to slash her way out.

Paloma untied the pirogue from the dock and stepped in. Immediately she dropped to her knees to keep the boat steady. She dipped the double-bladed kayak paddle into the still water, back-paddled away from the dock, and turned west.

First there was only one dolphin, rolling and bucking with the grace and precision of a carousel horse, exhaling a wheezy spray through the hole atop its head, its dorsal fin and glossy back shining in the low morning sun.

It crossed in front of her bow, then leaped clear of the water and dived and passed under the boat and rolled again in front. Then came another, and another, until there were a dozen, and then a score, and then more than Paloma could count.

They charged her boat in ranks of six and dived beneath it and surfaced on the other side, and in each rank one, only one, would leap *over* the boat, over her, and as its shadow passed, it rained droplets on her head. Then on some secret signal they ceased their frolicking and bounded off across the sea.

Paloma watched, thrilled. She felt as if she had been anointed by the dolphins. They had chosen her as their playmate in an interlude in their travels. It was an omen. Perhaps today would be a special day.

As the last of the dolphins leaped out of sight, Paloma dug her paddle into the water and continued toward the seamount.

The highest point on the seamount was not in shallow water—nowhere did it come closer to the surface than forty-five or fifty feet—so she could not see it from her boat. Nor could she hope to find it by timing her journey from the dock, for each day the winds and currents varied a bit from the day before.

Jobim had taught her to locate the seamount by using landmarks. A few miles to the west there was an island, and on the island grew giant cactus plants. From a distance it appeared that at the very highest point of the island was a particularly tall, thick cactus. But as Paloma paddled closer, her perspective on the cactus would change, and soon she would see that it was not one but two cacti. When she could barely discern a sliver of sky between the two plants, she knew she was on target.

The cactus plants told her only that she had come far enough westward. The wind or the current might have taken her too far north or south. She had to locate a second landmark that would tell her her north-south position.

As soon as she saw blue sky between the cactus plants, she shifted her gaze to a fisherman's shack at the end of a point of land on a neighboring island. If she was too far north, the shack appeared to be far inland; too far south, it seemed to be floating on the water. When the shack was precisely on the point, she knew she was directly over the seamount.

She tossed her anchor overboard and let the rope slip through her fingers. Her anchor was an old rusty piece of iron, called a killick, but it held the small boat as well as a proper one would have. And it was expendable. Anchors got caught in the rocks of the seamount and had to be cut away. But there was always another piece of rusted metal to be scavenged.

When the killick had set, Paloma dipped her face mask in the water, then spat in it and rubbed the spittle around with her fingertips to keep the glass from fogging—not even her father had been able to explain to her why spit kept glass from fogging, but it worked—and then she rinsed it again in salt water. She fitted her knife down the back of the rope belt wrapped around her shift, slipped her feet into her flippers, adjusted the snorkel tube in the mask strap, and slid over the side.

She kicked gently along the side of the boat until she reached the anchor line. There she paused, looking down through a blue haze streaked with butter-yellow shafts of sunlight, eager for the first glimpse of life on the seamount. Some days she would see a sailfish, some days a shark, a porpoise, or a pilot whale. But some days, like today, she saw only murky clouds of plankton driven up from the deep. The top of the seamount—a rough plain of rocks and corals—was all vague and misty.

If she couldn't see well enough from the surface, she had only one choice. She would go down to the seamount.

Paloma's training for a long breath-hold descent into the sea had come from Jobim, who had taken her down in stages of five feet, teaching her how to prepare for each depth, how each depth felt different in her lungs, how to avoid panic. And her training had come as well from four years of practice, and from instinct. She could hold her breath long enough to dive to the top of the seamount and spend enough time underwater to have fun—and return to the surface to dive again.

Lying on the water, facedown, with her snorkel poking up behind her head, she took half a dozen deep breaths, each one expanding her lungs farther than the one before. After the last breath, she inhaled until she felt she was about to burst, clamped her mouth shut, and dived. She pulled herself hand over hand down the anchor line and pushed herself with powerful strokes of her flippers. As she plunged downward, she let little spurts of bubble escape from her mouth, until the feeling in her lungs was comfortable.

She reached the seamount in a few seconds and, to keep from floating upward, wrapped her knees around a rock. She felt good, relaxed, her lungs pleasantly full. Time had a way of expanding underwater. She might be able to stay down for only a minute and a half, perhaps two minutes, but because her senses were alert, every sound, sight, and feeling registered sharply. Two minutes could seem as full as an hour.

For the first seconds after her descent the animals of the seamount retreated, wary of any disturbance. Now they began to return, as if accepting Paloma as part of life.

Something slammed her from behind, knocking her forward. She clutched at her rock perch and spun around, one arm up by her face. For a split second she couldn't see through the cloud of bubbles. Whatever it was had not been an accident; accidental collisions underwater were as rare as straight lines in nature.

Arm up, squinting through her bubbles, fighting to suppress panic, Paloma found herself face to face with her assailant. And she laughed into her snorkel.

It was a big grouper—three or four feet long, thirty or thirty-five pounds—and it hovered a foot from her face, its lower jaw pouting out from under the upper, its round eyes staring straight at her, waiting impatiently for her to do what it assumed she had come to do—feed it.

She had fed it often before. There was no mistaking this grouper. It was the only one of its size on this seamount, and it had prominent scars behind one of its gills, mementos of narrow escapes from larger predators. Today she had nothing for the grouper, so she held up a closed fist. The animal seemed to understand the gesture, for it made a halfhearted grab for her fist, then turned, flapped its tail in her face, and moved away.

Paloma pushed off the rock and swam down a few more feet, into a valley between two big boulders. There, in the sand, a triggerfish was darting back and forth, frantic, its tail quivering, its gill flaps fluttering. At first Paloma thought the triggerfish was wounded, for its movements were erratic and it was encircled by three, then five, then nine or ten other fish, all of which seemed determined to attack it.

A Scotch parrot fish—with tartanlike scales and beaked mouth—charged the smaller triggerfish, which parried with a flurry of twisting bites. The parrot fish retreated.

Immediately an angelfish dashed forward, feinted at the triggerfish, then banked and tried to get at the sand beneath the triggerfish, but it, too, was driven off.

Now Paloma realized what was happening. The triggerfish's egg deposit had been discovered by the other fish, and they were ganging up, trying to divert the triggerfish long enough for one of them to dash in and root out and eat the cache.

Paloma felt instinctively parental toward the eggs. She swam into the midst of the flurry and flashed her hands around; the invaders dispersed. But the triggerfish assumed that Paloma was another thief and it bit her earlobe.

Paloma moved away, smiling but sad, because she knew that once an egg deposit was discovered, it was as good as gone. Still, she told herself, this was the way it was supposed to be, an example of nature in balance. If all the eggs of every triggerfish hatched, the sea would be choked with triggerfish.

She began to feel the telltale ache in her lungs, the hollow sensation that she believed to be the lungs searching for air. Her temples began to pound. She pushed off the bottom and kicked easily toward the surface, trailing a stream of bubbles.

Her rule was to rest for five or ten minutes between dives, for then she could dive again and again without pain or fatigue. If she did not rest, she found that each successive dive would have to be shorter and the ache in her lungs would be sharper.

So she hung on the anchor line and drew deep breaths and occasionally looked underwater through her mask to see if anything new or special had arrived in the neighborhood.

Perhaps today she would see a golden *cabrío,* the rare, solitary grouper of a yellow so rich and unblemished that when it hung motionless in the water it appeared to be cast of solid gold. Or perhaps there would be a pulsing cloud of barracuda, whose silver backs caught the sunlight and were transformed into a shower of needles.

Once she had even seen a whale shark, but that was an encounter no reasonable person could hope to have again. Her first reaction had been shock, and then, for a fragment of a second, terror, and then, when she realized exactly what it was, a tingle of warmth flooded through her stomach. The whale shark had risen from the bottom, gliding so slowly that it seemed to be floating, an animal so huge that Paloma could not see its head and tail at the same time. But she could determine its color—a speckled, mustardy yellow—and that told her there was no danger: the whale shark ate plankton and tiny shrimps.

Jobim had tried to prepare her for the shock she would feel at her first sight of the leviathan.

"There is one way he can hurt you," Jobim had said without a hint of jest.

"Tell me." Paloma imagined stinging spines or molarlike teeth that could crush her bones.

"If you see his mouth open, and you swim to it and you squeeze yourself inside and force the jaws closed behind you."

"Papa!"

"Even then I don't think he'd like you very much. He'd shake his head and spit you out."

Paloma had jumped on her father and wrapped her arms and legs around him and tried to bite his neck.

When she had identified the whale shark, she had swum down to meet this largest of all fish, and it had slowed enough so that she could touch the head and run her hand down the endless ridges of the back. It did not show any signs of acknowledging her, but continued its lazy cruise, propelled by gentle sweeps of its tail. The tail fin alone was as tall as she was. And as it moved back and forth, it pushed before it a wave of water so powerful that it cast her away in a helpless tumble.

The whale shark had then moved off into the gray-green gloom, relentlessly, as if programmed to follow a course set by nature countless millions of years ago.

Today, as Paloma lay on the surface of the sea, a slight alteration in the way the water felt around her body told her something was about to happen. The water seemed to press on her, as if some great mass were moving toward her at high speed.

Reflexively she backpedaled in the water, trying to get away from this thing, whatever it was, that she could feel but couldn't see, that was coming closer, for the pressure on her body was beginning to lift her out of the water.

Then she saw it, a black thing.

It was larger than she was, larger even than her boat. It was soaring up at her. It was winged, and the wings swept up and down with such power that everything before them was scattered. She could see a mouth that was a black cavern, and it was flanked by two horns, and the horns were aimed at Paloma.

It was a manta ray. Even though she knew, rationally, that she had nothing to fear, she felt a rush of panic. Why was it coming straight at her? Her breath caught in her throat.

When it was no more than a few feet from Paloma, the manta tilted its wing and arched its back, changing its angle to display a belly of sheer and shiny white. Five trembling gills were on either side, crescent wings like slices of the winter moon.

The ray rushed up through the water and broke the surface, a perfect triangle of solid flesh as it broke free of the sea and reached for the sky. There was a deafening roar, an infernal boom, like the sound the wind makes at the height of a hurricane.

Paloma's eyes followed the manta as it flew high in the air, shedding diamonds of water. At the top of its arc it hung for a fraction of a second, a titan of shimmering black against the sun that rimmed it with a halo of gold.

Then it fell backward, showing its belly; it smashed flat against the pewter sea. The water erupted, and the sound seemed to carry the same violence as a thunderclap that cracks the clouds close by.

Paloma let out her breath, a whoosh of excitement. She had seen mantas jump before—young ones especially—but always from a distance, at twilight usually. They seemed to be flipping in happy somersaults.

But mantas couldn't be "happy." This was what the islanders called an "old" animal, and by old they meant low and primitive and stupid. The wisdom was that old animals could not know pleasure or pain, happiness or distress.

And Paloma agreed with most of this wisdom, for Jobim had taught her that it was wrong to think of animals in human terms. It deprived animals of what was most precious about them—their own place in nature. Jobim had had contempt for people who tried to tame wild animals. If an animal could be trained to, say, walk on its hind legs or beg for food, it seemed less threatening, more human. But the animal also seemed less whole.

What, then, was this manta doing? Why had it jumped right beside her, when the sea was empty for miles around? Mantas jumped out of water to rid themselves of parasites—small animals that attached themselves to a larger animal. Some of these parasites were burrowers, little crabs or snails or worms that dug holes in the manta and fed on its flesh. And according to Jobim, by leaping into the air the manta deprived the parasites of oxygen—for, like fish, the parasites got their oxygen from water, not air—and the sudden shock caused them to let go. If not, then being slammed down on the water surely would.

But on this manta Paloma had seen no parasites, and in its jump there was a sense of vigor, of excitement.

The island wisdom about manta rays had always encouraged Paloma to fear them. Careless sailors and fishermen were said to have been consumed by mantas. But a few months ago Paloma had been diving near the seamount and had seen a manta from the surface. It had been flying through the water with the grace of a hawk, rising and falling on its wind of water. She recalled now how surprised she had been that none of the other creatures on the seamount had acted afraid of the manta. They had not scurried out of its way, had not dashed for cover in the rocks. They had seemed to know that the manta would avoid them—gently lifting a wing to pass over a pair of groupers or dipping it to pass beneath a school of jacks.

On the edge of the seamount that day months ago, the water had been gray and turbid, signaling the presence of a cloud of plankton. The manta had headed for the plankton, and as it approached the cloud, it had surprised Paloma again. Its dreadful horns unfurled and showed themselves for what they actually were—floppy fins. The manta had used them like arms, sweeping the plankton-rich water into its mouth.

The manta had made three passes through the cloud of plankton and then, evidently satisfied, had flown up and away.

Now, holding on to her pirogue, feeling her pulse slow and her breathing become more regular, Paloma waited to see if today's manta would jump once more. She wanted to see it as it broke the surface, to hear the roar and the explosion again.

After a few moments she put her face in the water and turned in a circle. But the manta must have gone off into the deep, for life on the seamount had resumed its routine. Paloma decided to dive back down.

She took deep breaths and then sped down the anchor line. Finding the same rock on the seamount, she locked her legs around it. She half expected things to be different here, as if the drama on the surface should have provoked changes below. But all was the same. The same eels poked their heads out of the same holes, the same jacks searched for food.

There had been one change, though. Nearby, in the little valley, the triggerfish was still darting back and forth. But now the fish was alone. And its motion was less aggressive, more desperate. Paloma knew that the triggerfish's eggs had finally been taken and that it was searching for them in hopeless frenzy.

Another fish swam slowly before Paloma's mask. It was a fat

thing, with tiny fins that seemed far too small for its body. She waited until the fish was only a few inches away, then lashed out with both hands and grabbed it around the body. She held it very lightly, anticipating what would happen.

The fish struggled for a second and then, like a balloon, began to inflate. The scales on its back stood on end and became stiff white thorns. Its eyes receded into the swelling body and its fins, which now looked absurdly small, flapped in fury.

Paloma juggled this spiny football on her fingers for a moment, then held its bulbous face to hers. The puffer had done all it could—become a thoroughly unappetizing meal—so now it simply stared back at Paloma. Gently she released it in open water, and it fluttered quickly away. As it neared the shelter of the rocks, it gradually deflated. The thorns on its back lay down and once again became scales. By the time it reached a familiar crevice, it was slim enough to squirt through to safety.

Paloma began to hear anew the distant throbbing in her temples. It was still faint, not urgent; she had plenty of time to get to the surface. But by nature and Jobim's training, she was cautious. And so she kicked off and rose, facing the hill of rocks and coral.

She saw an oyster growing on the side of a boulder, reached behind her to slide her knife from her belt and, with a twist of her wrist, cut the oyster away.

The throbbing in her head was louder now, urging her to hurry up to where she belonged. Wanting air, she kicked hard, and her strong legs drove her upward with a speed that plastered her hair over the faceplate of her mask.

She popped through the surface, spat, and gulped a breath of air. She clung to the side of the pirogue and drew more breaths until her body was fully nourished with oxygen. Then she dropped the oyster into the pirogue, pulled herself aboard, and lay on the bottom, facing the sun and its warmth.

When she was warm and dry, she used her knife to split the mango and dig out the sweet, juicy fruit. She tossed the mango rind overboard and watched as it was savaged by a school of tiny, yellow-and-black striped fish. These sergeants major were everywhere, on reefs and rocks, in deep water and shallow. They appeared suddenly at the slightest trace of food. Voracious, they ate fruit, bones, bread, meat, vegetables and—now and then—nibbled on Paloma's toes.

She picked up the scraggly oyster and held it in one hand. With the other hand she guided the point of her knife to the rough slit between the two halves of the shell. Oysters weren't like clams, which you could open cleanly and easily with a cut and a twist and a scoop. Oysters were ragged and sharp and coated with slimy growths, and if you weren't very careful you'd stab yourself. And the cut would bleed, so you couldn't dive anymore that day.

Patiently she pried around the edges of the shell until she found a place where the knife could probe inside. She felt the knife point touch the muscle that held the shell together; slowly she sawed there.

Most people on the island would not eat oysters. They were thought to be unsafe. The truth was that the only bad oyster was one left too long in the sun. They died soon and spoiled instantly, and a spoiled oyster was a ticket to the hospital in La Paz.

But an oyster fresh from the sea was a delicacy, something cool and rich and salty and pure. Paloma cut through the last bit of muscle and pried open the shell and saw then that this oyster was the greatest delicacy of all.

Inside, nestled in the shimmering gray meat, was the prize. It was misshapen and wrinkled, its color mottled, and it was only half the size of Paloma's little fingernail. But it was a pearl.

PALOMA plucked the pearl from its shell and let it roll around in the palm of her hand.

Now she had twenty-seven.

It had taken her more than a year to find the others, but her progress had been steady, an average of two a month. It had been six weeks, however, since she had found the last one, and she had begun to wonder. Was it possible that on the whole seamount there were only twenty-six pearl-bearing oysters? She needed at least forty pearls.

She closed her fist around the little pearl and looked at the sky and said, "Thank you."

Her thanks were directed at her father. She could not accept that dead meant finished forever. She was lonely for, and needed, her father, and so in her mind she fashioned an existence for him, so that he was still available for her to talk to and ask for help and share private things with. He had been the only person she had felt comfortable sharing things with. Somehow, being able to explore events and alternatives with him seemed to guide and comfort her.

Shortly before he died, Jobim had recruited Paloma into a secret endeavor. Only a few months from now, Jobim and Miranda would have marked twenty years of marriage. He had wanted to give his wife something special. Since he had no money beyond that which fed and clothed them, he could not buy her something fine. He had decided to make the gift himself. And whatever he determined to make would have to be made in secret. And if it must be a secret, it must be small enough to conceal.

It would not be a wood carving or a clay figure or a decoration fashioned of seashells. Anyone could carve wood or collect seashells. It had to be something that only he could do, so that it would be a gift direct from his heart to Miranda's.

Once he had found the answer, it seemed obvious: pearls, a necklace of natural pearls. Of all the islanders, only he—and, through his teaching, Paloma—pursued the ancient skill of diving for pearl oysters. He had maintained the skill only for his own amusement, for pearling was no longer profitable. The pearl beds had been depleted more than a generation before, and anyhow the market for natural pearls had all but disappeared. People now preferred cultured pearls; they were rounder, had more luster.

Jobim did not like cultured pearls. "They are prettier, and they do come from the sea, and they make a nice necklace," he told Paloma. "But they are not natural. They are man trying to improve on nature. Man can't improve it; he can only change it."

Jobim had found just five pearls before he died, and Paloma had taken upon herself the task of completing the necklace. She wanted to be sure that Miranda knew it was a gift from Jobim, no matter who had gathered most of the pearls. So Paloma had decided to tell her mother a simple lie—that Jobim had collected all the pearls and had hidden them with the intention of stringing them just before the anniversary date.

"Thank heavens," Paloma would say to Miranda. "One day he swore me to secrecy and told me where they were, in case something should happen to him."

There would be happiness, nostalgia, and tears. The important thing for Paloma was that all the emotions would be directed not at her but at her father—at the memory Miranda still held of him.

Paloma tucked the pearl into a narrow crack in the wood on one side of the pirogue, so it couldn't spill out if the pirogue should tip. Then she lay back to rest for a few minutes, for she had found that to dive too soon after eating was to invite a painful knot in her side or, sometimes, to bring up bile in her throat, which could be very dangerous. There was nothing worse than to vomit underwater. The gag reflex would force a spasmodic intake of breath, which would bring salt water into her lungs, which would force a violent cough and another breath and would drown her.

She fell asleep. When she awoke about half an hour later, she slipped overboard and cleaned her mask. She grabbed the anchor line, took deep breaths, and pulled toward the bottom. Ten feet from the surface she stopped.

Something was wrong. The seamount had changed. She was disoriented. Nothing looked the same. An entire section of the seamount seemed covered in black.

She closed her eyes and willed herself to stay calm. When she felt more composed, she opened her eyes and looked down again.

And then she realized what had perplexed her. Not five feet away was the largest manta ray she had ever seen. It was like a black cloak that, from this short distance, blocked out most of her view of the seamount.

It was not only the proximity of the giant that had deceived her; it was also the fact that the animal was not moving at all. It was lying suspended, absolutely still in the water. It did not look alive.

But it had to be alive, for dead, it would have sunk to the bottom.

She dropped farther down, expecting the animal at any moment to move away. But the manta continued to hover, motionless. Her toes were within inches of the manta's back. The ray had to be more than twenty feet across, for she judged that she could have lain down four times across its wings and still not have covered them tip to tip.

Paloma had to go up for air. Making as little stir as possible, she floated up. As the distance between her and the manta grew, she gained perspective on the animal, and she could see the reason it was not behaving normally. Long, thin things were trailing beneath and behind it.

Her face broke water. She breathed in and out several times, each breath a bit deeper than the last, drew one final breath that seemed to suck air down into her feet, and went down again.

The manta had not moved. This time she approached it from the front, and she saw that behind the horn on the left side, the animal's flesh was torn in a broad, deep gash. Knotted ropes were embedded in its body, their ends dangling loose, like tails.

The manta must have become fouled in a fisherman's net, then panicked, and flailing to get free, driven its bulk against the taut ropes, forcing them to bite deeper into its flesh. Finally it had escaped, but the manta's victory was illusory. It was bound to die. Paloma knew that in the sea there was no truce, no mercy.

The wound had weakened the manta, and because the ropes still festered in the open sore, there had been no chance for healing to begin. Unable to pursue its food, the manta could not eat as much as it should. The less it ate, the weaker it would become; the weaker it became, the less it could eat.

Before long the manta would begin to emit the silent signals of distress that would be received by every animal on the seamount. First would come the tiny voracious fish, like the sergeants major. The signals would tell them that it was safe to ravage the bits of dying flesh in the wound, opening it further.

The manta would grow weaker still. It would appear to be, and would become, less formidable. Its sensory transmitters, incapable of human guile, would broadcast signals of increasing vulnerability. The manta would be committing inadvertent suicide. Sharks would begin to gather, their receivers assessing each new signal, until one of them—particularly hungry, or perhaps simply bold— would dart in at the manta and tear away a ragged bite of meat.

The end would come quickly then, in an explosion of blood and a cloud of shreds of skin and sinew.

Paloma's momentum was carrying her past the manta, over its head. She put out a hand to stop herself, and her fingers curled around a hard ledge above the mouth and between the two horns. The flesh felt firm—like taut muscle—but slick, for it was coated with mucus. Paloma had touched many fish and had felt the same slime. It was a shield against bacteria. Jobim had taught her to be careful not to scrape it off. If the protective coating was removed, a sore might develop on that spot, or a burrowing creature might discover the opening and settle in and begin to gnaw away. A fish that had been handled too much before being released usually didn't survive.

Apparently the manta was no more startled by her touch than was Paloma. It did not bolt from her; it did not twitch or shudder. It just lay there, floating, suspended in midwater.

It has no fear of me, Paloma thought. And why should it? It knows no enemies. But it is not a common occurrence in nature for a wild animal to allow a strange creature to touch it like this.

She reached with her other hand for the same ledge of muscle, and she tucked her knees up underneath her and knelt on the manta's back. The skin was like a carpet made up of millions of tiny toothlike things. They all faced to the rear, and so as Paloma's hand stroked the skin from front to back, it felt as smooth as a greased ceramic bowl. But as her knees inched up, back to front, the manta's skin, like coarse sandpaper, abraded them.

The terrible gash in the manta's flesh was beside Paloma's left hand. Some of the knotted ropes were buried several inches deep. Most of the flesh was whitish gray, but some was pink and some yellow. Once Jobim had pointed out to Paloma the different flesh tones of ailing fish: white gray was healthy, pink was inflamed, and yellow signaled the generation of a puslike substance that showed that the animal's body had activated its defense mechanisms.

Gripping the ledge above the mouth tightly with her right hand, Paloma reached with her left for the rope snarled nearest to the surface of the wound. It was a jumble of knots and vibrated as the water flowed through it.

Be quick, Paloma told herself, like when the doctor gives an injection. Grab it, pull it free, and cast it away, all before the manta knows what's happening.

She threaded her fingers deep into the mess of rope and made a fist around as much as her hand could grasp. Then she yanked.

It was as if she had thrown a switch that turned the manta on. The animal heaved both wings, churning up a maelstrom that threw Paloma off its back and tumbled her into a somersault.

By the time she had righted herself, cleared her mask, and waited for the storm of bubbles to dissipate, the manta was flying away into the dark water, the remaining ropes fluttering behind. It did not make a sound, but Paloma imagined that she heard an outraged wail of pain.

She kicked toward the surface, trailing rope in her hand, wishing she had had time to grab more, hoping that by removing some she had increased the manta's chances of survival.

II

THE sun was still high when Paloma left the seamount and started to paddle toward home. She was tired, hungry, and cold. Most of all, she was lonely. The better her day on the seamount, the lonelier she felt when it was over, and because today had been particularly exciting, she felt acutely lonely.

The problem was not that her experiences were solitary—she liked being alone—but that there was no one with whom she could share the wonder, the exhilaration of her day when she got home. There were no other girls Paloma's age on the island. Why, no one knew: a quirk of nature. There were plenty of older females— women now, with children of their own—and plenty of boys. But no girls. From the moment Paloma had been old enough to know what it was to be alone, she had been alone. She had no sister, no friend.

Paloma saw herself as different from all the other women of Santa Maria Island. She hoped, prayed, *knew* that she was special. At least she had been decreed special by her father. After he was convinced that his son would never be at home in the sea and would instead have to spend his life upon it, Jobim had begun to tutor Paloma. He had always recognized how naturally she took to the sea and he told Miranda that their daughter was not to be confined to the house and the pots and the washing of clothes. He would take her with him and would teach her things about the sea.

Miranda had tried to argue, but Jobim, when he had made up his mind about something important, became impossible to argue with. And Miranda knew that it was important—even vital—to Jobim that one of his children follow him into the sea.

What Jobim did not know, and what Miranda could not bring herself to tell him, was that by taking Paloma to sea he was depriving his wife of the solace that a daughter was supposed to supply to a woman. He was condemning Miranda to daily sadness. By the time of Jobim's death, not only did Paloma relish her independence, but she felt an obligation to her father to live as he had guided her. She recognized, however, that she also had responsibilities to her mother; it was important that her mother not think that Paloma considered herself too good for everyday chores.

"It is one thing to be quiet and alone and even a bit strange," Viejo had said to her one day. "People will call that growing pains and let it pass. But you must not remove yourself altogether. People will not understand. They will resent you and become your enemies." Paloma did not want enemies. And so every few days she returned home in time to help her mother hang out the wash or prepare the meal or clean the house.

Today when Paloma reached the dock, Miranda and the other women were washing clothes. At a shelf of flat rocks that led into the water, the women gathered and soaked their clothes and pounded soap into them with stones and rinsed them. They piled the clean clothes into baskets that would be taken up the hill for a final, freshwater rinsing.

Paloma knelt beside Miranda and pounded clothes. No one acknowledged her arrival; the women chattered on around her. They were not ignoring her. On the contrary, they were accepting her— quietly, naturally, as if she had been there all along. It was their gesture to Miranda, for to have greeted Paloma and asked her questions would have directed attention to what was regarded as Paloma's peculiarity.

As excited as she was when she returned to the dock, as tempted to tell everyone what wonders she had encountered today, Paloma restrained herself. To the women who never went on the water, the sea was alien and dangerous, populated by poisonous creatures starved for human flesh. They would not have welcomed contradictions from a young girl.

When the washing was done, Paloma picked up the heavy bas-
ket of wet clothes and followed Miranda up the hill. With a hand
pump they raised fresh water to wash the salt off the clothes, then
draped them over a line behind the house.

They worked in silence. Paloma wanted very much to tell her
mother about the manta ray. But she did not want to frighten
Miranda, so she could not say how big the manta was, nor how
close to it she had gotten—let alone that she had knelt on its back
and been tossed off violently. What Paloma did all day every day
caused enough public gossip; fooling around with a giant devilfish
might get her branded as a witch. Miranda had had a husband
reputed to be a rebel. She had a son who spent much of his time
concocting harebrained schemes to make money—enough money
to get him off the island and into a technical school in Mexico
City. A daughter who was a witch would be altogether too much for
Miranda to bear.

By now the sun had dropped low and had begun to turn red.
A light breeze was blowing through the hanging clothes, and the
tails of the shirts made soft snapping sounds. Miranda sniffed and
nodded and was satisfied; it was a good breeze.

They walked inside the house and began to prepare the fire for
the evening meal.

"I saw a giant manta ray today," Paloma said at last.

"That's nice," said Miranda, without looking up from the fireplace where she was laying wood.

"It was wounded. I think it got fouled in a fisherman's nets."

Miranda started to repeat, That's nice, but it seemed inappro-
priate, so all she said was, "Oh?"

"There were ropes hanging out of the wound. It must have been
in very bad pain."

This time Miranda nodded.

"I wanted to help it, but—"

"God will take care of it, He will decide." Miranda spoke fast,
as if spitting the words out in a rush would convince Paloma not
to meddle.

"Well, then," Paloma said, "He seems to want to let the manta die in agony, or get eaten by sharks."

"If that is His will, so be it."

"So be it," Paloma repeated. She did not intend to argue with her mother, an argument that could have only losers.

"What fairy tales are you telling now?" It was Jo's voice, and it came from behind Paloma. She spun around. Jo was slouching against the doorway, a smirk on his face.

"Nothing." Paloma could not know how much Jo had overheard, but she did not want to discuss the manta ray with him. A big wounded animal was something Jo could visualize in only one way: price per pound.

"Giant devilfish, wounded and bleeding, cared for by nurse Paloma." Jo snickered as he came into the room. "Sometimes I think you sit here all day and make up tales."

"Think what you like," Paloma said.

After a pause Jo asked, "Did you really see a manta ray?"

"Yes."

"And it didn't attack you?"

"No!"

"It must have been really hurt. Devilfish are mean."

Paloma didn't argue.

"How big was he?"

"Big," Paloma replied. "Bigger than this room."

Jo whistled. *"He'd* bring a fancy price."

"See, Mama?" Paloma said. "He hears about an injured animal, and right away he wants to kill it."

"Well, Paloma," her mother said, "that is how we live."

"A lot you bring into the house," Jo said. "Have you ever brought home a single fish?" He paused again. "Where *was* this manta ray?"

Paloma gestured vaguely. "Out there."

"Out where?"

"It doesn't matter. He's gone. I hurt him and he flew away."

"You hurt him how?"

Paloma did not think before she spoke. "I pulled some of the rope out of his wound and it hurt him."

Miranda stood up. She looked stricken. "You *what?*"

Jo said, "You got that close? I don't believe it."

"You *what?*" Miranda said again.

"Don't worry, Mama," Paloma said. "There wasn't any danger."

"She's right, Mama," Jo said. "There wasn't any danger, because it didn't happen."

Miranda looked from Jo to Paloma and back again, not knowing what to believe, certain only that if Paloma had done what she said, it was right to worry about her safety; if Paloma had not, then it was right to worry about a daughter who made up such stories.

Sensing Miranda's confusion, Paloma said again, "Don't worry, Mama. The important thing is, we're all here and we're all safe."

Miranda wanted to believe that, and she turned to her work.

Jo did not mention the manta again. During supper he spoke without bluster about the day's fishing, about how it was nice that the price for grouper had risen, but that the reason it had risen was that the fish were growing scarcer. Or perhaps they had just moved to other grounds.

"Do you see groupers out where you go?" he asked Paloma.

"Some."

"More than before, or less?"

Paloma shrugged. "About the same."

"Maybe I should come have a look where you are."

Paloma felt wary, but she forced herself to stay slouched in her chair, looking nonchalant. "Wouldn't be worth your time. There's not much there."

"What keeps you going, then?"

"I study different things." She glanced at Jo. "Things Papa wanted me to study."

Jo turned away and said, tight-lipped, "Sure."

After supper Miranda washed the plates and cups, and Paloma swabbed the table with a wet rag. Jo sat and watched.

Suddenly he said, "I'd like you to teach me to dive."

Paloma looked at Jo. "You would?" It was the first time Jo had ever asked her to teach him anything. "What do you want to dive for? You said yourself it's a waste of time."

"Yeah, well, maybe I've been wrong."

"But you know how to dive. At least, you did once."

"Yeah, well." Jo was blushing. "That didn't work out."

Paloma knew the story—how Jobim had led Jo into diving step by step, first in knee-deep water, then in water up to Jo's chin, then in water just over his head, then where the bottom was ten or fifteen feet away.

Jo had had all the lessons, knew all the rules, had done everything his father had asked him to do—and hated every minute of it. He had felt uncomfortable in the water, and he felt actually threatened by deep water. But he had never dared tell his father, for Jobim's approval was the most important thing in the world.

One day Jobim had taken Jo into the open sea for the first time. They went to where they could not see bottom, for Jobim wanted Jo to learn to gauge the depth by the feel of the water pressure and by looking up at the surface from underwater.

They went down the anchor line, and at about forty feet Jo was seized by a fit of claustrophobia. He felt trapped. The water was suffocating him. There was no land anywhere, not below, not on the sides, not above. Everything was blue and oppressive. He had to leave.

He had screamed underwater and flailed with his arms and clawed his way up the anchor line. The line caught between his snorkel and his mask. Thrashing to free himself, he twisted the rubber strap even tighter around the line.

Jobim had tried to subdue him, but panic made Jo even stronger than he was normally, and he kicked and punched and tore his father's mask from his face.

Jo might have drowned both of them if Jobim had not felt, blindly, for his son's throat and squeezed it until the boy lost consciousness and could be taken swiftly to the surface.

Recalling that, Paloma could not imagine why Jo suddenly

wanted to dive again, or why now he thought he could dive without panicking. But she said, "All right. If you want."

"Good. I want to see all the things you see. Tomorrow?"

Paloma spoke quickly. "No, not tomorrow. I've got . . . too many things to do." She had nothing to do, but tomorrow was too soon. She had to have time to think about what Jo could have in mind, for she could not believe that his request meant only what it said. Too many things about it were unlike him.

"Soon, then."

"Yes. Soon."

Jo stood and yawned and said good night and walked through the front door and disappeared into the night. His room was around the corner, connected to the house but separate in that it had its own entrance from outside.

Paloma thought how strange it was for Jo to have asked for her help. For him to acknowledge that she—a girl—might know more about something worthwhile than he did was remarkable. She was surprised to find that she truly cared about what this change in Jo might mean, and she realized it was a reflection of her loneliness, of the quiet desperation she had felt as she paddled home from the seamount that afternoon. To get along with Jo, perhaps even to make a friend—that would be a fine thing for Paloma.

THE last time the relationship between Paloma and Jo had resembled a friendship had been when she was five and he was four. Back then, they had played together happily. But soon Jo had found a pack of boys to run with, and Paloma had found herself either taunted or excluded, and she had begun to hate being a girl.

For a while she had dressed like a boy, cut her hair short, learned to laugh at jokes directed at her—as if laughing *with* the joke, saying, Yes, isn't it ridiculous to be a girl? Aren't I foolish? Well, I won't be a girl for long, and then we'll all have a good laugh at what I used to be.

As a male, Jobim could not have understood the depth of the

anxiety Paloma was feeling. But he knew generally what was wrong, deduced that it had to come from her being the only girl of her age on the island, and guessed that her feelings about herself and her sex were confused.

One day he had taken Paloma fishing. She was quite young then and had never been taken to sea before. In fact, she had rarely been in Jobim's boat, except for holiday excursions and a few trips to La Paz.

They were alone, and Paloma was thrilled. The sea was oily calm, so flat that the soft swells looked like bulges in a jelly, and Paloma had been able to kneel on the forward thwart and hang out over the bow.

Jobim had anchored the boat over the seamount, but Paloma had not yet been underwater, so she had no idea that the sea bottom was a landscape of different terrains. As far as she knew, the bottom was distant and dangerous, an unknown country.

Jobim had baited a big hook with half a needlefish, but he did not throw the line overboard. Instead, he handed her a face mask and snorkel and told her to put them on. Then, with his own mask propped up on his forehead, he told Paloma to jump overboard and hang on to the anchor line.

"Here?" Paloma was shocked. In the middle of the sea? "Why?"

"I want to show you something about girls," Jobim had said, and though what he said made no sense to her, she obeyed and slipped over the side.

Jobim jumped into the water and hung beside her, holding the anchor rope in the crook of an elbow so as not to drift away in the current. Slowly he fed the fishing line through his fingers, dropping the baited hook down toward the seamount.

Father and daughter lay on the surface, their faces in the water, breathing through the rubber snorkel tubes. Paloma's first sight of the seamount was breathtaking, a discovery as miraculous as if she had been given a secret glimpse of heaven, for here was a world she had not known existed. It was separate from her world, unquestionably real but wonderfully new, active, enchanted.

The nylon fishing line was invisible in the water, but the bait was unmistakable—a white morsel that dangled provocatively above the seamount. Small fish approached the bait and hovered around it, seeming to appraise it for delicacy and danger. Jobim had made no attempt to hide the hook, and now and then a glint of steel would flash in a ray of light. Whether the fish were not enticed by the needlefish, or were scared by the hook, Paloma could not tell, but none of them went for the bait.

Then the small fish vanished. The bait hung unattended, swaying in the current.

For a moment or two nothing happened. What had been a bustling community was now a barren plain.

And then from the darkness at the edge of the seamount came the sharks—three hammerheads, one of them half again as large as the other two: silent searchers moving with a relentless arrogance that broadcast their sovereignty over the seamount. Their bizarre T-shaped heads swung slowly from side to side, gathering signals from the sea and sending out signals of their own, giving fair warning.

Jobim jigged the bait, and Paloma could see the sharks swing in formation toward the dancing piece of meat. They circled it once, then again, and then one of the smaller sharks broke the circle and darted at it. Jobim jerked the line, and the bait popped away from the shark's mouth.

The three sharks circled again, faster now, each in turn shaking its head, perplexed. They were receiving signals that reported dead meat, but the prey was not behaving as if dead.

The second of the smaller sharks shot forward, and once more Jobim jerked the bait away. This time he pulled it up toward the surface, challenging the sharks to follow it. Only one did, the largest. The other two hung below, angrily circling nothing.

As the big shark drew near, Paloma saw that this animal, which down below had looked like a good-size fish, was enormous—bigger than Papa, almost as big as Papa's boat.

Paloma was terrified. Unable to take her eyes from the advancing shark, she flailed with her free hand, desperate to grab the gunwale of the boat and pull herself to safety. But because she trusted Papa totally, and would do anything he said she should, she forced herself to lie still, though she was sure the shark could hear her heart. She held her breath, hoping to mute the drums in her chest, but that only made her heartbeat seem louder.

The bait was six or eight feet away, and the shark a foot beyond it. Jobim kept pulling, but now the shark stopped coming. It circled instead, its black eye watching as Jobim reeled in the bait and, with a single twist, removed the hook.

Now the other two sharks were rising. They kept their distance from the larger one, seeming to defer to it, but they were growing bolder. And though they were definitely smaller, each of them was at least six feet long.

Jobim held the half a needlefish out to the big shark and wiggled it with his fingertips. The circling pattern grew tighter. Now the shark was missing Paloma by only three or four feet as it swept by. The head was shaking actively, the crescent mouth opening and closing in expectant cadence.

Jobim pushed the needlefish out into open water, released it, and quickly drew back his hand. The shark passed by, and the fish disappeared. There had been no snapping, no biting. The shark had simply inhaled the needlefish.

It made two more tight turns around Jobim and Paloma, then gradually loosened its pattern, like a spring unwinding. Its black eye never left them, but there was no urgency to its behavior.

Jobim reached inside his shorts, undid a knot, and came out with a whole needlefish. Paloma had not seen him do it, but in the boat he must have stuffed a plastic bag of needlefish inside his shorts—out of the sharks' sight and, because the neck of the bag was tied off, out of their range of smell.

Immediately the shark resumed its tight circling pattern.

This time Jobim broke the needlefish in two and shook both halves and then let them go. The smaller sharks sensed the food and rose toward it eagerly. At the same time the large shark dropped its head and snapped its tail back and forth, which drove the body downward like a spear.

All three raced toward the pieces of fish. Paloma thought the small sharks were bound to win, for the needlefish was falling toward them and away from the bigger shark.

When the pieces of needlefish were no more than a foot from the mouths of the smaller sharks, both, simultaneously and inexplicably, turned away. The big shark soared down upon the pieces of fish, sucking in the first one, then turning away and making a wide circle and letting the second morsel fall—utterly confident that there was no hurry—then banking and descending in a dive and gobbling the last bit of food.

The smaller sharks continued downward, away from the large one, away from the food, away from conflict. They shook their heads and hunched their backs and flailed their tails.

The big shark returned and began once again to circle. Jobim motioned to Paloma to climb back into the boat. She didn't hesitate. Keeping her eyes on the shark, she reached up and gripped the gunwale. She took a deep breath and tested the firmness of her grasp on the wood. When Jobim had first taught her to swim, he had told her always to get in and out of the water quickly, for it was in the marginal moments—half in, half out of the water—that a person looked like a wounded fish and was most vulnerable to shark attack.

She spun, grabbed the gunwale with both hands, hoisted herself out of the water, and tumbled into the boat. She lay there for a second, breathing heavily, then realized that Jobim hadn't followed her. Her mask was still on her face, so she leaned over the side and peered down into the water.

Jobim clung to the anchor line and turned with the shark as it circled. Paloma thought of dogs—two males, one an intruder into the other's neighborhood, circling each other, appraising each other, searching for weaknesses.

When the shark was at the most distant point in its circling pattern, on the far side of the boat, Jobim pulled the bag of fish from his shorts and dropped it. Then, as the shark started down after the bag, Jobim pulled himself aboard the boat.

They ate a lunch of mangoes and bananas and a slab of dried, salted *cabrío*, making sure to eat the fish first and the mango last so that the juice from the fruit would wash away the thirst caused by the salt in the *cabrío*.

They did not speak while they ate. Paloma was certain she was supposed to have learned something, but she didn't know what it was.

Jobim rinsed his fingers in the sea and said, "Were you afraid?"

"Yes," said Paloma, and then, worried: "Is that bad?"

Jobim laughed. "Of course not. I don't think there was much danger, but they're fearsome things."

"No danger?" Paloma felt almost disappointed.

"People aren't their normal food. If the water's clear and they can see you, and if you're not bleeding or dead, usually they'll leave you alone."

"Usually," Paloma repeated.

"Usually." Jobim smiled. "Now, what've you learned?"

"I learned that you don't know what sharks are going to do. I *knew* those two were going to take the needlefish from the big one, and then they didn't."

"Do you know why?"

"There's a reason?"

"I told you I was going to show you something about girls." Jobim smiled again. "The big shark was a female. A very young girl, as sharks go."

"How do you know?"

"How do I know she's a female? On the males you can see what are called claspers. They secure the connection during breeding. As for how I know the female's young, she had no scars on her at all. That's as it is with humans. The older you get, the more weather-beaten and scarred you are. An old shark looks like Viejo. An old female shark has even more scars, because during mating the males prevent the females from throwing them off by biting the females' backs."

"What were the other two?"

"Both males, both older. You saw the way they turned and ran when that young female came at them." Jobim paused, knowing what was going through Paloma's mind.

She frowned and said, "It doesn't make sense."

"Not to a human, because human males are bigger and do most of the physical work and must be obeyed, because . . . because why? Somewhere way back, when strength was all there was, the stronger you were, the more important you were. And that's true with a lot of animals—the bigger and stronger are the most important. With sharks, the females are almost always bigger and tougher and meaner. Sharks have a pecking order. When there's food around, the biggest eats first. *Then* the others get to feed, in the order of their size and bad temper."

"But with people," Paloma said, "females *aren't* the strongest or the toughest or the meanest. They're—"

"Who says?" Jobim cut her off. "Strong doesn't only mean biggest. Strong can mean smart and clever and creative. The toughest can be the one who knows how to survive without wasting energy, or how to swim from here to there against the tide without getting exhausted and drowning. Animals have to be what nature made them—big or not, strong or not. That's what sets their place. But people can set their own place. If they don't have one thing, they can make up for it with something else, with knowledge or experience. Do you understand?"

Paloma nodded.

Jobim knelt down beside her and spoke softly. The image of his brown forehead and black eyebrows and broad shoulders framed against the sunlit sky was engraved forever on her mind; the sound of his mellow voice reduced to a hoarse whisper was one she would recall whenever, after his death, she talked to him. "You are a female, and that is a fine thing. You are a young female, and that is finer still. But the finest thing is that you are a person who can decide for yourself what you want your life to be. You will teach people to respect you for that. More important, you will respect yourself for that."

Never, after that day, had Paloma wished to be a boy. She had let her hair grow longer. She had watched with fascination every change in her body.

A few months after Jobim's death, a big storm blew through, a chubasco as big, if not as sudden, as the one that had killed him. The first rumblings began in her body almost simultaneously with the onset of the storm, and the cramps seemed to her to be echoing the thunder. She was frightened briefly. But Jobim had prepared her well, so that soon she felt the comforting conviction that everything that was happening was natural and healthy and—she remembered his word—fine.

She hoped he knew what was happening to her, and how she was responding to it, that she was becoming a woman and was proud of it.

As PALOMA dried the last dish, she reprimanded herself for not being more receptive to Jo's request for diving instruction. He had been rather nice tonight, and she had put him off. He had given a little something, and she had given nothing. She decided to go to Jo's room and tell him that she had been mistaken, that tomorrow would be a good day to teach him.

As she walked outside the house, she heard something that made her stop. She waited, then peered around the corner and saw Jo going into his room. He must have gone for a walk, she thought, and she started again for his room. But again she stopped, and this time she wasn't sure why; she knew she didn't want to go on. She was sensing a warning—nothing she could have articulated, but something very strong. She could not take another step.

After a few moments she returned to the house and went to bed, resolving to let sleep clear her head.

By morning she had decided to give herself the day to settle the conflict in her mind. She accompanied Jo and his friend Indio down the path to the dock. Jo was still being genial, and as he untied his boat, he said casually, "You want to come with us today?"

"What?" Jo had never invited her into his boat.

"Manolo is sick."

"Sick with what?"

"I don't know. He says it's stomach cramps."

Paloma was tempted. If she could not make a gesture to Jo, at least she might accept his gesture to her.

She had never liked fishing, except with Jobim, and then it wasn't the fishing she liked so much as the being with Papa. Fishing was killing. She could not reconcile the communion she felt with the animals on the seamount with the sense of revulsion she felt on seeing those same animals lifeless, heaped in the bottom of a boat.

But if Jo needed her help, if they were going to be friends, it would be petty of her to refuse.

"All right," she said.

"Oh." Jo seemed surprised. "I mean, only if you want to."

"If you need the help, I'd like to help."

"Yes. I see." Jo seemed to be searching for something to say. "I don't really need your help, though."

"But I thought Manolo—"

"Sure, but . . . I mean . . . Indio and I can . . ." Jo was blushing. "We can manage. I shouldn't have asked. I know how you feel about fishing, and . . . today's not a good day. You said you had a lot of things to do, remember?"

"Yes, but—"

"We can manage. Really. You do what you have to do, then we'll spend a couple of days together. One day you can teach me to dive and the next day I'll take you fishing. A deal?"

"Okay." Paloma shrugged. She didn't know if she should say something more. Was he being considerate, or had he changed his mind? But no matter. The important thing was that she and Jo were being civil to one another.

Paloma uncleated the bow line and held the bow of the boat while Jo and Indio climbed aboard. Then Jo tried to start the outboard motor. He pulled the starter cord, and the wheels and gears made a purring sound like a feeding cat. He pulled again, and the purring sounded more anxious, then stopped abruptly. Jo cursed the motor and banged on the housing with his fist. Finally, with a sigh, he removed the housing and began to tinker with the insides.

Paloma felt sympathy for him. He knew motors as well as she knew fish—was at home with them, could understand them and talk to them and cajole them into cooperating. But the Sea of Cortez was a hostile environment for an internal-combustion engine. Salt corroded its innards, the sun burned out gaskets and hoses, sand clogged filters and destroyed lubricants.

No wonder Jo wanted to go away to school. He had a gift that was little more than useless here. There were a couple of outboard motors for him to work on, but no genuine challenge. He had no way of letting his talent earn him money and appreciation. He was like a gifted surgeon with no one to practice on.

He took something off the motor, cleaned it, blew on it, screwed it back in, and replaced the housing. He turned the choke up high and yanked on the cord. The motor gagged and protested its way to life with a belch of blue-gray smoke. Paloma carefully handed the bow line to Indio and pushed the bow of the boat around the end of the dock into open water.

Jo headed east, and soon he and Indio and the boat were black silhouettes against the pumpkin sun. Paloma went back to the house to fetch some food and a jar of fresh water. She let her mother wrap a slice of salted *cabrío* and a tortilla in a piece of paper for her to take along with her mango.

Then she returned to the dock and got in her pirogue and pushed off and paddled westward.

She did not look back, but even if she had, it was unlikely that she would have seen the figure squatting in the bushes at the top of the hill, who was tracking her through a pair of binoculars.

MANOLO, SUPPOSEDLY WRITHING with stomach cramps in his bed, had taken several precautions not to be seen. He had covered himself with the leaves and branches of the bushes. And the pocket mirror he had brought he placed facedown in the dirt so that it would not flash in the sunlight until the time came when he would need it.

He watched as Paloma paddled toward the west.

After a while she checked her landmarks, dropped her anchor, and held the line in her hands until she felt the iron set in the rocks. Then she put on her mask and fins and snorkel, slid her knife into her belt, and slipped overboard.

Not until then did Manolo step out of the bushes and hold the mirror to the morning sun and flash it twice toward the east.

PALOMA, with one hand on the anchor line, surveyed the seamount from one end to the other. With her vision restricted by the sides of her mask and by the turbidity of the water, she could not see a large area at a single glance. On the surface it was possible to see everything in the entire circle around her, all the way to the horizon, in a bit more than two looks. Down here she needed nine distinct surveys to see the same circle, and the distance she could see was never more than fifty or sixty feet.

In the first section she concentrated on, she saw only rocks. In the second, a few quickly flickering shadows told her that hammerheads were cruising near the bottom, the colors of their backs melding into the mottled green brown of the stony top of the seamount.

Paloma was doing what she did every day, looking over the seamount to see what was there. But also she was looking for the injured manta, hoping—not daring to voice the hope—that it had found its way back to the seamount.

As her eyes moved methodically on through the third, fourth, and fifth sections, hope gave way to resignation; the manta was not there. Mantas cruised ceaselessly, following the food, making their home, like petrels, on the wing. They were not territorial. Even if this manta contradicted the rule, Paloma reminded herself, the treatment it had received from her the day before would surely have driven it away.

In the eighth section she saw a manta ray, but it could not be the same one. It was smaller. She was about to shift her gaze when she suddenly realized that the ray below *was* the injured manta. The distance had deceived her; the ray was down very deep. Now she could see that small as the manta looked from up here, it dwarfed the terrain around it. Sea fans, half as tall as a man, looked like postage stamps beside the manta; a passing hammer-head looked no bigger than a spaniel. Also she could see a white slash behind the manta's left horn.

She guessed that the manta was hugging the bottom because there was less current there; the surrounding rocks and valleys would disperse the massive flow of water. And with less current, there would be less tug on the ropes that tore at the manta's battered flesh.

The manta was hovering in a temporary shelter, where the sea did not aggravate its wound.

Paloma guessed that it was instinct that told the manta it could find comforting shelter near the bottom. But she could not possibly help the animal if it was going to stay at a depth of sixty-five or seventy feet.

On the surface—but more dramatically underwater—the more you attempt to do, the more oxygen you consume. Paloma knew, for example, that she could easily make a breath-hold dive down to sixty or seventy feet if all she intended to do was wrap her legs around a rock and observe the creatures of the seamount—or, at the very most, swim calmly from perch to perch. But if she were to see a bed of oysters ten feet deeper still, and were to force herself down and begin to hack the oysters free and stuff them in a bag, the signals for immediate ascent would come right away, but too late. She would have consumed oxygen that should have been left in reserve for the trip to the surface.

Paloma knew that to try to help the manta where it now lay was well beyond her limits. So she floated on the surface and waited. The manta did not move, did not flap a wing tip or switch its tail.

Suddenly it occurred to Paloma that the manta could be dying. Maybe right then, as she watched, life was drifting away from the great animal. She felt helpless and frustrated and angry. She couldn't let the manta die. She had no choice. She had to go down and see for herself.

She took deep breaths and felt her lungs engage the rhythm of expansion and contraction, and when they were as empty as she could make them she slowly filled them to capacity, shut her mouth, and dived for the bottom.

She pulled herself down the anchor line, then released the line and swam over to the manta. It did not budge as she approached. It was hovering, evidently resting in a quirky swirl of water that flowed steadily over the top of the seamount and over its huge flat wings and permitted it to remain stable.

Paloma swam beneath it—she wanted to look at its gill slits to be sure they were pulsing, for that was the most reliable sign that the animal was extracting oxygen from the water. The big round eye swiveled and followed until she was out of sight.

She swam under the entire breadth of the manta, and it was like being in a cave, for the giant cloak shut out all light from above and cast a blanket of black shadow on the rocks.

The manta's left eye tracked her as she reappeared and swam up over the horn and hung above it, looking down at the deep laceration, with the skeins of rope still floating out like snakes among the shreds of flesh.

The wound did not look much different from when she had first seen it. There were fewer ropes in it, but those that remained were as solidly embedded as ever. There were no signs of healing. And the fact that the manta preferred to lie quietly, not to swim and feed, told Paloma that it was ill and very weary. Its instinctive impulses were weakening.

Left alone, the manta would languish, and left alone it surely would be. Only the whales and dolphins—the so-called higher animals of the sea—actively helped one another. Animals on the order of manta rays, however, were solitary in maturity, and therefore, when they were less than healthy, they were very vulnerable. They helped themselves or they died.

Paloma had to surface, yet she lingered for one more moment, feeling indignation—at nature, at fate, at mankind, at fishermen, at whatever had caused this fine animal to be hurt and helpless. At the last second before she kicked off from the seamount, Paloma impulsively wrapped her arms around the manta's cephalic fin—the dreaded horn—and pushed upward. In desperation, she sought to prod the manta into rising to a depth where she could help it. Then, with the drums pounding in her temples and the ache beginning to sear her lungs, she sped up toward the light.

On the surface she rested, waiting until her breathing had returned to normal. For good measure she waited a few minutes more until, from lack of exertion, she shivered. Her body had grown cold, and the shiver was its attempt to generate heat. Now she could dive again and exercise with no ill effect.

She put her face in the water and looked down. The manta was gone. First she thought she must be looking in the wrong place. She searched again, starting with the first sector, on the far right edge of the seamount, and moving methodically sector by sector toward the left.

The manta was nowhere.

As she had risen to the surface, it must have fled. Perhaps she had frightened it by grabbing its horn in her arms. But if so, why hadn't it bolted then?

Paloma felt remorse, condemning herself for driving the manta away, when suddenly the giant was soaring toward her, up from the depths like a black bomber flying from the edge of the gloom.

It passed fifteen or twenty feet beneath her as she hung on the anchor line. It made a wide, banking circle to the right, ropes fluttering behind, and returned. Then it stopped, directly under Paloma's boat, no more than ten feet beneath her toes.

The pressure wave from the movement of the enormous body through the water made Paloma and her boat bob like toys in a tub. She did not know why the manta had come into shallow water, why it had stopped beneath her boat. She was tempted, but refused, to believe that the manta knew she was trying to help, that her kindly gesture on the seamount had somehow communicated something.

Paloma slid her knife from her belt, took a deep breath, and dropped down onto the manta's back. She braced herself, prepared for the manta to burst to life and speed away, but it did not move. She gripped the lip of solid flesh between the horns and bent to the wound.

One long tail of rope fed out of it and down the manta's back. The end in the wound was snared in a mess of knots. Gently Paloma tugged on the rope. A foot or two more came free, and then it pulled tight. She felt a shudder course through the manta's body like a mild electric shock. The shudder subsided, and the manta lay still.

Carefully, with the knife's razor point, Paloma cut the rope away and probed the wound, snipping knots and snares, casting away bits of rotten flesh and pieces of rope.

Then, one by one, the alarms in Paloma's body began to sound.

She tried to ignore them all, for she feared that she had caused the manta such discomfort that when she left this time, the animal would depart permanently. She could make it to the surface in two or three seconds, and she knew she would have much warning before she lost consciousness.

She received that last warning—a tingling in her fingers and toes, a dullness in her shoulders and thighs, a thick feeling in her mouth and throat. She swept down with her arms, scissors-kicked twice with her flippers, and broke through to sunlight.

She held on to the side of the pirogue and gagged and gasped and cursed herself for taking such a chance. But she was unhurt, and she had cut away a lot of the rope. If the manta was gone—well, she had done what she could, and she hoped that that had been enough so the manta could survive on its own.

When she had rested, she looked down into the water. She expected to have to search for the manta, but it had not moved. It lay still at ten feet.

Paloma breathed deeply and held her breath and was about to plunge back down to the manta when she heard a high, very faint buzzing. She listened carefully. The sound was a bit louder now. She assumed it was coming from a boat, probably an outboard, passing in the distance.

Paloma checked to make sure her knife was secure in her belt, then took her breaths and dropped down to the manta. She saw the big round eye swivel up and follow her until she had passed out of its range. As she settled onto the broad back, she noticed that her knees were smudged with black. She touched the manta's flesh and looked at her fingers; they were black, too. The manta's protective mucous coating had come off on her skin like a stain.

She turned to the wound; there were very few ropes left, and she was able to reach them with the point of her knife. She removed them all, cleaned the wound with her fingertips, and cut away the dangling shreds of putrescent flesh.

The feelings in her head and in her chest told her that she still had some time—half a minute or more—before she would have to surface, so she began to pack the torn flesh together into the cavity of the wound, pressing it down as if to encourage it to adhere to itself and grow again.

Her moving around caused squeaky streams of bubbles, and the pulse in her temples drummed ever more insistently. These sounds, added to her intense concentration, obliterated the noise of the outboard motor as it approached overhead.

Now she had to surface. She pushed off the manta's back and kicked a few times. It was only habit that made her look up: Jobim had taught her always to do that as she ascended from a dive, to avoid knocking her head on the bottom of the boat.

When she did look up, she expected to see the surface. Instead, all she saw was Jo's face, peering down at her from the surface through a glass-bottomed bucket, his grin distorted by reflection into a gargoyle's leer.

III

PALOMA broke through the surface and reached up for the gunwale of her boat. Jo had put a line around her anchor rope, so they were moored together.

He was still looking through the glass-bottomed bucket. "I'll be! What a monster! How did you catch him?"

Paloma's heart was stuttering. She could hear it beat in her chest and feel it in her throat. She took a deep breath and tried to calm herself, for she had to be in control before she could hope to deal with Jo and Indio and—looking so smug, sitting in the bow—the miraculously recovered Manolo. Her first impulse was to shriek at Jo, to lash out at him. She felt betrayed, violated. But nothing would be accomplished by a display of rage, except that Jo and his mates would laugh, and she would feel even more humiliated.

"How did you catch him?" Jo asked again.

"I didn't catch him," Paloma said. "He's not caught."

"He's dead, then?"

"No."

Indio was looking through the bucket. "*Look* at 'em all! This place is a fish market. It's a gold mine! Let's get at 'em!"

A surge of nausea swept through Paloma and made her dizzy.

As if on cue, Manolo threw a baited hook overboard and fed the weighted line through his fingers.

"Don't!" Paloma shouted.

Manolo laughed. "There are fish down there. Are you saying I can't fish for them? That's what fish are for."

"You're wrong." Paloma pulled herself toward the bow of her boat. "You're not so important that God put *any*thing on earth just for you to kill."

With one hand Paloma grabbed her anchor rope; with the other she reached back into her belt and pulled out her knife and slashed the line that moored the other boat to hers.

Immediately the bow of Jo's boat swung wide, tangling Manolo's fishing line in the limp mooring line, and the boat slid away on the strong tide.

Furious, Jo leaped to his feet, cursed Paloma, and yanked on the starter cord of his outboard motor. The cord came away in his hand. He cursed the motor, and cursed Paloma again, and the cord and all boats and the sea. He rewrapped the cord and pulled a second time; the motor sputtered and died.

Paloma clung to her anchor rope and watched Jo teeter in the stern. Then she heard the outboard roar to life and saw the boat swing in a tight circle and head back toward her. Quickly she pulled herself aboard her own boat, for she knew that Jo's rages were sometimes blind and violent, and he could threaten to run her over with his boat. She didn't believe he would actually mean it, but he might hit her by accident.

Aiming directly at Paloma's pirogue, Jo kept his motor at full throttle until he was only ten feet from her, then cut the power altogether. His boat stopped six inches from Paloma's, and it caused a swell that tipped her boat and almost spilled her overboard.

Manolo, cheeks livid with anger, whipped his bow line around her anchor rope and made it fast. His fishing line was wrapped in a tight spiral around the bow line. He took a knife from his belt and cut the fishing line and snarled at Jo, "If you can't make her behave, *I* will."

"Don't worry," Jo said. "I'll take care of her."

"Jo, look!" said Indio, who had put the glass-bottomed bucket overboard and was surveying the seamount. "*Cabríos*. Dozens of them. And goldens! And jacks! A million jacks!"

Jo looked at Paloma and said, mocking her, "Not much out here, eh? Not many groupers. Just the same old stuff. I knew I couldn't trust you."

Paloma was stunned. "*You* couldn't trust *me?* Who was it who said he wanted to learn to dive?"

"I do, I do."

"To study things, to learn about animals."

"I do."

"No. All you want to do is kill things."

"No." Jo grinned. "I want to kill things and *then* I want to learn things. When I can sell enough fish to get enough money so I can get out of here, then I'll learn things—in Mexico City."

Paloma took the knife from her belt again and moved forward toward the mooring line.

"Paloma," Jo said in a tone reminiscent of Viejo's, "don't be so silly."

"Give up, you mean. Let you kill everything here."

"There you go again, exaggerating. Even if I wanted to, I couldn't kill everything on this seamount. If we take something, something else comes in to replace it. The sea goes on forever, you ought to know that."

"Jo . . ." Paloma hesitated before continuing. "Papa wanted this seamount saved, left as it is. He told me that we had to preserve it. It was his favorite place."

Jo flushed. "I know that. You think I didn't know that?" The words spilled from his mouth as he glared at her. "Papa is dead, Paloma! Dead, dead, dead!"

She put her hands to her ears, for she did not want to hear.

"I don't care if he told you to save the whole world! He is dead, and what he said doesn't mean a damn! Do you understand that? It is what I say that makes a damn, and I say I am more important than your stupid fish!"

There was nothing more Paloma could say, and so she raised her knife to cut the mooring line.

"That won't stop us."

"Yes, it will. I'll pull my anchor and go. You'll never find this place again."

"I'll buoy it."

"I'll cut your buoys away."

"I'll take landmarks."

"You?" Paloma sneered. "You couldn't find your way around the house with a landmark."

"I can learn."

Paloma knew he was right. And once he had the skill, he could find the seamount as easily as she did.

"Look, Paloma, we don't have to fight." Jo was trying to sound reasonable. "We can work it out. We can still be friends."

Paloma had been looking away from him. Now her eyes snapped back to his face, to see if he was mocking her. He was looking intensely sincere.

He said, "I'll make a deal with you."

"What deal?"

"I won't tell anybody about this place. It only makes sense that I'll keep my word; after all, it's good for me, too. We'll fish it with lines only, no nets. Anything we catch that we can't use, we'll throw back."

Paloma saw that Jo's mates were eyeing him as if they thought he had lost his mind, but they stayed silent.

"You have to admit that's fair," Jo said. "I don't *have* to do anything. I could even come out here and throw dynamite overboard."

"You could," Paloma agreed. "But you know that if you did, I'd get revenge. Somehow, someday, you'd pay." She hoped her voice had a tone of quiet menace.

Jo roared with laughter, but there was a brittle quality to his laughter, for he sensed that she was quicker and smarter, and driven by a passion that gave her courage.

Paloma thought Jo's deal was blackmail. Only if she agreed to let them fish as much as they wanted would they not spread the word to their competitors.

Worse still, Paloma doubted that they would keep their end of the agreement. The temptation to fish with nets would be too great to resist. They would see huge schools of *cabríos* and jacks beneath their boat, and each flashing body would ring in their minds as a silver coin. They would speak of the immense fortune that was escaping because they could not use nets. Then they would agree to try the nets just once, to see how many fish they could catch—an experiment, they would say. They would catch hundreds and hundreds, and then there would be no satisfying them with less.

"What about it?" Jo said. "Do we have a deal?"

She had no choice. By agreeing, she might buy time. "Okay."

"Smart," Jo said. "Very smart." Like a military commander ordering his troops to advance, Jo gestured at Indio and Manolo to start fishing. Obviously he was enjoying himself enormously: he was the leader who had negotiated a favorable truce that exploited his enemy's weakness.

Paloma watched as Indio and Manolo baited hooks and dropped their lines overboard. She put on her mask and leaned over the side of her boat and looked down into the water.

The manta was still there, still immobile, ten feet below the surface. The fishing lines passed four or five feet in front of the manta's left wing. If the manta were to decide suddenly to leave, its wing would collide with the fishing lines. If the wing were to strike the lines solidly, they might lodge in the flesh. The injury would be similar to the one Paloma had just treated, but more severe, for the thin monofilament line could cut through the flesh and perhaps even amputate part of the wing. The outcome then would be certain death.

Paloma put on her flippers and slipped the snorkel through her mask strap.

Manolo called out threateningly, "Stay away from my line."

"Don't worry," Jo said to him. "We made a deal. She knows she better not fool with me."

Paloma said nothing. She rolled over the side of her boat, breathed deeply, and dived to the manta. She checked the wound and saw that the flesh she had packed in was staying firm; perhaps it would heal and grow. There were no predators or parasites nearby, which told Paloma that the manta was not emitting distress signals.

What the manta did not need, however, was a new injury. So she hovered above the furled horn on the right side and reached down and pressed on it. She wanted to guide the manta toward the bottom, and since it had responded once before to her touch on one of its horns, she was guessing that the horns were as sensitive as a horse's mouth.

When the manta did not react at once, Paloma pressed harder. She felt a shudder as somewhere deep in the core of the giant a message was received. Silently the right wing dipped, the left wing lifted, and together they heaved once up and down. The pressure pushed Paloma away and forced an explosion of bubbles from her mouth. When the bubbles cleared, she saw the manta bank to the right and keep rolling, like an airplane in a spin, as it flew toward the bottom.

Jo had watched this through his glass-bottomed bucket on the surface. Now, as the others held their lines, he took up a honing stone and began to rub it in tight circles against the point of a harpoon.

"What are you going to do with that?" Manolo asked.

"The deal just said no nets." Jo gestured at the deep water where the manta had gone. "He'll be back."

Below, Paloma watched the manta swim toward the bottom. It was on its back, showing its brilliant white underbelly, and as it arrived at the top of the seamount, it continued its slow and easy roll, spinning and descending like a child falling down a sandpile, until the black of its back became one with the dark water of the abyss and Paloma could see it no more.

She wanted to follow it down the side of the seamount, to make discoveries with it and be part of the harmony of the sea. Instead, her body sent her signals that told her she was very much a human being and that if she intended to be a live human being, she had better ascend.

On her way up, she continued to look down, happy that she had been able to help the manta, hoping that it would survive. Then, at the distant limit of her vision, something began thrashing violently. For a second Paloma thought it was the manta, but as the animal was drawn a bit closer, she saw that it was far too small.

Then, as it drew still closer, she could see that whatever it was, was struggling to return to the bottom, fighting something that was forcing it to the surface. Because she had never seen such sights on the seamount, two or three seconds passed before she realized what she was watching: a fish caught on a hook, being dragged up to the boat. She felt a rush of bile into her throat. It was a trigger-fish, perhaps the very same one she had seen valiantly defending its egg cache.

Impulsively she put out a hand, hoping to grab the line and free the fish, but she was too far away. She looked up through the last three feet of water between her and the surface and saw the fish disappear into the shadow of Jo's boat.

She reached her own boat, broke through the surface, spat out her snorkel, and, choking, shouted, "Put it back! Quick!"

Manolo looked at her as if she were mad. "What?"

"Throw it back!" she gasped. "You don't have much time."

Manolo looked at Indio, and they smiled and shook their heads at one another.

Manolo said, "I've got all the time in the world."

"But . . . you . . ." The words were a jumble in Paloma's mind. She wanted to, *had* to, tell Manolo that the triggerfish must be returned to the water immediately; that in less than a minute the sun would begin to harm its skin and cause ulcers; that in two or three minutes the fish would be asphyxiated, for it could not draw oxygen from air. But in spite of all she wanted to say, nothing came out of her mouth except, "You don't understand."

Again Manolo smiled, and what should have been obvious to Paloma all along now struck her like a blow to the head. It was *she* who hadn't understood. Manolo had no intention of returning the triggerfish to the water. He regarded the fish as fairly caught and rightly his.

Now that she did understand, she could say only, "But why?"

"Why what?"

"You don't eat that fish. Nobody eats triggerfish."

"Cats do."

"But . . . but . . . that beautiful thing," Paloma sputtered. "You'd waste its life for . . ."

"What waste? Get a lot of 'em, they pay for 'em."

Paloma knew better than to argue. Every second she spent trying to save it, the fish was dying.

"Throw it *back!*" she screamed.

Manolo gazed at her, and there was no expression in his eyes. "Okay," he said. "You've convinced me."

He reached into the bottom of the boat and picked up the triggerfish by its tail. He pretended to examine it for a moment, then said, "Looks a little faint. Better wake it up." He swung the fish high and slammed it down on the gunwale of the boat. The sleek body, once purple and gold, now mustard and dull gray, shivered once and was still.

Manolo looked at Indio, who was grinning, and said, "That didn't work. I don't get it." Then he turned to Paloma. "You know so much about fish. Here. You try." And he threw the fish across the water.

It landed in front of Paloma and splashed water in her face. The flat body floated on its side. The gills did not pulse.

Paloma held the corpse, to keep it from drifting away in the tide. She said nothing, for there was nothing she could say that would change what was going to happen. She looked at Manolo, who was baiting his hook, and at Jo, who had quickly shifted his eyes away as soon as he saw her looking at him. Now he pretended to be deeply concerned about a knot in his fishing line.

Jo is trying not to look embarrassed, Paloma thought, but he *is* embarrassed, because he has no real control over the others. They only tolerated his pretense of leadership because the boat—which had been Jobim's—belonged to him. Jo wouldn't have pulled a stunt like Manolo's, but he could not stop his friend and would not have tried.

In a way, Manolo had done Paloma a favor. He had excised from her any softness or gullibility, any willingness to trust. Like one of the ancient pirates who used to sneak up on his victims flying a friendly flag and then, at the last moment, break out his pirate banner, Manolo had shown their true colors.

Without a word Paloma reached behind her for her knife. Swiftly she cut the triggerfish in quarters. As soon as blood began to billow in the water, tiny sergeants major materialized and searched in frenzy for the meal that must be there.

Paloma let the pieces of triggerfish fall one by one, and through her mask she watched each one as it was consumed by the swarming fish. She felt as if somehow she was compensating for Manolo's brutality. The triggerfish was now being returned to its home, serving to nourish the other creatures of the seamount and to prolong the life of the community.

Paloma climbed into her boat and removed her mask and flippers. In the other boat all three were now fishing, and they did not notice her as she went forward and tugged at her anchor line to shake the killick loose from the rocks below. Free of the rocks, Paloma's boat drifted off the seamount. Moored to her boat, Jo's boat drifted with it.

Jo was the first to sense that something was wrong. He was just letting his line down when the boat came adrift. He waited for his hook and sinker to strike bottom, but they kept falling, for by now the boats were away from the seamount and over a bottom that was four thousand feet away. The deeper Jo's line went the faster it fell, until his spool was all but empty.

He turned and looked at Paloma and saw her pull her killick aboard and cast his boat away from hers. He shouted, "Hey!"

"I have to go home," Paloma said calmly. "Put down your own anchor." Then she knelt in the pirogue and raised her paddle.

"But where's the bottom?"

"Right there," Paloma said, pointing vaguely to a spot in the sea a couple of hundred yards away. "You can't miss it. Not a fine navigator like you."

The others were already hauling in their lines, and Jo rushed to bring his aboard. He shaded his eyes and squinted at the shore, hoping to recall landmarks barely noted when he had approached the seamount. He started the outboard motor and aimed against the tide, reasoning that to recapture the seamount all he would have to do was reverse the direction of his drift.

"Put the bucket over," he ordered Indio. "Tell me when we're there."

Indio put the glass-bottomed bucket over the side, then gripped it tightly with both hands, for the movement of the boat against the strong tide tended to tear the bucket from him. All he saw below was blue.

"Well?" Jo said impatiently.

"Nothing."

"You got to be wrong."

Indio looked up from the bucket. "Look for yourself." He snickered and added, "Mister fine navigator."

Jo put the motor in neutral and took the bucket from Indio. The tide caught the boat and swung it, and it started to drift slowly in circles. Jo paid no attention. He stared through the bucket at the endless carpet of blue beneath him.

"Impossible!" he said.

He brought the bucket aboard and put the motor in gear and gave it full throttle. The boat lurched forward and traveled several hundred yards before he turned the bow against the flow of the tide. He continued uptide until he judged he had compensated for his movement sideways, then stopped and told Indio to look again.

"Nothing."

Manolo said, "I think you're way off to the side."

"I can't be," Jo insisted.

Manolo turned to Indio. "There's only one thing for sure. He doesn't know his butt from his bucket about where he is."

Jo said, "You could do better?"

"I couldn't do worse."

Manolo looked at Indio, who looked at Jo and shook his head and murmured, "What a goat."

Jo could not deal with sniping from two people at once. So he focused on one, on Indio, and said, "Get out."

"Get out of what?"

"The boat." Standing in the stern, Jo pointed at the sea. "Get out of my boat."

"And what?" Indio said, laughing. "Walk home?"

"I don't care. It's my boat, and I say get out!"

"And I say"—Indio mocked his imperious tone—"go suck a lemon!"

Jo took a step toward Indio, the boat yawed dramatically, and Jo lost his footing and started to fall overboard. To save himself he twisted in midair and fell across the hot motor. He yowled like a scorched cat, pulled away from the motor, lost his balance, and rolled headfirst into the water. He came up sputtering and clawing for a handhold.

Indio guided his hand to the side of the boat and said, feigning concern, "What'd you do that for? You always tell me you don't like swimming."

Jo tried to utter a threat, but all that came out was drool.

"If I were you," Manolo said, "I'd get back in the boat."

Jo struggled to haul himself aboard and then lay panting across the after thwart. He hated the other two for making fun of him. And there was nothing he could do about it. Except . . .

Jo shaded his eyes and stood up and looked across the water. Far away and moving still farther, appearing from this distance no bigger than a piece of driftwood, was Paloma's pirogue.

If she hadn't cast them loose, none of this would have happened.

With a single gesture, Paloma had destroyed his credibility with Indio and Manolo. The only way to restore it was to prove that he was stronger, more worthy, than Paloma. That would settle more than the matter of the moment. It would avenge the humiliation he had felt when his father had chosen her as his special child.

Jo turned and yanked on the motor's starter cord. The motor caught at once, which he took as a good omen, and he pushed the throttle open and spun the boat around.

"Where are we going?" Manolo asked. Pounded by the thumping bow, he half stood, letting the muscles in his legs absorb the strain.

"She's gonna put us back on that seamount," Jo shouted above the noise of the engine.

Indio said, "I bet we could find it ourselves."

"If we had a week," Jo replied. He poked a finger at Indio's chest. "Every minute we're not fishing that seamount, she's costing us money. You want to go to La Paz and see things and meet people?"

"Yeah. You know that."

"Then blame her." Now Jo pointed at Paloma's pirogue, which was growing larger and closer every moment. "She's the one got you chained to the island; she's taking the money from your pocket."

"I never thought of that."

"Well, think of it. Because we're gonna stop it right now."

PALOMA was more than halfway home when she heard the outboard bearing down on her. Immediately she recognized Jo's mood. Only someone ignorant of boats or out of control would run an engine at full speed in the open sea. It was dangerous to the sailors and damaging to the engine. Jo knew boats. The engine pitch was at peak hysteria, and so too, Paloma sensed, was Jo.

It had probably been a mistake to cast Jo's boat loose, for she had known he would soon be lost. He had never learned how to interpret tides and currents, couldn't differentiate the subtle shades of blue and green that would tell him how deep the water was. What she could not have known was how quickly his embarrassment would change to rage.

Paloma stopped paddling and waited, for there was no point in trying to outdistance him. She secured her mesh bag and her paddle to a cleat on the bow. The engine noise came closer, a shrill and painful scream. She saw the white hull rise out of the water and slam down, spewing rooster tails of spray from both sides of the bow. The boat was aimed directly at her.

Might Jo actually ram her pirogue? Could he be *so* stupid? He might sink the pirogue, true, but he would certainly damage his own boat as well. She wondered if she should jump overboard and go underwater and wait for him to pass. But then he might take her boat.

They were upon her.

For a split second she thought she would be crushed. Then suddenly and violently the bow skewed off to the left and she had a flashing glimpse of Jo's face before a mount of water struck the pirogue and lifted it nearly vertical. Paloma threw herself against the far bulwark, against the lean of the boat, and it righted itself and settled into a trough. Quickly she steadied herself and stood up to see where Jo had gone.

The boat was thirty or forty yards away, turning in a tight circle, running over its own wake, caught in crisscross patterns of swells and chop, the motor spewing smoke and screeching as the propeller bit through pockets of air instead of water. Manolo stood in the bow, bracing himself with the anchor rope, his head thrown back, laughing. Indio sat amidships, steadied by a hand pressed against each bulwark. And Jo knelt in the stern, turning the boat and aiming it once again at Paloma.

This time he turned a second sooner—Paloma was able to keep the pirogue from capsizing simply by shifting the weight on her knees and balancing with her hands—and then he stopped. His boat wallowed a couple of feet away.

"Get aboard," he said, indicating his boat.

"Why?"

"You're going to take us back to that seamount."

"Find it yourself."

"I'm not asking you; I'm telling you. Get aboard!"

Without thinking, Paloma ticked a thumbnail off her front teeth at Jo. As soon as she had done it, she knew it had been a mistake, for the rude gesture showed not only defiance but contempt.

Jo put his boat in gear and turned away, and Paloma could see the veins in his neck protruding thickly. He drove the boat perhaps thirty yards, then turned again toward her.

"One last time," he called to her. "Will you take us back to the seamount?"

Silently she shook her head.

"Yes you will. I gave you a chance to do it the easy way, but if you want to go the hard way, that's okay with me."

She heard his engine yowl as he revved it in neutral, and she knew what he intended to do. He wanted to capsize her pirogue so that she would have to beg him for a ride, and he would pick her out of the sea only if she would take him to the seamount.

Then she saw the oar.

His boat was directly in front of hers, his bow facing hers. He always carried two oars, and now he had fitted one into an oarlock and had directed Indio to hold it horizontal, so that the shaft stuck straight out from the side of the boat and the sharp edge of the blade faced straight at Paloma.

Now Paloma felt genuine fear; she had badly miscalculated. She was no longer dealing with Jo but with a mindless, violent creature who had surfaced once before and whose appearance had irrevocably ruined Jo's relationship with his father.

It had been late summer, at a time when the scars caused by Jo's panic underwater had healed. Jobim had not only forgiven him but had even come to regard the episode as his own fault for having pushed Jo too hard. Jobim had taken Jo's training back a few steps and had proceeded more slowly, more gently.

They had still been a team.

Every year at that time the islanders had a fiesta; its centerpiece was a fishing tournament. Anyone could enter and fish with hooks, harpoons, spears—anything except nets. The winner was the fisherman who returned with the most weight of fish.

What interested Jobim about the tournament was the challenge of trying to catch fish in ingenious ways, ways that gave the fish a more than even chance. This particular year he had entered with Jo as his partner. They were going to fish underwater, using spears that Jobim had fabricated. The spear was a steel rod, propelled by a rubber sling attached to a wooden sleeve.

Jo desperately wanted to win the tournament to give him stature with his friends. He had hoped that by fishing underwater with his father's invention, he would have an advantage over the competition. But by midday he and Jobim had caught nothing. There were plenty of fish, but neither of them could hit a thing and he was distressed. Finally he left his father alone in the water and returned to the boat. All around them other fishermen were hauling fish aboard their boats. Nearby were some of his friends, with their fathers, and when they saw that he had caught nothing, they taunted him.

And then Jo, frantic now beyond reason to be a winner, to be the best, pulled a small bag from a cubbyhole beneath a thwart. The bag contained firecrackers—the big canisterlike ones with the waterproof fuses—bought in La Paz for the fiesta.

He would show them who could catch the most fish. The firecrackers would explode underwater, so no one would hear them. Stunned fish would float to the surface. He would pile them in his boat and stick them with his spear to make it seem that he had caught them.

Jo lit one of the firecrackers and threw it overboard, from the side of the boat away from where he had last seen Jobim's shadowy form underwater. As he watched it sink and waited for it to explode, he wondered just how much damage a little explosion like that would do to a fish.

He never thought to wonder what it would do to a man—until

after he had heard the muffled *whump* and saw his father thrashing, struggling toward the surface, the clouds of blood streaming from his ears.

When Jobim's head had broken the surface, there had been a moment before he fainted from shock and pain. In that moment his eyes had locked on Jo's with an accusation of stupid, reckless cowardice.

Jo had screamed, "I'm sorry! I'm sorry!" over and over, but no one had heard him.

Now, waiting for Jo to charge, Paloma knew that the same kind of switch had been tripped again in his head. He was so obsessed with determination to capsize her that to succeed he was prepared to hurt her or perhaps even kill her.

At full speed, he would sweep the pirogue with his extended oar, from bow to stern. She could escape the oar completely only by lying flat, and in doing so would lose the ability that she had on her knees to balance the boat. She threw herself forward onto her face and covered the back of her head with the palms of her hands and braced her elbows against the sides of the pirogue.

She never saw the oar, never heard it, but she felt the blade nick the pirogue's wooden sides and bounce and nick again.

Then the wake of the motorboat slammed into the pirogue and heaved it upward. Paloma was no longer on her face but on her side, then over on her back, and then there was only grayness and a hollow, slapping sound and she was under the boat. She stayed there, breathing the air trapped beneath the overturned boat, trying to guess what Jo was planning to do next.

The engine noise dropped to the low mutter of idling speed, and she heard the wavelets lap at the motorboat's hull as it wallowed nearby.

"Where is she?" Indio's voice filtered into the chamber where Paloma's head stuck out of water. He sounded worried.

"You've drowned her!" said Manolo.

"She's not drowned," Jo said. "I'll show you where she is."

Suddenly Paloma's ears were battered by a hard, banging sound that echoed from side to side of the wooden cavern. Jo had hammered something against the upturned bottom of the boat.

"Hey!" he called. "Ready to take us to the seamount?"

Paloma didn't know what to say, didn't know what another flat refusal would goad him into doing. She hoped that by remaining silent she might scare him—even briefly—into believing she had drowned.

"I knew it!" came Manolo's voice. "She's dead!"

"No," said Jo, but there was a lilt of uncertainty in his voice. Again the heavy thing struck the bottom of the boat, but softer than before. "Paloma!" he called.

"Paloma!" Indio shouted.

"Leave it to me!" Jo snapped at him. And then Jo took a gamble: "Paloma, I know you can hear me. If you don't agree to take us to the seamount, I will punch a hole in the bottom of your boat with my harpoon. Your boat might not sink, but it won't paddle, either, so you will stay here and float with it till kingdom come . . . or you will take us to the seamount in return for a ride home. Your choice."

Paloma heard the harpoon's steel point grind into the wood fibers. The only reasonable thing to do was to surrender. But Jo hadn't used reason in what he had done, so why should she? Instead, she stayed beneath her overturned boat, listening to Jo's labored breathing as he gouged a hole in its bottom.

First she saw a pinprick of light, and then a shaft the size of a coin, and wood splinters fell on the water before her. Then the head of the harpoon jammed through the hole and turned a couple of times and was withdrawn.

"Good-bye, Paloma. You may think you're being proud, but all you are is pigheaded."

Paloma heard Jo pull on the starter cord of the motor. The motor sputtered but did not start.

"We can't leave her," she heard Indio say. "We have to make sure."

"Sure of what?" Jo said. As he talked, Paloma felt herself growing cold, not from the water but from the iciness of this person who was her brother. "Make sure she's under the boat? Make sure she's all right? Believe me, she is. Even if she isn't, what can you do about it? Nothing. When we get back to shore, we say we have no idea where she is, which is the truth."

Paloma heard the outboard wheeze and jump to life, and she could feel from shock waves in the water that Jo had put the motor in gear and was driving away.

IV

PALOMA waited for silence, and then waited some more, in case Jo had turned around and rowed back and was lurking nearby. At last she ducked her head underwater and came out beside the pirogue. She was alone on the sea.

Now she wondered whether she had been right or wrong, principled—as she believed—or pigheaded—as Jo had said. At best, she had delayed Jo a few days. He would find the seamount eventually and do his damage, perhaps destroy it. And the delaying tactic had cost her. Here she was in the middle of the sea, with the end of the day approaching and no way to get home unless she could devise a patch for the hole.

Paloma pulled herself up onto the overturned bottom of the pirogue. The hole was about the size of her fist, easy enough to patch with wood once ashore, but big enough to keep her from getting to shore.

She thought of her choices. She could stay with the overturned boat until she drifted to land. Or she could abandon the boat and swim for home. Or she could try to patch the pirogue here and now. With what? She had no wood, no canvas, no leather, no nails or tacks, no hammer.

And then suddenly she had the answer: her dress. She could stuff her dress into the hole. Packed tightly in a ball, the cloth fibers would bind and become nearly waterproof.

Paloma peeled the shift up over her head, then ducked under the pirogue and packed the cloth into the hole, making a plug that was secure enough for an easy paddle on calm water.

She ducked out again, hauled herself up onto the bottom, and grabbed the far edge. Bracing herself on one knee, she pulled, and there was a pop as the suction broke and the pirogue jumped free of the water and righted itself. It was full of water, though; only an inch of freeboard stuck above the surface. Since the boat was a hollow log, it would not sink, but if Paloma were to climb in, every tiny movement she made would allow more water to slosh aboard. She could not bail it out from inside.

So she clung to the side with one arm, and with the other hand began methodically to splash water overboard. She forced herself not to be impatient, for she knew that this was what she was going to be doing for the next several hours, probably well into the night. And she did not hurry, for she didn't want to tire herself and risk a cramp in an arm or leg. A muscle that had once gone into spasm was sure to cramp again unless it was rested for hours. Each succeeding cramp would be harder to relieve than the one before.

As she continued to bail, the muscles in her upper arm began to stiffen and ache. To massage them she had to release her grip on the boat. Immediately the tide caught her and dragged her away from the pirogue, but she was confident of her strength as a swimmer and was not worried.

She was more than fifty yards away from the pirogue when she finally felt her muscles relax, and she stopped massaging the arm. Unhurriedly she began to breaststroke against the tide.

After ten or fifteen minutes she seemed no closer to her boat than when she had started. But she had noted her beginning against a set of peculiarly shaped rocks on the bottom, and she knew she was making progress—very slowly, probably no more than a couple of feet with each stroke, and half of that she was losing before she could take her next one. She was not tiring; she could swim like this indefinitely, and eventually—it might be a couple of hours from now—the tide would ease and go slack and she would gain a little more with each stroke. Then the tide would turn, and she would make it to her boat.

Her left leg went first. She felt her toes begin to snarl. She reached down with her hand to squeeze the calf muscle, but it was too late. The muscle had already balled into a knot the size of an orange. She rolled onto her back, and kneading with her fingertips, she softened the knot. Suddenly it dissolved and she straightened out her leg, and then, before she knew what was happening, an even more violent spasm lashed the back of her thigh. Her heel snapped back against her buttock, like the blade of a jackknife closing.

She was drifting farther away from her boat. She tried to use her hands to straighten her leg, but her arms weren't long enough to give her adequate leverage. So she brought up her other foot and forced the toes between heel and buttock and pushed down.

Then the other leg went, a perfect mimic of the first. Now she felt like one of the beggars in La Paz whose legs had been lopped off below the knees. She had no balance, and she rolled in the water like a trussed hog. She knew then she had to attack the cramps with her mind.

She said to herself, You're drifting away. What is the worst thing that can happen? You'll drift so far that you can't get back to your boat on this tide. You won't drown because you know how to float forever. The tide will turn and take you back toward your boat. Even if you drift wide of it, all that will happen is that you'll travel until either you strike land or someone picks you up. So, really, you have nothing to worry about.

Then she looked down through the water and saw that there was one danger she had overlooked. Way down, in the blue shadows, were two sharks circling slowly. They were not the familiar hammerheads. Even from this distance she could discern the bullet shapes and the pointed snouts, and she knew they were a kind of bull shark—aggressive, ill tempered, and unpredictable.

Each circle brought the sharks a bit closer to the surface; each circle was a bit quicker than the one before. And Paloma knew that she was sending signals that she was an animal unable to defend itself, and she might make easy prey.

All right, she told herself. I've got to stop behaving like this or they'll home in on me and tear me to pieces. As she heard the words in her brain, she felt a rush of panic, and so she tried even harder to straighten out her legs; and the harder she tried the tighter they knotted.

She was now forced to use the extreme remedy. It was said that the only way to relieve a terrible cramp was to cause worse pain elsewhere in your body. As the mind can focus only on one pain center at a time, it will concentrate on the more severe and will stop sending cramp signals to the afflicted muscle. And so she asked herself, What's the worst pain you can imagine?

She bit her tongue. How that hurt! She bit harder. Nothing could hurt worse than this. She tasted blood in her mouth and saw little puffs of red seep from between her lips into the water. The blood might draw the sharks closer.

All she could focus on was the pain in her tongue. It was a blade, a flame, a needle.

The cramps collapsed.

She didn't know it until she stopped biting her tongue. As when you ease off on the throttle of an outboard motor, she expected the pain in her mouth to fade to a background, idle-speed sensation, and the pain in her legs to accelerate and take over. The pain in her mouth did fade, but nothing replaced it. Her legs had unlocked themselves, and the muscles in her calves were no longer twitching.

Very tentatively she began to swim, aiming vaguely at her boat, but more to test her muscles than to accomplish much. She used her arms and let her legs follow along in a weak scissors kick. Her arms were not enough to move her body against the tide. Still, she kept swimming to restore circulation. She maintained a smooth and easy stroke, hoping to convey a sense of calm and control.

After a few minutes she looked down again and searched for the circling sharks. She saw only a flicker of gray shadow, heading away. To the sharks she was now a healthy animal, even a formidable foe instead of vulnerable prey.

She swam on, watching her boat grow smaller and smaller against the sea. Once in a while a small muscle would give a warning twinge, and she would stop and massage it. She did not want to stop for long, though, for continual exercise kept her warm. If she allowed herself to grow cold, her circulation would drop, and her muscles would be starved for oxygen and would cramp. She focused on each stroke as an act independent of every other stroke and of all other acts, to be begun and completed with mechanical perfection. All other thoughts she forced from her mind.

The first sign she had that the tide was changing was a feeling of warm, still water on her skin. The sea, which had been merely calm, was now flat and slick. Such swells as there were, were so slow and lazy that she could not perceive them.

She saw a piece of floating weed and swam to it and threw it as hard as she could toward her faraway boat. It landed ten feet away from her and lay still. The tide was dead slack. Now if she swam, she could only gain, and soon the new tide would begin and would push her along. Her pirogue was anchored, so it would not move.

With every stroke she took, she imagined the boat growing infinitesimally larger. She traveled about a mile in the first hour. The second mile took her only twenty minutes, for the tide had turned. In another fifteen minutes she was hanging on to her pirogue.

She had been frightened, but now she felt proud, too, for she had survived on her own. Jobim had taught her the skills and given her the knowledge, but putting it all into practice, actually *doing* it, felt wonderful.

She shivered. The sun had dropped so far that the pirogue cast a sharp shadow on the sea. She bailed enough water out of the boat to get into it. Then, kneeling on the bottom, she scooped with her hands and splashed with her paddle, and scooped some more and splashed some more. She saw the sun slide to the horizon, hesitate, then plunge beneath it, leaving a sky of richer blue dotted in the east by faint stars. She saw a light or a campfire wink on a distant island.

The boat was as dry now as it would be until the sun could get at it. She had not been on the sea at night for a long time, so she double-checked the landmarks she could still see and stood up in the pirogue to search for the first lights of Santa Maria. Then she started to paddle toward home.

Miranda would be frantic. Paloma never stayed out this late, and her mother would *know* something had happened. She had drowned. Something had eaten her. Jo, of course, would be no help. He would feign innocence and concern.

The thought of that scene infuriated Paloma and made her paddle harder. But when she arrived, probably she would keep silent about what had happened today. For what would talking about it accomplish? Even if people believed her, Jo's offense would not seem serious. She had not been harmed. There was no way to convey the reckless willingness to hurt that she had seen in her brother. Paloma guessed that somewhere inside Jo there would be secret relief that she had returned, for she could not believe—despite his fits of rage—that his conscience could condone murder.

A three-quarter moon had risen in the black sky, and it cast a path of gold before the pirogue, a path that led Paloma home.

Her reception was almost exactly as she had imagined it: Miranda shrieked and clutched Paloma to her breast and thanked God for answering her prayers. She asked what had kept Paloma, and Paloma said she had been delayed by a little tidal maelstrom that had carried her too far from shore.

Jo crossed in front of Miranda and hugged Paloma—touching her with the same affection with which he would have caressed a leper—and said he had been worried about her.

Miranda sensed something awry between her children. She could feel a current of hostility surging back and forth. She was apprehensive but helpless, so she covered her anxiety with a veneer of relief that everyone was home safe and sound.

IN THE morning Paloma told Miranda that her terrible experience of the day before had frightened her and that she wanted to stay ashore for a day or two and help with the wash and the house. Miranda was pleased. Perhaps Paloma was outgrowing this foolishness with the sea.

The reason Paloma stayed ashore was that she knew that if she went out to the seamount, she would surely provoke another confrontation with Jo and his mates. And this time someone would get hurt.

She had walked to the top of the hill above the dock and watched them and the other fishermen prepare their boats for the day. She saw the last piece of gear that Jo and Indio and Manolo slung aboard: a big net, with lead weights at the bottom to drag the snare down to the top of the seamount.

After the other fishermen left, Jo started his motor and headed to sea. He did not yet know precisely where the seamount was, but he was certain to find it. With one of his mates peering through the glass-bottomed bucket, Jo would drive the motorboat in straight lines up and down the general area until he passed over the seamount.

Paloma watched until the wake from Jo's motor melted into the moving water and the white hull of the boat itself was consumed by the shining light on the sea.

The dock was empty, so she could work on her boat without bothering anyone. She found some pieces of canvas and plywood, and she cut and shaped them into patches that would block the hole inside and out, and nailed them in place, sealing them with daubs of pitch.

She spent the rest of the day helping Miranda. Late that afternoon, walking up the hill under a heavy load of wash, Paloma thought that if the day had accomplished nothing else, it had given her mother some happiness.

While she helped sweep the house and hang the wash to dry and stoke the cook fire, Paloma forced her thoughts to stay ashore. But as soon as the chores were done and Miranda turned to cooking the evening meal, Paloma went outside and looked at the sky to tell the time.

The sun was very low; it was late, later than Jo would normally stay out. On the path that led down to the dock she saw several fishermen strolling home, which meant that they had been ashore for an hour or more, for it took that long to unload the fish and clean them and swab the boat and stow the gear.

Perhaps some trouble had befallen Jo and his friends. Perhaps they had fouled their net on the bottom and had capsized trying to retrieve it. They would have to row home, for a saltwater-soaked motor would never start. Or perhaps they had cast their net into a mass of king mackerel or wahoos and seen it torn to shreds as they struggled to free the thrashing, snapping animals before they could drag the boat underwater.

But, walking toward the path to the dock, she suddenly realized there was a more likely reason for Jo's lateness—and it was a reason that made the palms of her hands go cold and sent a trickle of sweat down her brow.

From the top of the hill she saw that this was the true reason.

Jo's day had been successful beyond his dreams. They had netted so many fish that they had had to drive the boat home at its slowest speed to keep it from swamping and sinking.

As the boat docked, Paloma saw Jo and Indio and Manolo all sitting on fish, hip-deep in fish, surrounded by mounds of fish.

In a single day's netting they had caught more than in a month of line fishing. But that alone was not what distressed Paloma. The great schools of jacks and *cabríos* sustained heavy losses quite often, and they soon returned to full strength. No, worse for Paloma was that in the dwindling twilight she could see Jo and his mates pawing through the corpses in the boat and flinging overboard those species that did not measure up to their suddenly high standards. Now that they had the guarantee of endless fish, why bother to save those that did not bring the most lucrative prices? It was more economical to throw them away than to process them. And—to Paloma's horror—some of them were fish that did *not* school, did *not* breed countless young, did *not* exist in profusion on the seamount.

By the time Jo and Indio and Manolo had finished culling their catch, night had come, and they did the last of their work by the light of the rising moon. They were tired and hungry, so they did not bother to clean their boat or prepare their gear for the next day.

"We can do the boat in the morning," Jo said as they strode up the path. Paloma was crouching in the brush at the top, watching the three shadows approach.

"Now we know where the place is."

"And what's on it. I've never seen anything like that."

"I bet we could go late and be back by midday."

"We could go twice, do two trips a day."

"*You* go twice. One load like that's enough for me. My back's about to break."

"Maybe we ought to get another boat." This was Jo's voice, moving past Paloma and on up the hill.

"That'd mean more people."

"Why share?"

"We could double the catch," Jo said. "Let's meet after supper to talk. We don't have to decide anything."

"Okay."

The voices stopped and footsteps faded as the three dispersed, each to his home.

Paloma waited until she could hear no sound but the breeze rolling over the island. Then she crept down to the dock.

The moon was high enough so its light penetrated the shallow water by the shore and cast a faint mantle of white on the rocky bottom. But there was little bottom to see, for most of it was littered with the dead.

There were floating corpses and corpses that had sunk, corpses that tried to bob to the surface but were blocked by others, corpses battered and mangled and without color. And their eyes, all black and blank, stared glassily at nothing.

Jo and his mates must have thrown away a fourth of their catch, all but the biggest of the most valuable kinds. Here in the water by the dock were smaller jacks, little *cabríos* and other groupers that should have been pulled from the net alive and put back in the sea immediately, for they were the future of their species.

Here, too, were those beings Jobim had called the innocents, those that had no market value, could not be sold as individuals, and were not worth gathering in the numbers, the tons, that would produce fish meal or cat food and be worth a few pennies at the factory. There were puffers, gentle and shy and gallant in their defiant instant obesity; angelfish, whose chevrons changed color in every stage from infancy to adolescence to maturity. And there was a young turtle, still soft of carapace, its throat garroted by a strand of netting, its flippers limp. And other fish, like sergeants major, hogfish, and porgies, all killed and cast away to wash in the shallows and rot.

The carnage was immense; this was not fishing.

Kneeling on the dock, gazing into the water, Paloma saw her reflection in the moonlight, and she realized she was weeping.

She wanted to run up the hill and bring Viejo down, and point out to his dim eyes all the bodies, all the waste. But she did not, because she knew her outrage would not be shared. There would be some tongue clucking about teaching the young men how better to cull their catches. But that was all.

And by morning what she saw before her would be no more. As the tide ebbed, the bodies would be sucked out to deep water, so that when the other fishermen arrived at the dock, all that would remain of the carnage would be a few floating fish and a few half-eaten skeletons on the bottom—a normal amount of flotsam and jetsam from a day's work.

Even now the corpses on the surface were beginning slowly to drift away from the rocks onshore, obscuring her view of parts of the bottom but letting her see into new crannies. She saw an animal between two rocks. It looked to be curled up, like a sleeping puppy. She dropped to her stomach on the dock and lifted up a green moray eel, young and unscarred.

More than any other of the beings, it touched her. This moray was contorted in the agony of its death, frozen at its final moment. It was tied in a knot that made it seem that it would be dying forever. Paloma knew well that morays often died in this grotesque way. It was, in a strange sense, a natural death, for it reflected the animal's behavior in life.

Morays lived in holes or small caves or crevices or under rocks, and each lurked at the entrance to its lair, mouth open, gills pulsating rhythmically, hypnotically, skin color blending with its surroundings.

When prey passed by, the moray would shoot out its body—a single tube of muscle—and snatch the prey with mean-looking fangs. If the prey was large, larger than the eel's weak eyesight had anticipated, and if it threatened to yank the eel from its hole, the eel would anchor its tail around a rock or a coral boulder and contract its central muscles until no free-swimming prey could resist.

Thus, breath-hold divers were careful about poking around in holes in reefs. First there was the fear of being bitten, because the bite was excruciating and the eel's mouth was coated with a slime that contained virulent infectants. But even worse was the knowledge that if the eel grabbed a hand or a foot and could not sense the size of the prey—for it would not actually try to eat something so much bigger than itself as a human—it would anchor its tail and hold on until the victim stopped thrashing.

Once in a while a moray would snatch a prey and have no rock on which to fasten a grip. Then it would whip into a perfect knot, wrapping the tail around the head and back down through the loop made by neck and body, and pull its prey through the loop, flopping down the reef and out into open water—secure that it had an anchor and its prey did not.

Mostly the eels knotted themselves when they encountered a force stronger than they—like a steel-barbed hook that fastened in the back of the throat and was attached to a filament that slid between the fangs and could not be bitten off.

One day Jobim had hooked a moray and brought it up to the boat. It was tied in a knot, and as it struggled in the water it swung like the pendulum of a clock. Paloma had never seen a live moray before.

"Give me the pliers," Jobim had said.

She handed him the pliers and watched as he gently brought the eel to the surface.

"Hold this." He had passed her the fishing line, and she felt it twitch and thrum with the eel's desperation. He held the pliers in his right hand and, with the same hand, slid two fingers down the leader to within an inch of the eel's mouth. Then he pulled the eel clear of the water and, with his left hand, grabbed the eel behind the head and squeezed.

She had never imagined a creature like this. It wasn't a fish, it was a monster. Its black pig's eyes bulged and glistened. Its mouth was agape and strung with strands of slime. Its gills, what she could see of them amid the pile of bulbous green flesh, throbbed. It grunted. It hissed.

"Kill it!" she shrieked. "Kill it!"

"You want it dead, you kill it." Jobim had nodded at the cudgel he kept in the boat to stun sharks.

"Don't *you* want it dead?"

Jobim didn't answer. He was staring fixedly into one of the eel's eyes. The muscles in his arms and shoulders flexed as he fought to keep the eel from writhing free. He squeezed harder with his left hand, and the eel's jaws separated. Then he opened the pliers and pushed his hand into the eel's mouth.

"He'll bite off your hand!" Paloma grabbed the cudgel and raised it with both fists over the eel's yawning mouth.

Jobim pushed his hand farther down the gullet, and Paloma saw the eel's flesh bulge as his knuckles passed through. His hand was gone, and his wrist, and half his forearm. Still the eel writhed and hissed, and every fiber in Jobim's left arm danced. He probed with the pliers and found the barb of the hook. Slowly his arm and wrist began to withdraw, coated with shiny slime, and his hand came free, then the pliers and the hook.

Still holding the eel's head in his left hand, he lowered the entire body back into the water and slowly sloshed it back and forth to get water flowing once again over the gills. When he was sure the eel would not succumb to shock, he released it.

The ball of green muscle sank a foot or two, uncoiled like a waking snake, wriggled to stretch the tired tissues, and then—suddenly aware that it was vulnerable in open water—it darted with quick, snapping thrusts toward the bottom.

Paloma asked Jobim why he hadn't killed the moray.

"I hooked the animal by accident. But why should I kill it?"

As Paloma opened her mouth to speak, Jobim added quickly, "And don't say, Why not? Why not kill? is a question you must never ask. The question must always be Why kill? and the answer must be something for which there is no other answer."

Paloma had no good answer for Why kill? and so she said nothing.

That afternoon, when they had finished fishing, Jobim had moved the boat to the shallowest part of the seamount and told Paloma that he would take her for a dive.

He cut a fish into small pieces and put them in a plastic bag tied to his waist, and together they pulled themselves down the anchor line. On the seamount, Jobim motioned for her to stay at the anchor line, and he went off among the rocks, looking for something. Soon he had found whatever it was, and he waved her over to him. His face was six inches from a crevice in the rocks, and he pulled her down beside him.

In the second that it took her eyes to recognize what she was gazing at, she concluded that her father had gone mad.

Guarding the crevice with its gigantic head and black eyes and gaping mouth was a moray eel so large that it made the other one seem like a garden snake. Paloma believed that if the eel should shrug, it could consume her entire skull.

She jerked backward in reflex, but Jobim caught her arm and forced her to return to his side. He took a hunk of fish from the bag at his waist and held it up to the moray. For a moment the eel did not move. Then it slid slightly forward, as if on a mechanical track, and Jobim dropped the morsel of fish; the eel let it fall into its mouth and swallowed, and the gills rippled in unison, and the eel slid backward into its hole.

Jobim fed it another piece, and another, and by then he knew that Paloma was short of oxygen so he motioned that they would go up. As they rose, Paloma looked down and saw that the eel had slid more of its body—four or five feet—out of the hole and had turned its head and was looking up at them.

When, on the surface, Paloma tried to speak, Jobim waved her silent, signaling that he wanted to return to the seamount.

This time the eel seemed to have watched the last part of their descent, for its head was a foot outside the crevice and its eyes were tracking them.

Jobim handed Paloma the bag of bait. She shook her head no. She wouldn't do it. But he forced the bag into her fist and put a hand on her shoulder in assurance and embrace.

The first piece she held a full two feet from the eel's mouth, until Jobim pushed her hand closer. The eel slid forward; Paloma dropped the bit of fish; the eel swallowed.

With each new piece she grew bolder, for the eel made no motion to do anything but what she intended, and the last piece from the bag she actually laid within the eel's lower jaw.

Back on the surface again, she was elated and amazed. She wanted to cut up another fish and return to feed the moray.

"Not me," Jobim said somberly. "It's too dangerous."

"But—"

"I think we should kill him before he hurts somebody."

Now Paloma knew what Jobim was doing. She screamed and splashed water at him; he threw back his head and laughed.

While they rested, he cut up another fish into bigger pieces, for the moray had been larger than he had guessed it would be. This one was probably seven or eight feet long, and its head was more than a foot wide.

They had spent many minutes away from the eel, and it was not there when they returned. But as soon as one of their shadows crossed before the crevice in the rocks, the huge green head slid forward and hung there, gills and mouth pulsing together.

Each morsel Jobim held farther from the hole, urging the eel to slide out more. But he did not tease the animal. When Jobim had established where the food would be, there he left it. If he had pulled the food back after the animal had committed to exposing itself a certain distance, the eel might have registered betrayal and been driven to attack.

The eel would not come all the way out of the hole. Apparently it needed the security of knowing that its tail was anchored in the rocks so that if anything should go awry, it could dominate the encounter.

And as Jobim told Paloma when they were back in the boat, he saw no reason to encourage the animal beyond its own limits, especially on first meeting.

"You mean we can do it again?" It hadn't occurred to her that something so special could be repeated.

"We'll see. Some people can."

"What do you mean?"

"A few people have something special with animals. It may be the same thing some animals have with each other, that they send and receive each other's signals so they understand each other. By nature, animals in the wild don't trust people, and they shouldn't. But these few people, the people who have this good thing, animals trust."

"You have it, then."

"I have a little of it, but not a lot. I never know from animal to animal. Maybe we were lucky with this eel today."

Paloma said hopefully, "Maybe I have a lot of the good thing."

"Maybe. But don't hope too much. It's nice, the good thing, but it can be dangerous, too."

"Why?"

"You can believe in it too much, believe you can do anything. You take one step too many. If you're lucky, you end up with a good lesson. If you're unlucky, you get hurt. Or killed."

They had returned to feed the eel the next day after fishing. As Jobim set the anchor, Paloma had asked if he thought the eel would still be there.

"Moray eels will find a hole and make it their own as long as enough food passes by for them to grab. When it doesn't, they'll find another hole. This big fellow has no reason to move now; it has comfort, safety and, best of all, since yesterday doesn't even have to hunt. Some fools are bringing him dinner."

The eel was there, hovering in its hole, and had to be coaxed to take the first bite of fish.

Once the feeding reflex was stimulated, the eel became ravenous. More and more of it hung out of the hole, and Paloma, her confidence blooming, backed farther away, trying to bring the eel entirely out into the open.

She did not see, and never knew, that Jobim had a knife clenched in his fist behind his back.

There were half a dozen pieces of fish left in the bag, and now Paloma took one with her left hand and slowly, calmly, drew it wide and back toward her shoulder. With a brief shudder, the eel followed the fish.

Paloma drew it around her head, where she slipped it into her right hand and continued to lure the eel behind her. The eel's tail was over her left shoulder, its head over her right, when she gave it the fish. It swallowed the fish and stayed there, wrapped around her shoulders like a fine lady's stole.

She fed it two more pieces of fish, and there were three left. She glanced at Jobim and saw that his eyes were wide and the veins on either side of his throat were thick as anchor line. For a second she thought he was afraid for her, and perhaps he was, but then it struck her that both of them had to breathe.

Paloma took the last pieces of fish, squeezed them into a ball, and held them up before the eel's open mouth. She pushed them upward so the eel would have to rise slightly to reach them, and as it did she ducked down and pushed backward with her feet and shot on a sharp angle toward the surface.

Jobim didn't chastise her; he didn't have to. Each knew what the other was thinking: Paloma had been reckless but had succeeded; she had the good thing, but it was something she would have to learn how to use.

All the way home in the boat, they had only one exchange.

She had said, "I think I'll call him Pancho."

He had replied, "It's not a him. It's an it. It doesn't have a name, and don't give it one."

Every day she was out with Jobim she had looked forward at the end of the day to visiting the eel. It would curl around her shoulders, sometimes after only a bite or two of fish. Occasionally it would let its weight drop onto her shoulders, and it would lie there, and she could stroke its smooth skin while she fed it.

And then one day it was gone.

Paloma thought they had come to the wrong hole, but the landmarks underwater were too familiar. They searched that section of the seamount, hoping that if they passed the eel's new hole, it would come out. But it had gone.

"You said it wouldn't go away." Paloma felt hurt, deceived, as if Jobim had tricked her into believing that if she fed the eel, it would stay there, for her, forever.

"No, I didn't. I said it had no reason to move before. Maybe a secret clock or calendar inside him said it was time now to go somewhere else. Maybe to find a mate."

"I thought you said he wasn't a him. You said he was an it."

Jobim smiled and, seeing him smile, Paloma could not resist smiling, too.

"He was here yesterday and he isn't here today," her father said.

"But . . . he liked us. I could tell."

"Don't do that to yourself, Paloma." Jobim had stopped smiling. "We accustomed it to us as feeders. That's all. It didn't *like* us. It won't *miss* us. It doesn't have feelings like that."

"How do you know?"

"I . . ." Jobim stopped and looked at Paloma and smiled again. "I don't, not for sure."

"What about the good thing?"

"You have the good thing, as much as anyone can have it with an eel. With anyone else, it would have stayed in its hole or taken a bite out of them. It trusted you. That's what the good thing is, trust."

Now Paloma knelt on the dock in the moonlight and held the knotted eel in her lap. Gently she tried to undo the knot, to erase the reminder of the eel's last agony. But rigor mortis had already gripped the animal, and as she laid the body on the dock, it rocked on the wooden planks and banged its rigid snout.

She picked up the eel and dropped it off the dock. It fell on top of other corpses that were slowly being swept toward deeper water, and then it sank beneath them.

Still kneeling on the dock, Paloma let her glance travel along the path of gold cast on the water by the moon. It did not begin or end, but seemed simply to happen, magically, somewhere out there in the blackness this side of the horizon, and to disperse, spent, somewhere in the blackness behind her.

If ever she thought of trying to place her father, to locate him where he was now, she located him there, between the sky and the sea, at the source of the path of the moon.

"What can I do?" she said aloud to Jobim. "Don't say, Nothing, because that's what I've been doing, and look what's happened." Paloma gestured at the water. "They're going to kill our seamount. I can't do anything about it, because I'm alone and nobody will listen to me, and even if they did, they wouldn't do anything. Mama doesn't know anything about it, and if she did, she'd say it was

God's will." Paloma paused, fearing she had given offense. "I'm sorry, but that's the truth and you know it. Viejo says anyone can do anything he wants, and if all the fish are gone one day, well, that's the way of the world."

Now she shouted into the night. "But it's *not!* I won't let it be!" Her words echoed across the water.

She was gazing at the spot where the gold seemed to begin. She did not expect a response, and she did not receive one, not in the sense of an answer.

But something did begin to happen inside her.

It was a warmth that started at her fingertips and seemed to creep up her arms and over her shoulders and down into her chest and through her stomach and into her legs. It was a sensation of fullness, as if something missing had finally been put into place.

She felt a purpose and a sense of confidence and a sure knowledge that she would find an answer if she obeyed her natural instincts. What those instincts would tell her to do and what the answer would be, she had no idea.

But so suffused was she with this feeling, and so positive was she that it meant *some*thing, that once again she gazed at the spot in the sky where the gold began, and she nodded.

Supper was over by the time Paloma returned to the house, and the plate of food Miranda had left for her on the table was cold, but the new feeling that was running through her was consuming energy, so she was hungry and she sat down to eat.

Jo was there. Normally by now he would have been in his room, but he had lingered.

"Did you have a good day?" he asked Paloma.

Her mouth was full, and she did not respond right away.

Jo said, "I had a *fine* day. Many more days like this, I'll have enough money for school. I think Papa would have wanted it for me, too, don't you?"

Paloma looked at him but said nothing.

"Sometimes I think that's why I found the seamount. I think maybe he led me there." Jo smiled. "Don't you?"

Paloma clenched her teeth and kept silent.

Jo spoke this time to Miranda. "This seamount of Papa's is very rich. By the time I'm through with it, it will give me enough money to take care of all of us. You won't have to worry about money again, Mama." His eyes shifted to Paloma. "Viejo always says that the sea exists to serve men, and I know Papa would agree. Yes, this seamount is what he left us, and I will see that his will is carried out."

It took all Paloma's strength to keep her mouth shut. It outraged her that Jo was summoning their father's spirit to justify ravaging the seamount. But she knew Jo was trying to enrage her. So she busied herself with her food until Jo yawned and stretched and left the house to go to his room.

Preparing for bed, Paloma knew that Miranda was looking at her and was worried. Miranda sensed that something was afoot. She didn't know what. But then, neither did Paloma.

V

PALOMA stood on the hill and watched Jo and his mates prepare their boat for sea. Again they waited for the others to depart, for they were determined—especially now that they knew how rich the seamount was—to keep its location their secret.

Paloma guessed that they had been questioned by other fishermen about their formidable catch, for today they started out in the wrong direction and changed course only when they were confident they were being neither followed nor observed.

Paloma returned to the house and puttered around for a while.

She had no plan. She did not know why she had returned to the house, though it seemed as good a thing to do as any other. She felt an inner assurance—based on nothing rational—that whatever was going to happen would happen.

Miranda eyed Paloma nervously but made no comment. She suggested things for them to do—move this bed and sweep under it, take that mat outside and beat the dust out of it—and Paloma worked diligently. But Paloma was not really there.

At midday Paloma said she was going for a walk. As far as Paloma knew, she *was* going for a walk. But once she neared the top of the hill above the dock, the sea summoned her so powerfully that she could not possibly resist.

She went to the dock and pulled her boat out from beneath it and noted that her fins, mask, snorkel, and knife were in the pirogue and that her patch had sealed the hole in the bottom. She climbed aboard and paddled toward the seamount.

Their backs were to her as she approached. They were setting their net, letting it billow and sink in a wide, deep arc. Their boat sat high in the water, which meant that so far they had made no good casts or, perhaps, had not yet tried, waiting instead for the big schools to come by.

They did not see her or hear her, and she knelt in the pirogue uptide, watching. After a while Indio did chance to turn and he nudged Jo, whose head snapped around, eyes narrowed.

They eyed each other for a long moment, until Jo turned back to his net and said casually, over his shoulder, "Come to watch?"

She did not respond, but stayed where she was, a dozen or so yards from their boat. Jo was elaborately occupied with the net, but his mates were obviously unsettled by her presence. Even from a distance, Paloma could grasp the sense of the conversation.

"What does she want?"

"You think she'll do anything?"

"Like what?"

"What about the net? We said—"

"Forget it. She's beaten. She's given up."

"Then what's—"

"Forget it, I said. Watch this." Jo scooped a handful of rancid fish guts from the stern of the boat and flung the mess toward Paloma. It fell several feet short of the pirogue. Instantly a pack of sergeants major materialized and devoured it.

Paloma did nothing, said nothing, in no way acknowledged the gesture.

"See?" Jo said to the others. "She won't do anything. She knows what's what. Now. Look through the glass and tell me if they're still there."

Manolo put the bucket on the surface of the sea and looked down. "Right there. They haven't moved. Look at them all! We won't get 'em all in this boat."

"Then we'll tow 'em home in the net. Tomorrow we better bring a barge out here."

Though Jo did not look at Paloma as he spoke, she knew he was speaking for her ears, taunting her. But still she said and did nothing, for she didn't know what she could say, or what she could do. If her silence annoyed them, that was fine; speaking could only strip away the mystery about why she was there.

Their net was sinking, and they were concentrating to make sure it didn't snarl. When it was all the way out, they would let it sit for a few minutes before hauling it in—to give ample time for masses of fish to wander into the trap.

Paloma felt a slight surge that lifted her pirogue an inch, no more, and let it settle again. It might have been the wake of a distant boat, but there were no boats in the distance; it might have been the weakening signature of a long-distance seismic wave, but only her boat had moved, which meant that whatever was happening to cause the change in the water pressure was happening directly beneath her.

She cocked her head over the side of the pirogue and back-paddled so she would have a better angle on the water below. All the water looked black, which didn't strike her as peculiar until she realized that the water farther away was its normal blue.

Then she knew immediately and smiled to herself. The wounded manta had returned. It was lying a few feet below the surface, and the black carpet of its back was so close that it seemed to extend to the horizon.

Paloma held her mask to her face, bent over, and put the faceplate on the water. There were many manta rays around seamounts. And this could not be the same one, for there was no wound, no shredded flesh. Yet there was something strange about the area around the left horn. It looked dented or nicked, as if there had been an injury some time ago.

She decided to go down and look. She pitched her anchor overboard and let the line pay free. The fishermen were still setting their net, so they did not notice when Paloma slipped over the side and took a few deep breaths and disappeared.

When the net was set a moment later, however, Jo turned around and saw the empty pirogue. "Give me the glass," he said.

As soon as Paloma was underwater, she knew it was the same manta. But the wound looked ancient. The flesh had grown together—probably, Paloma thought with pride, because she packed it so tightly and took off the ragged pieces. All that remained were scars, and an indentation behind the horn. As Paloma stroked the animal, she saw that the abused flesh had even begun to regenerate the protective mucus that covered the rest of the body.

The manta lay perfectly quiet as her hands explored the injured horn, and against all her knowledge and all of Jobim's teachings, Paloma began to believe that the manta had returned to show her how successful her treatment had been.

Her body triggered the first familiar alarms to send her to the surface, and she resented them and dismissed them and pretended she was a fish, until the second set of alarms forced her to leave the manta. She looked down as she ascended, hoping the manta would remain until she could return, and because she did not look up she did not see that she was coming up alongside Jo's boat. He was standing in the bow, holding his harpoon.

"Bring the devilfish up," Jo said sharply.

"What are you talking about? I can't bring him up. But even if I could, why?"

"He has to weigh two tons. Good money."

"Money? For a *manta?*"

"A silver coin for every hundredweight. Cat food."

"You're crazy."

"Bring it up!" Jo said. "Now!" He raised the harpoon over his head threateningly, a gesture of defiance.

Paloma could feel, in her legs, movement in the water below. She looked down through her mask and saw that the manta was flexing its wings—not moving yet but about to. She felt a spasm of fear, for the manta could be about to come up on its own, and if it surfaced anywhere near Jo's boat—as sometimes they did out of playfulness or curiosity—Jo would surely plunge his harpoon into the animal. The manta would be dead before this day was done.

Quickly Paloma hyperventilated, and Jo, thinking she was obeying him, instructed Manolo to hold his legs and steady him so that when the giant rose to the surface his throw would be true.

Paloma dived to the manta. It had raised its wings, and she could see the motion begin that would drive the animal upward. She went directly to the horn on the right side, wrapping her arms around it and pressing down hard in an effort to make it change direction.

The animal stopped its rise and gently bent its head down and to the right, in perfect response to Paloma's hands. Together they began a graceful roll toward the bottom.

Paloma felt something sudden in the water, and she turned her head and saw Jo's harpoon hanging by its rope a foot from her head. Cast by the arm of one enraged, it had been driven six or eight feet into the water. Jo might easily have struck her with the harpoon.

The weapon hung for a second, then was retrieved.

Paloma released her grip on the horn. The manta eased out of its roll and leveled off at a depth of perhaps a dozen feet. Still moving away from the boats, it started to rise. Paloma would have to breathe soon, so she did not try to stop the manta's ascent. She had one hand on the manta's upper lip and one on a wing, and her legs and feet flew free as the manta banked and dipped and soared, changing direction on apparent whim but coming closer and closer to the surface. Paloma had no idea where she was, but she felt sure that the animal had changed course so many times that it must have traveled very far from the boats.

Then, as the surface swept closer and changed from a blue veil to the shimmering luster of wet glass, she saw the looming figure of Jo, standing in the bow of his boat, harpoon poised above his head.

She lurched forward, tried to grab a horn and drive the manta under again, but it was too late. The manta broke through the surface, not in a jump but like a turtle coming up for air. And it kept moving its wings just beneath the surface, carrying Paloma on its back, carrying her straight at the boats.

Looking over the hunch of the wing, Paloma saw Jo as he for the first time saw that Paloma was riding on the back of the beast. He let out a shriek of surprise and took a step backward, forgetting that his legs were gripped by Manolo. He started to fall, flung out his arms, let go the harpoon, and sprawled on his back in the boat.

The harpoon arced up into the air, askew, and Paloma saw it strike the water butt-first, before the manta once more dipped its horns, as Paloma took a breath and together they dived beneath the surface of the sea.

The manta was going deep, almost straight down. Ahead of its wings Paloma saw two streaks, and she realized that they were not shafts of sunlight but the lines that connected Jo's boat to the net. The manta passed between the lines and continued straight down, toward what Paloma could now see as a misty hump near the top of the seamount—the net itself, surrounding a clot of hundreds, thousands, of frantic fish.

If the manta did not turn, it would foul in the net and perhaps tangle Paloma in it as well. She tried to turn the manta, but it was flying hard and fast directly at the net.

It was in the last fraction of a second that Paloma suspected that the manta did see the net, did know what it was doing. From the immense ball of trapped animals the eyes of the desperate fish loomed vividly.

With a last thrust of its great wings the manta plunged forward into the net.

On the surface, in the boat, the fishermen stood ready for the manta to surface again. They searched for telltale bubbles or swirls. In the bow, Indio had his hand on the anchor line, prepared to pull the anchor up; in the stern, Manolo's hand was on the motor's starter cord. If they harpooned the manta, they would release their net and buoy it and leave it briefly.

Amidships, Jo held the harpoon high.

"She can't stay down this long."

"How do you know that?"

"Nobody can."

Jo was annoyed at the awe in their voices. "She has big lungs, that's all."

"And she rides the devilfish into the deep. That's all!"

Then they noticed that the anchor line was drawing taut, and that the lines connected to the deep net were stretched and throwing droplets of water as the rope trembled.

"Oh, God!" Jo shouted, the only coherent words he was able to utter, and then there were only screams and cries for help.

The manta had driven on, into the middle of the mass of fish, until Paloma was engulfed in jacks. They were under her arms, down her back, between her legs, flapping through her hair. They squirmed and gulped and shivered. The water roiled and clouded, and all she could see was fish.

In her brain, alarms began to sound, but there was no point trying to obey them. She knew she could never make it from here to the surface in time.

The manta flew on, pumping its massive wings up and down, its horns protruding through the net, its head pressing against it. The net held, and strained, and the manta slowed for a moment.

On the surface, the panicked fishermen felt their boat begin to move. The anchor and boat were being hauled through the water by the unseen creature that drove the net forward and down. And because the force was downward, the boat tipped and began to ship water; the fishermen didn't know what else to do but bail, frantically.

Then the net burst. The manta had simply overpowered it. It burst first in the center, and the fish squirted out the hole like grease from a tube. But the manta did not squirt out; it flew on and pulled the connecting lines even tighter until one line snapped. The net whipped free at one end, releasing the manta to start for the surface—with Paloma on its back—and destroying the equilibrium of pull, which was the only thing that had kept the boat steady above.

The change came suddenly, without prelude. The bow of the boat, from which the first line had snapped, jumped out of the water and spun. Indio, who had been kneeling on a thwart, found himself kneeling on air as the boat shot out from under him. Then he fell onto his back in the water and sank until his violent thrashing returned him to the surface.

Manolo had reached to steady himself on the motor, but the stern had sunk and the motor he reached for wasn't there. He pitched overboard and came up sputtering as the boat yawed away. Jo was alone in the boat, kneeling on knees bruised and bleeding, watching the sea with horrified eyes, wondering what next would erupt from the unknown below.

The manta flew for the surface, its wings pushing maelstroms that spun fish and blew sand and roiled water.

Paloma gripped lip and wing, but as the distant sunlight rushed toward her she knew she would not make it. All her alarms were in full cry—the pounding was thunderous in her head, the pain excruciating in her chest, her eyes seeing the light of safety as a pinpoint that expanded and contracted.

Air was only a few yards away, now a few feet, a split second in the flight time of the great animal rushing for the sun, when Paloma lost consciousness. All her muscles relaxed, including those in the fingers that held her grip on the manta ray, so she slid away as the broad plain of black back exploded from the water and launched itself high into the air.

It rose above the cringing Jo, higher and higher, until it blocked the sun and cast a black shadow on the boat. Water flew from it all around and caught the light and shone in a corona that lit the edges of the manta ray, and Jo knew he was being besieged by a creature from hell. His lips moved in prayer, and he threw his hands over his head to ward off doom.

The manta reached the height of its flight and for a moment hung in majesty against the brilliant sky. Then the heavier head and shoulders began to fall, leaving the tail where it was, and the giant embarked upon a graceful slow-motion backflip.

Jo saw it coming, and he screamed in fear of death and fell overboard. He splashed and sank, and even through several feet of water he could not block out the noise, the terminal, shattering crash as tons of cartilage and sinew came down upon the boat and disintegrated it.

The transom with the motor attached broke off and sank of its own weight. The rest of the hull, struck suddenly by such mighty force, splintered, fluttered into the sky, and rained down on Jo and on Paloma, who was still unconscious and floating on her back by her pirogue a dozen yards away.

The manta continued its roll down backward, beneath the surface, then righted itself and cruised slowly toward the sunlight again.

What woke Paloma was the lapping sound of the waves from the manta's splash against the wood of her pirogue. For a moment she didn't know where she was, and she grabbed her pirogue for safety. Before her and to the sides the sea was empty. Behind her, to the west, she heard sounds that could have been voices; perhaps they were sounds in her own addled brain.

Her feet touched bottom, a hard, slick rock ledge near the island, and though she wasn't sure how she had gotten there so fast she was glad to be home.

Bottom? She shook her head and looked at the pirogue and at the horizon and at the softly rolling sea swells. She was in at least ten, maybe twenty, fathoms of water. Then what was she standing on? She drained water from her mask and put her face down and saw the manta resting under her feet.

Did it want something? Was it injured again? Paloma took a breath and knelt on the manta's back, and very slowly it began to move. She stood, and the manta stopped. She knelt, and it started to move again; she stood, and again it stopped.

It's waiting for me, she thought. But that, she knew, was impossible; the animal didn't have such "higher" motives.

And yet she was impelled to respond, even if only to the appearance of a motive. She hyperventilated, dropped to her knees on the manta's back, and gripped with her hands.

This time the manta did not start slowly—it dived fast, shooting for the bottom. Within a few seconds the top of the seamount rose before Paloma. As the manta neared the upper rocks, it banked, like a fighter plane beginning a rollover dive, and aimed down the sheer side of the rock wall toward the blue mists.

Paloma's ears were popping, for she had never descended this fast or this far, and though she was nowhere near a crisis of oxygen, the new pressures in the strangely cold water made her pulse pound. She wanted to let go, but she didn't dare; she wasn't sure she could make it to the surface.

Down deep where there were no more reds or yellows or greens, where the blues looked indigo and the indigos violet and the violets black, the manta suddenly leveled out, banked sharply to the left, and entered a canyon in the wall of the seamount.

It slowed and stopped and hung above a sand bottom, its wings almost touching the rock sides of the canyon. Paloma looked up and could not see the surface—no sun, no shafts of light, just a vague lightening of the gray of the water—and panic shook her chest. She told herself not to look up again, for there was no point. She would either go up with the manta, or she would not go up at all.

What was this place? Below was sand, above was water, on the sides were walls of rock like any other, except . . . Something was strange about these rocks. They seemed to be studded with countless stones. She rose from the manta, praying that it would not suddenly decide to abandon her, and kicked quickly to one of the walls. She reached out to touch a stone, and before her fingertips had made contact she knew what these strange walls were made of. Each of the stones was an oyster.

At first they had been unrecognizable to her because they were larger than any she had ever seen—out of reach of all fishermen, they had been allowed to mature completely.

She reached immediately for her knife, but it was not there. She gripped an oyster with her hand and twisted and pulled until it came away. Her fingertips were scratched, her palm bleeding from little cuts, but she felt no pain. Using both hands now, she pulled the oysters free and stuffed them into her dress, dropping them down to her rope belt. When her front was full, she pushed the oysters around to her back, not feeling the shells slice her skin.

Finally she fell off the wall, exhausted and aching for breath. She landed on the manta's back. Had it been a horse, she would have spurred it on, for she needed to go now, and in but one direction—up.

And the manta took her up, flying with the swift grace of a bird seeking the sky. Soon she saw sunlight and blue crystal.

At the last second the manta slowed so it would not leap clear of the water, and, like a whale, it rolled through the surface and lay with its back in the air. And on its back lay Paloma, with her arms spread wide and blood running between her fingers.

The manta stayed with her until she had rested and swum to her pirogue and climbed aboard and emptied her dress of oysters. It stayed still as she knelt in the pirogue and watched it, silently, reverently.

And then, as the leading edge of the red sun touched the horizon, the great ray flipped a wing and dipped its head and kicked its tail in the air and was gone, leaving a ring of ripples that spread across the water and were soon gone, too.

For a long time, until the sun had sunk and the sky had darkened and the first stars were faintly seen, Paloma continued to kneel in the pirogue.

Far away in the night, she heard the voices of Jo and Indio and Manolo, and the words she could discern across the still water were contentious and accusing, for now they were safely floating and no longer feared for their lives. Later, she would get a motorboat and retrieve them. They would no longer want to return to the seamount.

The manta would not return, either. She felt certain of that, though she could not have said why she was so sure. Perhaps it was part of having the good thing. Perhaps it was a feeling that nature had needed to restore a balance that had been set askew, and to restore it had used the manta ray and, to an extent, had used Paloma as well. And now that the balance had been restored, the manta was released to fly free.

But what did she mean by nature? What was . . .

She stopped thinking, and she looked at the spot in the sky where soon the moon would rise and hang like an amulet and cast its golden path on the water, and she smiled and said aloud, "Thank you."

BEAST

CHAPTER ONE

IT HOVERED in the ink-dark water, waiting.

It was not a fish, had no air bladder to give it buoyancy, but because of the special chemistry of its flesh it did not sink into the abyss.

It was not a mammal, did not breathe air, so it felt no impulse to move to the surface. It hovered.

It was not asleep, for it did not know sleep. Sleep was not among its natural rhythms. It rested, nourishing itself with oxygen absorbed from the water it pumped through the caverns of its bullet-shaped body.

Its eight sinuous arms floated on the current; its two long tentacles were coiled tightly against its body. When it was threatened or in the frenzy of a kill, the tentacles would spring forward like tooth-studded whips.

It had but one enemy. All other creatures in its world were prey.

It had no sense of itself—of its great size or of the fact that its capacity for violence was unknown in other creatures of the deep.

It hung more than half a mile below the surface, far beyond the reach of any sunlight. Its enormous eyes registered only faint glimmers. Had it been observable to the human eye, the animal would have been seen as purplish maroon—but that was now, at rest. When aroused, it would change color again and again.

The only element of the sea that the animal's sensory system monitored constantly was temperature. It was most comfortable in a range between forty and fifty-five degrees Fahrenheit, and as it drifted with the currents and encountered thermoclines and upwellings that warmed or cooled the water, it moved up or down.

It sensed a change now. Its drift had brought it to the scarp of an extinct volcano, which rose like a needle from the ocean canyons. Cold water was driven upward around the mountain. And so, propelled by its tail fins, the beast rose slowly in the darkness.

Unlike many fish, it did not need community. It roamed the sea alone. It existed to survive. And to kill. For peculiarly in the world of living things, it often killed without need, as if nature, in a fit of perverse malevolence, had programmed it to that end.

From afar the boat might have been a grain of rice on a vast field of blue satin.

For days the wind had blown steadily from the southwest. Now it had faded, and the stillness was uncertain, as if the wind were trying to decide where to launch its next assault.

Howard Griffin sat in the cockpit, one bare foot resting on a spoke of the wheel. The boat, deprived of the driving force of the wind, rocked gently in the long swells.

Griffin glanced up at the flapping sails, then cursed himself for a fool. He hadn't anticipated a calm. He had plotted their course on the presumption of southerly winds. Stupid. They should have been well at sea by now. Instead, as Griffin turned and looked back at the fantail he could see the tall channel marker at the end of Bermuda's Eastern Blue Cut—a white speck in the lowering sun.

His wife came up through the hatch and handed him a cup of hot tea. He smiled his thanks, and as the thought suddenly came into his mind he said, "You look terrific."

Startled, Elizabeth smiled back. "You're not so bad yourself."

"I'm serious. Six months on a boat. I don't know how you do it." He looked at her legs, the color of oiled oak. She had not a stretch mark or a varicose vein to betray age or two children born more than fifteen years ago. He looked at her feet, brown and knobby and callused. He loved her feet.

"How am I ever going to wear shoes again?" she said. "Maybe I'll get a job at the Barefoot Bank and Trust Company."

"If we ever get there." He gestured at the luffing mainsail. Then he leaned forward to turn on the engine.

"Don't."

"You think I like it? The insurance man's gonna be at the dock Monday morning, and we better be there too."

"One second." She held up a hand. "Just let me check."

Griffin shrugged and sat back, and Elizabeth went below. He heard a burst of static as she adjusted the radio, then her voice. "Bermuda Harbor Radio, this is the yacht *Severance*."

"Yacht *Severance*, Bermuda Harbor Radio" came a voice from fifteen miles to the south. "Go to six eight and stand by."

"*Severance* going to six eight," Elizabeth said.

Griffin heard a little splash off the stern. He looked overboard and saw half a dozen gray chubs swarming on a patch of yellow sargasso weed, competing for tiny shrimps among the stalks. He liked sargasso weed. It spoke to him of life. It traveled on the water, pushed by the wind, bearing food for small animals, which became food for larger animals, and so on up the food chain.

"Yacht *Severance*, Bermuda Harbor Radio. Go ahead."

"Yes, Bermuda. We're sailing north for Connecticut. We'd like to get a weather forecast. Over."

"Right, *Severance*. Barometer three oh point four seven and steady. Wind southwest ten to fifteen, veering northwest. Tonight and tomorrow, winds northwest fifteen to twenty. Over."

"Many thanks, Bermuda." Elizabeth reappeared through the hatch and said, "This wasn't the way it was supposed to end."

"No." How they had envisioned their return was that they would ride a south wind all the way up the U.S. coast, and when they cleared Montauk Point, with Stonington harbor just ahead, they'd run up all the pennants and flags from all the countries and yacht clubs they'd visited in the last half year. When they reached Stonington, their kids would be waiting on the dock with Elizabeth's mother, and they'd have a bottle of champagne and then turn the boat over to the insurance broker for sale.

One chapter of their life would end, and the next would begin.

"There's still hope," Griffin said. "This time of year, a northwest wind doesn't last." He started the engine. The diesel sounded to him like a locomotive and smelled like midtown Manhattan.

Elizabeth said, "I hate that thing!" She went to haul in the jib.

"It's a machine," he called after her. "You can't hate a machine."

"I can so. I'm a terrific-looking person—you said so yourself. It's in the Constitution: terrific-looking people can hate whatever they want."

When Griffin saw that the jib was down, he pointed the bow into the breeze, which had begun to freshen. The boat's motion became uncomfortable now as it plowed into short, choppy seas. Elizabeth took down the mainsail and went below. To the west the sun was an orange ball slipping off the edge of the world.

The bow dipped under a wave, rose up and slapped the next wave hard. Spray flew aft like a chill rain. Griffin was about to call out to Elizabeth for his slicker when she reappeared, wearing her own slicker and carrying a cup of coffee.

"Let me take her for a while," she said. "You get some sleep." She slipped around the wheel into the seat beside him.

"Okay." He lifted one of her hands off the wheel and kissed it.

"What was that for?"

"Old sea custom. Always kiss the hand of your relief."

Below, he tucked himself into one of the two small bunks in the fo'c'sle. In port they slept together in the after cabin, but at sea it was better for whichever one was sleeping to sleep forward, to keep in touch with the motion of the boat, just in case.

The pillow smelled of Elizabeth. He slept.

THE ENGINE DRONED ON, DRIVING the boat north into the night. A pump drew seawater through a fitting in the hull, passed it through the engine, cooling it, and flushed it aft with the exhaust.

The engine was not old—had less than seven hundred hours on it when they bought the boat—and Griffin had nursed it like a cherished child. But the exhaust pipe was harder to tend. It exited beside the propeller shaft, under the floor of the after cabin. It was of good steel, but it had carried tons of salt water and gases. And when the engine was not running, salt and chemicals had lain in the pipe and begun gradually to eat away at the steel.

The minuscule hole in the exhaust pipe could have been there for weeks. They had had fair winds all the way up from the Bahamas and had used the engine only to power in and out of St. George's harbor. But now, with the engine running and the boat punching into the sea rather than sailing gently with it, the hole was growing. Bits of rusted metal flaked away from its edges, and before long the pipe buckled and tore, and then all the water from the cooling pump poured into the bilges. And when the boat's stern dipped and the exhaust outlet submerged, the sea rushed in.

ELIZABETH steered with her feet and leaned back against the cushions in the cockpit. To her right a crescent moon was rising, casting a streak of gold that tracked her on the surface of the sea.

No souls, she thought as she looked at the moon. It was an Arab idea in *The Discoverers,* one of a score of books she had devoured in these past six months. The new moon was an empty celestial vessel collecting the souls of the departed; and as the month passed, it swelled until, engorged with souls, it disappeared to deposit its cargo in heaven, then reappeared empty and began again.

She liked this idea because she was beginning to think she understood what a soul was. She was not a profound person. She and Griffin had always been too busy living to pause and reflect.

He had been on the fast track at Shearson Lehman Brothers; she, at Chemical Bank. The '80s were a time when they gathered toys: a million-dollar apartment in New York City, a half-million-dollar house in Stonington. The money came in; the money went out—twenty thousand dollars for private school, twenty thousand for vacations, fifty thousand for maintenance.

And then one day Griffin was laid off. A week later Elizabeth was given a choice: half time at half salary or quit.

Griffin's settlement would have allowed them to live for a year while he looked for another job. The other option was to take their severance money, buy a boat and see if there was more to the world than *confit de canard* and designer fizzy water.

They kept the house in Stonington, sold the apartment and put the proceeds in a trust to fund the children's education.

They were free, and with freedom came excitement and fear and discovery—discovery about themselves, about each other, about what was important and what was dispensable.

It could have been a disaster—confined twenty-four hours a day to a space forty feet by twelve—and for the first couple of weeks they got in each other's way and carped about this and that.

But then they became competent, and with competence came self-assurance and appreciation for one another. They fell in love again and, just as important, came to like themselves again.

They had no idea what they would do when they got home. But it didn't matter. Whatever they found would be better than what had been before, for they were new people. It had been a wonderful trip, with not a single regret. Well, except that they had had to turn on the engine.

Elizabeth was sleepy. She looked at her watch. Perhaps she should wake Griffin. No. Let him have another half hour.

A wave lapped over the stern of the boat and soaked her.

No problem. The water wasn't cold. It would—

A *wave?* How does a wave come over the stern of a boat when you're heading into the sea? She turned and looked. The stern was four inches from being awash. It dipped again, and more water rushed aboard.

Adrenaline shot up her back and down her arms. She reached forward of the wheel and switched on the electric bilge pump. Something was wrong. It sounded distant, faint and laboring.

"Howard!" she shouted. No answer.

She secured the wheel with a length of bungee cord and went down through the hatch. A stench of exhaust fumes choked her and burned her eyes. It was coming up through the floor.

"Howard!" She looked into the lighted after cabin. Six inches of water covered the carpet.

Griffin was in a dark dream when he heard his name called from what seemed a great distance. He willed himself awake, sensing that something was wrong with him. His head hurt, his mouth tasted foul, he felt drugged.

"What is it?" He sat up and looked aft through a bluish haze and saw Elizabeth running toward him, shouting something.

"We're sinking!" she was saying.

"Come on." He blinked, shook his head. Now he could smell the exhaust, recognize the taste.

Elizabeth peeled back the carpet in the main cabin and lifted the hatch covering the engine compartment. In seconds Griffin was standing over her. They saw that the engine was half underwater. The batteries were still dry, but the water was rising.

Griffin heard sloshing in the after cabin and knew what had happened. He said, "Shut down the engine."

Elizabeth found the lever and choked off the engine. The rumbling died and with it the circulating pump. No new water was being forced aboard, and they could hear the comforting whine of the bilge pump.

But there was still an open wound in the stern. Griffin grabbed two dish towels from the sink and handed them to Elizabeth. "Stick these up the exhaust pipe. Tight. Tight as you can."

She ran up through the hatch.

Griffin knelt on the deck and adjusted a wrench to one of the bolts holding the batteries to their mounts. If he could raise the batteries out of the engine compartment, he could give the bilge pump time to stop the water from rising. He had meant to move the batteries, but that would have involved dealing with island labor, which would have delayed them.

Delayed them from what?

He cursed and heaved against the first bolt. It was corroded, and the wrench skidded off.

With its way gone, the boat slewed broadside to the sea and fell into a rhythm of steep, jerky rolls. A cupboard door flew open, and a stack of plates crashed to the deck.

He tightened the wrench and leaned on the handle. The bolt moved. He managed half a turn, then yanked the wrench off, refitted it and turned again. The water rose.

In the cockpit, Elizabeth lay in the dark, face down on the fantail, spread-legged, her feet braced against the roll. One of the dish towels was balled in her fist. She reached for the exhaust outlet with her fingertips and tried to jam the towel inside. The pipe was too big. The towel slipped out and floated away.

She heard a new sound. Silence. The bilge pump had stopped.

Then she heard Griffin's voice below. "Bermuda Harbor Radio, this is the yacht *Severance*. Mayday, Mayday, Mayday—"

The boat yawed. Water rushed over the stern, and Elizabeth skidded. Her feet lost their grip. She was falling.

A hand grabbed her and pulled her back, and Griffin's voice said, "Never mind."

"Never *mind?* We're sinking!"

"Not anymore." His voice was flat. "We've sunk."

"No. I don't—"

"Hey," he said, and he gathered her to him. "The batteries are gone. The pump's gone. The radio's gone. We've got to get off before she slips away. Okay?"

She looked up at him and nodded.

"Good." He kissed her head. "Get the EPIRB."

Griffin went forward and uncovered the raft, lashed to the cabin roof. He checked to make sure all its cells were inflated and checked the rubberized box, screwed to the deck plates, containing flares and fishing lines and cans of food. Then he set a five-gallon plastic jug of fresh water in the raft.

Elizabeth came forward. She carried the EPIRB—the emergency position-indicating radio beacon—a red box covered in yellow Styrofoam, with a retractable antenna on one end.

The deck was awash now, and it was easy for them to heave the big raft into the sea. When Elizabeth was seated in the bow of the raft, Griffin stepped off the deck and dropped into the stern. He flicked on the EPIRB, pulled out the antenna and fitted the device into an elastic strap on one of the inflated rubber cells of the raft.

Because the raft was light and the northwest wind was brisk, it moved quickly away from the crippled sailboat.

Griffin took Elizabeth's hand, and they watched in silence.

The sailboat was a black silhouette against the stars. The stern sank lower, then slowly disappeared. Then suddenly the bow rose up and slipped backward down into the abyss. Enormous bubbles rushed to the surface and burst with muffled booms.

Griffin said, "Lord help us."

IT WAS alert, had been for several moments. Something large was approaching from above, from where its enemy always came. It could feel vast quantities of water being displaced.

It prepared to defend itself. Chemical triggers fired, sending fuel throughout the great body. Chromatophores ignited, and its color changed from maroon to a lighter, brighter red—a red designed by nature purely for intimidation.

It withdrew and cocked its two long whiplike tentacles, then turned in the direction of its enemy. It was not capable of fear; it did not consider flight.

But it was confused, for its enemy's signals were unusual. There was no acceleration, no aggression; there were none of the normal sounds of its enemy echolocating, no clicks or pings.

Whatever was coming, it passed without pause and continued into the deep, trailing strange creaks and pops. Dead sounds.

The creature's color changed back again, and its arms uncocked. Random drift had brought it to within a hundred feet of the surface, and its eyes gathered flickering shimmers of silver from the stars. Because light could signal prey, it allowed itself to rise toward the source.

When it was close to the surface, it sensed something new—a disturbance floating with the current, on the water but not part of it.

Two impulses drove the creature now—the impulse to kill and the impulse to feed. Hunger dominated. Once, hunger had been a simple cue, and it had responded routinely, feeding at will. But now food was a quest, for prey had become scarce.

Again the animal was alert—not to defend itself, but to attack.

THEY had not spoken.

Griffin had fired a flare, and they had watched the burst of orange brilliance against the black sky. A few bits of flotsam had drifted by the spot where the boat had been, but now there was no sign that it had ever existed.

Elizabeth reached for Griffin's hand. "What are you thinking?"

"I was doing the old 'if only' routine. You know. If only I hadn't been too lazy to check that pipe—"

"Don't do this, Howard. It wasn't anybody's fault."

"I suppose."

Elizabeth was about to say something when the raft dipped off the top of a wave and slid into a trough. She screamed. Then the raft evened out and bobbed gently up the next wave.

"Hey," Griffin said, and he edged over to her and put his arm around her shoulders. "It's okay. We're fine."

"No," she said into his chest. "We're not fine."

"Okay, we're not fine. What are you scared of?"

"What am I scared of?" she snapped. "We're in the middle of the ocean at night in a raft the size of a bottle cap, and you ask what am I scared of? How about *dying*?"

"Dying from what?"

"For heaven's sake, Howard. I don't want to talk about it."

"I'm serious. Come on, let's talk about it. Let's bring the demons out and crush them."

"Okay." She took a breath. "Sharks. I'm terrified of sharks."

"Sharks. Okay. We can forget about sharks. The water's too cold. And if one does come, as long as we stay in the raft we don't look or smell like anything he's used to eating. What else?"

"Suppose a storm—"

"Okay. Weather. Not a problem. The forecast is good. Even if a northeaster does come up, this raft is unsinkable. Worst can happen, it tips over. If it does, we right it again."

"And float around till we starve to death."

"Not gonna happen." Griffin found that the more he talked, the more he was able to push his own fears away. "One, the wind is pushing us back toward Bermuda. Two, there are ships in and out of here every day. Three, worst case: by Monday afternoon the kids and What's-his-name the insurance broker will report us missing, and Bermuda Harbor Radio knows all about us. But it won't get to that. This baby is beeping its heart out for us." He patted the EPIRB. "First plane that goes over will call out the cavalry."

Elizabeth was silent a moment, then said, "You believe all that?"

"Sure I believe all that."

"And you're not scared."

He hugged her and said, "Sure I am. But if you don't do something with fear—talk it away—it eats you up."

She put her head down into his chest. She smelled salt and sweat and comfort. She smelled seventeen years of her life. They stayed like that, huddled together, as the raft drifted slowly south.

Suddenly Elizabeth started. She sat up and turned toward the bow. "What was that scraping noise?"

"I didn't hear anything."

She crawled forward and touched the forwardmost cell of the raft. "Right here. Like fingernails scraping on the rubber."

"It could've been a flying fish."

"What's that smell?"

"What smell?" Griffin took a deep breath, and now he smelled it. "Ammonia?"

"That's what I thought."

"Something from the boat. Maybe something's spilled in here." He knelt toward the stern of the raft and unzipped the lid of the rubberized box. It was too dark to see, so he bent over to smell it.

He heard a noise like a grunt, and the raft lurched to one side. Then he heard some vague splashing sounds. "Hey!" He steadied himself. "Careful there."

There was no alien odor in the box. He zipped it closed. "Nothing." But the smell of ammonia was stronger now. He turned back to face the bow. "I don't know what—"

Elizabeth was gone. Just . . . gone.

He had a split second's sensation that he was hallucinating. He called out, "Elizabeth!" The word was swallowed by the breeze. He called again.

He sat back and took a deep breath and closed his eyes. After a moment he opened them, expecting to see her sitting in the bow and eyeing him quizzically.

He was still alone.

He got to his knees and hobbled around the entire raft, hoping—imagining—that she had fallen overboard and was clinging to a dangling loop of lifeline.

No.

He sat back again. Okay, he thought. Okay. Let's look at this rationally. What are the possibilities? She jumped overboard. She suddenly went out of her mind and decided to swim to shore. His pulse was thundering in his ears now. Or . . . Or what? She was kidnapped by terrorists from the Andromeda galaxy? He screamed her name over and over.

He heard a scraping noise, felt something touch the rubber beneath him. She was under the raft! She must have fallen over and gotten tangled in something, and now she was under the raft.

He leaned aft over the side and stretched his arms way under, feeling for her hair, her foot, her slicker—anything.

He heard the scraping noise again. He withdrew his arms and looked forward. In the yellow-gray moonlight he saw something move on the front of the rubber raft. It seemed to be clawing its way up the rubber, scrambling to come aboard.

A hand. It had to be a hand. She had freed herself from the tangle and now was struggling to climb aboard.

He flung himself forward and reached out, and when his fingers were an inch or two away from it—so close he could feel its radiant coolness—he realized that it wasn't human. It was slimy and undulant, an alien thing that moved toward him, reaching for him.

He recoiled and scrambled toward the stern. Then he watched, horrified, as the thing inched upward, until finally it was atop the rubber cell. It straightened up, fanned out, looking like a giant cobra. Its surface was crowded with circles, each quivering with a life of its own and dripping water like ghastly spittle.

Griffin screamed, a visceral shriek of terror, outrage, disbelief.

But the thing kept moving forward, always forward, slithering, it seemed, on its writhing circles; and as each circle touched the rubber it made a rasping sound, as if it contained claws. The thing came as if it knew that what it was searching for was there.

Griffin's eyes fell on the oar, tucked under the starboard cells. He grabbed it and raised it above his head, waiting as the thing came closer. And when he judged that the moment had come, he shouted, "Get away!" and slammed the oar down on it.

He was never to know whether the oar struck the thing or whether, somehow, the thing had anticipated it. All he knew was that the oar was torn from his hands and cast away into the sea.

Griffin stumbled backward, fell into the stern. He pushed himself back and back, desperate. He was mewling a litany of "Oh, God. . . . Oh, no. . . . Oh, God. . . . Oh, no."

The thing hovered over him, sensing exactly where he was, twitching, and spraying him with drops of water. Each of its circles twisted and contorted itself as if in hungry competition with its neighbors, and in the center of each was a curved hook that, as it reflected rays of moonlight, resembled a golden scimitar.

That was the last Griffin knew, save for pain.

CHAPTER TWO

Whip Darling took his cup of coffee out on the veranda, to have a look at the day. The wind had gone around during the night. The boats anchored in the bay were now facing northwest.

The sun was about to come up; the last of the stars had faded. Soon the wind would make up its mind what it was going to do.

Then he'd make up his mind too. He should put to sea, try to raise something worth a few dollars. On the other hand, there was always work to do ashore on the boat, like chipping paint.

He saw a splash in the bay, then another, and heard a fluttering sound: baitfish, a school of fry running for their lives and skittering over the glassy surface. Mackerel, he decided, from the vigor of the swirls and the relentlessness of the chase.

He loved this time of day before the din of traffic began across in Somerset. It was a time of peace and promise, when he could gaze at the water and let his memory dwell on what had been.

The screen door swung open behind him, and his wife, Charlotte—barefoot and wearing a summer cotton nightgown— came out with her cup of tea and, as she did every morning, stood beside him so close that he could smell the spice of sleep in her hair. He put an arm around her shoulder.

"Mackerel in the bay," he said.

"Good. First time in . . . what, six weeks? You going out?"

"I expect so. Chasing rainbows is more entertaining than chipping paint. Anyway, it's time to retrieve the aquarium's traps."

He finished his coffee, and as he turned to go inside he looked at the whitewashed house with its dark blue shutters—their paint flaking, slats cracked and sagging.

"Lord, this house is a mess."

"They want two hundred apiece to do the shutters," said Charlotte. "Three thousand for the lot."

"Thieves," he said, and he held the door for her.

"I suppose we could ask Dana." She paused.

"She's done enough, Charlie. Things aren't that bad."

"Maybe not yet, William." She went in. "But almost."

" 'William' now, is it?" he said. "It's pretty early in the day for your heavy artillery."

William Somers Darling was named after the Somers who settled Bermuda by shipwreck in 1609. Sir George Somers had been on his way to Virginia when his *Sea Venture* struck Bermuda, which Darling regarded as a triumph of seamanship, since to hit Bermuda in the millions of square miles of the Atlantic Ocean was akin to tripping over a paper clip on a football field. Still, Somers wasn't the first or the last: the twenty-two square miles of Bermuda were ringed by more than three hundred shipwrecks.

Most Bermudians, black and white, were named after the early settlers—Somers, Darling, Trimingham and a dozen more. And yet, as if in rebellion against mother-country pretension, most Bermudians soon cast off one of their names and assumed a nickname. Darling's was Buggywhip, in commemoration of the weapon with which his father had regularly thrashed him.

His friends called him Whip, and so did Charlotte, except when they argued. Then she called him William.

He was a fisherman, or rather, he had been; now he was an ex-fisherman, for being a fisherman in Bermuda had become about as practical as being a skiing instructor in the Congo. It was hard to make a living catching something that wasn't there.

They could live comfortably on twenty thousand dollars a year. They owned the house—it had been in his family, free and clear, since before the American Revolution. Upkeep cost five thousand dollars a year. Boat maintenance, which he and his mate, Mike Newstead, did themselves, cost another six thousand dollars. Food and clothing and other incidentals consumed the rest.

But twenty thousand dollars might as well have been a million, because he wasn't making it.

His daughter, Dana, was working downtown in an accounting firm, making good money instead of going to college, and she had tried to help. Darling had refused, more brusquely than he meant to, but unable to articulate the confusion of love and shame that his child's offer had triggered in him.

For a while Dana had succeeded in stealing some of their bills from their mailbox and paying them herself. When, inevitably, she had been discovered, she had advanced the defense that since the house was going to be hers one day, she saw no reason why she shouldn't contribute to its maintenance. The argument had slipped away from reason into dark regions of trust and mistrust and had ended in hurt and anger.

Maybe Charlotte was right. Maybe things *were* that bad. Darling had seen a folder from the bank in a pile of mail on the kitchen table, but before he could ask about it, it had vanished, and he had put it out of his mind. But now he forced himself to wonder: Was she already talking about mortgages or loans?

No. He wouldn't let it happen. There had to be ways. There was the aquarium retainer, which paid his fuel costs in exchange for exotic animals he fished up from the deep. And there was always the chance—about as long as winning the Irish sweepstakes, but a chance—that he'd find a shipwreck with some goodies on it.

In the kitchen Darling warmed up some of last night's barracuda. There was a barometer on the wall, and he consulted it. It was a tube of shark-liver oil. In good weather the oil was clear, a light amber color. In times of change, the oil clouded. He had faith in the shark-oil barometer, for it wasn't a machine, and he distrusted machines. Machines were made by man, and man was a chronic screwup. Nature rarely made mistakes.

The oil was clear.

He decided to go to sea. Maybe there was a robust grouper out there waiting to be caught, a wanderer from times gone by. A hundred-pound fish could net him four or five hundred dollars. Maybe he'd run into a school of tuna.

DARLING's mate showed up a little after seven. Darling liked to joke that Mike Newstead was the ultimate Bermudian, for he contained every ethnic strain ever represented in the colony. He had the short, curly hair of a black, the dark red skin of an Indian—a memento of eighteenth-century Tories bringing Mohawk Indians to the island as slaves—the bright blue eyes of an Englishman and the taciturn resignation of a Portuguese. He was thirty-six, five years younger than Darling, but he looked anything from thirty to fifty.

Mike stood six feet four and weighed over two hundred and twenty pounds, not a gram of which was fat. Though he was slow to anger, he possessed an explosive temper kept in check by his diminutive Portuguese wife and by Darling, whom he loved.

Darling considered him the perfect mate. Mike didn't like to make decisions, but preferred to be told what to do. He didn't talk much, but communicated intimately and joyfully with Darling's most hated enemies—machines. Utterly unschooled, Mike seemed to be able to seduce them into doing what he wanted.

Darling poured Mike some coffee, and they went outside.

"I guess it's time to pull the aquarium's traps," Darling said. "Might take along some bait, just in case."

Mike nodded, finished his coffee and went to the freezer in the toolshed to fetch some mackerel for bait.

Darling boarded the boat and started the big Cummings diesel and let it warm up. The *Privateer* was a shrimp dragger he had bought in Louisiana and had converted to an all-purpose Bermuda workboat. She was big and broad and strong, steel-plated and steel-decked. She had a dry and roomy house, two compressors, two generators and racks for twenty scuba tanks.

She'll knock you down, Whip would say, but she'll never drown you.

Mike hopped aboard and cast off. Darling eased the boat out of Mangrove Bay and around the point to Blue Cut.

Settling onto a hatch cover in the stern, Mike muttered at a recalcitrant pump motor as he cradled it in his lap.

Darling had set the aquarium's traps to the northwest, about six miles offshore in five hundred fathoms of water. Standing on the flying bridge, cooled by the northwest breeze and warmed by the young sun, he felt himself a happy man. He could forget that he didn't have any money, and could fantasize about silver coins and chains of gold. Sure it was fantasy, but it had been known to happen. Always his eyes searched for the signs of a shipwreck.

Bermuda had always been a ship trap, and it still was, even with modern miracles like loran and satellite navigation, because of its extinct volcano, which protruded from the bottom of the sea and was full of electromagnetic anomalies. Machines seized up and went berserk around Bermuda. Compasses reeled back and forth like drunks. The whims of the volcano had helped spawn all the legends of the Bermuda Triangle—from Atlantis to UFOs.

Darling didn't object to people indulging in nonsense about the Bermuda Triangle, but it seemed to him a waste of time. If people would make an effort to learn about the wonders that *did* exist, he thought, their appetite for dragons would be well satisfied. Even he, a nobody in a tiny corner of nowhere, had in his twenty-five years on the ocean seen enough dragons to fuel the nightmares of the entire human race: thirty-foot sharks that lived in the mud, crabs as big as motorcars, finless fish with heads like horses, viper eels that ate anything, fish with little lanterns that hung down off their eyebrows, and so on.

These days the Bermuda ship trap snared one or two victims every few years, but in the old days the reefs were capturing so many ships that an industry arose of people who made their living rowing out and salvaging stricken ships. Some, not content to wait, would wave phony lights to lure ships onto the reefs.

Today Darling saw no signs of shipwreck in the shallow water, but what he did see—for it was all he saw—drew the happiness out of him like a syringe pulling blood: one parrot fish, half a dozen flying fish and a few meandering breams.

Reefs that had once teemed with life were as empty as a train station after a bomb scare. He felt as if he were witnessing a funeral for a way of life—his way of life.

Soon the shallows sloped away to forty feet, sixty feet, a hundred feet, and he stopped looking at the bottom and began to search for the buoy marking the lines for his aquarium traps.

It was where he had left it.

"Coming up on it," Darling called down to Mike, who put his pump motor aside and reached for the boat hook.

The orange-and-white buoy slid alongside. Mike snagged it and pulled it aboard and wrapped the rope around the winch.

Darling put the boat in neutral, and came down from the flying bridge. He pushed the lever that turned on the winch, and as the rope began to come up, Mike fed it into a plastic drum.

They had put down three thousand feet of polyethylene rope, with the buoy on top and sash weights to keep the rope on the bottom. Starting at two thousand feet, they had attached, at every hundred-foot interval, a twenty-foot length of stainless steel airplane cable. At the end of each cable was one of the aquarium's gimmicks. Some were small wire boxes, some were contraptions of fine-mesh net. Most had bits of gurry inside to attract whatever creatures lived down in the dark.

Darling's hope was to bring the animals up and keep them alive in a cold-water tank on the boat. Every week or so a scientist from the aquarium would come to examine them, and the rare or unknown creatures he would take back to study in the laboratory.

Darling held the winch lever and kept his eye on the rope. He put his foot on the bulwark to steady himself against the boat's wallow and looked over the side, down into the blue gloom.

"Something's not right," Mike said. He had a hand on the rope.

"She's stuttery. Feel." Mike passed the rope to Darling and stepped back to take the lever from him.

Darling felt the rope. It was trembling erratically. There was a thud to it, like an engine misfiring.

Darling told Mike to slow the winch, and bent over the side to see the first trap come into view. He saw the glint of the first swivel holding the length of cable, saw the cable, and then . . . nothing. The trap was gone.

Impossible. The only animal large enough to take it was a shark, but there was no way a shark could have broken the cable.

He let the winch bring the cable up to him, and he unsnapped it from the rope and looked at the end. Then he held it up to Mike.

"Busted?" Mike asked.

"No. If she'd popped, the strands'd be all frizzy. Look. These strands are still as tight as in the factory." The cable had been sheared off, cut clean, as if by a scalpel. There were no gnaw marks, no worry marks.

"Bit," Darling said. "Bit clean through." He looked out over the water. "What has a mouth that can bite through steel?"

Mike said nothing. Darling gestured for him to start the winch again, and in a moment the second cable came up.

"Gone," he said, for that trap had vanished too, that cable bitten through.

"Gone," he said again as the next cable appeared, and the next and the next. They were all gone.

Now he saw the sash weights coming. He told Mike to stop the winch, and he pulled the last of the rope up by hand.

"I don't believe it," he said. "Look here."

One of the traps had been wrapped so hard around the weights, it was as if everything had been melted together in a furnace. They pulled the gnarled mass up and set it on the deck; it was a confusion of steel reinforcing rod, wire and lead.

Mike stared at it, then said, "What kind of thing do that?"

"No man, for sure," said Darling. "No animal, neither. At least, no animal I've ever seen."

THEY DIDN'T SPEAK AS THEY disassembled the rig, coiling the lengths of cable and jamming the final fathoms of rope into the drum. Darling was running through all the creatures in his head, trying to think of what might have destroyed that rig. Could it have been a man—some fisherman who was angry, resentful, jealous? No, he didn't think that any man could do it, and he was certain that nobody'd bother. There was no logic to it.

So what did that leave? What could have bitten through a cable woven of forty-eight strands of stainless steel?

Part of him hoped that they'd never know.

Mike, however, was not happy with the unknown. He didn't mind so much not having answers himself, but he didn't like it when Whip didn't have them. He preferred the security of knowing that somebody was in charge.

So now he was worried. Darling saw the signs and knew he would have to ease the man's misery.

"I take it back," he said. "I think it was a shark."

"What makes you think so?" Mike asked, wanting to believe.

"Had to be. I just remembered, *National Geographic* says some sharks can put out twenty tons per square inch when they bite. That'd be more than enough to cut those cables."

Mike thought for a moment, then said, "Oh."

Darling felt an odd desire to quit and go home. But it wasn't yet noon, and he'd already burned up thirty dollars' worth of fuel. If they went home now, he'd be out fifty bucks for nothing. And so he forced himself to say, "What say we try for a day's pay?"

Mike said, "Good enough," and together they began to rig a deep line with some big baited hooks.

Maybe they'd catch something worth selling, maybe just something worth eating. Even if they just caught *some*thing, it would be better than heading back to the dock and acknowledging another day's defeat.

Darling wasn't one to indulge in weepy bushwa about the good old days. He saw change and destruction as inevitable. But what did infuriate him, what shamed and disgusted him, was the change he had seen in Bermuda in only twenty years. By his reckoning, Bermuda had been ruined in the lifetime of a house cat.

In the late '60s and early '70s Darling could still go out on the reefs and catch his dinner. There were lobsters under every rock, schools of parrot fish, angelfish, surgeonfish, porgies. When he worked on a shipwreck, goatfish dug in the sand beside him, rays skittered by and, more than once, reef sharks had chased him off.

Just over the edge, in deeper water, were whole colonies of groupers. There were moray eels and hinds and snappers. And in the deep, wahoo fought with barracudas for the bait. Bonitos and Alison tuna swarmed around the back of the boat. A good day was a thousand pounds of tuna, and the hotels took pride in listing their daily special as fresh Bermuda fish.

No more. Some of the hotels still listed Bermuda fish, but not with pride, for all that was left was trash—the fish that had survived because nothing wanted them.

Darling listened with bitter amusement to the explanations of the fishermen. Pollution! they cried; and to that he replied, Bull.

What had killed Bermuda's fishing industry was fishermen. Fishermen who weren't content with making a living and wanted to make a killing, treating the ocean as if it were a pit to be strip-mined. And the chief villain was a piece of equipment they had invented: the fish trap.

In times past, fishermen had *fished*—with handlines—and what limited their catch was their grit. They stopped when they fell down in a stupor. Then someone thought of putting down wire cages with bait inside and buoys to the surface. The fish would swim in and, thanks to the construction of the traps, not be able to find their way out again.

Soon everybody was putting traps down, as many as they wanted. There was supposed to be a limit, but nobody paid any attention to it. And did they catch fish! So many fish that they threw away all but the best—dead or dying, but who cared?

Darling had never used traps, didn't like them, because to him trapping wasn't fishing. He thought, If you can't enjoy what you do for a living, then find something else.

The first problem with the traps was that they caught everything—big, small, young, old, pregnant, whatever. A handline fisherman could pick and choose among his catch, but with traps, by the time the fish had been jammed together in the wire for a few days, they had little chance of surviving even if the fishermen put them back—which most of them didn't.

The second problem was lost traps. If the buoy broke away or the rope chafed off, so that the trap sank beyond reach, it would keep on killing. The fish inside would die and become bait for more fish, which would come in and be trapped and die and become bait for more fish, forever and ever.

Darling had found lost traps on the bottom that looked like a jam-packed Tokyo subway car at rush hour. The sight saddened and enraged him. More than once, he had lost time and money diving down to deep traps and cutting away the doors with wire snips. The perplexed and exhausted prisoners would meander within the now open trap for several moments, as if unable to believe their sudden good fortune. Only when he moved away would they seem to share some silent cue and burst free.

Finally, in 1990, the Bermuda government outlawed trap fishing. Now the hope was that the fish would come back, but Darling had his doubts. Bermuda was not like the Bahamas, a chain of islands that had a chance to replenish each other if one or another was fished out. Bermuda was a single rock in the middle of nowhere. What was there was there; and what wasn't, never would be again.

Fishing had once given Darling a feeling of vitality, an appreciation of and wonder at the richness and diversity of life. Now all it made him think of was death.

It took them an hour to bait and set their deep line. When it was down, Darling snapped a rubber buoy onto the end of a line and tossed it overboard, letting it drift with the tide.

Mike sat aft on the hatch cover and tinkered some more with the pump motor. Darling went into the wheelhouse to listen to the radio to hear if anyone was catching anything. No one had seen a thing.

The sun had just begun to slide westward when they pulled in the line. They exchanged hopeful guesses.

"Coupla coneys."

"I say snappers."

The eight hooks had caught two small red snappers. Darling tossed them into the bait box and looked at the sea. Not a fin, not a feeding bird. Nothing. "Well then, forget it," he said.

He was about to step forward to start the engine when Mike said, "Look there." He was pointing to the southern sky.

A navy helicopter was heading their way from the south.

"Wonder where he's going," Darling said.

"Nowhere. They never do. Just loggin' time."

But this pilot wasn't idling; he was heading north with speed on.

"I don't know," Darling said. "Unless he's late for supper up in Nova Scotia, I'd say he's on a mission with some clout to it." He turned into the wheelhouse and picked up the radio microphone.

"Huey One, Huey One, this is *Privateer*. Come back."

CHAPTER THREE

LIEUTENANT Marcus Sharp had been shooting baskets that Friday when the operations officer called him inside and said that a British Airways pilot on his way to Miami had picked up an emergency signal twenty miles north of Bermuda.

The pilot hadn't seen anything, of course, the ops officer said, but the signal had been loud and clear. Someone was in trouble.

Sharp had quickly showered and pulled on his flight suit, while the operations officer had rounded up a copilot and a rescue diver and made sure one of the helicopters was gassed up. Then Sharp had scribbled down the coordinates reported in by the British Airways pilot, and trotted out to the waiting chopper.

As they had lifted off, for the first time in weeks Marcus Sharp felt alive. Something was happening—not much, but anything was better than the nothing that had become his routine.

Sharp's problem wasn't only that he was bored. It was worse than boredom. He had a weird, amorphous sense that he was dying—not physically, but in other, less tangible ways. He had always needed adventure, courted danger, thrived on change. And, until lately, life had always provided nourishment enough.

The navy recruiter at Michigan State had recognized the need in Sharp for action. He persuaded Marcus that the navy offered him a chance to spend his career doing what others could do only on occasional vacations. He could "stretch his envelope" on the sea and in the sky, and in the process contribute to the nation's defense.

The first few years met all his expectations. He became expert in underwater demolition. He qualified as a helicopter pilot. He served a stint of sea duty and saw combat, in Panama. He studied meteorology and oceanography. Life was rich, varied and fun.

But in the past year and a half, variety and fun had ceased to satisfy. And at the core of his discontent lay the only thing close to tragedy that the twenty-nine-year-old Sharp had ever known.

He had fallen in love with a flight attendant—a skier and scuba diver—and they had been all over the world together. They were young and immortal. Marriage was a possibility, but not a necessity. They lived in and for the present.

And then one day in 1989 they were snorkeling in northern Queensland. They had heard routine warnings about dangerous animals, but they hadn't worried. They had been swimming with sharks and barracudas before; they could take care of themselves.

They had seen a turtle swimming by, and they had followed it. The turtle had slowed and opened its mouth as if to eat something, though they saw nothing, and they glided up to it, entranced by its grace and efficiency in the water.

Karen had reached out to touch it, and she suddenly convulsed and clawed at her breast. Her snorkel slipped from her mouth. Her eyes went wide, and she screamed, tearing at her flesh.

Sharp grabbed her and pulled her to the surface and tried to get her to speak, but all she could do was shriek.

By the time he got her to shore, she was dead.

The turtle had been feeding on sea wasps—box jellyfish all but invisible in the water and so toxic that a brush with them could stop a human heart. And so it had.

When Karen had been buried in Indiana, and Sharp's grief had begun to scar over, he had found himself possessed by darker thoughts. He became plagued by the emptiness of his life.

The navy had given him the best billet available, a two-year tour in Bermuda—sunny, comfortable, undemanding. Quiet, however, was not what Sharp needed. He needed action, but now action alone wasn't enough. There had to be a purpose to it.

From time to time he thought of quitting the navy, but he had no idea what he would do. Meanwhile, he volunteered for any task that would keep his mind off himself.

HE WAS heading northwest now at five hundred feet, intending to set a search pattern up along the north side of the island.

Six miles offshore, where the reefs ended and the water changed from dappled turquoise to deep cerulean, he heard a beep—faint but persistent. Sharp scanned his instruments, turning the helicopter slowly until he found the direction in which the beeping was loudest. He took a compass bearing.

Then a voice came over his marine radio. "Huey One, Huey One, this is *Privateer*. Come back."

"*Privateer*, Huey One." Sharp smiled. "Hey, Whip, where you at?"

Whip recognized the voice; Marcus Sharp was a friend. "Right underneath you, lad. Going for an outing?"

"B.A. pilot picked up an EPIRB signal a while ago. You hear it?"

"Not a peep. How far out?"

"Ten, fifteen miles. I've got it on one twenty-one five now."

"Maybe I'll chase your wake."

Sharp hesitated, then said, "Okay, do that, Whip. Who knows? Might use your help."

"Done and done, Marcus. *Privateer* standing by."

Good, Sharp thought. If a boat was sinking out there, Whip would arrive a lot faster than any vessel from the base. He could check it out while Sharp searched for floaters.

Besides, maybe there'd be something worthwhile for Whip if nobody claimed it. A raft. A radio. Something worth selling or using. Sharp knew Whip needed money.

Besides, Sharp thought, I owe him one.

One? No, he owed Whip Darling about a hundred.

Whip had saved Sharp's sanity at a time when his weekends had become unbearable. Sharp had dived with every commercial tour group on the island, visited every fort and museum, spent money in every saloon. He was on the brink of doing the unthinkable— taking up golf—when he met Whip at a base function.

He had listened, fascinated, to Whip's discourse on the techniques of discovering shipwrecks, and had asked enough intelligent questions to secure an invitation to come out on the boat some Sunday—which had quickly become every Sunday and most Saturdays. Here was a man with six years' schooling who had taught himself to be a walking encyclopedia of the sea. Whip had shown him photographs of what old shipwrecks look like from the air, and suddenly Marcus saw the prospect of new goals.

Whip taught him not to look for the classic fairy-tale image of a shipwreck—the ship upright and ready on its keel, sails rigged. The old ships had been wooden, and for the most part, storm seas had broken them to pieces. The sea bottom had absorbed them, and corals grew on them, taking the dead to their bosoms.

There were giveaways, Whip said, to a shipwreck on the bottom. When a ship was driven over the reefs, it would crush them, leaving a scrub mark that from a couple of hundred feet in the air would look like a giant tire track.

Another giveaway—visible from the air but most difficult to identify—was a ballast pile, for Whip insisted that where a ship dropped her ballast was where she had died. Yes, her deck might have drifted away or her rigging, but her heart and soul—her cargo, her treasure—lay with her ballast. Usually the old-timers ballasted with rocks from rivers near their home ports. The rocks were smooth and round and small enough for a man to lift. All the cobblestones, Whip told Sharp, in places like Nantucket had been ballast stones, carried to keep a ship upright on her way from England, then replaced with oil barrels for the journey home.

Now, whenever Sharp flew, he always kept an eye out for shipwrecks. He flew as low as possible, yawing back and forth, and if one of his crew ever asked what he was doing, he would reply with something vague like, Just putting her through her paces. So far he had found two ballast piles, two wrecks. One, Whip said, had been explored in the '60s. One was new. They'd go have a dig on it one of these days.

THE beeping was loud and regular now, and Sharp could see something yellow sliding up and down the rolling seas. He dropped the helicopter to a hundred feet and saw that it was a raft, small and empty and apparently undamaged.

"*Privateer,* Huey One."

"Yeah, Marcus" came Whip's voice.

"It's just a raft. Nobody aboard. False alarm, I guess."

"Whyn't I pick it up? I'll cruise around, see if there's any swimmers, then bring it in. Nobody has to get wet."

"You got it. Meantime, we'll set a search grid and swing back and forth till fuel sends us home."

"Roger that, Marcus. *Privateer* standing by."

"MAYBE THE DAY ISN'T A DEAD loss after all," Darling said as he climbed the ladder to the flying bridge.

"Why's that?" Mike was stowing the last of the wire leaders.

"Got us a chance to pick up a raft. If nobody's name's on her, there's a couple thousand, maybe more."

They spotted the raft in less than an hour, and Darling made a slow circle around it, studying it. "Switlik," he said, pleased.

"Looks brand-new, like nobody was ever on it."

Darling nodded. "That, or they were rescued right quick."

"Sharks got 'em?" Mike said.

Darling shook his head. "Shark would've bit through the rubber, maybe burred it with his skin. You'd see it. Whale, maybe."

Darling kept circling as he pondered that possibility. Orcas, the so-called killer whales, had been known to attack rafts, even big boats, but they'd never gone on and attacked the people. Perhaps they just got to playing with a raft and didn't know their own strength. "No," he said, "everything would be upside down."

Mike said, "Maybe she just slipped off the deck into the ocean."

"Then what turned on the EPIRB?" Darling pointed to the Styrofoam-cased beacon. "That's not automatic. Somebody turned it on." Darling paused. "I'd say they tossed the raft in and jumped for it and missed and drowned themselves."

Mike seemed to like that answer, so Darling didn't articulate the hazy idea he had of another option. They snagged the raft with a grappling hook and hauled it aboard.

After turning off the EPIRB, Mike knelt down and poked around, opening the supply box, feeling under the rubber cells. "Nothing," he said. "Nothing missing, nothing wrong."

"No." But something was bothering Darling, something he knew he should be seeing.

The oar. That was it. There wasn't any. Every raft carried at least one oar. There were oarlocks. But no oar.

And then his eye was attracted to sunlight glinting off something on one of the rubber cells. He put his face close to the rubber. There were scratch marks, and around each scratch mark was a patch of some kind of slime. He touched his fingers to the slime and raised them. They stank of ammonia.

Darling called Sharp on the radio and told him he had the raft and intended to keep searching a bit farther to the north. A person in the water wouldn't have traveled nearly as far as the raft had.

And so they drove north for an hour, then turned south again and began to zigzag. By the time they reached the area where they had recovered the raft, they had found only two seat cushions.

Darling looked out over the water. There were no other signs of life, so he took a bearing on Bermuda and headed for home.

By six o'clock they had left the deep behind. The ocean swell had faded, and the water's color had changed from blued steel to dark green. When they rounded the point into Mangrove Bay, the sky was turning violet, and the departing sun had tinted the western clouds the color of salmon.

A single light bulb burned on the dock, and beneath it, moored to a piling, was a white outboard motorboat with the word POLICE stenciled on the side. Two young policemen stood on the dock—one white, one black—watching as Darling eased the boat in.

Darling knew the policemen. He had taken these two to sea on their days off, had helped them learn to read the reefs.

He leaned on the railing of the flying bridge and said, "Colin. Barnett. What brings you fellas out of a night?"

"Hear you found a raft," Barnett, the black one, said. He stepped aboard and pointed to the raft lying athwart the cockpit. "That it?"

"That's the one."

Barnett shone a flashlight on it and leaned down. "My, it stinks!"

Colin came up next to Barnett and said hesitantly, "Whip . . . we gotta take it."

Darling paused. "Why's that? Somebody claim to have lost it?"

"No. Not exactly." Colin seemed uneasy.

Darling waited, feeling a roil of anger in his stomach, fighting it down. "Well? What then?"

"Dr. St. John," Colin said. "He wants it."

"Dr. St. John." Now Darling knew he was bound to lose, and his temper was bound to win. "I see."

Liam St. John was one of the few men in Bermuda whom Darling took the trouble to loathe. A second-generation Irish immigrant, he had gone away to school in Montana and graduated with a doctorate from some diploma mill. Exactly what the doctorate was in, nobody knew. All anybody knew for certain was that little, redheaded Liam had left Bermuda pronouncing his name Saint John and had returned pronouncing it SINjin.

Armed with an alphabet appended to his name, St. John had rallied a few powerful friends of his parents' and besieged the local government, arguing that disciplines such as maritime history and wildlife management should be turned over to a certified, qualified expert—which meant him.

The politicians, who were unconcerned with shipwrecks and nettled by loudmouthed fishermen, were pleased to remove both from their agendas, and for Liam St. John, Ph.D., they created the position of minister of cultural heritage. With no precise job description, St. John just defined the job as he went along, assuming more and more authority. He had decreed, for example, that no one was permitted to touch any shipwreck without first securing a license from him and agreeing to pay one of his staff two hundred dollars a day to supervise work on the wreck. The result was that nobody reported finding anything, and if they did dig up something, they smuggled it out of Bermuda. Thanks to the minister of cultural heritage, Bermuda's heritage was being sold in galleries on Madison Avenue in New York City.

For almost a year Darling and his diver friends had fantasized about ways to get rid of St. John. In fact, Darling wouldn't have been surprised if St. John were simply to vanish some night.

"Colin," he said, "I want you to do me a favor."

"Name it."

"You go back and tell Dr. St. John that I'll give him the raft if he'll come over here himself and let me shove it down his throat."

Barnett stepped away from the raft and came forward and stood at the bottom of the ladder, looking up at Whip on the bridge.

"Whip," he said, "you don't want to do this."

"That raft is mine, Barnett. I can't let you take it."

Barnett sighed. Something made him look aft, and he saw Mike standing in the darkness, holding a three-foot gaff with a honed four-inch hook on the end. "You know what we're gonna have to do. Get a dozen more coppers and come back and take the raft."

"Not without somebody getting bruised."

"That may be, Whip, but think about it. That happens, you're gonna end up in jail, we're gonna end up with the raft. And who's gonna get the last laugh? Dr. St. John."

Darling looked away, across the dark water of Mangrove Bay. He wanted to fight, wanted to rage and storm around. But he swallowed it because he knew Barnett was right.

"Barnett," he said at last, "you are the soul of wisdom."

Barnett looked over at Colin, who let out a big breath.

"Dr. SINjin wants my raft," Darling said as he came down the ladder and strode aft, "Dr. SINjin shall have my raft."

He took the gaff from Mike, raised it above his shoulder and slashed downward at the bow of the raft. The hook plunged through the rubber, and with a pop the cell collapsed.

"Whoops!" Darling said. "Sorry." And he slammed the hook into another cell. It deflated, and he hauled the sagging rubber up onto the bulwark. Something small fell from the raft with a click and rattled away. He yanked the raft upward and dropped it into the police boat, then turned back to the two policemen and said, "There. Dr. St. John can have his bloody raft."

The policemen looked at one another. "Okay," said Colin quickly. "We'll tell Dr. St. John that's how you found it."

"Right," said Barnett, and he stepped off onto the dock. "Looks to me like a shark got it."

"And there *was* a sea on," said Colin. "Night, Whip."

Darling watched as the policemen piled the raft in the stern of their boat and motored away into the darkness. He felt drained—half pleased with himself and half ashamed.

Later, as he and Mike cleaned up the boat, Darling felt something small and sharp under his foot. He picked it up and looked at it, but the light was bad, so he dropped it into his pocket.

"See you in the morning?" Mike said when he was ready to go.

"Right. We'll give the aquarium the bad news, see if they want to trust us with more gear. If not, we'll start chipping paint."

Darling followed Mike up the path to the house, waited till Mike had started his motorbike and driven away, then shut off the outside lights and went inside. He poured himself a couple of fingers of dark rum and sat in the kitchen.

Charlotte came in, smiled and sat down across the counter from him. She took a sip from his glass, then reached for one of his hands. "That was childish," she said quietly.

"You saw?"

"Police don't stop by every evening."

He shook his head. "You know, it makes me sick to feel so helpless. I had to do *some*thing."

"Did it make you feel better?"

"Sort of." He looked at her. She was smiling. "Okay, so I'm an old fool with a baby's brain."

"Well, you're cute anyway." She leaned across the counter to him.

As he rose up to kiss her, something stabbed him in the thigh, and he yipped and jerked backward.

"What?" she said.

"I've been punctured." He reached into his pocket and pulled out the thing he had stepped on and put it on the counter.

It was a crescent-shaped hook—hard, shiny, bony.

"It looks like a claw," said Charlotte. "Or even a fang. Where'd you find it?"

"Fell out of that raft." He hesitated as he recalled the marks he had seen on the raft, like cuts in the rubber. He looked at Charlotte, then at the thing, and he frowned. "What in the devil . . . ?"

CHAPTER FOUR

IT HUNG invisible in the deep and waited for the vibrations that would signal the approach of prey.

Its skills were those of a killer, not a hunter. It had never needed to hunt, for the cold, nutrient-rich water had always been host to countless animals of all sizes.

But now the rhythmic cycles that had propelled the creature through life had been disrupted. Food was no longer abundant. It was confused by the discomfort caused by the unfamiliar sensation of hunger. Instinct was telling it to hunt.

At that moment it felt an interruption in the flow of the sea, a sudden irregular static in the water's pulse.

Prey. In numbers. Passing by somewhere above.

The creature drew quantities of water through the muscular collar of its mantle, then expelled it through the funnel in its belly, driving itself up and backward with the force of a racing locomotive. Chemicals coursed through its flesh, altering its colors. It homed on the signals—many fish, many big fish—and thrust itself through the water with spasmodic expulsions.

When it judged itself close enough, it spun and faced the direction of its prey. Its huge eyes registered a flash of silver, and it lashed out with its whips. The two club-shaped ends fastened on flesh; the toothed circles tore at it. The curving hooks, erect within each circle, slashed it to shreds, and the retrieving arms fed the gnashing beak. Within seconds all that remained of the fish was a shower of scales and a billow of blood.

The creature's hunger was not allayed, however—it was increased. It needed more, much more. But the school of tuna had

fled. Now the searching whips found nothing. The shorter arms at
the base of its body gradually ceased moving; the beak closed its
jaws and withdrew into the body cavity.

It drifted, hungry and confused. The current that swept up from
the abyss propelled the creature slowly along a slope to a plateau at
five hundred feet. The cool water eddied here, so the creature rose
no farther.

On another slope, up ahead, was something large and unnatural, something that its senses told it was dead, except for the routine life-forms that grew upon it.

The creature ignored it and waited, gathering strength.

Lucas Coven was so annoyed and so impatient to get this day
over with that he put his boat in gear and leaned on the throttle
before the winch had the anchor snugged up. He heard the big steel
flukes thud against the hull, and he could envision the gouges in
the fiberglass, which made him even angrier.

He was always doing this, getting himself in over his head and
then, captive of his bullheaded pride, refusing to back off. He was
just a fisherman—so where did he get off playing Jacques Cousteau? It was his mouth that betrayed him every time.

Once clear of Ely's Harbor, he turned south. He looked down
from the flying bridge. His two passengers were on the stern, as-
sembling their diving gear—computers, buoyancy vests, still cameras, video cameras. Enough to equip an astronaut.

They had said they were expert divers, but to Lucas, people who
decked themselves out in all that machinery weren't divers, they
were shoppers. Besides, on the girl, gear just spoiled the picture. It
covered up the golden skin, the mane of yellow hair.

But they were high-tekkies, these two. Like most everybody
these days, they relied on electronic doodads to do their work for
them. Common sense was becoming a thing of the past.

Well, he hoped one of them, the boy or the girl, had a ration
of common sense because, where they were going, the only

thing the toys might do was provide a record for the coroner.

That thought brought Lucas another fit of anger. Maybe he'd pay someone to remove his vocal cords.

His first mistake had been to go to the Hog Penny Pub for his five-o'clock smile. He never went to any of the tourist bars on Front Street—the drinks were overpriced. But a pretty girl had stopped to ask him directions, and she'd said she went to the Hog Penny every day and why didn't he come by for a drink, and so he'd dropped by. Naturally the girl never did.

His second mistake had been to hang around long enough to destroy a twenty-dollar bill on vodkas because, even at tourist prices, that bought him enough fuel to tamp down his native quietness.

His third mistake had been to put his mouth where it didn't belong—into a conversation between two people he didn't know.

He'd been dazzled by the girl from the moment he saw her, but he had no ambitions about her, because the boy she was with was just as good-looking as she was, just as blond and tan. They looked so much alike they could have been brother and sister— which, he later learned, was exactly what they were: twins, just out of college, down here staying in their parents' house. He gathered that their father was some big shot in broadcasting, up in the States.

Because Dr. Smirnoff had Lucas well in tow by then, he began to fancy that he might actually have a chance with this heartstopper. Her getup alone should have been warning enough. No girl with a real gold Rolex watch was likely to give a thought to some ragged-haired boat jockey. But Dr. Smirnoff was driving.

They were standing next to him at the bar, consulting a set of decompression tables, planning how deep they could go on the next day's dives, which should have rung alarm bells in Lucas's head, since no visitors were ever taken on deep dives in Bermuda. Deep diving wasn't something sensible people did by choice.

Lucas hadn't said a thing while the two discussed the depths of the various shipwrecks they had been on—none of which lay deeper than forty feet, an average breath-hold range. He had found his opening when the boy—Scott, his name was—said something like, "The boat guy said the deepest wreck around's the *Pelinaion*."

"Will he take us to it?" asked the girl, Susie.

Lucas leaned forward and said, " 'Scuse me. None of my business, but I'm afraid somebody's pulling your chain."

"Really?" Susie's eyes opened wide.

"Yep. Like I say, none of my business, but I hate to see you get a bum steer."

"What is, then?" said Scott. "The deepest wreck."

"The deepest shipwreck in Bermuda," Lucas said, pleased to find that his mouth was working even though his lips felt numb, "is the *Admiral Durham*. It's off the south shore."

"How deep is that?" Scott looked as if he didn't believe a word.

"She starts at a hundred and ninety, then angles down the slope to about three hundred."

Scott said, "Gimme a break."

But Susie gave him a punch. "Scott! Listen, for once." So Lucas had let his mouth keep running.

"Saw her once, years back. She's not so easy to find."

"What was it like?" Susie asked, all eager.

"Gets your blood to racing. I call her the Widowmaker." He didn't, but it sounded good. "All of a sudden she looms up out of the deep, and you see a great iron ship that looks to be sailing right up at you. Just about the time your head clears, it's time to go. You only get about five minutes at that depth."

"I don't believe it," said Scott.

Lucas said, "That's your privilege," and motioned for a refill.

Susie put a hand on Lucas's arm and, with a glance at her brother that told him to keep quiet, said, "Our treat." That was the moment when Lucas knew he had them.

When his drink came, Susie said, "Excuse us a minute," and she took Scott's arm and led him off by some empty tables. They whispered for three or four minutes, and when they came back, it was Scott who started the ball rolling.

Would he be willing to try to find the *Admiral Durham* again?

Well . . . he didn't know. He was pretty busy. He had a charter party on hold for tomorrow. (Charter party! Where had he come up with *that?*) He wished he could help them, but he couldn't sacrifice that charter fee.

They'd make it worth his while. How much was the charter?

Well . . . full day . . . fifteen hundred—a fat figure, plucked out of the air.

No problem. In fact, if he could guarantee to put them on the shipwreck, they'd pay two thousand. But if he didn't find it—Scott was playing Mr. Big-time Hard-nose—they'd ride for free.

Fair enough. But Lucas had to ask, Were they really up to a two-hundred-foot dive? Did they know about the bends, about nitrogen narcosis, about the other stuff that happened at depth?

Oh, sure. They were super careful. And if they hadn't actually gone to two hundred feet before, they'd both been down well over a hundred—Scott was positive, Susie pretty sure.

Okay, then, he'd take them, but he'd have to send them down the anchor line alone. He couldn't go with them, 'cause he didn't have a mate, and he couldn't leave the boat unmanned.

Susie said that was fine. They'd swim right down the anchor line, take a lot of pictures and be back before he knew it.

Scott said, "So let's raise a glass to the dive of a lifetime."

And they had done just that—several glasses, in fact, until the time came when Lucas decided to make his move on Susie and suggested they slip away for a quiet dinner somewhere.

She had laughed at him—not a nasty laugh, but a kind of sweet, motherly laugh he couldn't get mad at—and ruffled his hair and said, "See you tomorrow."

LUCAS gave Southwest Breaker a wide berth. There was no breeze to speak of, but the sea still boiled around the treacherous fang of rock sticking up from the bottom.

The reef line was close on the south shore; deep water came fast, so it wasn't long before Lucas started looking for his landmarks. There was a purple house with twin tall casuarina trees directly behind it. His eye was supposed to line up those trees, at the same time triangulating so that the peach-colored cottage to the west sat at the foot of Gibbs Hill Lighthouse.

Landmarks weren't foolproof, though. And close wasn't good enough with a wreck as deep as the *Admiral Durham*. With five minutes' bottom time—which meant five minutes from the time you left the surface till the time you started up from the bottom— you didn't have leisure to go hunting around. Lucas had to anchor *on* it, drop the hook on the deck and let it drag along till it found a purchase on a rail or some chain.

He switched on his fish-finder. The readout of lines and lumps showed nothing between the surface and the bottom. He turned the wheel, nosing the boat to port, then to starboard, and suddenly it was there, a giant hulk rising up from the bottom.

Lucas nudged forward a hair—to compensate for the current that would grip the anchor—and pushed the release button.

He closed his eyes and wished the anchor all the way down, seeing it in his mind, dropping through the darkening blue and striking steel with a hearty clang.

THE creature was in a state close to hibernation. Its respiration had slowed. Its arms and whips floated freely, like gigantic snakes. It was gaining strength, as if sucking sustenance from the cool and silent darkness.

Suddenly the silence was broken by a shower of sound vibrations, amplified by the salt water. To a human ear the sound would have been resonant, metallic—solid steel striking hollow steel. To the creature the sound was alien and alarming, and so its respiration increased. Its arms curled; its whips cocked; its color brightened.

It located the noise as coming from above, so it rose toward the large, unnatural, lifeless thing it had sensed there earlier.

Any sound, any change whatever in the normal rhythms of the sea, could mean prey. And the need that was overwhelming it, now that it was moving and consuming energy, was hunger.

LUCAS stood on the bow and let the anchor rope run through his hands until it reached fifty fathoms. Then he took a turn around a cleat and went aft. "Dive, dive, dive!" he said, grinning at Scott and Susie, who looked like heroes from one of those comic books.

They were wearing matching wet suits, blue with yellow chevrons the color of their blond hair, and strapped to their legs were big red-handled knives. Both of them were lashed up with straps, buckles and snaps. Lucas ushered them down onto the swim step, off the stern. Susie's face had taken on an ashy hue.

"You okay?" Lucas asked, touching her arm.

"Yes. . . . I guess."

"You don't have to go. There's no shame."

"We're going," Scott said. "She'll be fine."

Lucas looked at Susie, who nodded.

"It's your party." Serious now, Lucas said, "When you're ready, one of you go first, the other right behind. And I tell you, *fire* for the bottom. You got precious little time."

They nodded, and put on their masks. Lucas passed them their cameras: a video for Scott, a Nikonos V for Susie.

They gave one another the thumbs-up sign.

As soon as they hit the water they inflated their vests and kicked against the tide toward the bow of the boat. At the anchor line they fiddled with this and checked that. Then they put their mouthpieces in, vented their vests and dropped beneath the surface.

Lucas looked at his watch: 10:52. By eleven o'clock he'd either be two thousand dollars richer or in a mess he didn't want to think about.

THE CREATURE HAD TWICE COVERED the length and breadth of the large, unnatural thing. The sound vibrations had ceased, and no other signs of prey had followed, so it had moved away from the thing and begun to drop back into the darkness.

But then it sensed movement again, something coming closer, and a sound that signaled a life-form.

It moved back to the unnatural thing, its great body resting in shadows, waiting.

SCOTT pulled himself down the anchor rope hand over hand. He was in dim nothingness now, surrounded by blue. He saw no shipwreck below him, no bottom.

The feeling was eerie, lonely, but there was solace in the taut anchor line. Something was down there; the anchor had caught in it. If it was the shipwreck, fine; if not, well, he and Susie would save two thousand dollars.

Where was Susie? He turned and looked back up the anchor line. She was way above, hanging on the rope at fifty or sixty feet— afraid, maybe, or having trouble with her ears.

There was nothing he could do for her. As long as she was above him, she'd be okay. He kicked for the bottom.

At one hundred and sixty feet he saw it, and his breath caught. It was exactly as Coven had described it—a ghost ship seeming to sail right up at him, enormous beyond imagining.

Fantastic! He stopped his descent long enough to unsnap the video camera from his belt and adjust its settings. He checked his air gauge and told himself to control his breathing.

Then he aimed his camera at the bow, pressed the trigger and, wielding a light, let himself drift gradually downward.

IT WAS alive, whatever this thing was. And it was coming.

The creature cocked its whips and fluttered its tail fins and, very slowly, moved up out of the shadows toward the prey.

Scott dropped down onto the bow of the ship. He was breathing too fast, but he didn't care. This was incredible! The size of it!

He found a railing to wrap his legs around to steady himself, and tucking the flashlight under his arm, he brought the camera's viewfinder up to his mask, trying somehow to get it all in the frame. He felt a change in the rhythm of the water around him, but he didn't turn to look. Perhaps Susie was arriving nearby.

He sensed a shadowy movement at his left, and something touched him. He jerked, turned, but all he could see was a blur.

And then the something had him around the chest and was squeezing. He dropped the camera, twisted around, but the something kept squeezing. Now there were stabbing things in it, like knives. He heard a crack—his ribs, breaking like sticks.

The last thing he saw, in his mask, was a bubble of blood.

Susie could see nothing above, nothing below. She was fighting to stay in control, not to panic. Why hadn't Scott waited for her? They were supposed to go down together; they had agreed. But no, Scott had gone off on his own. Impatient, selfish. As usual.

She checked her air gauge—fifteen hundred pounds. She'd never make it. She was gasping and could envision air disappearing with every breath. She was going to die!

Stop it! she told herself. Everything's fine. She clung to the anchor line and closed her eyes, willing herself to take slow, deep breaths. Oxygen nourished her, her brain cleared.

She decided to drop down another fifty feet. Maybe she could see the shipwreck from there. Then she'd start up.

Still clutching the rope, she let herself fall. One hundred and twenty feet, one thirty, one forty, then . . . What was that? Something was moving below. Something was coming up at her.

It had to be Scott. He had seen the wreck and taken his pictures and was already on the way back.

She'd never get to see it. She'd have to settle for Scott's description, have to endure his sly asides about this being a man's dive, too tough for the girls. Too bad, but . . .

This thing, this purplish thing—it wasn't Scott rising at her. It was huge, so huge it couldn't possibly be alive. But what was it? What could it—

Her last sensation was surprise.

Lucas looked at his watch: 10:59. They'd better be on their way up in the next sixty seconds. If not, he'd have to get on the radio and find out where the nearest decompression chamber was. Because these two were gonna be bent up like corkscrews.

That is, unless they chickened out, maybe hung at one hundred and fifty feet or so, from where they could just see the shipwreck. That was it. They were at one twenty-five, one fifty. They could stay another five minutes. It was 11:02.

He lay on the bow and stared hard down the anchor line, looking for even a glimmer of one of those snazzy wet suits.

He heard a noise down aft. Stupid kids had come up away from the anchor line, probably run out of air and shot for the surface. Be lucky if one of them didn't have an embolism.

He stood up and started aft. The noise was still going on—a weird noise, a wet, sucking kind of noise.

Now he smelled something. Ammonia. *Ammonia?* Here?

As he edged along the side of the cabin the boat suddenly heaved sharply to starboard. He heard wood crack and splinter.

The boat was listing badly; he had to struggle to keep his footing. He jumped down into the cockpit and looked over the transom. What he saw drove the breath from him. It was an eye as big as the moon in a field of quivering slime the color of blood.

He shouted—not words, just noise—and snapped upright, to flee the eye. He lurched to the right, took a step, but the boat heaved again and he was thrown backward. His knees struck the transom, his arms flailed out and he tumbled overboard.

MARCUS SHARP CHECKED HIS fuel gauges and saw that in another twenty minutes he'd have to turn back to the base.

He had been aloft for a couple of hours—ostensibly on a routine training patrol, in fact trying to spot shipwrecks. He had circled the island, flown low over the reefs in the north and northwest looking for ballast piles. He had spotted the known wrecks, the *Cristóbal Colón* and the *Caraquet*, but nothing new. He had hoped to find a virgin wreck for Whip, preferably a late-sixteenth-century Spanish ship laden with ingots and gold chains. But he'd settle for anything old and untouched, to replenish Whip's rapidly depleting reserves of hope and money.

Sharp was feeling guilty because he'd all but promised Whip he could keep that raft, and he'd heard that that self-important little jerk St. John had confiscated it.

Now Sharp was cruising along the south shore, off Elbow Beach. He could see scores of people frolicking in the surf and a few snorkelers offshore exploring the wreck of the *Pollockshields*.

Sharp's copilot finished the copy of *People* he'd been reading and said, "Let's head home."

"Almost there," Sharp said. He was about to give up and turn back to the northeast when his radio came alive.

"Huey One, Kindley Field."

"Go ahead, Kindley."

"Feel like a little flake patrol, Lieutenant?"

"If it doesn't take more'n ten minutes. Otherwise we use up our fuel and swim home. What's up?"

"A woman called the cops. Said she saw a boat go to pieces a mile south of Sou'west Breaker."

"Go to pieces? What did she mean. Blow up?"

"No. That's the strange part. She said she was looking through her telescope for humpback whales—sometimes she can see 'em from her house—and she saw this fishing boat just . . . go to pieces. No flame, no smoke, no nothing. It came apart."

"Okay, I'll look," Sharp said. "It's on the way home anyway."

He banked the helicopter off to the south. The sun was almost directly overhead and slightly behind him, and there was no glare on the water. He could see perfectly.

But there was nothing to see. He flew south for two minutes, then turned east. Nothing broke the endless roll of swells.

"Kindley, Huey One," Sharp said into his radio. "I gotta break off. Nothing down there."

"Come on home, Huey One. Probably nothing to it."

"Hey!" The copilot pointed downward.

Sharp banked to the left and looked. He saw two white rubber fenders; then, half-submerged, looking like a white blanket covered with blue haze, the entire roof of a boat's cabin.

"We're out of fuel," Sharp said. "Can't stop now or we'll be down there with it." He set his course straight for the base.

He had crossed the reef line when he saw the *Privateer* chugging slowly westward along the shore. *"Privateer, Privateer,"* he said into his microphone, "this is Huey One."

Darling was in the wheelhouse, drinking a cup of tea and wondering how much he could get if he sold his Masonic bottle—it was rare, one hundred and seventy years old—when the call came.

He picked up the microphone from its hook. *"Privateer."*

"Privateer, Huey One," said Sharp. "Whip, there's a boat wrecked about two miles dead ahead of you."

"Wrecked how?"

"Don't know. I haven't got fuel left to look for survivors. Police boat's probably on the way, but you're closest."

"Roger that, Marcus. I'll go check it out." Darling started to hang up, but then a kindness occurred to him. The raft wasn't Marcus's fault. "Hey, Marcus. Probably be going out this weekend, if you're interested."

There was relief in Sharp's voice as he replied, *"I'll say."*

Darling replaced the microphone and pushed his throttle forward. Finally something to do. Little by little, Darling had found, his opportunities were disappearing—and all turning up in Liam St. John's hands.

Whip and Mike had returned the damaged gear to the aquarium and had explained the little they knew about what had happened to it. Darling had begun to outline how to improve new gear when the deputy director—a mousy, nervous man—said, "I'm afraid not."

"Afraid not what?"

"We'll be . . . ah . . . terminating our agreement with you."

"*What?* Why?"

"Well, this was . . . expensive equipment . . . after all."

"Sharks are big animals . . . *after all.* Look, Milton, if you want me to hang the gear down where the action is, there are risks."

"Yes, but . . . I'm afraid that's that."

"Who's gonna catch your critters for you?"

"Well . . . that's yet to be decided."

Darling had taken a deep breath, trying to suppress his rage—and fear—at the loss of eight hundred dollars a month.

"It's St. John, isn't it?"

Milton had looked away. "I don't—"

"He's gonna take *my* eight hundred a month and go out with a dip net and a case of Budweiser, and when he doesn't come back with anything, he can blame it on the oil spills off California."

Milton was sweating. "For heaven's sake, Whip—"

"You're right, Milton, I'm overreacting." He had walked to the door and opened it. "But you know what? I feel sorrier for you. I may not make much of a living, but at least I don't have to earn my pay by kissing up to that Irish lizard."

Darling was convinced that St. John saw him as a threat, that he was determined to bring Darling to heel. And what rankled Darling was the fact that St. John was succeeding. He had all the weapons.

"There," said Mike, pointing to some floating wood. It was about three by five feet, with two short chains dangling from it.

"It's a swim step," Darling said. "Bring it aboard."

Mike went aft with the boat hook, while Darling climbed the ladder to the flying bridge. From up here he could see debris everywhere: fenders, planks, cushions, life jackets.

"Sling it all aboard," he called down to Mike.

For an hour they cruised among the debris as Mike grabbed piece after piece of flotsam and tossed it into the cockpit.

"Want that too?" Mike said, pointing to a white wooden rectangle twelve by fifteen feet, that hung just beneath the surface.

"No. That's his roof," Darling said from the flying bridge. Then a corner of the roof bobbed up out of the water, and he had a glimpse of pea-soup green on its underside. "Hang on," he said. He put the boat in neutral and went down the ladder to get a better look at it.

"It's Lucas Coven's boat," he said.

"How d'you know that?"

"I saw him painting it last spring. He was doing the whole inside in that sick green. Said he'd got the paint on sale."

"What was he doing out here?"

"You know Lucas," Darling said. "Probably had some half-baked scheme to make two dollars in a hurry."

"How do you make two dollars out here? Nothing here."

"No," Darling agreed. "Nothing but the *Durham*."

"Nobody dives on the *Durham*. Nobody with sense."

"Right again. Let's have a look." Darling picked up a rubber fender. There were no marks on it—no scars, no burns.

"Look here," Darling said. "No char, no stink. He didn't blow up, he was busted up . . . somehow."

"By what? Nothing out here for him to hit."

"I don't know. Killer whales?"

"Killer whales? In hailing distance of the beach?"

"*You* come up with something then." Darling felt anger welling up. Mike always wanted answers, and it seemed he had fewer and fewer of those. He said, "Damn!" and kicked a life jacket, which would have gone overboard if Mike hadn't caught it.

Mike was about to toss it aside when he noticed something. "What's this?"

Darling looked. The orange cloth covering the kapok had been shredded, and the buoyant material beneath was exposed. There were two marks in it—circles about six inches in diameter. The rim of each circle was ragged, and in the center of each was a deep slash.

"Look at this," Darling said. "Looks like a scuttle."

"Sure." Mike thought Darling was joking. An octopus? "You ever seen a scuttle with teeth in its suckers?"

"No." Mike was right. The suckers on an octopus's arms were soft, pliable. A man could unwrap them from around his arm as easily as removing a bandage.

But what was it, then? An animal for certain. This boat hadn't blown up or disintegrated. Something had destroyed it.

Darling tossed the life jacket onto the deck and kicked some pieces of wood aside to clear his way forward. Something popped out of one of the planks and landed with a click.

It was a claw like the other one—crescent shaped, two inches long and sharp as a razor.

He looked overboard as a swell heaved the boat upward. As the boat settled again, something floated out from underneath it: rubber, blue with a yellow chevron on either side. A wet-suit hood.

Darling picked up the boat hook and scooped up the hood with it. The hood came up like a cup, full of water, and in it were two little striped fish. They were feeding on something.

Darling held the hood in his hand. A smell rose from it, sharp and acrid. Like ammonia. He turned to let the sunlight fall into the dark pocket.

What the fish were feeding on looked like a big marble.

Mike came up behind Darling and looked over his shoulder. "What've you—Oh, my God!" Mike gasped. "Is that human?"

"It is," said Darling, and he stood aside to let Mike retch into the sea.

CHAPTER FIVE

DR. HERBERT Talley hunched his shoulders against the wind, a roaring northeaster that drove salt water off the ocean and blended it with rain. He stepped in a puddle of icy water.

It might as well be winter. The only difference between summer and winter in Nova Scotia was that by winter all the leaves had been blown away.

He crossed the quadrangle, stopped at Commons to pick up his mail and climbed the stairs to his tiny office. He was winded by the exertion, which annoyed him. He had taken pride in being a young fifty, but he was beginning to feel like an old fifty-one.

He vowed to start jogging tomorrow, even in a whole gale. He had to. To go to flab would be to accept the loss of his dreams, to resign himself to whiling away his days as a teacher. Some might say that academia was the graveyard of science, but Herbert Talley wasn't ready to be buried yet.

Days like today didn't help. A total of six stuporous summer school students had shown up for his lecture on cephalopods. He had done his best to infuse them with his enthusiasm. He was among the world's experts on cephalopods, and he found it incredible that they couldn't share his appreciation of the wondrous head-foots. Perhaps the fault lay in him. He was an impatient teacher, who preferred showing to instructing. On expeditions he was a wizard. But there weren't any new expeditions—not with the economy of the western world about to implode.

Talley's office had room for a desk and a desk chair, a bookcase, and a table for his radio. One wall was taken up with a *National Geographic* world map, which Talley had dotted with pushpins representing events in malacology: ongoing expeditions, sightings of rare species, depredations by pollution, and cyclical calamities. The other walls contained photographs of the celebrities of his field: octopuses, squid, oysters, conchs.

Talley hung his hat and raincoat on the back of the door, turned on the radio and sat with his airmail copy of the *Boston Globe*. There was no news, really, and lulled by a symphony and the patter of rain, he struggled to stay awake.

Suddenly his eyes snapped open. A phrase out of all the thousands on the page in his lap had awakened him like an alarm.

Sea monster.

What sea monster? He scanned the page, ran down each column, and then . . . there it was, a tiny item on the bottom of the page, a filler.

> Bermuda (AP)—Three persons died yesterday when their boat sank from unknown causes off the shore of this island colony in the Atlantic Ocean. The victims included the two children of media magnate Osborn Manning.
>
> There was no evidence of explosion or fire, and some local residents, recalling the mysteries of the Bermuda Triangle, blamed the incident on a sea monster. The only clues noted by police were strange marks on wooden planks and an odor of ammonia in some of the debris.

Talley held his breath. He read the item again and again. He rose and went to the wall map. His pushpins were color-coded, and he searched for red ones. There were only two, both off Newfoundland, both marked with reference dates from the early 1960s. Off Bermuda there was nothing.

Until now.

Obviously the reporter hadn't known what he was writing about. He had gathered facts and lumped them together, not realizing that he had included the key to the puzzle.

Ammonia. Ammonia was the key. Talley felt a thrill of discovery; it was his old nemesis, a creature he had spent most of his professional life seeking, a creature he had written books about.

He tore the item from the paper and read it again. "Can it be?"

he said aloud. "After all these years?" It had to be. And it was only a thousand miles away, waiting for him.

He had to get to Bermuda. But how? He must mount a search, a proper scientific search, but how would he pay for it? The university was funding nothing these days. He had no cash of his own. The solution was simple enough. The world was full of money. How could he get some of it?

He smoothed the newspaper clipping on the desk before him. He read, "media magnate Osborn Manning."

There was his answer. He picked up the telephone.

OSBORN Manning sat in his office and tried to focus on a report from one of his vice presidents. The news was good. With the economy heading for the dumper, people weren't willing to pay seven dollars for a movie. They were opting for cheap entertainment, his entertainment—cable television. Subscriptions were up, and his people had been able to buy new franchises at distress prices. Manning now had more cash than many emerging nations.

So what? Would cash bring back his kids? Would cash make his wife whole? Could cash restore a family?

Cash couldn't even buy him revenge, and revenge was one thing he craved, as if it could help expiate his sin of having been a distant, almost an absentee, father. But he didn't even have the luxury of imagining revenge, for he had no idea what had killed his children. No one knew. Freak accident. Terribly sorry.

He tossed the report aside, leaned back in his chair and looked out his Fifth Avenue window at the sprawl of Central Park, a view he used to love. The intercom buzzed on his desk. He spun around and punched a button and said, "Helen, I told you I—"

"Mr. Manning, it's about the children," his secretary said. "There's a Canadian scientist on the phone. A man who says he knows what killed them."

Manning suddenly felt cold. He reached for the phone, and he saw that his hand was shaking.

THEY HAD RESTED, MOTHER AND calf, on the surface of the sea, with the others in the small pod, since the sun had lowered in the western sky. It was a daily gathering, fulfilling a need for socialization. No matter where they were, no matter how dispersed during the day, as night began to fall, the pod came together to experience the comfort of community.

In times past, long ago but still within the memory of the eldest of the pod, there had been many more of them. There was no questioning, for these whales—with the largest brains on earth—did not question. They accepted. They accepted their smaller numbers, would accept even when the pod was perhaps reduced to two or three.

But these sophisticated brains, unique among animals, did recognize loss, did know sadness, did, in their way, feel. And accept though they might, they also lamented.

Now, as darkness fell, the pod disbanded. In ones and twos and threes they drew breaths through the tops of their heads, filled their enormous lungs and dove into the darkness.

Mother and calf dove as one. When the calf was younger, its lungs had lacked the capacity to sustain an hour-long dive into the deep. But now the calf was two years old, had grown to twenty-five feet long and more than twenty tons of weight. It had ceased to nurse, and now it fed on live prey.

As they dove in the black water, propelling themselves with powerful sweeps of their horizontal tails, from their blunt foreheads they emitted the pings and clicks of sonar impulses that, on return, would identify prey.

THE creature hung in the dark, letting itself be carried by the current. Its arms and whips floated loose, its fins barely moved.

Suddenly it was struck a blow, and another, and what passed for hearing in the creature registered a sharp and penetrating ping.

Its enemy was coming.

THE SONAR RETURN WAS unmistakable: prey. The mother thrust downward with her tail, accelerating as she drove herself ever deeper. The calf strove to keep up.

The mother's brain fired sonar missiles again and again, for this was to be the calf's first mature kill. The prey must be stunned by sonar hammers before the calf could set upon it.

BESIEGED, the creature recoiled. Chemical triggers fired, nourishing the flesh, galvanizing it and streaking it with luminescence. Other reflexes voided a sac within the body cavity, flushing a cloud of black ink into the water.

Sonar blows struck it again and again, confusing the small brain. Defense impulse changed to attack. It turned to fight.

As THE mother closed in on the prey, she slowed, permitting the calf to draw even, then to pass her. She unleashed a final burst of sonar blows, then swerved and began to circle the prey.

The calf plunged downward, excited by the prospect of the kill, impelled by a million years of imprinting. It opened its mouth.

THE creature felt the pressure wave. The enemy was upon it.

It lashed out with its whips. They flailed blindly, then found flesh, hard and slick. Automatically they surrounded it and their circles fastened to it and their hooks dug in, drawing the enemy to the creature and the creature to the enemy, like two boxers in a clinch.

THE calf closed its mouth on . . . nothing. It was perplexed. Something was wrong. It felt pressure behind its head, confining it, slowing its movement.

It struggled, pumping with its tail, frantic to rid itself of whatever was holding it down. It was consuming oxygen too fast.

Now its lungs began to send out signals of need. Deprived of oxygen, the muscles were shutting down. An unknown agony coursed through its lungs. The calf was drowning.

The mother circled, alarmed, sensing danger to her calf, but incapable of helping it. She knew aggression, she knew defense, but in the programming of her brain there was no code for response to a threat to another, even to her own offspring. She made noises— high pitched, desperate and futile.

THE creature held on, anchored to its enemy. The enemy thrashed, and from its motion the creature sensed a change: no longer was its enemy the aggressor; it was trying to escape. The more its enemy struggled to rise, the more the creature forced them both down into the abyss.

Finally the creature felt its enemy stop struggling and begin to sink. Though it still clutched the flesh, gradually the creature released the tension and let itself fall with its kill, slowly spiraling. The whips tore away a chunk of blubber and fed it to the arms, which passed it back to the snapping protuberant beak.

THE mother, circling, followed her calf with sonar pings. She sent clicks and whistles of distress, bleats of helpless despair.

At last her lungs, too, were exhausted, and with a final sonic burst, she thrust up toward the life-giving air above.

MARCUS Sharp sat on the beach and wished he were somewhere else. He didn't like beaches much, didn't like sitting while his skin fried in the tropical sun. A misguided impulse born of desperate frustration had led him to jump on his motorbike and drive the fifteen miles from the base to Horseshoe Bay.

It was Saturday and he had hoped to go diving with Whip Darling. But Darling had told him that he and Mike intended to chip paint all day. So Sharp had read for an hour and then, at eleven o'clock, had found himself scanning the titles in the video store. He realized that in order to get through the rest of Saturday he would have to rent not one, not two, but three movies.

He had tried to find a tennis game instead, but all the tennis players he knew were out. So he had gone to the beach, impelled, he guessed, by some vague hope that he might meet a girl worth talking to, having lunch with, maybe even making a date with.

It had been a mistake. As he sat and watched children frolicking in the wave wash and couples strolling under palm trees, he felt more and more lonely, more and more hopeless.

He had seen two girls with potential—tourists, pretty and vivacious. They had even stopped and spoken to him. One had fair skin and red hair, the other was deeply tanned and raven-haired.

He had wanted to talk to them; his mind had flooded with conversational gambits—the navy, helicopters, shipwrecks, diving, Bermuda. But he was out of practice in the dating game, and after he had answered their questions about moderately priced restaurants in Hamilton, he had let them get away.

He was hungry, and so he got to his feet and started toward the concession stand. He was about to turn in to the trees when he saw the girls again. They saw him watching them, and they waved at him, ran into the water and began to swim.

Okay, he thought, he'd wait till they stopped swimming; then he'd go in and swim out to them.

When they were thirty or forty yards offshore, the girls stopped and treaded water, talking and laughing. Sharp walked down to the water's edge. He saw one of them wave, and he waved back.

The girl waved again, with both hands, and then she disappeared underwater; and now the other one was waving too, and shouting. No, not shouting, Sharp realized. Screaming.

"Omigod," he said, and he ran and dove in and swam, sprinting.

When he looked up to get his bearings, he was almost there. He saw the redheaded girl, flailing and shrieking. The other girl was trying to grab her under her arms and stop her hysterics.

Sharp swam up behind the redhead and pinned her arms to her
sides and wrapped his arms around her and leaned back, kicking
to keep himself afloat and her head out of water. He looked for the
shark, the barracuda, the man-of-war.

"I've got you," he said. "You're okay. Calm down."

The girl's shrieks were subsiding now into sobs.

"Are you hurt? What happened?"

"Something horrible and slimy . . ." she said.

"Bit you?" Sharp asked.

"No, it . . ." She rolled over and clung to Sharp, weeping and
almost sinking him.

Sharp said, "Let's get you to shore." He took one of her arms
and gestured for the other girl to take the other arm. Together they
sidestroked toward shore, holding the girl between them. Soon they
could touch bottom.

Trying to smile, the girl said, "I'm okay. I just . . . Thanks."

"Back in a minute," Sharp said, and he turned toward deep
water and swam an easy breaststroke. When he reached the spot
where the girls had been, he stopped swimming and spun in a slow
circle, searching the water. He didn't know what he was looking
for. Box jellyfish didn't exist in Bermuda. Besides, the girl was unhurt, just scared. He supposed there were big, harmless jellyfish
under the surface, but she'd have seen them.

He started for the shore slowly, and then his hand touched
something. He looked at the water. There was something creamy
white and roundish, about the size of a watermelon. Gingerly he
reached forward and touched it. It was slimy, ragged, pulpy, like
rotten meat. He put his hand under it. The underside was hard and
slick. When he brought it up out of the water, his nostrils were assailed by a vile smell of putrefaction.

It wasn't meat. It was fat. Blubber. He rolled it over. The skin
side was blue-black and newly scarred with a circle, six inches
across, of what looked like cuts. In the center of the circle was a
deep gash that went through the skin and into the blubber.

"Good Lord," Sharp said.

Pushing the thing ahead of him, he swam to shore.

On the beach a group of children were gathered around something that had washed up. They were prodding it with a stick. When Sharp looked, he realized that it was another piece of blubber, smaller, with two half circles, one on either end.

Sharp held the thing as far away from his face as he could. The girls were sitting together, the redhead wrapped in a towel, the other's arm around her shoulder.

"She's okay," said the dark-haired girl, smiling, and added, "We want to thank you. Can we—" The breeze carried the stench of Sharp's prize to her. "What's *that?*"

"Gotta go," Sharp said. He scooped up his towel, wrapped the blubber in it and walked up to the lot, to his motorbike.

DARLING and Mike were on their knees, sanding in the after hold of the *Privateer*. They wore surgical masks to keep the paint dust out of their lungs, and goggles to protect their eyes.

Darling felt the boat dip as a weight came aboard. He looked up and saw Sharp standing by the open hatch. "Hey, Marcus," he said.

"Sorry to interrupt."

"Don't be. I'd welcome Lucifer himself to get me away from this rotten work."

"Could you look at something for me?"

"You bet." Darling removed his mask and goggles and started up the ladder. Mike kept sanding until Darling said, "Come look, Michael boy. Don't miss a chance for a breather."

Sharp had set the bundle on a cutting table amidships. As Darling approached, the stench hit him, and he said, "Whoa, lad! What you brung me? Something dead?"

"Very," Sharp said, and he told Darling what had happened at Horseshoe Bay. While Whip unrolled the towel, flies materialized from nowhere, and two gulls began to circle over the boat.

"Sperm whale," Mike said.

Darling nodded. "Young too. See? The blubber's thin."

Sharp said, "Turn it over."

Darling used a knife blade to flip the blubber. In the direct sunlight the circle of marks shone like a necklace.

Mike and Darling looked at each other; then Darling shook his head. He walked into the cabin and came back holding an amber-colored claw. He slid the claw into the slash in the blue-black skin. It fit perfectly.

Sharp said, "What is it, Whip? What did this?"

"I hope it isn't what I think it is." Darling pointed to the blubber and said to Mike, "Drop that mess over the side." Then he turned to Sharp. "Come on."

"Where to?"

"Need to consult a book or two." As Darling led the way up the path to his house he noticed his daughter's car in the driveway. "Dana's here," he said. "Wonder what about."

Sharp had never been inside Darling's house before, and he looked quickly around. It was a classic eighteenth-century Bermuda house, built like an upside-down ship. Sturdy wooden knees supported the ceilings; twelve-by-twelve beams braced the walls. The old chests, cabinets, tables and floors were all of wide-board Bermuda cedar. The rooms were cool and dark.

The two women sitting in the dining room jumped when they saw Darling in the doorway.

The younger woman—tanned and sharp-featured, with sun-bleached hair—quickly shuffled the papers on the table before her, covering some with others.

Darling didn't seem to notice. He said, "Hey, Lizard," and went to kiss her on the cheek. "You know Marcus Sharp? Marcus, this is Dana."

"Know *of* you," said Dana. She looked uneasy, awkward, though she smiled and shook Sharp's hand.

Darling led Sharp through the living room to a small room beyond, lined with bookcases and furnished only with a huge cedar desk and two chairs. Sharp scanned the titles on the shelves. It seemed that every book ever written about the sea was here, from Jacques Cousteau to Herman Melville.

"Now, let's see." Darling pulled a volume from a shelf and read the title aloud: *"Mysteries of the Sea."* He opened the book.

"About ten years ago," he said as he leafed through the pages, "I was on a boat in the Sea of Cortés, helping some aquarium people from California gather strange critters. There were some big squid in the water—Humboldt squid—four or five feet long, fifty or sixty pounds. I'd never seen the big ones before, so I decided to get in the water with them. As soon as my mask cleared, one of them made a run at me. I swatted at him, and faster than I could believe, one of his whips shot out and grabbed my wrist. I thought a hundred needles were stabbing me. I punched him in the eye and he let go and I started up. Then all of a sudden I felt myself being dragged down. *Three* of the things had me, and they were yanking me down into the gloom. I tell you, the Lord must have a special place in his heart for stupid Bermudians, 'cause everything they grabbed broke away—one of my flippers, my depth gauge, a collecting bag. I took off for the surface and made it back to the boat. But I had nightmares for a month."

"Wow," Sharp said.

Darling turned some pages, then said, "There," and pushed the book toward Sharp.

"What's *that?*" Sharp asked as he stared at the picture on the page. It was a nineteenth-century woodcut of a hideous creature with a huge bulbous body that ended in a tail shaped like an arrowhead. It had eight writhing arms, two whips twice the length of the body and two gigantic eyes. In the picture the beast was destroying a sailing ship. Bodies were flying, and a woman, her eyes wide with terror, was hanging from the creature's beak.

"That," Whip said, "is the granddaddy of the critter that grabbed me. It's *Architeuthis dux,* the oceanic giant squid."

"Talk about nightmares. It can't be real . . . can it?"

"It's real, all right—rare, but real." Darling paused. "In fact, it's more than real. It's out there now. It's here."

Sharp looked at Darling. "Come on, Whip," he said.

"You don't believe me? Okay." Darling pulled out another book and read the spine: " '*The Last Dragon* by Herbert Talley, Ph.D.' " Years before, he had turned pages down as marks, and he opened the book to the first mark. " 'Giant squid have been written about since the sixteenth century, maybe even earlier,' " he read. Then he asked Marcus, "You've heard the word *kraken?* It's Swedish for uprooted tree. That's what people thought the monsters looked like, with all those tentacles snaking around like roots. Nowadays scientists like the word cephalopod."

"Why?" asked Sharp. "What's it mean?"

"Head-footed. It's 'cause their arms spring right out from their head." He turned to another mark. "Here, Marcus," he said. "One came up in the Indian Ocean and dragged down a schooner called the *Pearl*. There were more than a hundred witnesses." Darling slapped the book. "I can't believe I didn't figure this out sooner," he said. "It's so obvious. There's *nothing* else that could have torn up our gear like that." He paused. "And nothing else is so all-out, bone-deep evil."

"But Whip. Look at the date." Sharp pointed at the first book. "Eighteen seventy-four. That's not today."

"Marcus, those marks on the whale skin—you saw for yourself." Darling took one of the claws from his pocket. "What kind of beast has knives like that?" Darling felt a growing sense of urgency. Suppose there was a giant squid. What could they possibly do to get rid of it?

He pulled more books down from the shelf, handed a few to Sharp, then sat on the couch and opened one. "Read," he said. "We better learn everything we can about this beast."

They pored through Darling's books about the sea. The references to giant squid were sketchy and often contradictory. Some experts claimed that the animals grew no bigger than fifty or sixty feet long; others insisted that there were hundred-footers, or bigger. Some said that the sucker disks of giant squid contained teeth and hooks; some said they contained one or the other, or neither.

Darling passed the Talley book to Sharp. "Says here, in 1941 some sailors in a lifeboat were attacked by one. Tore off pieces of flesh the size of an American quarter. They figure the animal was . . . what?"

Sharp ran his finger down the page. "Twenty-three feet."

Darling thought a moment, then said, "How big would you say those marks on that whale skin were?"

"Five, six inches?"

"Judas priest. This squid may be as big as a blue whale."

"A blue whale!" Sharp said. "Whip, that's twice as big as your boat. It's bigger than a dinosaur. A blue whale's the biggest animal that's ever been."

"In body mass maybe, but not in length. And not in nastiness."

As THEY headed outside, they passed the dining room. Charlotte looked up and said, "Whip, what's this about a giant squid?"

"Giant squid? What are you? Some kind of psychic?"

"It was on the radio just now. Somebody found something on a beach, and scientists at the aquarium said—"

"Yes, Charlie," Darling said. "It looks like we've got ourselves a giant squid."

"They're having a big meeting about it tomorrow night. Down at the lodge hall. The whole island's in an uproar."

"I don't wonder."

"William," Charlotte said, and she rose from the table and came over and took Darling's arm. "Promise me."

"Come on, Charlie. Nobody but a certified idiot would make a run at a beast like that."

"Like Liam St. John, for instance."

"What do you mean?"

"On the radio he said he's going to catch it. To save Bermuda."

"Fat chance," Darling said. "St. John's gonna end up in the belly of the beast, and good riddance." He looked beyond her at the pile of papers on the table. "What are you girls doing? Taking over General Motors?"

"Nothing," Charlotte said. "Go away." She started toward the table, stopped and said, "You had a call."

"Who from? What'd they want?"

"They didn't say. Foreigners. The one I talked to sounded Canadian. They just wanted to know if you were available."

"Available for what?" Darling said. "Never mind. I can guess. If they call again, you can tell 'em I *was* available until about ten minutes ago. Now, all of a sudden, I think I've retired."

CHAPTER SIX

WHAT a joke, Darling thought as he left the lodge hall. They had called it an island forum, but it had really been nothing but a charade to show the citizenry that the politicians were concerned—without their ever having to do anything. Not that there was anything anybody could do.

Darling took a deep breath of night air and decided to walk home. He figured the meeting would go on for at least another hour, with people squabbling over how to deal with a monster that few had heard of and none had seen.

It was probably too late to worry. Thanks to St. John and his crusade for personal publicity, the morning's headlines—MONSTER IS GIANT SQUID, ST. JOHN CONFIRMS—would be burning up the wires all around the world.

Predictably, Liam St. John had waited till things seemed at an impasse before he rose from his seat in the row of Cabinet ministers and, after a vain attempt to make himself appear taller than his five feet four by fluffing up his helmet of pumpkin-colored curls, asked for public support for his plan of action.

Since nobody knew enough about the monster to pass judgment on St. John's plan, a clamor had gone up to get Darling to say what he thought. After all, somebody said, "Whip's caught at least one of everything God ever put in the ocean around here."

And Darling had told them what he'd read and his conclusions: that the appearance of a giant squid around Bermuda was probably a fluke; that since human beings weren't its normal food, in all likelihood it would eventually go away; and that to set out to catch or destroy it was pointless because in his opinion no one could do it. In sum, Darling had said, leave it alone and wait.

St. John had termed Darling's approach "do-nothing defeatism," and that had set off a new round of arguing.

Darling had left soon after, elbowing through the crowd of standees. Now he walked along the road to Somerset and thought about what to do. Part of the problem, he decided, was that people were spoiled; they couldn't accept a situation that demanded patience and offered no easy solutions. A car approached from behind. It slowed as it passed him, and stopped just ahead. Darling saw it was a BMW. Somebody rich. A man got out of the passenger's side and started back toward him. "Captain Darling?" he said.

Darling saw a tweed jacket and tan-colored pants, but he couldn't see the man's face. "Do I know you?" he said.

"My name is Dr. Herbert Talley, Captain."

Talley, Darling thought. There was something familiar about that name, but he couldn't place it. "Doctor of what?"

"Malac— Well, squid, Captain. Doctor of squid, you could say."

"You don't have to talk down to me. I know it's malacology, the study of mollusks."

"Sorry. Of course. Could we give you a lift home?"

"I'm happy to walk," Darling said, and he started around the car, but then he remembered, and he stopped and said, "Talley. You wrote *The Last Dragon*."

Talley smiled and said, "Yes. I did."

"Good book. Full of facts."

"Thank you. Ah . . . Captain, we'd like to talk to you about *Architeuthis*. Could you spare us a few minutes?"

An alarm bell rang in Darling's brain: this must be the man who had telephoned. Charlotte had said he sounded Canadian, and Talley's pronunciation of the word "about"—as if it were "a boat"— was a giveaway. Darling said, "I've said all I have to say."

"Perhaps you could listen, then, over a drink?"

"Who's 'we'?"

Talley gestured toward the car. "Mr. Osborn Manning." When Darling said nothing, seeming not to register, Talley said, "Manning . . . the father of the—"

"Oh, yeah. Sorry."

"We would appreciate a word with you."

Darling hesitated. He didn't want to be rude, not to a man who had just lost both his children. Finally he said, "All right."

"Fine," Talley said, holding open the back door of the car. "There's a nice hotel around the—"

Darling shook his head. "Go up the road a hundred yards. Pull in under a sign that says SHILLY'S. I'll meet you there."

"We'll drive you."

"I'll walk." Darling stepped around the car.

Shilly's had once been a one-pump gas station. Now it was a one-room restaurant. It advertised itself as "the home of Bermuda's famous conch fritters," which was a local joke, since Bermuda's conchs had been fished out years ago. The skeleton of the old gas pump still stood in the parking lot, painted purple.

Darling could have let them take him up to the hotel, but they would have been comfortable there, and he didn't want them to feel comfortable. He wanted to make the conversation short.

He walked into Shilly's and stood for a moment, letting his eyes adjust to the darkness. He smelled stale beer and cigarette smoke. A dozen men crowded around the snooker table, shouting and placing bets. They were hard men, all of them black.

There were several empty tables near the door, but Talley and Manning were standing together in a corner, as if they had been sent there as punishment by a teacher.

An enormous man slid off a barstool and ambled over to Darling. "Whip," he said.

"Shilly."

"They with you?" Shilly nodded toward the corner.

"They are."

"Good enough." Shilly lumbered to a nearby table and let his face crack into a grin. "Gentlemen," he said, "please be seated."

When they were seated, Shilly said, "What's your pleasure?"

Manning said, "I'd like a Stolichnaya on the—"

"Rum or beer."

"Make it three Dark and Stormys, Shilly," Darling said.

"You got it," Shilly said, and turned back to the bar.

Darling looked at Osborn Manning, who appeared to be in his early fifties. He was impeccably tended. His blue suit looked as if it had been pressed while he waited to be seated. His white shirt was starched and spotless; his silk tie held in place by a gold pin.

But it was Manning's eyes that Darling couldn't stop looking at. In the best of times they would have seemed sunken, but now they looked like two black tunnels. Maybe it's just dark in here, Darling thought. Or maybe that's what grief does to a man.

Shilly brought the drinks, and Talley took a gulp and said, "Splendid." Darling watched Manning's reaction as he took a sip: he winced. To a mouth used to vodka and ice, rum and ginger beer must taste like anchovies with peanut butter.

There was an awkward silence, as if Talley and Manning didn't know how to begin. Darling had a fair notion of what they wanted, but he resisted telling them to get to the point. He had made quite a few dollars keeping his mouth shut. Manning sat stiffly, his hands folded, and stared at the candle on the table.

Well, no harm in being polite, Darling thought. He said to Manning, "Sorry about your youngsters."

"Yes" was all Manning said.

Talley took another gulp of his drink and said, "Captain Darling, we liked what you said at the meeting."

"You were there? Why?"

"We wanted to see how people are reacting to all this."

"That's easy," Darling said. "They're scared to death. They see their world being threatened by something they can't even understand, much less do anything about."

"But you're not. Scared, I mean."

"You heard what I said back there. It's like anything else big and awful in nature. You leave it alone, it'll leave you alone." He thought of Manning's children, and added, "As a rule."

"That doctor back there. St. John. He's a fool."

"That's one way to put it."

"But there is something I disagree with you on. What's happening here is not an accident."

"What is it, then?"

Darling saw Talley glance at Manning, then Talley said, "Tell me, Captain, what do you know about *Architeuthis?*"

"What I read, what you wrote, other stuff. Not a whole lot."

"What do you *think* about it?"

Darling paused. "Whenever I hear talk about monsters," he said, "I think about *Jaws*. People forget *Jaws* was fiction. As soon as that picture came out, everyone started fantasizing about fifty-foot white sharks. My rule is, When someone tells me about a critter as big as a truck, I right away cut a half off what he says."

"Sound," said Talley, "very sound. But—"

"But," Darling said, "with this beast, seems to me, when you hear stories about him, the smart thing to do is double 'em."

"Exactly!" Talley said. He leaned toward Darling, as if pleased to have discovered a kindred spirit. "I told you I'm a malacologist, but my specialty is teuthology—squid. Specifically, *Architeuthis*. I've spent my life studying them. Ever seen a live one?"

"Never," Darling said, "and I'd like to keep it that way."

"The more I've studied, the more I've realized how little anybody knows about the giant squid. Nobody knows how big they grow, how old they get, why they strand sometimes and wash up dead—not even how many species there are." Talley stopped suddenly, looking embarrassed, and said, "Sorry. I get carried away. I can cut this short—"

"Go on," said Manning. "Captain Darling has to know."

They're setting me up, Darling thought.

"I have a theory," Talley said. "Up to the middle of the last century there were few sightings of *Architeuthis*, or of *any* giant squid.

Then all of a sudden in the 1870s there was a rash of sightings and strandings, and even attacks on boats. Then it all stopped again until the early 1900s, when for no reason, there were more sightings and strandings. I wondered if there was a pattern, so I collected reports of every sighting and every stranding, and I fed them into the computer with all the data on major weather events, current shifts and so forth. The computer found that sightings and strandings coincided with cyclical fluctuations in branches of the Labrador Current, the big cold-water funnel that sweeps up the whole Atlantic coast. For most of the cycle, *Architeuthis* is never seen. But in the first few years of the change, for some reason, the beast shows up."

"How long are the cycles?" Darling asked.

"Thirty years. The last one began in 1960."

"I see."

"Yes," Talley said, leaning forward. "It's here because it's time."

Darling thought, This man is in love with giant squid. "Doc," he said, "this is all very interesting, but it doesn't say a lick about why the beast is suddenly eating people."

"But it does!" Talley said. "*Architeuthis* is what we call an adventitious feeder. He feeds by accident, and he'll eat *any*thing. Let's say that cyclical currents are bringing him up from the three-thousand-foot level, where he usually stays. And let's say he's finding his food sources are gone—I hear Bermuda's almost fished out—and all he's finding to eat is—"

There was a sharp *snap!* that sounded like a rifle shot, and something flew past Darling's face.

Osborn Manning had been clutching his plastic swizzle stick so hard that it shattered. "Sorry," he said. "Excuse me."

"No," said Talley. "*I'm* sorry. I'm very sorry."

"Doc," Darling said after a pause, "there's one thing you haven't talked about—nature's number-one rule: Balance. When there are too many sea lions, up jump the white sharks. Seems to me, this critter being here is saying nature's out of whack. Why?"

"Because," Talley said, "people have *put* nature out of whack. Only one animal preys on *Architeuthis*, and that's the sperm whale.

Man has been killing off the sperm whales, so it's possible that more and more giant squid are surviving."

More questions crowded into Darling's mind, but suddenly he realized that he was taking the bait. He made a show of looking at his watch. "It's late," he said, "and I get up early."

"Ah, Captain," Talley said, "the thing is, this animal can be caught."

Darling shook his head. "Why in the world do you want to?"

It was Manning who interrupted. "Captain Darling," he said, squeezing his hands together, "this . . . this beast killed my children. It has destroyed my life—our lives. My wife has been sedated since . . . she tried to—"

"Mr. Manning," Darling said, "this beast is just an animal."

"It is a sentient being. Dr. Talley has told me—and I believe— that it knows a form of rage. It knows vengeance. Well, so do I. Believe me. So do I."

"But it's still just an animal. What good will it—"

"How much do you charge for a day's charter?" Manning said.

Here we go, Darling thought. I never should have come here. "A thousand dollars," he said.

"I'll give you five thousand a day."

When Darling didn't reply, Talley said, "This isn't only personal, Captain. This animal *must* be caught."

"Why? Why not just let it go away?"

"Because you were wrong. It won't stop killing people. If it's found a food source, I see no reason why it will move on. And I don't believe there's a living thing out there that can stop it."

"Well, neither can I. Look, Mr. Manning, you've got all that money. Hire yourself some big-time experts. Bring in a ship."

"Don't think I didn't try. You think I want to work with you . . . with locals? I know Bermudians." Manning leaned toward Darling. His voice was low, but its intensity made it seem like a shout. "I've had a house here for years. I know all about small islands and small minds; I know how you people strut around and bray about your independence. As far as you're concerned, I'm just another rich Yankee jerk."

Talley looked stricken. Darling leaned back, smiled and said to Manning, "You do have a way with words."

"I'm tired of this, Captain. Yes, I could have chartered a boat, but your pigheaded government has so many rules that it would have taken months to set it up. So I have to use locals, and that means you. You're the best. As I see it, we've got only one problem, and that's your price."

Darling looked at him for a long moment; then he said, "Let me tell you how *I* see it, Mr. Manning. You are rich and you are a Yankee, but what makes you a jerk is that you think money will bring your children back. You think killing the beast will. Well, it won't. You can't buy yourself peace."

"I have to try, Captain."

"Okay," Darling said. "You've laid down your cards; here are mine. There's no question I could use your money. But the only asset I've got is wrapped up in these clothes, and if I lose that asset, my personal worth is zero." He stood up. "So thanks but no thanks." He nodded at Talley and walked out.

WHEN Darling had gone, Talley finished his drink, sighed and said, "I must say, Osborn, you were—"

"Don't tell me how to do business," Manning said. "Charm wouldn't have worked any better. Now at least we understand one another." He signaled to Shilly for the check.

Talley and Manning did not speak again until they were in the parking lot, and then Manning said, "How much do we know about Darling?"

"Just he's the best around. Nothing about *him*, personally."

"Nose around. See what you can learn. There's not a man alive who doesn't have enemies. Find one. Throw money at him. Tell him you want to know everything there is to know."

"You want to destroy the man?"

"No. I want to control him, but I can't until I know what there is to know. Old truism, Talley: Knowledge is power."

CHAPTER SEVEN

As DARLING took a breath he realized that the air was coming slowly, reluctantly. His tank was almost out. He might get one more breath, two at most, before he'd have to surface.

He was only five feet down, but he didn't want to have to go up now and change tanks, just to finish this stupid job. He hadn't had to work on the government's buoys in years, had hoped he'd never have to again. But there was little other work. The aquarium retainer was gone. He hadn't gotten a single dive charter. It had been nearly two weeks since anybody had seen a sign of the squid, and still not a single diver had gone into the water. He didn't know how Charlotte was keeping food on the table.

Sometimes Darling regretted turning down Manning and Talley, especially on days like today, when his mouth ached from biting on a regulator mouthpiece and he was whipped to the point of coma—all for a few hundred bucks he'd split with Mike. Darling had never stopped to think what was worth risking his life for—outside of Charlotte and Dana—but he knew for sure it was not some creature that ate people for breakfast and boats for lunch.

The job finally finished, Darling surfaced on his last breath of air. He washed the salt off in the boat's shower and put on a pair of shorts, while Mike stowed the dive gear and fried a mackerel from the cold box. After lunch they cruised southwest along the outer edge of the reefs, meandering toward home.

"Look there," Mike said, pointing down from the flying bridge. Something shiny was floating between two swells.

Darling swung the wheel. "Looks like a six-foot jellyfish," he said. He put the boat in neutral and watched the thing. It was a

huge clear jelly oblong, with a hole in the middle, and it appeared
to have some sort of life, for it rotated as if to expose new parts of
itself to the sunlight every few seconds.

Mike said, "No jellyfish *I've* ever seen."

"Beats me," Darling agreed. "Spawn of some kind, I guess. We
should take some back for that Dr. Talley to look at."

"Want me to dip it up?"

"Why not?"

Mike went down the ladder, found the long-handled dip net and
went aft, where he could reach the water easily. As the net touched
the jelly it fragmented. "Lost it," he said. "Lemme try again." He
held the handle of the net and stretched his arm out.

As the net touched water something grabbed it and pulled.
Mike's shins struck the low bulwark, and he started to fall.

"Hey!" He flailed with his free hand but found only air.

"Let it go!" shouted Darling. But Mike didn't, and he slipped
overboard. He landed in the water on his back. Only then did he
let go of the net.

Darling ran to the back of the flying bridge and half jumped
down the ladder and hurried aft. The boat was out of gear, so Mike
was in no danger from the propeller, but Darling was worried he
might panic and swallow water and drown himself.

And panicked Mike was. He forgot how to swim. He screamed
incoherently and windmilled with his arms—not five feet from the
boat.

Darling grabbed a rope. "Michael!" he shouted. He threw it at
Mike's head. It hit him in the face, but Mike ignored it until his
hands found it and, in reflex, fastened on. Then Darling pulled him
to the dive step at the stern of the boat and hauled him up.

Mike lay there, whimpering and spitting water. Then he coughed
and rose to his knees and said, "To hell with this."

"Why, Michael," Darling said, smiling, "it was just a big old turtle. I saw him. Must've decided to fight you for the spawn."

Mike coughed again. "I'm gonna go be a taxi driver."

When Mike had wrung out his clothes and wrapped a towel
around himself, Darling returned to the wheel and circled around

to where the dip net was floating on the surface. He snagged it with the boat hook and brought it aboard.

The turtle had torn a hole in the netting, but a few globs of jelly clung to some of it. Darling looked closely at one of the globs. There were little things inside, too small to make out. He debated storing it in a jar, but there probably wasn't enough of it to be worthwhile. So he washed the jelly away in the water, dropped the net on the deck and went up to the flying bridge.

A few minutes later Mike appeared with two cups of tea. "I don't like this," he said, handing Darling a cup. "Everything's making me go crazy. That squid's got me spooked."

Darling looked at Mike, huddled in the towel, his hands shaking, and he thought, This thing has opened a dark door inside this young man. It's weird how things we don't understand can arouse demons we don't even know we have.

THEY were well up in the shallows, with the pink cottages of the Cambridge Beaches resort to the right, when Mike, who was facing aft, said, "Never seen that fella before."

Darling looked back. To the north, at least three miles away, was a small ship with a white hull and a single black stack.

"Looks like one of those private research vessels," said Mike.

Darling picked up the binoculars and focused on the ship. Aft of the cabin he could see a huge steel crane. On a cradle beneath the crane was something oval with portholes in it.

"Look at that," Darling said. "Whoever he is, he's got a submersible, a little submarine, mounted on his stern."

MARCUS Sharp's commander, Captain Wallingford, was at his desk when Sharp rapped twice on the door and said, "Captain?"

"Sharp. What is it?" Wallingford spoke without looking up. "No, don't tell me. You've heard there's a research vessel with a two-million-dollar submersible here that some journalist types are using to look for the giant squid. You've heard that we're going to put a navy man in it, and you've come to volunteer." Wallingford looked up and smiled. "Well?"

"I . . . Yes, sir." Sharp stepped into the office and stood before the captain's desk.

"Why you, Sharp? You're a chopper jockey, not a submariner. And why should I send an officer? Why not just a seaman? All I need down there is a pair of eyes—somebody to make sure these turkeys don't poke around where they shouldn't."

"I'm a diver, sir," Sharp said. "I know what the underwater looks like. I might be able to see things other people wouldn't." He paused. "I've had underwater demolition training."

"Sharp, these people aren't here to blow anything up," said Wallingford. "They're not even in research. They're just magazine hotshots who want to be the first to take pictures of a live giant squid."

"What's the deal with the Bermuda government? I'd've thought the last thing Bermuda wanted was any more publicity."

"Money. What else? Bermuda's hurting. Tourism is in the dumper. Sport fishing has pretty well stopped. The diving business is *out* of business." He paused. "So tell me, what makes you want to go down into the ocean in a little steel coffin to look for something that probably isn't there and might kill you if it is?"

"Because . . ." Sharp hesitated, knowing that most people would have trouble understanding his reasoning. "It's something I've never done before. I want to see what it's like."

"You've never been to the moon before, either. Would you go to the moon if somebody asked you?"

"Yes, sir. Yes, I surely would."

"You're nuts, Sharp," Wallingford said, shaking his head. "Okay. Be at dockside at 1600. They're gonna go out and anchor tonight and put the sub down first thing tomorrow."

"Thank you, sir." Sharp saluted.

"I was gonna send you, even if you hadn't volunteered." Wallingford grinned. "I just wanted to hear you make your case."

BACK IN HIS QUARTERS, SHARP packed an overnight bag. By the time he had showered and dressed, it was nearly 1500. He picked up his bag and started out of the room. At the door he remembered that he had been scheduled to go diving the next day with Darling, and so he went back and picked up the phone.

"Glad you called, Marcus," Darling said when he answered. "How about a rain check for tomorrow? There's a bunch of people here from some magazine. They want to put a submarine down to take pictures of the squid, and they've hired me as escort."

"You're going? What do you mean, escort?"

"They don't know where to look for the thing."

"And you agreed to go? I thought—"

"Marcus. It's a thousand dollars a day. I'll just show 'em where to go float around over their submarine." Darling laughed. "You can be sure I'm not going down in that sub."

"Whip," Sharp said, and he paused, feeling his enthusiasm begin to ebb. "I'm supposed to go with them. The navy's worried they'll snoop around our sonar gear."

There was silence on the line; then Darling said, "You don't mean you're going down in that submarine."

"I have to, Whip."

"No you don't, Marcus." Darling paused, then said, "There's one thing we both have to remember: there's a big difference between being brave and being foolish."

THE Royal Navy Dockyard had been built in the nineteenth century by convicts transported out from England. Its stone walls were more than ten feet thick; its cobbled streets had been paved by hand. It had once been a civilization unto itself. There had been barracks, cookhouses, jail cells, sail lofts, rope lockers and armories. Now as Sharp walked along the quay toward the little ship tied to the dock, he passed boutiques, cafés, a museum.

The ship's name was the *Ellis Explorer*, from Fort Lauderdale.

Measuring his paces, Sharp walked alongside the ship. She was one hundred and fifty feet long, and most of her was open stern. Clearly, she was brand-new and meticulously tended. About halfway between the fantail and the cabin the submersible rested on its cradle, covered by a tarpaulin. A woman stood in the bow, tossing pieces of bread to a school of little fish.

"Hello," Sharp said.

She turned to him and said, "Hi." She was in her late twenties, tall and lithe and deeply tanned. She wore cutoff jeans, a man's oxford shirt with its tails tied at her waist and a Rolex diver's watch. Her sun-bleached brown hair was cut short.

"I'm Marcus Sharp. Lieutenant Sharp."

"Oh," she said. "Right. Come on aboard."

Sharp walked up the gangway and stepped onto the deck.

"I'm Stephanie Carr," the woman said, smiling and holding out her hand. "I take pictures." She led him aft into the cabin.

The cabin was large and comfortably furnished. There were two tables, two vinyl-covered sofas bolted to the deck, some plastic stacking chairs, and a television set and VCR. Steps led up to the bridge forward, and down to the galley and the staterooms aft.

A short, wiry man with a crew cut sat on the deck watching a James Bond movie. "That's Eddie," Stephanie said. "He drives the sub. Eddie, this is Marcus."

Eddie gestured distractedly and said, "Hey."

Sharp noticed that one of the tables was littered with camera equipment. "Do you have a writer with you?" he asked Stephanie.

"No," she said. "I do it all. Besides, if we get pictures of this monster, no one's going to care about words."

Sharp tossed his bag onto a chair. "Who's Ellis?" he said. "The name—*Ellis Explorer.*"

"Barnaby Ellis. Ellis Publications."

"You work for him?"

"No, I'm freelance. I work for whoever pays me."

"Hey, navy man," a voice called down from the bridge.

"Come meet Hector," Stephanie said, and she led the way up onto the bridge.

Hector was dark-skinned and beefy, and he wore a starched white shirt with captain's shoulder boards. He was working on a chart of the waters around Bermuda. "This Darling," he said, "he tells me to go anchor out here"—he tapped a spot on the chart—"but out here there's no bottom."

"Do what he says," said Sharp. "If he says there's a bottom there, there's a bottom there."

"But the chart—"

"Captain," Sharp said, "in Bermuda, if I had to choose between some map and Whip Darling, I'd go with Darling every time."

It was after five when they left Dockyard behind and headed north toward the channel markers. Sharp and Stephanie stood on the observation deck, atop the cabin, and watched the puffs of cumulus cloud change color with the lowering sun.

"Where do you live?" Sharp asked.

"San Francisco, sort of. I keep a tiny apartment there, but I'm away ten or eleven months a year."

"So you're not married."

"Hardly," she said, smiling. "Who'd have me? He'd never see me. When I got started in this business I knew I'd have to make a choice, and so far it's been worth it. I've been everywhere in the world, photographed everything from tigers to army ants. Now and then I think about settling down. But then the phone rings, and I'm off"—she waved her hand at the sea—"like now."

"How much do you know about giant squid?"

"Nothing. Well, almost nothing. I read a couple of articles on the way over. I gather that nobody's ever gotten a picture of one, and that's enough for me."

"There's a reason, you know. They're dangerous."

"Well," she said, "that's the fun of it, right? We get paid to do what other people couldn't do if they had all the money in the world: take chances and make discoveries. It's called living."

As Sharp looked at her he suddenly felt a pain he hadn't felt in many months—the pain of remembering Karen.

SURE enough, there was a bottom—a little outcropping from a cliff, right where Darling had said it would be.

They had dinner in the cabin: microwaved hamburgers, pasta and salad. Then Eddie and the two crewmen watched *The Hunt for Red October,* and Hector returned to the bridge.

Stephanie poured coffee for herself and Sharp, and led him outside onto the open stern. The moon was so bright that it extinguished the stars around it; the sea was as flat as glass.

"What about you?" she asked him. "Are you married?"

"No," Sharp said, and then—he wasn't sure why—he told her about Karen.

"That's rough," she said when he had finished. "I don't think I could deal with that kind of pain."

Before Sharp could say anything else, they heard Hector shout, "Hey, navy man!" from the bridge.

They walked forward along a passageway on the port side and up four steel steps to the outside door of the bridge.

"Come here," Hector said.

Sharp stepped inside the dark bridge. Little colored lights glowed from the electronic gear.

"What do you make of that?" Hector said, and he gestured at the side-scan sonar.

Sharp looked and saw a shapeless smear on the screen. He looked at the calibration numbers on the side. The smear seemed to be twenty or thirty meters long.

"It could be a shipwreck," he said.

"Have a look at it from the sub tomorrow," said Hector. "A lot of ships were lost around here in the war. Maybe it's one of them."

None of them looked at the sonar screen again. If they had, they would have seen a change in the shapeless smear. They would have seen some lines fade, others appear, as the thing three thousand feet beneath them began to move.

CHAPTER EIGHT

WHEN Sharp awoke in the morning, he didn't know where he was. The bed was small—not his—and there was a buzzing somewhere near his head. He rolled over and saw an intercom phone on the bulkhead. He picked it up and mumbled his name.

"Rise and shine, Marcus," said Stephanie. "Time to go."

As he hung up, Sharp felt a rush of adrenaline. He had volunteered for this, but what yesterday had seemed exciting was fast becoming frightening. He had never ridden in a submarine, let alone a submarine a third the size of a subway car. He didn't like crowded elevators, and he felt uneasy in interior cabins on ships. As he dressed in wool socks and a sweater—it would be cold three thousand feet down—he wondered if he was a closet claustrophobe.

The sun had barely cleared the horizon when Sharp arrived in the cabin. Through the windows in the rear he saw Eddie and one of the crewmen removing the tarpaulin from the submersible. Stephanie was on the afterdeck, mounting a video camera in an underwater housing. Then he saw that the *Privateer* was tied to the port side of the ship and heard Darling's voice behind him, up on the bridge, talking to Hector.

"Morning, Marcus," Darling said when Sharp appeared on the bridge. "Are you sure you still want to go down there?"

"Yes," Sharp said. "I'm sure."

Darling turned to Hector and said, "I'll have my mate hang off a ways till you launch. Then he'll track the sub on my gear." He left the bridge and walked aft to talk to Mike, on the *Privateer*.

Sharp went down to the stern. At the top of a ladder he met Stephanie on her way up, and she gestured for him to follow her through a watertight door aft of the bridge.

It was the control room for the submersible, and it was dark, lit only by a red bulb in the overhead and by four television monitors. One of the crewmen sat before a panel dotted with colored lights and keyboard buttons, wearing a headset and a microphone.

"Andy keeps tabs on all our systems," Stephanie said. "Your friend Whip will be in here too. We can talk to him anytime."

Sharp pointed at the TV monitors. "The submersible is hard wired to the surface?"

"Everything's videotaped. One fiberoptic cable does it all. I've got video cameras inside and outside the sub, plus my still cameras. Can I give you a camera? We'll be at different portholes."

"Sure," Sharp said. "What do you want pictures of?"

Stephanie grinned. "Monsters. Nothing but monsters."

AT CLOSE range the submersible looked to Sharp like a giant antihistamine capsule—a Dristan with arms. Each arm had steel pincers on the end, and mounted between them was a video camera in a globular housing.

The sun was higher now, and there wasn't a breath of breeze. Perspiration poured from Sharp as he lowered himself through the hatch in the top of the submersible. Stephanie, who had changed into warmer clothing, was already inside, as was Eddie.

The interior of the capsule was a tube twelve feet long, six feet wide and five feet high. There were three small portholes—one in the bow for Eddie, one on either side for Stephanie and Sharp. He found that he could sit, with his legs curled beneath him, or kneel, with his face pressed to the porthole. But there was no way he could straighten out. Don't think about it, he told himself.

"How long does it take to get to the bottom?" he asked.

"Half an hour," said Stephanie. "A hundred feet a minute."

Not too bad. He could survive for an hour, anyway. "And how long do we spend down there?"

"Up to four hours."

"Four hours!" Never, Sharp thought. Not a chance.

He heard the hatch slam above him and a metallic hiss as it was dogged down.

Stephanie passed him a small 35-mm camera with a wide-angle lens. Sharp tried to take it, but it slipped from his sweaty palms, and Stephanie caught it an inch above the steel deck. "You look like death," she said.

"No kidding." Sharp wiped his hands on his trousers and took the camera from her.

"What are you worried about? This is a state-of-the-art sub, and Eddie is a state-of-the-art pilot." She smiled. "Right, Eddie?"

Eddie nodded and mumbled into the microphone on his head-set, and suddenly the capsule jerked and began to rise as the crane lifted it off its cradle and swung it out over the side of the ship. It dropped slowly until it thudded into the water.

Sharp saw the sea lapping at the porthole glass. Then the capsule began to sink into monochromatic blue. All noise ceased except for the soft whirring of the electric motor aboard the submersible.

Sweat was quickly evaporating from under Sharp's arms and down his back, and he felt chilly. In less than a minute the temperature had dropped thirty degrees. Yet he was still sweating—not from heat but from fear and the creeping onset of claustrophobia.

He looked through the porthole and saw that the blue outside was fast deepening to violet. He dared his eyes to wander downward. Below, blue yielded to black and all was night.

SHARP was freezing. His wool socks were soaked with the condensation on the inside of the steel capsule, and his toes were numb. He tucked his hands under his arms and leaned away from the porthole to look over Eddie's shoulder at his gauges. The outside temperature was about forty degrees Fahrenheit. Inside, it was just above fifty. They were at two thousand feet and falling.

Into his microphone Eddie said, "Activating illumination,"

and he flicked a switch. Two thousand-watt lamps on top of the submersible flashed on, casting a flood of yellow that penetrated twenty feet before being swallowed by the blackness.

And then a universe of life exploded before Sharp's eyes. Tiny planktonic animals swirled in and out of the light, a living snowstorm. An infinitesimal shrimp adhered to his porthole. And something resembling a gray-and-red ribbon with a pompadour of spikes wriggled up to the porthole, then darted away.

"Look," Eddie said, pointing out his porthole. Sharp craned to see, but it was gone. A moment later it appeared at his own porthole, the creation of some disturbed imagination: an anglerfish. It looked like a brownish yellow cyst with teeth. Its eyes protruded like blue-green sores; it had fangs like needles; its flesh was crisscrossed with black veins. Where its nose should have been was a white stalk, and atop that, glowing like a beacon, was a light.

Sharp had seen pictures of anglerfish. They used their stalks as lures to attract curious and unwary prey.

He heard the motor-drive on Stephanie's camera firing frame after frame. "I thought you only wanted monsters," he said.

"What do you think these are?" Stephanie pointed out her porthole. "Look at that!"

Sharp saw a flicker of yellow pass Stephanie's porthole. He turned back and waited for the animal to make its way around the capsule. This creature might have been a yellow arrow, save that its entire digestive system—gut and stomach—hung down from a pouch and trailed along, pulsing.

Soon other animals swarmed around the capsule, drawn by the light, inquisitive and unafraid. There were snakelike creatures that seemed to trail hairs along their backs; large-eyed eels with lumps on their heads that looked like tumors; translucent globes that seemed to be all mouth.

Darling's voice suddenly boomed over the capsule's speaker. "You've got a regular zoo down there, Marcus."

"Wait'll the aquarium sees these pictures, Whip," Sharp said.

"They'll come back to you on their hands and knees." Forgetting his fear, he picked up the camera Stephanie had given him and waited for the next miniature mystery to swim by.

MIKE slapped himself in the face, and the sting roused him for a moment. But as soon as his eyes returned to the screen of the fish-finder, he felt his lids begin to droop. He stood up, stretched, yawned and looked out the window. The research ship was about a quarter of a mile away. Otherwise the sea was empty.

Whip had told him to keep his eyes glued to the fish-finder, and for more than an hour Mike had. But the image hadn't changed at all. There was the line of the bottom and just above it the little dot of the submersible. Nothing else. The radio crackled to life, and Mike heard Whip's voice. *"Privateer, Privateer."*

Mike picked up the microphone, pushed the TALK button and said, "Go ahead, Whip."

"How you doing, Michael?"

" 'Bout to fall asleep. This is worse than watching paint dry."

"Nothing's going on—take a breather."

"I'll do that. Get some air and fiddle with that pump."

"Leave the volume up so you'll hear me if I call."

"Roger that, Whip." Mike replaced the microphone. He looked at the fish-finder one more time, then went outside.

In the wheelhouse the fish-finder continued to glow. For several moments the image stayed steady. Then on the right side of the screen a new mark appeared. It was a solid mass, and slowly it began to move across the screen toward the submersible.

"YOU look cold, Marcus," Stephanie said.

Sharp nodded. "You got that right," he said. He couldn't stop shivering. "How come you're not?"

"I've got a layer of wool over silk over cotton." Stephanie reached into a plastic box and took out a thermos bottle. She poured the top full of coffee and passed it to Sharp.

The coffee was strong, and as it pooled in his stomach Sharp welcomed the warmth. "Thanks," he said.

He looked at his watch. They had been down for nearly three hours, drifting at twenty-five hundred feet, and they had seen nothing but the small, strange creatures that gathered around the capsule and then vanished into the darkness.

"Shall I put her on the bottom?" Eddie said into his microphone.

Darling's voice came over the speaker. "Might's well," he said.

Eddie pushed the control stick forward, and the capsule began to drop. The bottom was like pictures Sharp had seen of the surface of the moon: barren, dusty, undulating. Suddenly Eddie said, "What's that?"

"What?" Sharp said. "What is it?"

Eddie pointed at Sharp's porthole, and Sharp pressed his face to the glass. He saw snakes. No, they were some kind of weird fish, all swarming on something dead. Bits of flesh broke loose and floated away, and were mobbed by other, smaller scavengers.

Eddie swung the submersible over the fish, driving them away, and then Sharp could see what they had been feeding on.

"A sperm whale!" he said. "It's the lower jaw of a sperm whale. Do you see that, Whip?"

"Yes," Darling's voice said, sounding flat and distant.

"What could possibly kill a sperm whale?"

Darling didn't answer, but in the silence Sharp suddenly thought, I know. And he began to sweat. He strained his eyes to see beyond the perimeter of light. Fish darted back and forth, phantoms suddenly appearing and disappearing. He was comforted by them. Whip had once said that as long as fish were around, you didn't have to worry about sharks, because fish read the electromagnetic impulses that warned of a shark's intention to attack. It was when the fish vanished that you worried.

THE creature sensed a change in its surroundings, as if energy had suddenly surged into its world. A great light, emitting a pulsing sound, was galvanizing other animals. Something was there, not far away, and it was moving.

The creature's olfactories detected no signs of life. If it had been less hungry, it might have been more cautious. But it had not eaten in days, and its needs were impelling it. So it continued to move. It could no longer live as a scavenger; it had been forced to become a hunter.

Soon it saw the lights, little pinpoints of brightness piercing the black, and throughout its body it felt the thrumming vibrations emanating from the thing.

Motion meant life; vibrations meant life. And so it determined that the thing was alive.

It attacked.

"THE thing's not down here," Eddie said. "We're going up." He pulled back on the control stick.

Sharp looked at the digital depth readout on the console. As he watched, the numbers changed—ever so slowly, he thought, and he tried to will the numbers to flash faster—from 970 meters to 969. He sighed and massaged his toes.

Suddenly the capsule jolted and yawed to one side. Sharp was knocked off his knees, and he grabbed for a handhold. The capsule righted itself and continued upward.

"What was that?" Sharp said.

Eddie didn't answer. He was hunched forward, his shoulders tensed.

Stephanie's back was pressed against the bulkhead, her hands braced on the deck. "What was it, Eddie?" she said.

"I didn't see," Eddie said. "It felt like we hit a current."

Over the speaker Darling said, "Not a chance. There *are* no currents down there." He paused. "Something's there."

As Darling's words registered with Sharp, he felt a weight like a sack of rocks in his stomach. Here we go, he thought.

He looked over at Stephanie. She had her back to him, and her camera was firing frames against the porthole. "Take some pictures, Marcus," she said over her shoulder.

"Of what?" Sharp said. "I didn't see anything."

"The lens is wider than your eye. Maybe it'll see something."

Before Sharp could reply, the capsule was jolted again, hard, and it careened to the left. A shadow passed before the lights, dimming them, then disappeared.

"Whoa!" Eddie shouted, and he fought the stick, righting the capsule.

With trembling hands Sharp put his camera to the porthole and pressed the shutter release, advanced the film and shot again.

The capsule was rising again. Sharp looked at the digital depth readout on the controls: 960 meters, 959, 958 . . .

THE giant squid rushed through the darkness, seized by paroxysms of frustrated rage. Its whips lashed out, hooks erect; its colors flashed from gray to brown to maroon to red to pink.

It had passed once over the lighted thing, appraising it; then it had tried to kill it. The thing had been hard, an impenetrable carapace, and it had fought back with vigorous movement.

Because its attack had created no encouraging spoor of blood or torn flesh, the squid had not pressed the attack. It had moved on in search of other nourishment.

But its digestive juices had begun to flow; now they were causing the creature pain, confusion and rage.

Seeking food, any food, it moved slowly upward behind the retreating thing, not pursuing it, but following it nevertheless.

"THAT was *something*," Stephanie said as she pulled herself up through the open hatch and sat on its rim. She grinned down at Darling and Hector, who stood below, on the ship's deck.

Sharp squeezed through the hatch and sat beside her. He took a deep breath, savoring the fresh air. Savoring safety.

"Did you see it?" Hector asked. "The thing that knocked you around down there?"

"Not really." Stephanie looked at Sharp. "Did you?"

"No," Sharp said, looking at Darling. "Did you get anything on the video, Whip?"

"Just a shadow," Darling said.

Eddie said, "Whatever it was, it didn't want to tackle the sub. It gave us a once-over and took off."

"Maybe," said Darling. He was making a circuit of the capsule, examining it. He stopped and touched something.

Sharp leaned over the side and looked where Whip's fingers were rubbing the paint. He saw five ragged scratch marks, two or three feet long, that had slashed through the paint to bare metal. "It's the squid, isn't it?" he said.

Darling nodded and said, "Looks like it to me."

"We'll be ready for him next time," said Stephanie. She pulled her legs out of the hatch, slid down off the capsule and said to Eddie, "What's your turnaround time?"

"Four hours," Eddie replied, looking at his watch. "We should be ready to go down again at about four o'clock."

Not me, Sharp thought. "I'll stay topside," he said. "I can see plenty on the TV screens to keep the navy happy."

"You've already been bumped anyway," said Hector.

"By whom?"

"The Bermuda government's got someone on it this afternoon. That St. John fellow. It seems he's got a plan to kill the squid."

Sharp looked at Darling and saw a look of disgust on his face. Then Darling turned away and spit over the side of the ship.

CHAPTER NINE

SHARP and Darling stood on the observation deck and watched St. John unload his gear from the aquarium boat. There were four aluminum cases, two boxes of fresh fish, and a modified fish trap, about three feet square, made of chicken wire and steel reinforcing rod.

St. John consulted with Eddie and Stephanie. Then Eddie called the two crewmen over, and they hauled the cases to the submersible and began to fasten the wire cage to the top.

Stephanie climbed to the observation deck. "This should be interesting," she said to Marcus and Whip. "He's even got Hector jazzed, and that takes some doing." She pointed to the afterdeck, and they saw Hector following St. John around, asking questions.

Sharp said, "You think he's got a chance?"

"A chance, yes. And he's sure got enough bait. A hundred pounds of fresh tuna should keep anything down there busy long enough for us to do what we have to do."

"How does he think he's gonna kill it?" Darling asked.

"With two weapons," Stephanie said, gesturing at the mechanical arms of the submersible. "Both are attached to the sub's arms, and he can work them from inside the capsule. One's a spear gun loaded with enough strychnine to kill a dozen elephants. The other fires a twelve-gauge-shotgun shell loaded with globs of mercury that disperse like poisonous shrapnel. And if the weapons don't kill the squid, he thinks it might wrap itself around the capsule, and then it can be brought to the surface on the cables and killed up here."

"That's crazy," Darling said. "That's like trying to catch a tiger by sticking your arm in his mouth and shouting, 'I've got him!' "

"He can't crush the submersible," Stephanie said. "I think it sounds like a pretty good idea."

"Well, I think it sounds like bloody foolishness," said Darling, and he left the deck.

"Don't go down," Sharp said to Stephanie when Darling had gone. "Let St. John try it alone. You can go the next time."

"You're nice to care, Marcus," she said, and she touched his cheek. "But I want to go. That's what I'm here to do."

DARLING entered the bridge and called over to the *Privateer*, which by now had drifted a mile to the north.

"Just checking in, Michael," he said. "You awake?"

"Barely. Okay if I put a line down for some snappers?"

"Sure, but drive over here first, then kill the engine and let her drift. That way you'll be in position to track the sub."

"Roger that, Whip," Mike said. "*Privateer* standing by."

Mike brought the boat closer, took it out of gear and let it settle. He looked across the still water and tried to gauge his distance from the research ship now. A hundred and fifty yards, he guessed. Just about right. The sub was still aboard.

He turned off the engine and went aft to cut up some mackerel. He rigged two hooks on a line, put half the mackerel on each, then tied a weight to the end of the line and tossed the rig overboard. The bucket the mackerel had been in was half full of bloody water and bits of flesh. He tossed its contents overboard.

When after five minutes he hadn't had a nibble, it occurred to him that if there were any fish around, they might be above or below his bait. The fish-finder was still on; he might as well take advantage of it, see if it could give him any clues. He cleated the line off and went into the wheelhouse.

The screen was a mess. He'd never seen a pattern like this before. If he hadn't known for a fact that he was in three thousand feet of water, he'd have sworn the boat was aground. Maybe something had gotten caught in the through-hull fitting that held the machine's transponder. When they got to shore, he'd put on a scuba tank and go under the boat and have a look.

He went aft and uncleated his line. Something was wrong with it; it was too light. The weight was gone and probably the hooks and bait as well. He cursed and began to reel in the line.

THE creature blew a volume of water from its funnel and propelled itself through the blue water, searching for the faint trail of food scent that it had found and then lost again.

It was not comfortable this close to the warm surface and would not have been up here if hunger had not driven it. It had found two bits of food and consumed them. Then it had rested in the cool shadow of something above. But it had felt itself tapped by a barrage of annoying impulses from that thing above, and so had moved again.

It plunged from blue water to violet, then rose once more.

It found nothing.

The higher it went, however, the more promising the water seemed. There were tantalizing hints, as if the water near the surface contained the residue of food.

It rose still higher, close to something dark above, and soared directly beneath it, pushing a vast mass of water above itself.

DAMN puppy sharks, Mike thought as he examined the end of the monofilament line. Leave a line cleated for one minute, and they sneak up on you and bit it off.

The boat rose beneath him as if lifted by a sudden sea, and he raised his eyes from the line and looked at the flat water. It was weird how ground swells could appear like that, out of nowhere. In the distance he saw the crane on the *Ellis Explorer* pick the submersible up and swing it out over the side of the ship.

How long did it take the submersible to get to the bottom? Half an hour? He still had time to put another line down. He took a new wire leader off the hatch cover, leaned against the bulwark and held the eye of the swivel on the end of the leader up to his face so he could see to thread the monofilament through it.

There was a squishing noise behind him. Part of his mind registered this, but he was concentrating on the monofilament.

He heard the squishing noise again, closer this time, and there was a sound of scratching. There was a smell to it, too, a familiar smell, but he couldn't quite place it.

And then suddenly something had him around the chest and head, something tight and wet. Mike's hands grabbed at it, then slipped off as the thing began to squeeze. He felt as if a thousand ice picks were piercing his flesh.

As his feet lifted off the deck and he felt himself dragged through the air, he realized what had happened.

ANDY, THE SUBMERSIBLE'S CONTACT, sat at the console in the ship's control room. Darling stood behind him, wearing a headset, and Sharp stood beside Darling.

Because only two television cameras were in use, two of the four monitors were blank. The third showed the inside of the capsule: Eddie holding the stick and looking out his porthole, St. John testing the manipulators of the arms, Stephanie adjusting the lens of one of her cameras. The fourth monitor showed the scene outside the capsule: the bright aura from the lamps, the shower of plankton, and evanescent swirls of red as the eddying currents swept fish blood from the wire cage.

"Twenty-eight hundred," Andy said. "They're nearly there."

Soon they saw the bottom rise up. The turbulence of the submersible's propeller stirred the mud into a cloud. Then the capsule settled, and the cloud cleared.

Suddenly a shadow passed over the bottom, disappeared and passed again, going the other way.

"Shark," said Darling. "Liam didn't figure on sharks. It'll probably go for his bait."

The image on the monitor jiggled as the capsule shook.

"What's that?" they heard St. John say.

"A shark, Doctor," Andy said into his microphone.

"Well, do something!" said St. John.

Darling laughed. "We're half a bloody mile away, Liam."

Andy grabbed a control lever. The monitor of the exterior camera turned and faced upward. Now they could see the wire cage.

"It's a six-gill shark," Darling said. "Rare enough."

It was chocolate brown, with a bright green eye and six rippling gills. It was small, less than twice the size of the cage, but tenacious. It bit down on the corner of the cage and rolled its body, first one way, then the other, trying to tear a hole in the wire.

On the other monitor they saw St. John crawl forward and take the handles that operated one of the mechanical arms. Recessed in the arm's control panel was a monitor showing the image seen by the outside camera. Consulting it, St. John pulled the handle, and the arm turned, pointing its needle toward the wire cage filled with tuna bait.

"Uh-oh," Darling said. "Don't do it, Liam. Leave it alone. A six-gill can't wreck your cage."

"So *you* say." St. John's voice came over the speaker. "Why should I let the shark take all the bait?"

They saw Stephanie move toward St. John and heard her say, "Doctor, if we waste one of your weapons on a shark, we're cutting our odds in half."

"Don't worry, Miss Carr," St. John said. "We'll still have plenty left to do the job."

On one monitor they saw St. John push a button; on the other they saw a burst of bubbles as the dart fired from the spear gun and struck the shark just behind its gill slits.

For a few seconds the shark seemed to take no notice of the sting. Then suddenly its body arched, and its mouth jerked away from the cage and gaped. Rigid and quivering, it hung suspended in the water, and then rolled over and fell into the mud.

"Won't a dead shark just bring *more* sharks?" Sharp asked.

"No," said Darling. "Sharks are strange that way. They'll kill each other, but if one of their own dies, they stay away. It's like they can read their own death in it." Darling paused and looked at the monitor. "Some things can't deal with death," he said. "Others thrive on it."

THE squid had fed, but after so long a deprivation the protein it had consumed had not satisfied its hunger. And so the beast continued to hunt, drifting down to the bottom.

Suddenly its senses were assaulted by new, conflicting signals— live prey, dead prey, light, movement, sound. It began to charge back and forth, confused, defensive, aggressive.

The rods in its eyes detected light nearby. Then more light flooded in, and more. Agitated, it drew water into its body and expelled it, propelling itself across the bottom.

As the beast drew closer to the source of light, the light became harsh, repellent. Reflex told it to retreat, but its olfactory sensors began to receive strong waves of food spoor—fresh kill.

Hunger drove it onward.

SHARP yawned, stretched and shook his head; he was having trouble staying awake. He had been watching for over an hour, and there had been no movement on either monitor. It was hypnotic, like watching test patterns.

In the submersible, Stephanie, St. John and Eddie had hardly spoken. Stephanie had taken a few pictures, but now she just knelt at her porthole and watched.

Aboard the *Explorer,* the control room door opened, and Darling entered, carrying two cups of coffee. He passed one to Sharp and said, "I couldn't find any cream, so . . . Oh, my God!"

"What?" Sharp followed Darling's eyes to the monitors.

"The fish. They're gone."

As Darling put on a headset and fumbled for the TALK button on the microphone, Sharp realized what he meant: no abyssal creatures were patrolling; no tiny scavengers gulped the bits of tuna that floated down from the wire cage.

"Liam," Darling shouted into the microphone. "Look out!"

St. John started at the sound of the voice. "Look out for—?"

There was a hollow sound then, a scraping, almost like a ship running aground. Then the capsule was jerked up and tilted forward. The interior camera showed Stephanie and St. John being hurled into Eddie, and all of them tumbling over the control panel. The exterior camera showed nothing but mud.

Eddie cursed. St. John grabbed for the mechanical arm and tried to work the handles. "It's stuck in the mud!" he yelled.

"Put power to her!" Darling said to Eddie. "That beast won't like the propeller."

They saw Eddie pull back on the stick and apply power, and they heard the submersible's motor shriek as it raced. The capsule tilted up; the mechanical arm came free.

"The camera!" St. John said.

Eddie reached for the controls for the outside camera as St. John raised the mechanical arm, his finger poised over the firing button.

The monitor showed the camera turning. Mud gave way to water, then to a blur on the side of the capsule, then to—

"What the hell is that?" Sharp said.

The camera showed a field of circles, pinkish gray, each quivering on its own stalk, each apparently rimmed with teeth and each containing an amber-colored claw.

"Bad news, that's what," said Darling, and he shouted into the microphone, "Fire it, Liam!"

Then the screen went blank.

THE creature crushed the camera in its whip and cast it away.

Then it turned back to the shredded remains of the food, its eight short arms scratching and clawing as it searched for more to feed to the snapping beak. But there was no more.

The creature was confused. The spoor of food was everywhere. All its senses told it there was food. But where was it?

It perceived a large, hard carapace and associated it with food. It encircled the prey with its whips and set about to destroy it.

"I CAN'T see!" St. John shouted. "Where did it go?"

"Fire it, Liam!" Darling shouted. "Fire the dart! That thing is so big you can't miss."

They saw St. John push the button to fire the dart. "It didn't fire!" he cried, and he pushed the button again and again.

Stephanie yelled, "Look!" She was pointing out her porthole. "In the mud. The spear gun. The thing tore it *off*."

The capsule shuddered then and rolled from side to side, knocking them all over. The images through the portholes flashed like patterns in a kaleidoscope: mud, water, light, darkness.

Watching the single television monitor, Sharp felt sick with helplessness. "We've got to *do* something!" he said. "Bring it up. Start the winch. Maybe the motion will scare it off."

"It'd take ten minutes to reel in the slack in the cable," Darling said. "And they don't have ten minutes. Whatever's gonna happen is gonna happen now."

THE creature sought weakness. There was weakness some- where. There was weakness in all prey. It was less than half the creature's size, and although it was strong and dense, it did not struggle.

The creature lifted it easily in its two long whips and drew it into its eight short arms, probing for a soft spot. It opened its beak and let its rasping tongue slowly search the skin.

"WHAT's that noise?" St. John hissed. It sounded as if a coarse file were scraping at the hull.

The capsule was upside down now, and the three of them knelt on the overhead and braced themselves with their hands.

"It's playing with you," Darling said over the mike. "With any luck it'll get bored and leave you be. Then we'll winch you up."

Sharp waited until Darling had released the TALK button, then said, "You believe that?"

Darling paused before he said, "No. It's gonna find a way in."

THE tongue snaked across the skin, examining texture, seek- ing difference. But the skin was all the same: hard, tasteless, dead. Then a signal flashed across the creature's brain and vanished.

The tongue stopped, retreated, began to lick again, slower. There. The signal reappeared, steady.

The texture here was different: smoother, thinner. Weaker.

STEPHANIE HEARD A NOISE BEHIND her and turned to look at her porthole. What she saw made her scream and back away.

St. John looked, and gasped.

"What?" Darling said into the microphone.

"I think . . ." St. John said, "a tongue."

Andy changed the angle of the camera in the submersible and focused on the porthole. Then he and Whip and Marcus could see it too: a tongue. It licked in circles, covering the glass with pink flesh. Then it withdrew, and for a moment the porthole was black. There was the sound of a deafening screech.

St. John grabbed a flashlight from a clip on the bulkhead and shone it on the porthole.

They could see only part of it, for it was bigger than the porthole, much bigger: a curved, scythelike beak, amber-colored, its sharply pointed end pressing on the glass.

Stephanie flattened herself against the opposite bulkhead, while St. John silently pointed the flashlight at the porthole. Eddie turned his face to the camera and said, "Damn!"

In the control room the three men could hear a cracking noise and then an explosion of water, a booming sound and screams. Then silence as the monitor went dead.

They all continued mutely to stare at the blank screen.

CHAPTER TEN

As SOON as Darling got into the taxi, he took off his tie and stuffed it into his jacket pocket. He rolled the window down and let the breeze wash over his face.

He hated funerals, but at least this one had been simple—just Mike's family and Darling, with a few words from a Portuguese preacher. Mike and he had made a pact long ago that if one of them died, the other would simply bury him at sea. Well, Mike had been buried at sea, all right, but not the way they had planned.

There had been no questions, no recriminations. In fact, Mike's widow and her two brothers and two sisters had made a special effort to comfort Darling.

Which, of course, had made him feel even worse.

He hadn't told them the truth about how Mike died. Only he and Sharp knew the truth, but Whip had seen no point in painting pictures that would haunt them for the rest of their lives. So he had said Mike had fallen overboard and drowned; that he must have struck his head on the dive step and knocked himself out.

They had told that tale to the authorities too, with no conscience about suppressing evidence. There was enough carnage on the videotapes of the submersible's destruction to satisfy all the ghouls. One more victim wouldn't make any difference.

When Darling had gotten no answer to his calls to the *Privateer*, he had been ready to chew Mike out for falling asleep on watch. He and Sharp had borrowed Hector's Zodiac and sped across to the drifting boat. Sharp had still been in shock from the sub disaster; he had ridden in the speedboat like a zombie. But when they had found Mike missing, he had quickly come around.

At first they were convinced that Mike *had* fallen overboard. Then they had seen scratch marks in the boat's paint, had felt a telltale slime and smelled a telltale odor.

Because Darling hadn't been on the boat when the accident happened, he heaped blame on himself. Mike had always relied on Whip to tell him the right thing to do; he had never liked being alone on the boat, and Whip had known it.

Stop it, Darling told himself. There's no point to this.

The taxi driver had the radio on, and the midafternoon newscast began with more gloomy news about the Bermuda economy. In the week since the disaster, tourism had dropped by almost half.

Nobody wanted to tangle with the beast anymore—nobody except that Dr. Talley and Osborn Manning. They had written to Darling, upping their ante to two hundred thousand dollars. Darling's response had been simple: What good is money to a dead man? As he saw it, they were, each in his own way, next to nuts.

His own concern was to find an immediate way to make a living. He had decided that the time had come at last to sell his cherished Masonic bottle, and a dealer in Hamilton had told him there was some interest in it. He thought he might go through the artifacts in the house and see if there was anything else rare enough to be worth selling. He hated to do it—it was like selling pieces of himself—but he had no choice.

He did have one hope, however: the aquarium had called, and they were interested in discussing a new retainer agreement. Now that St. John was gone, they could make decisions based on practicality. That might pay for some fuel.

Still, he and Charlotte had to eat.

At the dirt road to his house, Darling paid the driver and got out of the taxi. He saw Dana's car in the driveway. What was she doing here this early in the day?

Then he heard a voice. "Captain Darling?"

He turned and saw Talley and Manning walking down the road toward him. Manning was in front, immaculate in a gray suit, a blue shirt and a striped tie. He was carrying a briefcase. Talley followed, looking, Darling thought, nervous and uneasy.

"What do you want?" Darling said.

"We want to talk to you," Manning said.

"I've got nothing to say." Darling turned toward the house.

"Talk to us now, Captain," Manning said, "or talk to the law later."

Darling stopped. "The law?" he said. "What law? You got nothing better to do than threaten people?"

"I didn't threaten anybody, Captain. I stated a fact."

"Okay. Say your piece and go along."

"May we perhaps"—Manning gestured at the house—"go to the house and discuss this like—"

"I'm not a civilized person, Mr. Manning. I'm an angry fisherman who's sick to death of having people tell me—"

"As you wish, Captain. Here it is. Within ten days you are to deliver to me a certified check for twelve thousand dollars. If you fail to make the deadline, you will then have thirty days to move yourself and your belongings out of your house."

Darling stared at Manning. Then he looked at Talley, who was staring at the ground.

"Wait a second," Darling said. He couldn't have heard right; there had to be a mistake. "Let me get this straight. I give you twelve thousand dollars or you kick me out of my house."

"Correct. You see, Captain, I own your house. Or, to be precise, I will very soon."

Darling laughed. "Right. And you're my great-great-grandfather."

"Captain"—Manning took a piece of paper from his briefcase and held it out to Darling—"read this."

The paper was in legalese, and the only elements Darling could parse were the name of the house, its location, an assignment of something or other to Osborn Manning, and some numbers. "I'll have to get my specs," he said.

"By all means. But why don't I tell you the substance? Your wife has been borrowing money, using the house as collateral. She is three months behind in the payments and has been notified that she is in danger of default. I bought the note from the lender. In ten days I will foreclose on the note."

"That's a lie," Darling said, staring at the paper. "Charlie wouldn't have done that. Not ever."

"She did it, Captain."

"It's a lie," Darling said again, and he turned back to the house.

Charlotte and Dana were sitting together in the kitchen.

The screen door slammed behind Darling, and he marched in from the hallway. "You won't believe what—" He stopped when he saw their faces. They were both crying. "No," he said. "No."

And then he asked them, "Why?"

"Because we had to live, William."

"We were living. We had food. We had fuel."

"We had food because Dana brought us food. How was I supposed to pay our electricity? How was I supposed to pay the taxes? They were going to cut off our gas." Charlotte wiped her eyes. "What do you think we've been *living* on?"

"But . . . I mean . . . There were things we could sell."

"I sold everything already. The coins. The three-mold bottles. The bellarmine jug. All of it. There was nothing more."

"I'll go talk to the bank. They can't just—"

"It wasn't the bank," said Dana. "They wouldn't give you a mortgage. You had no steady income."

"Who lent the money, then?"

"Aram Agajanian," said Charlotte.

"Agajanian!" Darling shouted. Aram Agajanian was an immigrant to Bermuda who had made a fortune producing soft-core pornography for Canadian cable television and had chosen Bermuda as a tax haven. "Why did you go to *him?*"

"Because he offered. Dana had done the accounts for one of his companies, and she asked him a couple of questions about securing loans, and . . . well, he offered."

"I don't believe it!" Darling said, turning to Dana. "You hung out our dirty laundry in front of that pervert?"

"You want me to say I'm sorry, Daddy? Well, I am. I'm sorry. There." Dana was struggling not to sob. "But the fact is, he offered. No strings, no payment schedule. I never thought he'd sell the note. He didn't want to."

"Why did he?"

"I think Mr. Manning made him one of those offers you can't refuse. Mr. Manning owns a lot of cable companies."

"Wonderful. Great." Darling felt betrayed and confused. He looked around and, for no reason, touched one of the walls. "Two hundred and twenty years," he said.

"It's just a house, William," Charlotte said. "We'll find somewhere else to live. It's just a house."

"No, Charlie, it's not. It's more than two centuries of Darlings. It's our family." He looked at his wife and his daughter.

"Let it go, William. We're together. That's all that counts."

"Like hell," Darling said, and he turned and left the room.

WHEN Darling returned to the end of his driveway, he found the tableau unchanged. Talley still paced and fidgeted; Manning still stood like a Bond Street mannequin.

Darling motioned for them to follow him, and as he led them up the driveway he imagined Manning was gloating, and he had to fight to keep from spinning on the man.

He gestured for them to sit at a table on the porch. "You're pretty sure that beast is still around, then," he said to Talley.

"Yes. Nothing's changed yet. The seasons haven't changed, currents haven't changed. *Architeuthis* is finding food. There's been no reason for it to leave."

"There was no reason for it to come, either."

"Yes, but it did. It's here. The important thing to remember, Captain, is not to make *Architeuthis* into a demon. It is an animal with its own cycles; it responds to natural rhythms. I think it's hungry and confused. It's not finding its normal prey. I think I can coax it to respond to an illusion of normalcy."

"Whatever that means. Do you believe you can get the best of this thing?"

"I think so, yes."

"How?"

Talley hesitated. "I'll tell you . . . soon."

"Is it a state secret or something?"

"No. I'm sorry. I'm not playing games. It depends on how the animal behaves. What I want to try to do is make it destroy itself."

Darling looked at Manning and saw him staring, stone-faced, at the bay, as if the details bored him. "I wouldn't count on it, Doc," Darling said. "I think I've got a right to—"

"No, Captain," Manning said, suddenly interested again. There was a thin smile on his lips. "You have no rights. You have a duty: to drive the boat and to help us."

"Now, Osborn," Talley said, "I don't think—"

"Why not, Herbert? We're not civilized people here; Captain Darling said so himself. Politeness wastes time. Better that we all know exactly where we stand, right from the start."

Darling felt a sharp pain behind his eyes, sparked, he knew, by rage and a feeling of impotence. Manning was correct: he had found Darling's price. There was no point in pretending otherwise.

Darling said, "When do you want to go?"

"As soon as we can," Manning replied.

"I'll have to get fuel, food. We could go tomorrow."

"Fuel." Manning reached into his briefcase and brought out a packet of hundred-dollar bills. "Ten thousand enough?"

"Should do."

"Now, the terms." Manning snapped his briefcase shut. "Dr. Talley is confident he'll be able to attract the squid within seventy-two hours, so you'll provision the boat for three days. Whether or not we catch it, on our return I'll destroy the note and pay you the balance of the two hundred thousand." He stood up. "Agreed?"

"No," Darling said.

"What do you mean, 'no'?"

"Here are *my* terms," Darling said, looking at Manning. "You'll burn the note now, in front of me. Before we leave the dock, you'll give me fifty thousand dollars in cash, which will stay ashore here with my wife. The balance in her name in escrow in the bank, in case we don't come back."

Manning hesitated, then opened his briefcase again and took out the note and a gold lighter. "You're an honorable man, Captain," he said as he held the note and touched the flame to it. "But so am I. You shouldn't distrust me."

"This has nothing to do with trust," Darling said. "I want to provide for my wife."

It took Darling almost three hours to pump two thousand gallons of diesel fuel into the *Privateer* and to buy six bags of groceries—fruits and vegetables, corned beef, canned tuna, blocks of cheese, loaves of bread. By the time they'd eaten all that food, he figured, they'd either be home or they'd be dead.

When he returned to his dock, evening was coming on. He removed extraneous gear from the boat: broken traps, scuba tanks, compressor parts. He came across the pump Mike had been working on. He held it in his hands and looked at it. He thought he could feel Mike's energy in it.

Don't be stupid, he said to himself. He was alone now. Well, not quite alone. He had one ally, in a box down in the hold, and he'd use it if he had to.

I'm giving you one chance, Mr. Manning, he thought. And if you screw up, I'm gonna blow that sucker to kingdom come.

CHARLOTTE was in the kitchen doing what she always did when things were bad and she didn't know what else to do: cooking. She had roasted an entire leg of lamb and made a salad big enough to feed a regiment.

"Company coming?" Darling said, and he went to her and kissed the back of her neck.

"After twenty-one years," she said, "you'd think I would have known what you'd do."

"I even surprised myself. Until today I thought there were only two things in the world that really mattered to me. I wonder what my old man would say."

"He'd say you're a fool."

"I doubt it. He was a big one for roots—that's why they all loved this house. It was their roots. It's our roots too."

"What about us?" Charlotte turned to face him, and there were tears in her eyes. "Aren't we roots enough—Dana and I?"

"We wouldn't *be* us without this house, Charlie. What would we be, living in a condo or Dana's spare room? That's not us."

Charlotte turned back to her cooking. "Marcus called."

"Did you tell him what's going on?"

"I did. I thought maybe he could think of a way to stop you."

"And could he?"

"Of course not. He thinks you walk on water."

"He's a good lad."

"No, just another fool."

Darling looked at her back. "I love you, Charlie," he said. "I don't say it too often, but you know I do."

"Not enough, I guess."

"Well . . ." He sighed, wishing he could think of comforting words to weave. But he couldn't think of any, so he turned on the television to get the weather forecast.

They left the television on while they ate, letting it fill the silence, for they both sensed there was nothing more to say and any attempts at conversation would result in words they would regret.

After supper Darling went out onto the lawn and looked at the bay. There was still some light—the soft violet that ushers in the night—and he could see two egrets standing like sentries in the shallows by the point. A gentle, fluttering sound heralded the arrival of a school of fry, skittering across the glassy water.

When he was a child, he spent his evenings watching the sights and sounds of the bay, as enraptured by it as other children were by radio or television. The bay was life and death, and it still gave him a feeling of peace, the reassurance of continuity.

The crown of a full moon peeked above the trees in the east and cast arrows of gold that lit the egrets like golden statues.

"Charlie," Darling called, "come look."

He heard her footsteps in the house, but they stopped at the screen door. "No," she said.

"Why not?" he asked.

She didn't answer. Instead, she thought, Oh, William, you look like an old Indian, sitting on a hillside, getting ready to die.

CHAPTER ELEVEN

DARLING was awakened by the sound of the wind whistling through the casuarinas behind the house. It was still dark, but he didn't need to see to know the weather; his ears told him that the wind was out of the northwest and blowing fifteen to twenty knots. He half hoped it would crank up into a gale. Maybe a rough ride would make Manning and Talley get sick and decide to quit.

Charlotte lay on her side, breathing deeply. He bent down and kissed her, inhaling her aroma and holding his breath, as if trying to carry the memory of her with him.

By the time he had shaved and made coffee, the sky was lightening in the east. There was still a stiff breeze on, but a ridge of high cirrus was creeping northward, signaling that the wind would soon shift back to the south. By noon the swell would have faded.

He headed down to the dock. The boat was straining against its lines, rocking gently. He was about to step aboard when suddenly he sensed someone was there, in the cabin. He stopped and listened. Over the noise of the lines creaking and water lapping against the hull, he heard breathing sounds.

Some reporter, he thought. One of those kids who think they've got a right to invade a man's privacy.

He crossed the gangplank and stepped down onto the steel deck and said, "By the time I count three, you better be up and ashore, or you're goin' for a long, long swim." He stepped over the threshold into the cabin, said, "One . . ." and saw Marcus Sharp sit up with a start.

Sharp yawned, smiled and said, "Morning, Whip."

"Marcus," Darling said, "to what do I owe the pleasure?"

"I heard you were going out today. I thought maybe you could use some help."

"I'd welcome a pair of friendly hands, that's for sure. But what does Uncle Sam have to say about this?"

"Uncle Sam sent me. Sort of. Scientists from all over have been trying to push the navy into launching an expedition to hunt for the squid, but the navy claims it doesn't have the money. When I told Captain Wallingford you were going out, he thought it would look good to have the navy go too—sort of show the flag." Sharp paused. "I tried to call. I hope you don't mind."

"Of course not. But look, Marcus, I want you to know up front what you're signing on for. These folks—"

"I've seen the beast, Whip. Or almost."

"Okay, then. You've had demolition training, right?"

"A year."

"Good. We're gonna need it."

At six thirty they cast off, and motored slowly across the bay, tying up at the town dock, where Talley and Manning waited beside a rented pickup truck piled high with cases. They unloaded twenty-two in all, placing them aboard the boat under Talley's supervision. When all were aboard, Manning reached inside the cab of the truck and brought out a long case. From the way he carried it aboard the boat, Darling could see that it was heavy; and from the care Manning took not to bang it on anything, Darling could tell that it was precious.

"What's that?" Darling asked him.

"Never mind," Manning said, disappearing into the cabin.

Well, we'll see about that, Darling said to himself.

He went up to the flying bridge, looked aft and said, "Cast her off, Marcus." When he saw that the last of the lines was aboard, he put the boat in gear and began to move slowly through the bay.

He waited until they were well out; then he leaned over the side of the flying bridge and said, "Mr. Manning, would you come up here a second?"

Manning climbed the ladder impatiently. "What is it?"

"What's in the case?"

"I told you all you need to know."

"I see," Darling said. Fifty yards dead ahead a schooner lay broadside to their path. "Okay, here you go. It's your show; you run it." Then he turned and headed for the ladder.

"*What?*" Manning cried. "Come back here!" They were closing in on the schooner. "Help!" he shouted.

Darling waited another second, and then he stepped quickly across the deck and took the wheel again, nosing the boat past the schooner's bow by six inches. "Look, Mr. Manning," Darling said. "We have to work together. We can't have folks running all over the boat with their own agendas. Talley knows the animal, but doesn't know anything about the ocean. Marcus knows the ocean, but doesn't know the animal. I know something about each; and you, I figure, don't know nothing about anything but making money. Now, tell me: What's in the case?"

Manning hesitated. "A rifle."

"What kind of rifle?"

"A Finnish assault rifle. A Valmet. I've fixed the clips so that every third bullet is a phosphorous tracer, and the others are filled with cyanide slugs."

"And you think you can kill the beast with that?"

"That's our arrangement. Talley will find it, do whatever studies he wants, and then I'll kill it."

"It has to be you?"

"Yes."

"I see," Darling said with a sigh. "Okay, Mr. Manning, but do it right the first time, 'cause then it's my show. I'm taking over."

"And doing what?"

"I'm gonna blow him into dust. Or try to."

"Fair enough," Manning said. "Want some coffee?"

"Sure. Black."

Manning walked aft toward the ladder and said, "I'll tell the mate to bring you some."

"The mate," Darling said, "is a lieutenant in your United States Navy. Don't tell him. Ask him. And say please."

Manning opened his mouth, closed it. "Excuse me," he said, and he went below.

At the mouth of the bay Darling turned to the north. As he rounded the point he looked back. Between two Norfolk pines on the end of the point stood Charlotte, her nightgown billowing in the breeze. He waved to her, and she waved back, then turned away and walked up the lawn toward the house.

Sharp brought Darling up some coffee and stood beside him.

For a moment neither of them spoke. Then Darling said, "You liked that girl."

"Yes. I even thought . . . Well, it doesn't matter."

"Sure it matters."

Talley came up to the bridge and stood to one side. He looked edgy, excited.

"Spend much time at sea, Doc?" Darling asked.

"Some, years ago. But nothing like this. I've spent my life reading and writing books about the giant squid. Do you know what a privilege it is to finally get close to one?"

"Seems to me," Darling said, "some critters are better left alone."

They came upon a trail of sargasso weed—floating patches of yellow vegetation, unconnected and yet apparently following one another, like ants, toward the horizon.

"Does it always make a straight line?" Talley asked.

"Seems to. It's a mystery, like that spawn Mike and I saw. I can't figure out what that thing was, or where it came from."

"What thing? What did it look like?"

Darling described the huge gelatinous oblong with the hole in the center, and Talley asked questions. With every answer he grew more excited. "It's an egg sac," he said finally. "Nobody's ever seen one before—at least not in a hundred years."

"What lives in a sac like that?"

Talley looked out over the sea, then slowly turned to look at Darling. "What do *you* think, Captain?"

"How should I . . ." Then Darling paused and said, "Good heavens! Little baby beasts? In that jelly thing?"

"Hundreds," Talley said. "Maybe thousands."

"But they'll die, right?" Sharp said. "Something'll eat them."

"Normally, yes." Talley said. "Most of them. That is, if there's anything left down there to do that."

AT THE edge of the deep, near where the *Ellis Explorer* had anchored, they stopped. It took them an hour to lower the gear—what Talley referred to as phase one of his operation. From three thousand feet of half-inch rope, six umbrella rigs fanned out at intervals, on different levels, each with ten mackerel baits on titanium leaders. The wire was unbreakable; the hooks securing the bait were unbendable and four inches across at the base. If *Architeuthis* should take one of the baits, it would flail with its many arms and—or so Talley theorized—foul itself onto many more of the hooks until, finally, it would be immobilized.

"How much is the beast likely to weigh?" Darling had asked when Talley had outlined his plan.

"There's no telling. I've weighed the flesh of dead ones; it's almost exactly the weight of water. So it's possible a truly big squid could weigh as much as ten tons."

"*Ten tons!* I couldn't put ten tons of meat in this boat—"

"Nobody's asking you to. We'll winch it up, and when Osborn has killed it, I'll cut specimen samples from it."

"With what, your penknife?"

"I saw you have a chain saw below."

"You're ambitious, Doc. I'll give you that," Darling had said. "But suppose the critter doesn't want to play by your rules?"

"It's an animal, Captain," Talley had replied. "Just an animal. Never forget that."

When the rope was down, Darling and Sharp snapped three large pink mooring buoys to its end and tossed them overboard.

"What now?" Sharp asked.

"Let's eat," said Darling.

AFTER LUNCH TALLEY UNPACKED some of his cases and set up a video monitor and tested two of his cameras, while Manning sat on one of the bunks and read a magazine. Darling beckoned Sharp to follow him outside. The boat had been drifting slightly faster than the buoys, so by now the buoys had fallen a hundred yards astern.

"Doc's right about one thing," Darling said as he watched the buoys from the stern of the boat. "Anything tangles with that rigmarole, it'll know it's hooked."

"Maybe it'll beat itself to death on the line."

"Sure, Marcus," Darling said with a smile. "But just in case the beast has other ideas, let's be ready. Get me the boat hook."

By the time Sharp had found the boat hook on the bow and brought it aft, Darling was standing beside the midships hatch cover and opening a cardboard carton. Stenciled on the side of the carton was a single word.

"What's that?" Sharp asked.

Darling reached into the carton and pulled out what looked like a six-inch-long salami, roughly three inches in diameter, covered with a dark red skin of plastic. He smiled. "Semtex," he said.

"Semtex!" said Sharp. "Whip, that's terrorist stuff." Manufactured in Czechoslovakia, it was the explosive of choice of the world's most sophisticated terrorists, for it was extremely powerful, malleable and, best of all, stable. "Where did you get it?"

"If people knew what was flying around the world with them, Marcus, they'd never leave home. It came with a shipment of parts I ordered from Germany; it must have been an accident in packing. I didn't know what it was at first. It wasn't till a couple weeks later that I saw a picture of Semtex and realized what I had." Darling turned the end of the salami toward Sharp. "We've got enough here to blow the end of Bermuda all the way to Haiti. But we do have one little problem."

"What's that?"

"No detonators. Mike must have put 'em ashore. He doesn't . . . *didn't* like sailing with things that might sink us."

"We may be able to make one," Sharp said.

"What do you need?"

"Benzine. Or regular gasoline."

"There's a can for the outboard down below."

"Glycerine. You have any Lux flakes?"

"In the galley, under the sink. That it?"

"No. I need a trigger; something to ignite it. Phosphorous would be best. If you've got a box of kitchen matches . . ."

"No problem. Manning's got a couple hundred rounds of phosphorous tracers. How many?"

"Just one. But Whip. I've never done this before. I've read about it, but I've never actually done it."

"I've never chased a ten-ton squid before, either."

"IT DOESN'T look like a bomb," Sharp said an hour later, when they finished. "More like a piece of cheap fireworks."

"Think it'll work?" said Darling.

"It better, hadn't it."

They had blended the gasoline and the soap flakes into a thick paste, which they pressed, like a wad of gum, to the end of the stick of Semtex. Then Sharp had opened one of Manning's phosphorous tracer bullets. Working with his hands in water—for phosphorous ignites on contact with air—he had mixed phosphorous and gunpowder and put it with some water into a small glass pill bottle, which he then sealed off and embedded in the paste.

Now they used duct tape to affix the bomb to the end of the ten-foot-long boat hook.

"What happens if he swallows it before he breaks the pill bottle?" Darling asked.

"It won't go off," Sharp said. "If air doesn't get to the phosphorous, it won't ignite. It'll be a dud."

"Well, with any luck Talley's plan will work, and we won't need it." Darling paused. "Of course, with any *real* luck we won't find the beast to begin with."

He climbed to the flying bridge, turned the boat to the south and began to look for the floating buoys. He was surprised to find that he didn't see them right away. The boat couldn't have drifted that far from them, and on a clear day like this they should have been visible for at least a mile. There was probably more of a swell on than he'd realized, and they were in a trough. He'd pick them up in a minute.

But he didn't. Not in a minute or two or three. By that time he knew from his landmarks that he was beyond the spot where he'd left them. They were gone.

He heard footsteps behind him, then Manning saying, "Have you lost the buoys?"

"No," Darling said. "I just haven't found 'em yet."

"If you hadn't wasted so much time—"

Darling held up a hand, suddenly tensing; he had heard something or felt something—sensed something. The feeling was coming through his feet, a weird thumping sensation.

"What are you—"

Now Darling recognized the sensation, even though he could hardly believe it. "Incredible!" he said, and he went to the railing and looked down into the bottomless blue.

One of them came into view then—the only one left intact— and it was rushing for the surface like a runaway missile. It broke water with a loud, sucking *whoosh* sound and flew half a dozen feet into the air, spraying them, before it settled back onto the surface, trailing beneath it the burst tatters of the two other buoys.

Talley and Sharp had come out of the cabin, and by the time Darling reached the deck Sharp had snagged the rope with a grapnel and was hauling the buoy aboard. Darling unsnapped the buoy, then wrapped the rope around the winch and turned it on.

"Is it him?" Manning said. "Is it the squid?"

The rope was quivering and shedding drops of water. Darling felt it with his fingertips. "I can't say, Mr. Manning, but anything strong enough to yank the stretch out of half a mile of poly rope, plus sink three mooring buoys, each designed to float half a ton—

that is one humongous creature." Darling leaned over the side, then said, "I can't tell if it's still there or not."

"If it was hooked," Talley said, "it's there. It can't break those wires or bend the hooks."

"Never say never, Doc." Darling ran the winch as Sharp fed the rope into a plastic drum.

Talley set up a tripod with a video camera on the flying bridge, while Manning positioned himself against the railing, his rifle loaded with a thirty-round banana clip.

When the drum was half full, Darling reached out and strummed the rope with his fingers. Then he stopped the winch and wrapped a hand around the rope and tugged on it.

"It's gone," he said. "If it was ever there. It's gone now; there's nothing on this rope but rope."

"It can't be," Talley said.

"We'll know in a minute," Darling said, and he started the winch again.

"It wasn't really hooked, then."

"You mean it pulled those buoys down just for sport?"

The first of the umbrella rigs came up, and Sharp lifted it aboard. The baits were there, untouched. A moment later the second rig came up, then the third. Nothing had eaten any of them.

As the fourth umbrella rig came into view Sharp held up a hand, and Darling slowed the winch.

"Man, look at this," Sharp said, reaching for the rig. "It looks like it was run over by a train."

The rig had been crushed, and its wires had been wrapped tight around the rope. Intertwined with the rope and wires were strands of a white musclelike fiber. Two of the baits were whole, still secured to the hooks, but the other baits were gone, and nothing was left of the hooks but a couple of inches of gnarled shaft.

Darling held one of the hooks up for Talley as he ran the camera. "Can't bend 'em out, huh? Can't bust 'em off? Well, Doc, whatever's down there didn't just bend 'em out, it *bit* 'em off."

Sharp plucked some of the white fibers from the rig, and they left a pungent stench on his fingers. He grimaced and wiped his hands on his trousers.

"It's *Architeuthis*," Talley said. "Smell the ammonia. It left us its calling card." He turned off the camera. "Their flesh is full of ammonium ions. The dead ones I saw *reeked* of it."

"Listen, Doc," Darling said, "either you're crazy or you've been holding out on us. You can't catch a giant squid on a hook. You can't catch one with a submarine. So how do you really plan to catch it?"

Talley said, "Living things are driven by two primal instincts, Captain. The first one is hunger. What's the other?"

Darling looked at Sharp, who shrugged and said, "Sex?"

"Yes," Talley said, "sex. I intend to capture the giant squid with sex."

CHAPTER TWELVE

TALLEY had numbered his cases, and now, with the help of Sharp and Darling, he sorted them and arranged them on the afterdeck in a precise order.

Manning stood aside, his rifle held against his chest, and stared out at the water. He seemed to be reducing himself to a single core, a naked compulsion with a single purpose: to kill.

When Talley was satisfied with the arrangement of his cases, he beckoned Darling and Sharp over to a long aluminum box the size of a coffin and lifted the lid. "Admit it," he said proudly. "Isn't this the sexiest thing you ever saw?"

Cushioned in foam rubber was what looked to Darling like a six-foot-long bowling pin made of plastic and painted bright red. Hundreds of tiny steel hooks hung from swivels all over it, and a three-inch steel ring was embedded in its top.

Talley lifted the thing by the ring and passed it to Darling. It couldn't have weighed more than ten pounds, and when Darling tapped it, he heard a hollow sound.

"I give up," he said simply.

Talley took the thing from Darling and put a hand on either end and held it up before him. "Think of this," he said, "as the mantle—the main body—of *Architeuthis*. As a general rule the body of a giant squid constitutes about a third of its total length. So this represents an animal whose total length, counting the whips, would be about eighteen or twenty feet."

"A baby," Sharp said. "A squirt."

"Not necessarily. But even if our animal is five times as big as this thing, male or female, its impulse will be to breed with this." Talley unscrewed the steel ring. "I've spent years developing a chemical that perfectly replicates the breeding attractant of *Architeuthis*. I've been able to synthesize the chemical trigger."

"You're positive?" Darling said. "Have you tried it?"

"In the field? No. But in the laboratory, yes. I won't burden you with the specifics, but just as a dog in heat emits a musk, a giant squid responds to chemicals released by others of its species." He put his finger in the hole left by the steel ring. "A vial of liquid poured in here and diluted with seawater will seep out through tiny holes behind each hook. It will create a spoor that will travel for miles—a call of nature the beast won't be able to resist."

"Won't the thing know it's a phony?" Sharp asked.

"No. There's almost no light down there, remember, so it doesn't depend on its eyes for much. To be on the safe side, the surrogate is red, one of the colors of excitation. And we'll hang chemical lights beside it, so in case the animal is accustomed to using its eyes for confirmation, the lights should cast a convincing glow."

"Okay," Darling said. "Say it works. Then what?"

"The beast has eight arms and two whips. It will wrap all of them around the object. It will press its body to it." Talley flipped a few of the little hooks, and they tinkled. "Each one of these will set into its flesh—not enough to alarm it. But when it tries to get away, it won't be able to. That's when we bring it up—just close enough on the surface for me to take pictures of it and for Osborn to kill it. Then I'll cut some specimens."

"Well, one thing's for sure," Darling said. "By the time he gets up here, that's gonna be one angry squid."

"I don't think so. I think it will be concerned with only one thing: survival. The rapid change in water temperature may stun it. The change in pressure may kill it before it reaches the surface. But whatever happens," Talley said, turning and gesturing at Manning, "that's when Osborn takes over."

Manning acknowledged Talley with a curt nod and gestured with his rifle.

"You know what scares me?" Darling said. "You're too sure of all this." He turned to Sharp. "Marcus, I'm glad we built ourselves that bomb."

"You won't need explosives, Captain," Talley said.

"I hope not. But this is not a critter to underestimate."

It took them more than three hours to set Talley's rig, which was a masterpiece of complexity. It involved thousands of feet of rope and cable, and a low-light surveillance video camera that could be controlled from the boat and was housed in a Plexiglas sphere the size of a fortune-teller's crystal ball. Darling had to fetch his chain saw to cut a two-by-four, which he lashed between the camera and the lure, as a connecting brace. It was twilight when at last all was ready. The wind had died, and the sea was a meadow of steely swells.

Sharp watched a pair of gulls wheel toward the sunset. Then he recognized something on the surface of the sea.

"Look, Whip," he said, pointing. "Whales."

"Nice. Sperm whales. They always gather at twilight. I don't know why—maybe to get together for a gam."

Talley went into the cabin, and when he came back, he held a six-ounce vial of clear liquid. At his direction Darling and Sharp held the plastic lure upright and poured in buckets of seawater.

Then Talley unscrewed the cap from the vial, emptied the liquid into the lure and screwed the steel ring tight. They shackled the ring to the cable, and with Darling holding one end and Sharp the other, they lowered the rig over the stern. It floated for a moment, then slipped away in a flurry of bubbles.

Darling and Sharp manned two hand-crank winches clamped on either side of the stern. Simultaneously they fed first the cables, then the ropes, over into the sea, securing the camera's cable to the rope every twelve feet.

Darkness fell on the still ocean, and the rising moon cast a golden path from the eastern horizon to the stern of the boat. From behind them came the warm glow of the cabin lights.

Finally, at nine o'clock they reached the four-hundred-and-eighty-fathom marks on the ropes, and they wrapped them around the winches and tied them off to an iron towing post that ran down into the keel.

"Want some food, Mr. Manning?" Darling asked as he and Sharp started forward.

Manning shook his head and continued to stare at the water.

Talley had returned to the cabin, and sat at the table adjusting a timer on the video recorder, which could, while they slept, turn off the camera at intervals to conserve tape. The monitor was on, and Darling walked up behind Talley to look at it. The lure was in frame, swaying back and forth, and from the hundreds of holes in its skin shimmering strands of spoor trickled out and trailed off into the blackness.

Darling noticed that Talley was sweating. "Is it getting to you?" he said. "Sometimes it's better if our dreams don't come true."

"I'm not afraid, Captain," Talley said sharply. "I'm excited. I've been waiting thirty years for this. No, I'm not afraid."

"Well, I am," said Darling. He stepped up into the wheelhouse and turned on the Fathometer. The bottom was three thousand feet away, so if he and Sharp had measured the lines correctly, the lure and camera were suspended one hundred and twenty feet above it. He reached over and switched on the fish-finder and calibrated its reading depth to five hundred fathoms. The bottom glowed as a straight line. Otherwise, it was blank.

"That spoor's driving everything away, from here to the Azores," Darling said as he stepped back down into the cabin. "There isn't a porgy or a shark between us and the bottom."

"No," Talley said. "They know to stay away." He turned off the camera and set the timer.

Darling walked to the door and flicked a switch. The halogen lamps mounted on the flying bridge flashed on, and the afterdeck was flooded with light. Through the window Darling saw that Manning hadn't budged. He sat on the midships hatch cover, his shoulders hunched, his rifle cradled in his lap.

Sharp passed Darling a sandwich. He nodded toward Manning and said, "Should I take him one?"

"He's not interested in food," Darling said. "The man's eating himself up inside."

By ten thirty the timer had activated the camera a dozen times, and each time they had gathered around the monitor and seen the lure swinging back and forth across the frame, leaking ribbons of spoor. Up-current from the lure a few tiny crustaceans flashed like fireflies across the screen. Down-current there was nothing but black.

The boat drifted on the calm sea, rocking gently.

"Suppose he doesn't come tonight?" Darling said to Talley.

"In the morning, then, or the afternoon. But it will come."

"We might's well get some sleep, then."

"If you can."

Sharp went to the bunk room below to lie down. Talley turned off the monitor, then lay back on the bench seat and closed his eyes. Darling went outside.

Manning was still sitting on the hatch cover, but he was slumped over, asleep.

Darling checked the ropes; they hung straight down, unmoving, untouched. Then he looked toward shore. The loom of Bermuda was a rosy glow against the black sky. They were ten miles away, but he took comfort in the knowledge that home was still there. He thought of Charlotte in their house, in their bed, and suddenly he was suffused with loneliness.

He went into the cabin and lay down on one of the bunks. He longed for sleep, but he was sure that his mind would refuse to retreat into the comfort of numbness. Ever since he had first gone to sea as a boy, whenever he slept on a boat, a part of his brain always stood watch, alert to any change in the wind, to the slightest alteration in the rhythms of the ocean.

The watchman in his head had been on duty in the best of times, when the boat had floated over an apparently infinite resource of life. And he knew that the watchman would be on duty now, when for the first time in his life his most fervent hope was that the sea beneath him would remain a barren, lifeless plain.

THE giant squid expanded its mantle, propelling its great mass through the night sea. Driven by the most basic of all impulses, it rushed in one direction, then another, extending its many senses to gather in more and more of the scattered signals that were exciting it into a frenzy. Its color changed from pale gray to pink to maroon to red, reflecting emotions from anxiety to passion.

Suddenly it encountered a stream of the signals; it was a trail, strong and true. The creature homed in on it.

DARLING awoke in the dark without knowing what had woken him. He lay quietly for a moment, listening and feeling.

He heard the familiar sounds: the hum of the refrigerator, the scratch of the stylus across the Fathometer paper. But he felt a difference in the motion of the boat. There was a reluctance, as if the boat was fighting the flow of the sea.

He rolled off the bunk, walked to the door and stepped outside. The instant his eye caught the movement of the water, he knew what had woken him: something was pulling the boat backward.

Then he looked at the stern and saw little waves slapping against it. The ropes still angled straight downward, but they were trembling, and he could hear the squeak of straining fibers.

So, he thought. Here we go. He ducked back inside. "Turn your TV monitor on, Doc," Darling said, then shouted, "Marcus. Marcus! Let's go."

"Why?" Talley sat up, still groggy. "What . . . ?"

"Because we've hooked your squid, that's why. And he's dragging us backward." Darling reached across Talley and pressed the switch. The monitor flickered, then glowed.

The image was without definition—a swirl of bubbles and shadows. "The lure!" Talley said. "Where's the lure?"

"He's got it," said Darling. "And he's running with it."

Just then Sharp came up from below. Darling beckoned to him and went outside.

Manning was standing in the stern, soaked with spray, staring at the thrumming ropes. "Is it . . . ?" he asked.

"Either it's the beast, or we've hooked the devil himself." Darling directed Sharp to the starboard winch, while he took the one on the port side, and together they began to wind in the ropes.

For a minute or two they made no headway; the weight on the winches was too great for them to get traction, so the winch drums skidded under the ropes. The boat continued to move backward. Then the ropes suddenly eased, and the boat stopped.

"The strain's gone," Sharp said. "Did it get off?"

"Could be. Or else he's just turning. Keep cranking."

They wound in tandem, retrieving a foot of rope every second, ten fathoms a minute. Darling's arm muscles began to burn.

"Whip, he's got to have busted away," Sharp said when the two-hundred-fathom marks on the ropes rolled over the drums.

"I don't think so," said Darling. He had a hand on the rope. There was weight, but no strain; pull, but no action. "It feels like he's there, but not pulling. Maybe taking a breather."

"Or maybe dead," Sharp said, sounding hopeful.

"Keep cranking, Marcus," Darling said.

Talley came out of the cabin. "I can't see anything on the video," he said. "It's a mess."

"Leave it run anyway," said Darling.

"I am." Talley took a position behind them. He had another video camera and was hurrying to load a tape.

Suddenly Sharp said, "Whip, look!" And he pointed. The ropes no longer hung vertically; they had started to move slowly out, away from the boat. Still there was no stutter on the winches; the rope kept coming aboard.

"He's coming up!" Darling shouted. He looked at Manning and said, "Cock your gun now. This is what you've been waiting for."

For the next few minutes no one spoke. Darling and Sharp cranked the winches, and the rope flowed aboard, then ended, and the big shackles rattled over the bulwarks, followed by the first lengths of cable. "Fifty fathoms, Marcus," Darling said.

The cables angled out behind them, not quite horizontal, taut and quivering but still coming aboard. The creature must be nearing the surface now. They stared at the water off the stern, trying to follow the silver threads of cable, to see beyond the edge of the pool of light cast by the halogen lamps.

"Show yourself, you bastard!" Darling called, and he realized suddenly that his fear had changed. What he was feeling now was not dread or foreboding or horror, but the galvanic fear of meeting an opponent. It was almost like an electric charge.

Just then the winches jolted, skidded, and the cable that had just come aboard leaped from its coils on the deck and began to snake overboard.

"What's he doing?" Sharp shouted.

"He's running again!" Darling cried. He grabbed the winch handle and leaned on it, but the winch refused—the spool spun; the cable kept backing off into the water.

"No!" Manning screamed. "Stop him!"

"I can't!" Darling said. "Nothing can."

"You mean you *won't*. You're afraid. I'll show you how." Manning put down his rifle, reached into the coil of cable at his feet and grabbed a length of slack.

"Don't!" Darling yelled, but before he could stop him, Manning had flung the cable at the iron post that ran down into the keel, looped it around the post and tied it off.

"There," Manning said. The cable continued to run off the stern, buzzing as it passed over the steel bulwark. Manning turned and picked up his rifle. But as he was turning, he slipped, and just then the creature must have accelerated, for suddenly the coils of cables jumped off the deck and flew. As Manning staggered to regain his balance he stepped through a snarl of cable. The cable snapped tight around his thigh, and he was lifted off the deck like a puppet. For a fraction of a second he hung suspended in the lights. He made no sound, and the rifle fell away from his hands.

Then a great force slammed the cables taut, and Manning flew backward, pulled by his leg, his arms out in a swan dive.

Light flashed on Manning's face for an instant, and Darling saw no horror, no agony—only surprise, as if Manning's last sensation was amazement that fate had had the temerity to thwart him.

The rifle struck the deck and discharged a bullet, which ricocheted off the bulwark and whined away overhead.

Darling thought he saw Manning's leg pull away from his body, for something seemed to fall from the cable. But he heard no splash, for all sounds were overwhelmed by the *sproing!* of the cable setting against the iron post.

Instantly the cable rose to the horizontal, and the boat was dragged backward. Waves splashed against the transom.

Then Darling saw the cable rise above the horizontal, and he yelled, "It's up!"

"Where?" Talley cried. "Where?"

They heard a splash then, and they smelled a stinging stench. The spray that fell on them became a rain of black ink.

Ten or fifteen feet behind the stern, Darling saw a little flicker of silver, and instinctively he knew what it was. The threads of the cable were snapping, and rolling back on themselves.

He shouted, "Duck!"

"What?" said Talley.

Darling dove at him and tackled him to the deck, and as they fell, there was a booming sound from behind the boat, followed instantly by a high-pitched whistle.

A length of cable screamed overhead and shattered the windows in the back of the cabin. The second length followed immediately, and they heard the crash of Talley's camera housing disintegrating against a steel bulkhead.

The boat pitched and yawed for a moment, then settled back into the sea.

"Good God . . ." Talley said.

Darling rolled away from him and stood up. He looked aft, out into the darkness. There was no sign that anything had ever been there. Only the soft whisper of breeze over the silent sea.

CHAPTER THIRTEEN

TALLEY'S face was the color of cardboard, and as he got up off the deck he trembled so badly that he could barely stand. "I never thought . . ." he began, but his voice trailed off.

"Forget it," Darling said. He and Sharp were pulling in the skeins of rope that littered the surface beside the boat.

"You were right all along," Talley said. "There was no way we—"

"Listen, Doc." Darling looked at Talley and thought, The man's gonna collapse. "When we get to shore, there'll be time enough to moan and groan. We'll say nice words for Mr. Manning and do all the proper things. But right now all I want to do is get us out of here. Go inside and lie down."

"Yes," Talley said. "Right." And he went into the cabin.

When they had hauled the last of the rope aboard, Darling followed Talley into the cabin. He was sitting at the table. He had rewound the videotape, and was starting to play it back.

"What are you looking for?" Darling asked.

"Anything," Talley said. "Any images at all."

Darling took a step up toward the wheelhouse and said over his shoulder to Sharp, "Check the oil pressure for me, Marcus."

Sharp opened the engine-room hatch and started below.

Suddenly Talley shouted, "It's there!" His eyes were wide as he stared at the monitor, and he groped blindly for the controls.

Sharp and Darling crowded behind Talley as he found the tape controls and pressed the PAUSE button.

On the monitor was an image of froth and bubbles. Talley pressed the FRAME ADVANCE button, and the picture jumped. "There's the lure," he said, pointing to a flicker of something dense and shiny. In the next frame it had disappeared; then it reappeared at the top of the screen. Talley pointed to the bottom of the screen, and he said, "Now watch."

A grayish hump rose from the bottom until it covered the entire screen. The frames kept changing, and the gray shade kept climbing. And then the bottom of the screen was invaded by something off-white, curved on top. It moved upward.

The thing must have moved away from the camera, for gradually the image widened out, and the thing showed itself as a perfect off-white circle, and in its center was another perfect circle, blacker than ebony.

"Is that an *eye?*" Sharp said.

Talley nodded.

"What kind of size?" asked Darling.

"I can't tell," Talley said. "But if the focal length of the camera was about six feet, and the eye fills the frame, it has to be . . . like so." He held his hands two feet apart. In a voice barely above a whisper he said, "This could be a hundred-foot animal."

"And when we get home," Darling said, "We're gonna get down on our knees and give thanks that we never got any closer to it." Then he turned and climbed the two steps to the wheelhouse.

Dawn was breaking, and the advancing sun cast a line of pink on the horizon. Darling pushed the starter button and waited to hear the rumbling cough as the engine came to life.

But all he heard was a click; then nothing.

He pushed it again. This time, nothing at all. He swore to himself, then whacked the wheel with the heel of his hand, for as soon as he knew that the engine wouldn't start, he knew why. Sometime during the night the generator had run out of fuel. The batteries had taken over automatically, but eventually, after being drained for hours by the lights and the Fathometer and the fish-finder, they had run down. They were still putting out some power, but they couldn't muster the juice to fire up the big diesel engine.

After he had calmed down, Darling considered which of the two fully charged compressor batteries would be easiest to shift over to the main engine, selected one and reviewed in his mind the procedure for removing it from its mounts and mounting it beside the engine. It was nasty work, but not the end of the world.

As he crossed the wheelhouse on his way down to the engine room it occurred to him to turn off the instruments to save power. He turned the knob on the Fathometer. As he reached for the switch on the fish-finder his eyes glanced at the screen.

It wasn't blank anymore. For a moment he thought, Good. Life is coming back. Then he looked closer, and he realized that he had never seen an image like this on the screen. It was a single, solid mass rising toward the surface, and rising fast.

THE beast shot upward through the sea like a torpedo. It moved backward, its tentacles trailing like a tail; but it was not retreating. It was attacking, and its triangular tail was like an arrow point, guiding it to its target.

Its chemistry was agitated, and its colors had changed many times as its senses struggled to decipher conflicting messages. First there had been the irresistible impulse to breed; then perplexity when it had tried to mate and been unable to; then anxiety as it had tried to shed the alien thing and found it could not; then rage as it had perceived a threat from the thing and proceeded with its tentacles and its beak to destroy the threatener.

Now what remained was rage, and it was rage of a new dimension. Before, the giant squid had always responded to impulses of rage with instantaneous explosive spasms of destruction, which had consumed the rage. But this time the rage did not abate; it evolved. And now it had a purpose, a goal.

The beast rose, driven to cause not only destruction, but death.

A THOUSAND feet, Darling guessed, as he calibrated the fish-finder. The thing was at a thousand feet, and it was coming up like a bullet. They had five minutes, no more—probably less.

He jumped down into the cabin. "Get the boat hook, Marcus," he said. "And make sure that detonator's ready to fire."

"What's wrong?" Talley asked.

"The thing's coming up at us again," said Darling, "and my bloody battery's dead." He disappeared down into the engine room.

Sharp climbed up to the flying bridge, where they had left the boat hook, and he examined the bomb. It was simple. As soon as air got to the phosphorous, it would ignite and set off the Semtex. All they had to do was feed it to a hundred-foot monster and jump out of the way before they were blown to tatters. That was all.

Sharp suddenly felt sick. Stop it, he told himself. And get ready.

DARLING crawled across the engine room and pushed the heavy twelve-volt battery in front of him. His knuckles were bloody and his legs cramped. When he judged that the battery was close enough for the cables to reach it, he unbolted them from the dead battery. He didn't care if the fresh battery tumbled around; once he got it to kick over the engine, he wouldn't need it.

He paused long enough to be sure he was attaching the cables to the proper poles and bolted them down.

Then he got to his feet and raced up the ladder.

Its prey was directly above.

It could see it with its eyes, could feel it with the sensors in its body. But because the prey was alien, instinct told the creature to be wary, to appraise it first. And so, as a shark circles unknown objects in the sea, *Architeuthis dux* passed once beneath the quarry and scanned it with its eyes. The force of its passage cast a pressure wave upward.

Suddenly the prey above it erupted with noise and began to move. The beast interpreted the noise and movement as signs of flight. Quickly it turned in its own length and attacked.

When Darling had felt the boat surge beneath him, he had held his breath and pushed the starter button and then, a second later, had heard the rumble of the big diesel. He didn't wait for the engine to warm up. He rammed the throttle forward.

At first the boat leaped ahead, and then suddenly it stopped, as if it were anchored by the stern. It tipped backward; the bow rose, and Darling was thrown back against the bulkhead. Then the boat fell forward again. But still it didn't move.

The pitch of the engine had changed from a roar to a complaining whine. Then it began to sputter. It coughed twice, then died; and the boat lay dead in the water.

This is it, Darling thought. The beast has wrecked the propeller. He felt suddenly cold.

He dropped down into the cabin and went out onto the afterdeck.

Talley was out there, staring numbly at the sea. When he saw Darling, he said, "Where is he? I thought you said—"

"Right underneath us," Darling said. "He's ruined us good and proper." They went to the stern and looked down over the transom into the water. A few feet beneath the swim step, snaking out from beneath the boat, was the tip of a tentacle.

Talley said, "He must have tried to grab the propeller."

"He's lost an arm," said Darling. "That'll discourage him."

"No, it won't," Talley said. "All it will do is enrage him."

Darling looked up at the flying bridge and saw Sharp standing at the railing, holding Manning's rifle. He started up the ladder to join him. Sharp had stood the boat hook vertically in a rod holder. Darling removed it and felt its heft.

"I'll do it," Sharp said, gesturing at the bomb.

"No, Marcus." Darling tried to smile. "Captain's prerogative."

IN THE darkness below, the beast writhed, berserk with pain. Green fluid seeped from the stump of its missing tentacle.

It was not disabled; it sensed no loss of power. It knew only that what it had perceived as prey was more than prey. It was an enemy. The creature rose again toward the surface.

DARLING and Sharp were gazing off the bow when suddenly from behind them came Talley's voice screaming, "No!"

They whirled around to the stern and froze.

Something was coming over the bulwark. It seemed to ooze like a giant purple slug. Then the front of it curled back and began to rise and fan out until it was four feet across and eight feet high, blocking the sun. It was covered with quivering circles, like hungry mouths, and in each one was a shining amber blade.

"Shoot it, Marcus!" Darling shouted. "Shoot!"

But Sharp stood agape, the rifle useless in his hands. Below them, Talley heard something, and he turned and screamed. Amidships, slithering aboard, was the beast's other whip.

The scream startled Sharp, and he fired three shots. One went high; one struck the bulkhead; the third hit the club of the whip dead center. The flesh did not react. It seemed to swallow the bullet.

More and more of both whips came aboard, writhing like snakes and falling in heaps of purple flesh, which moved and pulsed and quivered. They seemed to sense life aboard, and movement, for the clubs bent forward and began to move on their circles, like searching spiders.

Talley seemed paralyzed. He did not flinch, made no move to flee, but stood still, frozen.

"Doc!" Darling shouted. "Get out of there!"

When both whips were heaped in the stern, they stopped moving for a moment, then suddenly expanded with muscle tension, and the stern was pressed downward. Behind the boat the ocean seemed to rise up, as if giving birth to a mountain. There was a sucking sound and a roar.

"Look out!" Darling yelled. "It's coming aboard!" He backed away, holding the boat hook like a lance.

They saw the tentacles first—seven thrashing arms that grasped the stern and pushed downward to bring the body up. Then they saw an eye, impossibly huge, rising like a moon.

The stern was forced downward until it was awash. Water poured aboard and ran forward, flooding into the after hatches.

It's gonna do it, Darling thought. It's gonna sink us and then pick us off one by one.

The other eye came up now, and as the creature turned its head and faced them the eyes seemed to fix on them. Between the eyes the arms quivered and roiled, and at the juncture of the arms the two-foot beak, sharp and protuberant, snapped reflexively.

Talley suddenly came to. He turned and ran to the ladder and began to climb. He was halfway to the flying bridge when one of the whips rose in the air and sprang forward, reaching for him. Talley saw it coming, and as he tried to dodge it his feet skidded off the ladder, and he hung by his hands from one of the rungs. The whip coiled around the ladder, tore it away from the bulkhead and held it suspended over the flying bridge, with Talley dangling from it like a marionette.

"Drop, Doc!" Darling shouted.

Talley let go, and fell. His feet struck the outboard lip of the flying bridge, and for a second he teetered there, his arms cartwheeling as he groped for the railing. His eyes were wide, and his mouth hung open. Then he toppled backward into the sea. The whip crushed the ladder and cast it away.

Sharp fired the rifle until the clip was empty. Tracer bullets streaked into the oozing flesh and vanished.

The tail of the creature thrust forward, driving the body farther up on the boat, driving the stern farther down. The bow rose out of the water, and from below came the sounds of tools and chairs and crockery crashing into steel bulkheads.

"Go, Marcus!" Darling said.

"You go. Let me—"

"*Go*, dammit!"

Sharp looked at Darling, wanted to speak, but there was nothing to say. He dove overboard.

Darling turned aft. He could barely stand; the deck sloped out from under him, and he crouched, bracing himself with one foot on the railing.

The creature was tearing the boat to pieces. The whips flailed randomly, clutching anything they touched—a drum of rope, a hatch cover, an antenna mast—and flinging it into the sea. As it drew air into its mantle and expelled it through its funnel, the creature made sounds like a grunting pig.

And then its rampage ceased, and—as if it had suddenly remembered something—the great head, with its face like a nest of vipers, turned toward Darling. The whips lashed out; each one fastened on a steel stanchion on the flying bridge. The whips pulled, and the creature lunged forward.

Darling balanced one foot on the railing and one on the deck, and he raised the boat hook over his head like a harpoon. He tried to gauge how far he was from the beak. The creature's arms reached out. Darling focused on the gnashing beak, and he struck.

The boat hook was torn from his hands. He saw one of the whips raise it and drop it into the sea.

His only thought was, I am going to die.

The arms reached for him. He ducked; his feet slipped out from under him, and he fell, skidding over the edge of the flying bridge and dropping onto the sloping afterdeck.

He found himself in waist-deep water. He started to slog toward the railing. If he could get overboard, away from the boat, maybe he could hide in the wreckage, maybe the creature would lose interest, maybe . . .

The beast appeared around the edge of the cabin then, looming above him, its whips waving like cobras. Seven arms reached for him to push him into the amber beak.

He turned and struggled toward the other side of the boat. One of the arms slapped the water beside him, and he dodged to the side, stumbled and regained his footing. How many steps to go? Five? Ten? He'd never make it. But he kept going because something deep inside him refused to surrender.

An obstacle blocked him, and he looked at it, wondering if he could dive under it. It was the big midships hatch cover, floating. Lying atop it was the chain saw.

Darling didn't consider, didn't hesitate, didn't think. He grabbed the chain saw and pulled the starter cord. It caught on the first try, and the little motor came to life. He pressed the trigger, and the saw blade spun, shedding drops of oil.

He said, "Okay," and he turned and faced the beast.

It seemed to pause for a moment, and then, with a grunt of expelled air, it lunged for him. Darling squeezed the trigger again, and the sound of the saw rose to a shrill screech.

One of the writhing arms flashed before his face, and Darling swung the saw at it. The saw's teeth bit into flesh, and he was bathed in a stench of ammonia. The motor labored, slowing as it might when cutting wet wood, and he thought, No! Don't quit. Not now!

The pitch of the motor rose again, and the teeth cut deep, spraying bits of flesh into Darling's face. The arm severed and fell away. A sound burst from the beast—a sound of rage and pain.

Another arm assailed Darling, and another, and he slashed with the saw. As the teeth touched each arm, all the arms flinched and withdrew and then, as if goaded by the creature's frenzied brain, attacked again. A shower of flesh exploded, and Darling was drenched with green slime and black ink.

Suddenly he felt something touch one of his legs underwater, and it began to crawl up his leg and circle his waist.

One of the whips had him. He tried to find it, but in the mass of curling, twisting tentacles he couldn't distinguish it from the arms.

When the whip had circled his waist, it began to squeeze, like a python, and Darling felt a stabbing pain as the hook in each sucker disk tore into his skin. He felt his feet leave the deck and knew that once he was in the air, he was dead.

He twisted his body so that he faced the snapping beak. As the whip squeezed and drove the breath from him, Darling leaned toward the beak, holding the saw before him. The beak opened, and for a second Darling could see a flicking tongue within—pink, and studded with toothlike rasps.

"Here!" he shouted, and he drove the saw deep into the yawning beak.

The saw stuttered as its teeth failed to slice through the bony beak, and skidded off. As Darling raised the saw again, one of the arms wrenched it from his hands and flung it away.

Now, Darling thought, now I am truly dead.

The whip squeezed, and a mist dimmed his eyes, signaling the onset of oblivion. He felt himself rising, saw the beak reaching for him, smelled a rancid stench.

He saw one of the eyes, blank and relentless.

Then suddenly the beast itself seemed to rise up, as if propelled by a force from below. There was a sound unlike anything Darling had ever heard—a rushing, roaring noise. Something huge and blue-black exploded from the sea, holding the squid in its mouth.

The whip that had him contorted violently, and he felt himself flying, then falling into nothingness.

"PULL!" Sharp shouted.

Talley reached into the water and groped for Darling's belt. He found it and pulled, and with Sharp hauling on Darling's arms, they brought him aboard the overturned hatch cover. Its wood was thick and sound, and it was large enough to hold three of them.

Darling's shirt was in tatters. Streaks of blood crisscrossed his chest where the creature's hooks had torn at his skin.

Sharp touched an artery in Darling's neck. The pulse was strong and steady. "Unless something's busted inside," he said, "he should be okay."

In a dark fog Darling heard the word okay, and he felt himself swimming up toward light. He opened his eyes.

"How do you feel, Whip?"

"Like a truck ran over me. A truck full of knives."

Sharp lifted Darling up and supported his back. "Look," he said.

Darling looked. The boat was gone. The animal was gone.

"What was it?" Darling asked. "What did it?"

"One of the sperm whales," said Sharp. "It took the whole damn squid. Bit it off just behind the head."

There was sudden movement in the water, and Darling started.

"It's all right," Talley said. "Just life, just nature."

The surface of the sea was littered with flesh—masses of it—and each piece was being assaulted. The tumult around the boat had been like a dinner bell, summoning creatures both from shallow and from deep. The dorsal fin of a shark crossed the debris. The head of a turtle poked up and looked around. Triggerfish, yellowtails and jacks darted through the rich broth.

"Nice," Darling said. He lay back. "That kind of life I like."

"I don't know where we are or where we're going," said Sharp. "I can't see land. I can't see a thing."

Darling wet a finger and held it up. "Home," he said. "Northwest wind. We're going home."

IT HAD been created in the abyss, and had remained there for weeks, adhering to a rock overhang on the mountainside. Then it had broken away, as nature planned it should, and had begun slowly to drift toward the surface. In times past it might have been eaten on the way up, for it was a rich food source.

But nothing had attacked it; nothing had shattered its integrity and permitted a rush of seawater, which would have killed the tiny creatures within. So it had arrived safely on the surface and bathed itself in the sunlight vital to its survival.

It had floated on the still water, oblivious to wind and weather, so thin as to be nearly transparent. But its jelly skin was remarkably strong. Still, it was vulnerable. A turtle might have fed on it; a passing shark might have slashed at it. Nature had ordained that many of its members would die, feeding other species and maintaining the balance of the food chain.

But since nature itself was out of balance, the gelatinous oblong rotated through days and nights until its cycle was complete. At last, ripe, it broke apart and scattered into the sea thousands of little sacs, each containing a complete creature. As each creature's time came, it struggled free of its sac and began to search for food.

They were cannibals, these creatures, and those that could, turned on their brethren and ate them. But there were so many, and they dispersed so fast in the water, that most survived and dove for the comfort of the cold abyss.

Almost all should have been eaten before they reached the bottom, or the safe crevices on the submerged volcano; at most, one creature in a hundred should have survived.

But the predators were gone, and while a few lone hunters did appear, and took their toll, there were no longer the great gatherings that had once acted as natural monitors. The vast schools of bonito and mackerel, the pelagic jacks, the herds of tuna, the voracious wahoo and barracuda—all were gone.

And so, by the time the creatures had crossed three thousand feet of open water and taken shelter in the cliffs, perhaps a hundred individual animals still lived.

They hovered, each alone, for each was completely self-sufficient.

Their bodies would mature slowly, and for a year or more they would be wary of other predators. But the time would come when they would sense their uniqueness, their superiority, and then they would venture out.

They hovered, and they waited.

PETER Benchley's first famous ancestor was the humorist Robert Benchley, a member of the legendary Algonquin Round Table known for both his writing, especially for the *New Yorker*, and also as a successful Hollywood personality. Nathaniel Benchley, Robert's elder son, also became a professional writer, starting with young people's literature and later branching out to adult novels and nonfiction. Peter Benchley, born May 8, 1940, in New York City, was the elder son of Nathaniel.

When Peter was in his teens, Nathaniel offered him encouragement to take up the family writing business in the form of a summer salary if the boy would write each morning. "I wrote a thousand words a day—and it was gibberish," Benchley reported, but he felt the experience was invaluable in teaching him discipline. Like his father and grandfather, he studied at the Phillips Exeter Academy in

New Hampshire, then Harvard, where he majored in English. He had started writing articles for the *New York Herald Tribune* while still in school. After graduating in 1961, Peter traveled around the world for a year and wrote a book about his experiences entitled *Time and a Ticket*. He next worked as a reporter for the *Washington Post*, and then joined the staff of *Newsweek*, where he spent three years as TV-Radio editor. From March 1967 until the end of Lyndon Johnson's presidency, Benchley was a speechwriter for the White House.

After that, Benchley began freelancing as a television commentator and as a contributor to magazines as diverse as the *New Yorker, National Geographic, Vogue* and *TV Guide*. His interest in sharks, he said, "began during my summers spent on Nantucket, when my parents and I would charter boats and go shark fishing." They had originally intended to catch swordfish, but they couldn't find any. "But the ocean was littered with sharks, so we started catching them." It had been in the 1920s that Robert Benchley had started summering on the island of Nantucket, and Peter's parents eventually moved there to become year-round residents.

The story of the publication of *Jaws* is legendary. Tom Congdon, an editor at Doubleday and Sons, had seen some of Benchley's articles and invited him to lunch to discuss possible book ideas. Mostly Benchley was pushing nonfiction projects, but he did have a possible story based on some white sharks that had turned up in the 1960s off the coast of Long Island. He had already written a couple of nonfiction articles about those sharks, and the idea for *Jaws* was simply, "What would happen if one of those came around and wouldn't go away?" A notoriously brief one-page outline from the publisher earned Benchley an advance of $1000 to give the book a shot. Its working title was *Silence in the Water*.

When the book was published in 1974, it was a publishing phenomenon, one of the first of the blockbuster meganovels that redefined the meaning of bestseller in the United States, selling over 20 million copies. If that wasn't enough, the 1975 film, the script of which was cowritten by Benchley, was the first of the blockbuster megahits that redefined the motion picture business in the United

States, taking in over $100 million at the box office; adjusting for inflation, it remains one of the highest grossing pictures of all time. If Benchley did nothing else with his career, he would have had a hand in irrevocably changing both the publishing and the movie business in ways that are still with us today.

Following *Jaws*, Benchley wrote *The Deep* (1976) and *The Island* (1979), both of which were made into films, with Benchley either writing or cowriting the screenplays. As he said at the time, "I write about what I like, and what I like is the ocean. I can do my own research on the sea." And, in fact, his inspiration for *The Girl of the Sea of Cortez* came from a personal experience.

In the summer of 1980, Benchley was working on a television special about hammerhead sharks in the Sea of Cortez. One day the film crew spotted an enormous manta ray lying some twenty feet beneath their boat. The animal was injured, with fishnet caught in an open wound, just like the manta befriended by Paloma in the novel. One of the crew members dived toward it, hoping to remove some of the ropes before the creature fled. To everyone's amazement, the manta, after being helped, allowed the diver to sit on it, and proceeded to swim peacefully around a seamount. For three days the manta lingered near the boat, cruising the sea with human riders, including Benchley himself. "It was really exciting, but very dangerous," he noted. "*You* go where *it* wants you to go."

Benchley wrote two non-nautical novels before returning to the water with *Beast* in 1991. "Everything I've written," said Benchley, "is based on something that has happened to me or something I know a great deal about . . . With *Beast*, I had been fishing for giant squid for years with no luck . . . It was a speculation, a 'what if' story. Almost all my stories are 'what ifs.'" According to the author, the scariest thing about this novel was that the monster actually exists. And it's even bigger in real life. In fact, the giant oceanic squid can grow to two hundred feet. Benchley said, "I made it smaller because I thought it would be too much for readers to believe if I made it as big as it really is."

Benchley's hobbies included scuba diving, a sport he pursued all over the world, from the Caribbean to Australia's Great Barrier Reef. He was especially fond of looking for shipwrecks around Bermuda. He also enjoyed tennis and the guitar. He and his wife, Wendy, had a son and a daughter.

There is no question that *Jaws* inspired a fascination with sharks that remains strong to this day. Benchley, however, came to regret his villainous depiction of the creature. As he put it, "Sharks rarely take more than one bite out of people because we're so lean and bony and unappetizing to them."

Benchley passed away on February 12, 2006.